THE UNDEAD. DAY TWENTY ONE

RR HAYWOOD

rrhaywood.com

The boy will be a boy.

Not a killer.

CHAPTER ONE

D ay Seven

T he evening is warm, sultry even. The sun slowly gives way for the moon to take the night. In other parts of the world people wake and give prayers to whatever Gods they hold dear that they are alive to see another day.

Give hope for what you have and hold your loved ones close because monsters now roam your land and darkness is upon you. This is the end of times. The end of days.

Not here though. Not in Northern England. Here the tranquil rural lanes are bordered by high hedgerows and vast fields of crops rolling away to the horizon. Here is many miles from the fort where a former supermarket manager is preparing to make a stand against an army led by Darren.

The CD plays in the stereo. The windows are down. Sunlight streams through the canopy dappling the windscreen. The red Skoda Octavia 1.9 TDI holds a steady course.

The driver reads the road ahead. Seeing the camber of the road. The bends. The width. The junctions. His eyes glance frequently at the mirrors and down to the instrument panel on the dashboard. He holds the steering wheel with both hands. His thumbs do not loop to grip the wheel. If there is a sudden accident, the jolt could break his thumbs and he needs his thumbs. How can he hold his pistols or knives with broken thumbs?

He glances to the boy. The boy never normally stops talking but he is quiet now. Almost reflective in his manner and lost in his thoughts.

'Plane with hands?'

The boy blinks, re-focussing with a distinct motion of his head that turns to look at Gregori.

'You do plane with hands?' Gregori asks again.

The boy shakes his head but doesn't say anything. The boy always says something. He never not says something, and normally repeats it at least fifty times.

'See,' Gregori pushes his right hand out the open driver's window. His palm open and held flat against so the wind goes equally over and under the blade of his hand. The boy leans forward to watch. 'Plane,' Gregori says. He tilts his hand slowly, feeling the wind give lift to his palm. He tilts more. The force is greater. Another tilt and he submits for the wind to lift his arm up. The boy watches intently. His whole face focussed with an intense gaze.

'You do this,' Gregori says, nodding at the boy.

The boy shuffles closer to his window to hold his hand out. He glances back to see Gregori's hand now held blade forward again and copies the action, locking his arm out with his palm flat.

Gregori tilts his hand. The boy does the same to feel the rush of air giving lift to his arm that starts rising like a plane taking off. A wing is created. Natural lift is given. The boy's eyes widen that such a thing can happen. He watches his own arm soar up until it hits the window frame.

'Plane,' Gregori says.

The boy brings his arm down to do it again. Flat first, tilt then rise. He turns to grin toothy and wide at Gregori but still he doesn't say anything. He tries again. Flat, tilt, rise. He does it again and tenses his little arm to resist the push, feeling the wind buffeting the open sail of his palm. Twitches of tilt send his arm up and down as he rides the power of wind. Then he goes still and loses that focus in his eyes. The smile freezes and slowly fades.

Gregori looks at the back of the boy's head then to the passenger wing mirror to see the reflection of the boy's face. Maybe he is tired. The day has been long and hot and this quiet journey in the car has already been a couple of hours.

He goes back to searching for a place to stay. Somewhere remote that is detached and isolated. Somewhere they can stay safely away from other people. Somewhere the boy can be a boy, not a killer. He has seen plenty of houses, farms and cottages but none were right. Some had obstructed views of the land around them. Some were too big. Some were too close to towns and villages. It's no matter. He will keep searching until the right one is found.

A single set of power lines overhead. He tracks the direction and gains a glimpse of a roof in the distance. His right foot eases to slow the car as he commences an assessment of the area.

No other dwellings nearby. Thick forests and copses break up the rolling fields and meadows. The land rises and falls with hills and valleys.

He spots the driveway and slows the vehicle again, cruising to a gentle speed to take in the house in the distance set in vast open grounds that gives perfect line of sight.

This is good.

He steers in towards the mouth of the driveway and brings the vehicle to a stop. Engine off. He listens first. Breathing easy and slow to detect any noises. Nothing.

He has a non-threatening profile. The vehicle is a family saloon. He is an adult male with a young boy. A father and son. They have taken the family car to try and escape the towns. Yes. This is the approach. He will drive slowly as though nervous. He will lean forward to peer through the windscreen and make sure that anyone looking sees someone who is afraid. When they get out, he will hold the boy's hand and retain that look of fear. Yes. This is the way.

'Boy,' Gregori says, drawing the child's attention to him. 'We go house. You hold hand.'

'Okay,' the boy says, unsmiling, unlaughing, unresponsive.

'What wrong?' Gregori asks, leaning forward to peer through the windscreen. He takes in every window. Every door. Every angle, corner, recess and every possible point of danger.

Maintaining his nervous persona, Gregori makes a show of staring to the left and right and even lifts his hand as though ready to wave should anyone show themselves.

As he nears the house he slows the Skoda while turning the wheel to let the tyres crunch the gravel to make more noise. Still no response. He stops the car but waits while leaning forward to scan the front of the house and spots the discrete cameras fitted above the door and more on the sides of the house and under the eaves. A prickle inside. His senses coming to the fore.

He opens his door and pauses. Nothing. He gets out, stretches and looks scared. Nothing. He puts his hands behind his back as though to tug his trousers up and checks the pistol is secure in his waistband. He hates not using a holster. Only amateurs and gangsters shove pistols in waistbands.

'Boy, we walk to house.'

The boy drops down to walk silently to the front of the car. When he holds his hand out the boy takes it instantly and walks quietly at his side towards the door.

'HELLO?' Gregori shouts, adopting an English accent.

Nothing. No reply.

'ANYONE THERE?' he knows to speak only small words when adopting an English accent. Anything more than two simple words shows his accent.

He walks on with the boy holding his hand. Silence save for the crunch of gravel underfoot and the dull clicks coming from the cooling engine of the car but the prickle is there. This house is not empty.

A thump inside. A series of low bangs of wood hitting wood. A voice. Male and hushed. Someone runs up the stairs inside. Seconds later the banging ends.

Gregori pretends not to have noticed and continues calling out while looking round as though scared and nervous. He even makes his gait change to show a tremble in his legs and his hand shakes when he lifts it to shield his eyes. The boy looks up at him as though studying the change in manner.

'WHAT D'YA WANT?'

A rough voice calls out. London accent. East end. Harsh and strong.

'Hello?' Gregori calls back the second he hears the voice. He falters as though startled.

Benny curses under his breath behind the front door. It's been eight fucking days since they got here. Eight days of being cooped up in a house. The power went out the day after they got here. They don't even have a radio. No phone signal. No landline. They were only meant to be here for three days and now there's some twat and his kid outside. He peers through the spyhole to the nervous looking man and the sulky looking kid. They've obviously got lost or broken down. There's no phone signal for miles round here.

'HELLO?'

Benny tuts at the man calling out again. They could have pretended no one was here but the bitch started making noise. He glares at Scott who wilts back with a shrug and a shake of his head to show it wasn't his fault. It was Todd's turn to look after her.

Shit. This is all they need. The geezer outside looks like a bleeding accountant or something. The nosey type that like calling the pigs to say they knocked on a door and heard people inside but no one answered *so perhaps an officer should pop along and check? You know, it might be an old person that fell over or something.*

'Shit,' Benny whispers.

'You going out?' Scott asks.

'Gotta ain't I now,' Benny hisses. He reaches back to check his pistol is secure in his waistband then pulls his shirt out to cover the bulge of the weapon. 'Keep that bitch quiet...put ya fackin' gun to her head.'

'What's goin' on?' Todd asks from the landing upstairs.

'Geezer outside,' Scott says, running up with his pistol in hand. 'Broke down or sommit. Benny goin' out to speak to him...he said to put our guns to the bitch's head so she stays schtum.'

'Don't fackin' shoot her for fack's sake,' Benny whispers up.

'What's happening?' Carl asks, yawning and stretching in the doorway to the living room.

'Some fackin' twat broke down or sommit,' Benny says. 'Go back to sleep.'

'You want me to get the shotgun?' Carl asks.

'No I don't want the fackin' shotgun for fack's sake. What for? Shoot some fackin' accountant for breakin' down in his motor? Get the filth here quicker than anyfin that will ya fackin' plank. Fack off back to sleep...'

'Alright, Benny. Was only saying,' Carl says with a huff.

'What's up with Benny?' Andy asks as Carl goes back into the living room to grab the packet of smokes from the coffee table littered with handguns, shotgun shells and overflowing ashtrays.

'Some fackin' twat broke down outside,' Carl says. 'Ere', Jerry, get the kettle on.'

'Will do,' Jerry says from the kitchen. 'Brian awake is he?'

'I am now,' Brian grumbles from the depths of an armchair in the living room.

'What's going on?' Chris asks, coming out of one of the bedrooms upstairs.

'Geezer broke down,' Scott says, walking past him towards the end bedroom.

'Tom, you best wake up mate,' Chris says going back into his room. 'And you Charlie, Benny's going out to talk to some geezer with a broken motor.'

'Fack me backwards,' Benny mutters, pulling the bolts back on the front door before turning the key to swing the door in. He strides out with a big grin and charm oozing from his friendly manner.

'Alright, mate! What's up? Broken down have ya? We don't got no phone here...alright, nipper...'

A blink of an eye. A beat of a heart. A lifetime of experience. The weathered complexion of the man. The faded tattoos on his arms and hands and on the side of his neck. The solid bulk of his shoulders. The thick gold chain and the creases in his shirttails that tell Gregori the man just untucked his shirt before coming out. An isolated house with clear line of sight. Cameras fitted. A muffled thump from inside. Whispered voices. As the man walks out so he brings the pungent stench of body odour and cigarette smoke with him. A combination Gregori has smelled the world over. The very essence of the criminal fraternity.

The boy smiles suddenly wide and toothy. His eyes twinkling as he pulls his hand from Gregori's to clap in excitement.

Benny stops dead. The sight of the boy isn't right. Something jars him. A lifetime of experience. He takes in the man. The pock marked skin. The bulging eyes. It's not possible. Not here. Not for this.

'FACK IT!' Benny roars, reaching back to snatch his pistol. 'UGLYMAN....'

Gregori lets him draw. It makes life easier for Gregori if the opponent has his pistol in hand. He leans right as the first shot is fired while bringing his own pistol up to fire a single shot that sends the nine millimetre round spinning through the air that forms a neatly cauterised entry wound in the middle of Benny's head but takes the back of his skull off in a burst of pink mist.

'Brains!' The boy laughs, still clapping.

Gregori moves fast. A blur of motion to run and dip to grab Benny's gun then rising as he goes on towards the front door with two pistols now up and aimed.

'More brains,' the boy laughs, jumping up and down on the spot.

The *Uglyman* goes to work. There is no thinking. Only instinct. He strides in through the door and clocks the movement of men lunging for weapons in the living room on his right. He fires while turning. Always one at a time. Never both pistols together. Aim and fire. Aim and fire. Left and right. Each bullet counts. Each bullets strikes a mark.

Carl goes for the sawn off shotgun at the side of the sofa and dies instantly from the bullets slamming into his body that go through his heart and lungs. Brian roars up from the armchair and slumps straight back down again with the back of his head blown off. Andy grabs a pistol as he dives and his last thought before he's killed is that he's always wanted to dive across a room and snatch a gun from a table in a shootout. He always thought it would end differently though and not with his brains splodging on the carpet.

Men shouting. Men screaming out scared and panicked. Gregori drops the pistols as he walks and leans back to slide the single knife from his belt. He ducks as Jerry comes out from the kitchen firing his handgun. A flick of the wrist and the knife spins across the short distance into Jerry's throat. Gregori dives across the floor, twisting as he goes to catch the pistol dropped by Jerry that he uses to fire up into Jerry's arse and groin.

Another man in the kitchen frantically trying to unjam a poorly maintained submachine gun. He screams out in terror at the sight of the *Uglyman* staring at him with an absolute lack of expression.

Gregori fires two shots into the man. One in the shoulder to make him spin and the next in the head. More blood sprays. More brains splashing out.

'Haha,' the boy says from outside. 'I Gregori,' he adds in a mock deep voice. 'Come, we go...'

Gregori tuts as he rises effortlessly to his feet, takes his knife back, wipes the blade clean and goes through the kitchen to check the ground floor rooms before moving down the hallway to the base of the stairs.

Feet thunder down the stairs. Gregori lets Chris reach the bottom before shooting him dead. He also waits for Charlie to thunder down and reach the bottom before shooting him dead too. Tom goes slower but goes nonetheless and even fires down a few rounds as he descends. Plucking shots at the doorway and the walls. Gregori fires through the banister rails into his legs. Tom falls down to land screaming at the bottom then looks up into the face of Gregori aiming at his head. A flash of light and his brains also come out while outside a young boy claps his hands and laughs.

Upstairs, Scott and Todd stare at each other. Both wide eyed. Both suddenly pale and terrified. They both flinch at the sound of the first step being taken on the stairs. A second. A third. Clump. Clump. Slow and steady to instil fear.

'WE'LL BLOW HER FACKING BRAINS OUT...' Scott screams. 'WE WILL...DON'T FINK WE WON'T DO IT...'

'I not here for woman.' A quiet voice. A calm voice. A thick accent.

'Gregori? I need a wee wee.'

'One minute. Wait.' Gregori calls back.

'I can't wait...' the boy whines.

'I'M TELLIN' YA...WE'LL FACKIN SHOOT HER IN THE HEAD...'

'Gregori? Gregori? Gregori?'

'What, Boy? I work now.'

'Can I do a wee wee outside, Gregori?'

'Yes. Do the wee wee outside.'

'YAY! Can I wee wee on the car?'

'No! Not wee wee on the car. Wee wee on the grass.'

'Ah but...on the wheel. Just on the wheel, Gregori. Please, Gregori. Please...'

'Okay,' Gregori snaps, halfway up the stairs and rubbing his forehead with the back of one hand clutching a pistol. 'Wheel. Not wee in car. No wee wee in car.'

'Yay!'

'What the fuck?' Todd asks Scott.

'Boy...No wee wee in car.'

'Okay, Gregori.'

'He wee in car. I know he wee wee in car.'

'WHO THE FUCK ARE YOU?'

'I Gregori.'

'Gregory? Who the fuck is Gregory?'

'No. Gregoree. Not Greg Rory.'

'WHAT D'YA WANT?'

'House.'

'Eh? What?'

'House. I want house.'

'The fackin' house? You robbin' us? You dumb prick...do ya know who we are?'

'I not know,' Gregori mutters, glancing back down the stairs while frowning. 'BOY! NO WEE IN THE CAR.'

'Okay, Gregori.'

'Mmmm. Mmmm. Mmmmmmm.'

Gregori cocks his head at the new sound then nods in understanding.

'YOU DON'T FACKIN' ROB US YOU FACKIN' NUMPTY...'

'Mmmmm. Mmmmm.'

'SHUT UP BITCH. I'LL BLOW HER BRAINS OUT,' Scott screams.

'Mmmm. Mmmmm.'

'HAHA! I'M DOING A WEE WEE ON THE CAR, GREGOREEEEE.'

'Oh my god,' Todd whimpers.

'Mmmmm. Mmmm.'

Gregori clumped the first half of the stairs to make sure they heard him. He stopped to talk to make sure they heard him and by doing so, he gained position and distance. He rises silently up the next half, unseen and unheard.

'MMMMM. MMMMMMMMMMMMMM...' she squirms on the chair. Huge eyes staring at the open door. Scott and Todd on either side. Gaffer tape across her mouth.

'SERIOUSLY MATE...YOU'D BEST...

A single shot. Blood sprays across her face. Hot and wet. Scott slumps over her lap leaking clumps of grey matter and gooey bone shards over her thighs. Todd screams.

'MMMMMMMMMMMMM...'

Another shot. Todd falls on Scott. The woman stares down at the bleeding heads and bits of gore pulsing out.

Footsteps in the hallway outside. A shot. A scream. Another shot.

Silence. Footsteps. A submachine gun opens up filling the air with a solid staccato. When it ends, the footsteps continue.

A scream. A single shot. Silence.

She tries to move to shift the bodies weighing down on her lap. Her thighs now hot from the blood and juices leaking. The smell of it. The sight of it. She looks away with an urge to gag and puke while knowing her mouth is taped shut and listens to the footsteps coming closer down the hallway outside the room. A fresh surge of terror hits that only gets worse when the Gregori walks into the room. Pocked marked skin. Bulging eyes. Ugly and cold. A pistol in his right hand.

He takes in the bodies over her lap and the solid wooden chair bolted to the floor and turns to walk out.

'MMMMMMM,' she tries screaming while squirming to shift the crushing hot wet bodies lying across her legs. Gregori pauses at the door, looking back at her frantic expression partly concealed by the thick tape. For a second he considers killing her then forms the judgement she is not a threat and that singular decision not only saves her life but renders her as a meaningless entity. He goes to leave. She is nothing to him. She murmurs harder, thrashing her body side to side. Her eyes wide and clearly imploring. He shrugs mildly, walks over and yanks the gaffer tape from her mouth. As she screams out from the sensation he pokes the bodies with the barrel of the gun to slide them from her lap.

It's too much. She gags, coughs, composes herself for a second then pukes with projectile vomit spewing down her front. Gregori steps back with a mild look of distaste on his face. She retches, gasps, pukes and sobs with eyes watering, mouth stinging and ears ringing all with a chorus of gargled noises.

'WHERE ARE YOU? I HAD A WEE WEE.'

'Here,' Gregori calls back, not looking away from the woman.

'Haha! His brains came out...and his brains too...urgh that man did a poo I can smell it...GREGOREE!' the boy runs in and stops dead at seeing the woman sobbing, puking and heaving. Drool hanging from her mouth. Snot hanging from her nose. Tears streaming from her red eyes. She goes to speak but gargles instead. Gregori and the boy stare at her. Mesmerised at the sight and sounds.

She snatches a big fast breath, desperate and terrified. 'Please,' she gasps. 'Untie me...'

Gregori stares. She begs again with a whispered voice all strangled and choked that makes the boy's mouth drop open. 'Please...please help me...'

Gregori glances round the room seeing the single bed at one end. No other furniture. A sturdy lock on the outside of the door. A second of thought and he crosses the room while drawing his knife with an action that makes her scream out and screw her eyes closed. A few quick slices and the ropes securing her drop away. Gregori even tuts at people using rope. Rope is for the movies. Chains and handcuffs are used by professionals.

It takes second for the woman to realise she has been freed and not stabbed to death. She rubs her wrists, frantic and clearly terrified. 'Where's my father?' she asks weakly, tracking Gregor as he crosses back to the boy still gawping in wonder.

'Come, we go.'

'What's...I...I mean...are the police...' the woman staggers away from the chair, stepping too high over the bodies and slipping on the blood and gore. 'Is...oh god...is my father...'

'I like this house,' the boy says.

'No. Mess. No clean this.'

'Please...please... who are you? Did my father...are you the police?' she looks in confusion at the child, looking but not processing. 'Did...please...did my father send you?'

Gregori looks back at her. The boy too.

'My father sent you, yes?' she asks with a frantic nod while wiping the back of a trembling hand across her mouth. She looks at the child, at Gregori, at the child again. Looking but still not seeing. Too panicked to understand. 'What...please...is my father here?'

'No. We look for house....'

'House? Who...I...what the...' she blinks rapidly, shaking from head to toe. Blood, gore, tears, snot and puke dripping from her chin.

'How long men keep you in this place?'

'What?'

'How long be here?' Gregori asks again. 'This place...how long in this place?'

'Eight days. I...they took me...I was...I mean there was a van and...please...'

'This place eight days?' Gregori asks.

She nods frantically, her eyes imploring him to understand while not having a clue of anything herself. 'They took me...eight days ago...'

'Seven days,' Gregori says.

'No, eight days,' she cuts in quickly, stumbling towards him on shaking legs. 'My father sent you didn't he? Are you from the police? Why is there a...' she looks again at the boy then over to the bodies. 'Child...why is a child...who are you?'

Gregori speaks slowly and deliberately, choosing his words. 'It happen seven days. Father no send. Nobody send.'

'What? What are you...who is that child? Where is...what was seven days ago?'

'World,' Gregori says. 'It end. Seven days. Boy, come, we go.'

CHAPTER TWO

'Can you ask him to stop staring at me please?'

'Boy. No stare.'

The boy twists round in his seat to face forward as the Skoda drives on through country lanes in a landscape growing darker by the minute. Night is coming. The darkness will soon be here. Gregori flicks his eyes to the rear-view mirror and the red hair of the woman. Pale skin. Full sensual lips. Green eyes. Quintessentially English in appearance with perfect pronunciation of words that comes from a private education.

'You don't work for my father then?' she asks again.

Gregori stays quiet.

'He always told me to do what they say and wait. I waited. I waited eight days. You killed them all. He must have sent you...'

Gregori stays quiet. The boy twists round to stare at her again. His sullenness and withdrawn manner now gone.

'What did you say about seven days? Say it again.'

'Disease.'

She waits for more but more doesn't come. 'What disease?'

'Everywhere.'

'What disease?! What does that mean?'

Gregori reads the road. Glimpses of buildings in the distance. Sign boards for a town.

'Where am I? Are we close to London?'

'No.'

'Will you please tell me what's going on?'

'Brains come out and poo.'

'What? Is he your son?'

'No.'

'And we went to the park and Gregoreee made a Happy Meal in MacDonald's and...'

'What? Stop staring at me. Listen, my father is a famous MP. Everyone knows him. You're from London right?'

'Albania.'

'No I mean from London now.'

'And I got new shoes and I made them all sit down and stand up and...'

'Jesus, what he is on about? Kid, stop looking at me.'

'Boy, no stare.'

'I like your hair.'

'What? Stop staring at me!'

'Find car. You go.'

'Jesus Christ! What the hell...' she squeezes her eyes closed and draws a big breath to bite the frustration away. 'How far from London are we?'

'Darren is going to the fort.'

'What? Who is Darren?' she asks with increasing confusion.

'Who Darren?' Gregori asks, glancing across at the boy.

'HAHA! Can we get a Happy Meal, Gregoreee? Please, Gregoreee, can we make burgers and cheese burgers and fishy fingers and...'

'Is he sick? Why does it stink of piss in here?'

'Where stink of wee?'

'Back here. It stinks of urine.'

'Boy, you wee wee in car. I say wee wee on wheel.'

'But I did!'

'It smell of wee wee in car.'

'Some went in,' the boy says innocently. 'Can we go to the park, Gregoreee?'

She pushes her hands through her hair. Tense, scared and not having a clue what's going on.

Gregori tuts. 'We get new car now,' he mutters.

'Yay! We can have a blue one and...'

'I choose. You wee wee in car.'

'No! I choose. I wanna blue one with a white roof and a sports car.'

'Can you just call my father? Tell him where we are. I know his number...'

'No phones.'

'Find one. Please...we just need a payphone or...there's a town! Look...' she points at the sign board going past. 'Go there. Go into the town and...I'll find a phone and call my father. He'll pay you...whatever you want he'll pay it...please...he's really wealthy and...' she lapses into silence as they pass the first buildings at the edge of the town. A sight that catches her attention instantly. Doors smashed in. Windows broken. Houses dark and unlit. An immediate feeling of an empty ruined place. Like something from a war zone. The further into the town they go the more she sees. Her head turning left and right as she leans to look closer, her mouth hanging open and a feeling of dread growing. Cars left abandoned with doors open. Shop windows smashed and broken. Blood smeared on walls and across the panels of a small white van. Debris everywhere and the whole of it so silent and empty. Not a soul anywhere. No ambulances or fire engines. No police. No people.

'Oh my god,' she whispers in shock at the sight of the first bodies on the pavement. An old lady with a knife buried to the hilt in her chest with the corpse of a man across her legs, his neck bitten deep and the puddle of congealed blood now dried and sickening in appearance.

'Did you see that?' she gasps, twisting to look back through the rear windscreen. 'What's...Jesus...' she flinches again as they pass another corpse, then another. Men and women. Children. Elderly.

Some are bloated from decomposition. Others writhe with maggots and swarms of flies hanging over them. Gaping wounds in limbs, torsos, on necks and faces. Like wild animals have run the town through biting everyone in their path. Too many things to see at once. Her mind closes in as she picks out individual details, noticing with abstract attention that she has a dress of the same colour worn by that dead woman. She can't think. She can't speak and she doesn't notice at first when Gregori brings the car to a stop and switches the engine off. A second of silence before the electric whine of motors as he lowers the windows in the front. The boy stares up at the darkening sky.

'Why are we stopping?' she blurts at finally realising they're not moving. 'We can't stop...please...what's...' she casts round, snatching glances of bodies and carnage with that sense of dread growing in her gut.

'Listen,' Gregori says quietly.

'What? Listen? What do...why are...please...what for? To what? What's...' she turns and twists about to see through the still closed windows in the back of the car. Silence outside. The boy shuffles on his seat to pop his head out of the window as he stares intently at the sky. Gregori waits with both hands on the wheel. His face impassive as he watches the last rays of sunlight slowly fade from the street in front of him. Shadows grow deeper and darker as twilight gives way to night proper.

It comes a minute later. An instant howl of voices screeching out primeval and malevolent. Voices from every direction. Human but not people. So many too.

She flinches again, the blood in her veins running cold as ice that sends a shock through her body and makes her stomach flip and sink. Her heart booms, missing beats, making her breathless. Adrenalin dumps into her system readying her body for flight or fight. The noise goes on and on. A screeching awful sound that fills the air and grows louder with every second.

The noise ends with a jarring suddenness that makes the silence so much worse. She can feel her own heart beating. She can hear the blood roaring through her skull. 'Please,' she whispers, 'what's happening? What's happened? I don't think we...what was that noise?'

Gregori doesn't reply. He opens his door and steps out to stand in the dark street. A pistol in each hand. He moves to the front of the car then looks back to see the boy still staring up at the sky.

'What the hell are you doing?' she claws at the door handle to get out from the piss smelling car and the weird kid. It's hot and humid but she wraps her arms round her chest and shivers as she looks round at the devastation so macabre in the dark night. 'Please...what's...'

A drumming. Faint and distant but growing louder and closer.

'What is that?' She spins round while her stomach drops and her legs go weak. Fear inside that screams at her to run and never stop until she's away from that awful sound. A drumming that grows closer. A drumming that grows louder. The sound of feet running on a road in a town with no other noise to absorb the vibration.

She moves towards Gregori without realising she does so. She stops next to him without knowing she does so and stares in horror at the sight of the figures running towards them. More pouring from roads and junctions. More staggering from buildings to charge down the street towards the car. People but not people.

Gregori watches them come. His hands holding the pistols at his sides. He has to know. He has to see it again to be sure.

She turns to run but more are running from behind already blocking any way to escape. Her vision becomes almost strobe like. Snatching glimpses of wounds and injuries. Of bones jutting through skin and faces bitten away. Noses gone. Hair lank and greasy. Skin smeared with blood. An old woman with her left arm just a bloodied pulp but still running as fast as the others. Fat people. Old, young, children, men and women. All races. All colours. All of them running directly towards her. People but not people. Like animals. Wild and feral. Something from a nightmare, a movie, this is isn't real. It can't be real.

The boy stares at the sky. Gregori watches them coming. The woman feels her chest tightening, ready to pass out from a sensory overload of fear and panic.

The infected swarm in with red bloodshot eyes and hands clawed to talons. Vicious and animalistic in nature and bearing. The sight is too much. She staggers in shock. The back of her legs hit the car making her stumble and trip. She cries out with absolute terror at the people charging in from all sides in such stark contrast to the utter calmness of the man holding his pistols at his sides and the boy leaning out the car staring up at the night sky.

Gregori waits. Expecting them to stop but they come fast with no sign of slowing. His eyes flick to the boy.

The woman whimpers with a keening noise that rises louder as she snatches views of the gaping wounds and awful bite marks. Eight days of fear. Eight days of confinement and staying passive. Eight days of waiting, then a taste of freedom and suddenly the world around her is twisted and broken.

Gregori tenses. His eyes narrowing. He widens his stance and readies his body to lift the pistols. A glance to the boy still gawping at the sky. A look round to the oncoming things closing the distance. Twenty metres away. Fifteen. Ten. Five.

'BOY,' Gregori yells out at the last second as his pistols come up to aim at the closest two who suddenly stop inches from the barrels as the whole of the horde do the same and come to a sudden standstill.

She cries out at seeing it. At the tiny gap between the pistols and the awful things now frozen in place and the low chuckling coming from the child in the car.

'Is not funny,' Gregori mutters.

The boy laughs on in amusement as he opens his door and drops out to run over.

The woman tracks him with horror on her face at the surrealness and abstract notions flashing through her mind.

'I shoot them,' Gregori says in admonishment, making the boy giggle again.

All around her they stand. A circle closed in by human form but these things are not human. The stench of them hit her. The putrid smell of rotten meat, unclean bodies, faeces, urine and stale sweat. She gags and covers her mouth as the horror goes on. In the midst of the sheer panic, she notices not one of them is looking at her or the man but only at the boy.

She translates the awful sight of them into a threat against the child and thinks any second they will close in and tear him apart but the child skips round singing and laughing as he starts weaving round the legs of the things. The Albanian watches him. Everyone watches him but he acts as though he pays no heed. A child playing, a child without a care in the world.

'They no kill him,' Gregori says quietly.

The woman stays frozen, her hand still clamped over her mouth and it takes seconds to realise the man was talking to her. She turns slowly to look at him, at the complete calmness on his face. Not calmness, something else.

'They,' Gregori says, using a pistol to sweep round at the horde, 'kill to make more...more them. They not kill boy...'

'I...' she stammers.

Gregori shrugs with a gesture that makes him almost seem human for a second. She clocks his eyes are white. The boy's eyes are white. The things all have red eyes. The man and child look healthy and clean. The things are dirty, filthy and just different, markedly different.

'Disease,' Gregori says quietly. 'Blood...bite, cut...make bleed you get disease...'

'How?' she whispers.

'I not know this,' Gregori says.

'London?' she asks, breathing harder. She swallows to try and gain composure, to try and think clearly.

'I not see London but it...it,' he stops to think of the words, 'it move fast...'

'Spread,' she whispers.

'This word...spread.'

She nods once and promptly passes out from the combined shock, horror and stress sucking the blood from her brain rendering her legs rubbery and weak.

A second of silence as the boy and Gregori look at each other then over to the woman lying on the floor. 'Did she die, Gregoreee?'

'No.'

'Why did she lie down?'

'She sleep,' Gregori says, walking to the woman, he squats, pulls her close and rises easily with her draped over his arms.

'Did she have milk?' the boy asks, running after them in apparent fascination at someone who can fall asleep in the middle of the road.

'Milk?'

'Mummy made me have hot milk and I got sleepy.'

'She no have milk.'

'Did she have hot choclit?'

'No.'

'But but...'

'Car smell of wee,' Gregori says, scowling as he pulls back from placing the woman in the car. 'You wash car tomorrow.'

'But but...'

'Come, we go.'

'But but,' the boy says, running round to clamber back in the passenger seat. He closes the door then twists to stare at the woman. 'She doesn't have a nightie, Gregoreee. She should have pyjamas or a nightie...'

Gregori starts the engine, selects a gear and starts moving forward. A quick press on the horn that sounds out clear and distinct.

'And she didn't brush her teeth,' the boy says.

'Boy, make move,' Gregori says, waving at the horde still encircling the car.

The things move back instantly. Walking backwards to create a path for the car to roll through. 'But but...' the boy twists back to stare at the woman. 'And she didn't wash her face or have a wee...'

The car drives on through the ruined town and out into the country lanes. The boy stares at the woman sleeping before sitting back in his seat to stare up at the same night sky the people in the fort work under to get ready.

CHAPTER THREE

It makes sense now. The rising tension in the house she was held captive in. The increasingly hostile snatched conversations she overheard. The power going out. They didn't have a radio or television. Just long days of waiting.

Her face glistens with sweat. Her hair wet against her scalp. Her mouth feels dry. Thirst and hunger mixed with panic and confusion. She woke to feel the car in motion and sat up to stare out at the night sky. It took a few seconds to remember where she was.

'Do you have any water?' she whispers. Gregori leans to reach into the passenger footwell then passes a bottle back. The water is warm but she is thirsty and drinks deep.

'Where are we going?'

A pause. 'Find house.'

'Your house?'

Another pause. 'No.'

She drinks again and stares at nothing while trying to process everything she saw. For a second or two she even doubted her own memory and thought it was a dream or something. 'What about me? I need to get to London…'

Gregori stays silent but glances across at the boy who has lapsed back into the quiet reflection he had earlier.

'I need to go home,' she whispers. 'I need to go home,' she adds louder and waits for a response but none comes. 'Is he dead?'

The same pause. Like he is thinking before replying. 'Who?'

'My father?'

Gregori exhales noisily through his nose.

'Did you hear anything about London?'

An entrance ahead. Gregori spots the darkened recess and slows the vehicle as he approaches. A wide dirt track leads away between fields. He leans out of his open window at the power lines overhead and sniffs the air for smoke or scent of life. Nothing.

'Where are we going? Is this where you live? Do you know anything about London?'

He blinks at the barrage of questions while the Skoda bounces on the rough track. High hedges on both sides with snatches of woodland and fields. He goes slowly and turns the headlights off to use just the light of the moon to navigate.

'Why did you do that? You can't see...is this where you live? What about me?'

'Boy?' Gregori looks down at the child. 'The things. They in this place? Boy?'

The boy stares fixed at the sky. His eyes focussed and far away.

'Boy?' Gregori taps his arm but the child stares motionless and silent.

'Why isn't he talking?' she leans forward to look down at him. 'Is he okay? Where are we going?'

Gregori brings the car to a gradual stop and scans ahead then up at the sides. A glimmer of a reflection from a tiled roof in the distance. He moves closer to the window to inhale.

'Why have we stopped? Wait! Where are you going?' she gabbles the words as Gregori opens his door and steps out to stand and listen. She tumbles out with wide eyes.

'Come, we go.'

'Go? Go where?' she asks.

'House.'

'What house? Where? Your house? Please just...I'm so confused...'

she runs after him as he walks round the front of the car to open the boy's door.

'Please, just...what house?' she spins to look but sees nothing. 'Please...just hang on...'

'House,' Gregori says. He bends in to unfasten the seatbelt and lifts the child up to hold in the crook of one arm. 'What wrong with you?'

'Nothing,' the boy says quietly, finally looking down from the sky to Gregori.

'Sick?' Gregori presses his hand to the boy's warm forehead. He sets off walking. The two pistols tucked in his waistband.

'Wait,' she rushes after them, stumbling and tripping on the stones and dips on the track. 'I really need to...'

'No speak,' Gregori cuts her off.

'No listen I...'

A look. A glare. His pock-marked face shadowed and awful. His bulging eyes so cold and hard. She falls instantly quiet and even thinks to go back to the car but the memory of the things in the town make her stay with the man and child.

She spots the roof after another minute of walking. Slate tiles reflecting the silver glow of the moon. A chimney stack jutting up. An old stone built cottage nestled in open grounds bordered by dark tree-lines. A hand on her arm makes her flinch and jump back as he guides her to the side of the track. Gregori scans, listens, absorbs and reads the ground. The windows are all dark. The door intact. Big sheds and outbuildings off to one side. A low stonewall marking the edge of the front garden.

She eases back as he takes the lead. The house looks foreboding and frightening but she stays close as he walks to the end of the track then stops to listen and stare.

'Stay,' he lowers the boy and glances back to the woman, 'wait.'

He draws one of the pistols and walks off. She watches him then looks down to see the kid staring up at the sky.

'Darren.'

'What?' she asks. 'What did you say?' The boy frowns. 'Is that your name?' He shakes his head but doesn't speak. 'Who is Darren? Is that man Darren? I thought he said Gregory…'

'Gregoreee,' the boy whispers, placing the emphasis on the last elongated sound.

'You said Darren. Who is Darren?'

Movement in her peripheral vision. Gregori coming back in view from the other side and moving across the front of the cottage to the front door. A test for locks. Pressure applied to the top and bottom. A pause. A grunt and he slams his shoulder into the door making it pop open. Pistol up and aimed and he strides inside.

'What's a cunt runt?'

'What?!'

The boy looks at her. 'What's a cunt runt?'

'What the hell? That's really rude. Don't say that. Who said that? Did someone say that?'

He shrugs and peers past her to the house then sets off towards it.

'Wait, he said to…er…little boy? He said to…' she reaches for his arm to pull him back.

'Gregoreeee?'

'Shush!' she whispers frantically at him calling out. For a second she feared he would pull away or scream at her touching him but he just stops and looks again up at the sky. 'What are you staring at?' she looks up but sees nothing.

'We get car,' Gregori says, walking from the house. He bends to scoop the boy as he passes. Lifting him up to settle back in his left arm as he strides up the lane. She follows again. Running behind to catch up.

'Who's house is it? Was anyone home? I mean…what if they come back? They might come back? What about the police? Have you tried the police? Did you see a phone in there?'

'What's a cunt runt?'

Gregori scowls at the child. 'Is bad word.'

'Runt?'

'No.'

'Cunt.'

'Yes.'

'Is it naughty?'

'Yes. Where hear this word? This woman say this word?'

'I didn't say it!'

'Don't say bad word.'

'I didn't say a bad word. He asked me what it meant. He said Darren then said cunt runt...'

'She said cunt runt.'

'No say this word. Bad word.'

'I didn't! He said it.'

'Who Darren?' Gregori asks. 'You say name again. Who this man?'

'I'm tired. Can I have some warm milk now please, Gregoreee.'

'We get car.'

'Do I have my pyjamas?'

'Yes. In car.'

'Will you read me a story?'

'No.'

'Does the woman have pyjamas?'

'No.'

'What's her name?'

'Er excuse me. I'm right here. My name is Cassie. Cassie Appleton.'

They drive the short distance to the cottage. Lights off. Engine low. Gregori backs the car in with the nose pointing at the lane ready for a fast egress. Cassie stays in the back, still confused, still fearful, still with no clear idea of what's going on. She gets out when Gregori gets out and follows him and the boy to the front door.

'Phone,' she rushes into the hallway to snatch the handset up. No dial tone. She presses the clickers down several times but hears nothing. 'The phone's dead,' she calls out. 'Have you got a mobile?'

'No.'

She follows the sound of his voice down the darkened hallway. Polished floorboards under foot. Walls painted a light colour. Prints and pictures hanging from hooks. The air musty and stale but otherwise clean. Gregori stands by the kitchen sink running water from the tap. The boy next to him quiet and pensive. She looks round at the modern décor. Pine units. A tiled floor. A pine table off to one side. Everything neat and tidy. Gregori tastes the water before grunting and filling a cup for the boy.

'Drink.'

'Want milk.'

'No milk. Drink.'

'Want warm milk.'

'No milk now. Drink.'

'Okay, Gregoreee.'

'Hungry? You eat?'

The boy shakes his head.

'You eat now?'

The boy shakes his head again. Gregori presses his palm to his forehead again. His whole manner so cold, his voice so hard but his actions jarringly caring. 'Sick?'

The boy shakes his head.

'Drink water.'

'Okay, Gregoreee.'

Gregori watches him drink. Waiting patiently. His eyes on the boy and nothing else. She studies his features. The scarred skin. The bulging eyes. His broad shoulders and the striations of muscle in his forearms. Lean but not bulky. Strong but not overly muscular and as ugly as anything. She steps back without realising as though to create distance. He detects the motion but pays no heed.

'More?' he asks the boy when the cup is empty.

'No,' the boy shakes his head and holds the cup out.

'Come,' Gregori lifts him up to carry down the hallway to the stairs. Cassie follows after them. Afraid to be with them but more afraid to be alone. More pictures and paintings on the walls.

She watches them go into the bathroom. Gregori positions the boy in front of the basin, pulls a toothbrush from his pocket and runs the tap. A squeeze of toothpaste and he watches the boy brush his teeth. Once done he helps the boy pull his top off and wash his face, arms and upper body. 'Go toilet,' Gregori says, stepping out and pulling the door closed. 'Three room.'

'Pardon?'

'Three room,' Gregori says.

'Oh I see, three bedrooms, right, yes...yes of course. Listen, I really need to get to London.'

'Find car tomorrow. You go.'

'Thank you.'

She slides into the bathroom after the boy is taken to one of the rooms. A thin bolt on the door that she slides across then tugs her jeans and knickers down to wee in the bowl. She only had two sets of clothes in the house. They made her wear one set for three days before letting her change. It was rank. She felt filthy from sweating through long hot days and even longer hotter nights and all the time they had no clue what was going on outside in the world. She knows that lack of knowledge probably saved her life. They would have killed her without question if they realised there was no ransom coming. She thinks back to Gregori moving through the house executing them one after the other. He was so fast. So brutal. So efficient. She saw the bodies after and almost threw up again. Then the car journey and those things in the town. More bodies. More horror. More than she can take but she's alive and safe at least for now.

Her hair is in desperate need of a wash. It feels greasy, matted and knotted but she rushes to rinse her face and uses her finger loaded with paste to clean her teeth. When she steps out she hears the rhythmic breathing of a sleeping child and hears the noise of Gregori moving around downstairs and hesitates. She doesn't want to go down but she doesn't know which room to use, is there a protocol in place? Should she ask?

When she heads into the kitchen she stops in surprise at the blue jet of flame hissing from the gas hob under the pans of water. Gregori doesn't say anything but goes through the bags he brought in from the car at the table. The two pistols now on the table top but she spots the hilt of a knife in his waistband.

He crosses to the hobs and checks the water. She watches him then glances back to the pistols.

'No touch guns,' his voice is hard and low.

'I wouldn't,' she replies instantly.

'Eat?'

'I'm not...no thank you but...'

Pasta goes in a pan. The rustle of the plastic packet so distinct and loud. He takes a tin from the cupboard, examines the front then finds a tin opener and sets about removing the lid. She stays put. Unmoving. Unspeaking. Not knowing what to do or say.

The contents of the tin go into the pan with the pasta. She smells the rich scent of tinned tomatoes. When the other pan comes to boil he lifts it to pour into two mugs. The aroma of coffee adds to the smells of cooking. He stirs, lifts a mug and holds it out to her.

She has to go closer to take it and realises without the presence of the boy she is afraid of him. His face is so hard and ugly. His whole manner so cold and ruthless. His voice harsh and brutal. She takes the mug and retreats. 'Thank you.'

'Sugar,' he says, moving a metal pot down the counter.

'No thank you,' the coffee smells divine. They gave her one cup of tea a day in the house. She ate basic food. A single slice of toast in the morning. Baked beans in the evening. She's never farted as much in her life from eating beans for eight days. 'Is he asleep?' she asks, feeling the need to fill the silence.

Gregori doesn't reply but stirs the pan of pasta and tomatoes.

'He's not your son then?'

'No.'

'How do you know him? I mean...is he family?'

'No.'

She sips her coffee, the awkwardness of his one word replies hanging in the air.

'His mother die.'

'His mother?'

'Yes. I see this.'

'So...you took him?'

Gregori stirs the pasta.

'What's his name?'

Gregori stirs the pasta.

'I thought he said he was called Darren.'

Gregori drains the pasts in a colander over the sink. Steam rises to evaporate in the air.

'What will you do?'

Gregori swills the colander to rid the excess water before tipping the contents on a plate. Simple pasta and tinned tomatoes. Her mouth waters at the sight. She clears her throat and sips from the mug. He freezes. Holding still. She holds her breath. Unsure of why. A flick of his eyes at her. Her heart beats harder. She flinches when he moves to take another plate from the cupboard and spoons half the pasta and tomatoes across. He takes another fork, places it on the second plate then carries his to the table. She lets go of the breath, trying desperately not to show she was so afraid.

He sits down and starts eating. Hidden in the shadows. She can't go to the table. She can't sit with him. She's so hungry though. She walks briskly to the plate, grabs the fork and starts eating. It does taste good. Eight days of toast and beans. The pasta is firm. The tomatoes rich and so full of taste. They eat in near silence. She twists round so she can see his form as though afraid he will sneak up on her. She reminds herself he saved her. He came into a house full of armed men and killed them one by one. He didn't have to do that. He didn't have to take her with them. If anything, those thoughts make it worse. That she is in a house in the middle of nowhere with a man so capable of doing that. He didn't flinch earlier either when those things ran at him. Not a shred of fear showed.

She fills quickly and steps away to drink the coffee. Gregori eats methodically. Chewing precisely. Food is nutrition. Food is energy. When he finishes he drinks his coffee.

'I should er...tired and...' she falters, his face hidden from view, a shiver runs up her spine at his silence. 'Night then...' she starts walking, feeling the urge to run from the room. She climbs the stairs with her heart hammering and rushes into one of the bedrooms. A single bed. Everything in beige. A spare room bland and awful but she doesn't notice and doesn't care. What she worries about is the lack of a lock on the door. Not that a lock would stop him. She tells herself what he did today but again the fear rises. She starts undressing then worries about being undressed but it's too hot to sleep in clothes. She strips to knickers and t-shirt and climbs under the covers to stare at the door.

A clunk of cutlery on a plate downstairs. A tap running. Footsteps moving to the front door. The sound of a bolt going home. His feet on the stairs climbing up. She tenses, staring at the door. Silence on the other side. Silence that stretches. She imagines his hand on the door handle, his bulging eyes full of lust and sadistic desire.

The toilet flushes. Silence. The sound of a bed creaking. Silence.

CHAPTER FOUR

Day Eight

'NO!'

Gregori launches from his bed, pistol gripped and the safety off before he reaches the door.

'NOOOOO...'

He runs into the boy's room, weapon up and ready. Weak light coming through the windows of a new dawn and a new day. The boy screams out again. His little body tensing rigid. His face flushed. Gregori drops to one knee at the side of the bed and places a hand on the child's head as he thrashes side to side, convulsing as though having a fit.

Cassie staggers bleary eyed and full of panic from her room. Her hair wild and dishevelled. Lines on her face made by the creases of the pillow. She stops in the doorway to see the man leaning over the thrashing child. 'GET OFF HIM...' she screams out and goes forward without thinking or seeing properly. An instinct telling her the man is hurting the child. She slams into his side, expecting to knock him away but his form absorbs the blow without flinch or concern.

'He dream.'

'Oh my god, I am...I'm so...I thought...'

'NOOOOOOOO...'

'Boy, is dream...is dream...'

The boy thrashes then goes still. His face flushed red. His little fists clenched into hard balls. He releases the tension then falls still and quiet, breathing hard with his eyes clamped shut and a look of fury etched on his sleeping face.

'Boy, is dream,' Gregori says again, his hand still on the child's forehead.

'I am so sorry,' Cassie whispers, backing away towards the door. 'I didn't mean...' her words cut off as the boy's eyes open to glare at Gregori. He sits up and looks nothing like a child. Breathing hard, seething with fury. The fists bunched hard. His top lip curling up. His whole face twisting in pure rage.

'CUNTRUNT...' the boy roars and how the hell a child can make such a noise is beyond Cassie. The hairs on the back of her neck stand up. Shivers run down her spine. Her skin prickles. The look on the child's face. A depth of years in his eyes.

'Our Father who art in heaven...' a growl of a voice, whispered and low.

'Oh shit,' she covers her mouth in horror.

'Hallowed be thy name...'

'What this?'

'Thy kingdom come, thy will be done in earth as it is in heaven,' the boy's head cocks to one side to stare at Cassie. Unblinking with an intensity pouring from him.

Silence holds. The air thick and charged. Cassie's eyes widen. The silence stretches yet the boy holds that air of expectation with malicious glee and the face of a demon, small, defined, angelic and with a crop of blond hair but with an ageless seething rage. A twisted smile, humourless and cold. When he speaks, he does not speak alone. When he continues, he does not continue alone.

'Give us this day our daily bread...' voices join him. Hundreds of voices all speaking in perfect unison. Gregori lurches to the window to look down at the dense horde packed into the front garden and spilling down the access track and the lines of infected pouring across the fields towards them.

'And forgive us our trespasses as we forgive them that trespass against us…'

'Jesus…' Cassie reels back from the window at the sight of hundreds of red bloodshot eyes staring up.

'And lead us not into temptation but deliver us from evil…'

The voices rise in volume. Perfect in delivery yet flat and without undulation of tone or pitch.

'No,' Gregori whispers. Cassie's stomach twists and heaves. A thing like this isn't possible. It's not real. She's dead. She died in the house. This is hell or a dream or a nightmare. It cannot be happening.

'For thine is the kingdom…'

'No,' Gregori strides to the bed. The boy lifts his head with defiance in his eyes.

'The power and the glory…' the voices come louder, taunting, goading, powerful. They send a fresh chill running down Cassie's spine. The fine hairs on the back of her neck and arms stand on end. Electricity in the air.

'You challenge me?' Gregori says, his tone growling with fury.

'For ever and ever…' louder, stronger, defiance shown and another step taken towards the house. Cassie sees the faces of the undead. A hand on her arm wrenching her across the room

'YOU CHALLENGE ME?' Gregori roars, dragging Cassie to the doorway. 'I SHOW YOU WHAT I DO BOY, I SHOW WHAT I DO…boy not leave room,' he tells Cassie and strides out, slamming the door behind him so hard a chunk of plaster falls from the wall. She trembles from head to toe. Staring at the child that's not a child as his head cocks over.

'AMEN…'

A thunderous chant. A roaring of voices that almost drown out the tread of Gregori as he runs down the stairs. The boy surges towards the window. Cassie goes after him, convinced he will launch himself through the glass. She grabs his arm, yanking him back. He twists to pull away as the front door is opened and Gregori's pistols boom to life one after the other with huge retorts that blow heads from necks and blast brains from skulls. Eighteen shots in rapid succession. Eighteen people killed instantly.

'YOU CHALLENGE ME?'

'NO,' the boy screeches. His voice back to that of a child. He thrashes to pull free but Cassie holds on.

Gregori's thumbs hit the release switches that drop the magazines from the pistols. He lifts his hands as though to throw the pistols up then lets go and drops to pull two magazines from his pockets that he launches up like rockets. As the pistols reach the apex of their lift and start to drop, so he grabs the butts and thrusts them down to slot the magazines in. All within a second. All within the blink of an eye. All within a blur of motion then the arms go out and eighteen more die as he moves left towards the Skoda.

'DON'T,' the boy screams out, wrenching and yanking to get free. He kicks Cassie in the shins and throws himself at her. The infected outside growl as the boy's temper grows. His face flushing deeper shades of red while outside Gregori guns them down, picking targets so fast it's near on impossible to track. When the pistol in his left hand empties he ditches it to thrust a hand in his pocket and presses the boot release catch on the Skoda. The lid pops as he reaches it and pulls the pump action shotgun taken from the dead guards in the house. The boom is louder, deeper and the damage more widespread. Several are blown off their feet with each shot.

'NO NO NO,' the boy screeches with each shot, fighting with every ounce of strength to get free from Cassie hanging on for dear life. She wraps her arms round his chest. Pinning his limbs to his sides. He rakes nails down her forearms and sinks his teeth into her shoulder. His feet cycle, battering her shins. She screams out but holds on with no idea of what is happening or why. She doesn't know a thing only that Gregori told her to stop him leaving the room. She snatches glimpses to the man below slaughtering as he fires the shotgun at the crowd still standing passive and unmoving.

The boy slams his elbows into her stomach and headbutts backwards. A vicious demented crazed action that suddenly ends when he goes rigid with his head fixed and staring and his eyes unblinking.

Dozens lie dead. Dozens more lie injured from the shotgun blasts but not a sound they make. Not a bleat or cry of pain. Not a whimper of regret or remorse. Not a beg or plead to stop.

It becomes sickening. One man slaughtering passive watchers. Tears stream the boy's face to spill over and drop to land on the cuts on Cassie's arms. Gregori carries on as though this is work and nothing more. As though to kill for him is to breathe for anyone else.

She watches as men and women are shot down. She watches skulls blow out and his aim that never misses. She watches them die one after the other. All ages. All colours. No hesitation and no remorse. Her eyes fill with moisture that spill out as thick tears that roll down her cheeks. To see such a thing, to see human forms killed so easily. She breathes harder, deeper. The boy starts shaking in her arms, his sobs growing louder.

'Stop,' she whispers the word, unable to see them being killed like that. The speed at which she was repulsed to feeling horrified at their death is quick but such is human nature that a simple act can make the switch from abhorrence to sympathy to outrage and disgust. 'Stop...' she whispers in a voice breaking from the tragedy witnessed. The boy's grip on her changes from trying to break free to a child seeking comfort from an adult. Her tears fall on his head. His tears fall on her arms. Still Gregori fires. Still he kills. Still they fall and die. Passive. Unthreatening. Just standing there. He has to stop. It's too much. They're not doing anything.

Gregori places the pistols in the boot of the car. He changes the magazines for fresh ones then tucks one in his waistband. His right hand grips the hilt of the knife as he steps away from the car and flicks the blade over so it presses up against his forearm. The boy will be a boy. The boy will live normally. The boy will be shown what happens if he brings the things to him.

It gets worse. So much worse. Killing with guns is one thing but with a single blade to throats is something else. The speed of him. The fluidity of his motion as he ducks, weaves and glides through them whispering the blade across neck after neck. They fall like dominoes. Literally dropping as their jugulars are opened with an almost synchronised act of arterial sprays jetting out one after the other.

'THIS WHAT I DO.'

They both flinch at the thick accent and the strength of his voice. She squeezes her eyes closed as her lip trembles and the tears fall faster. She wants to move away but she can't do a thing other than stand and watch. He gets faster. Moving faster. Killing quicker.

She can't stand it. She can't see it. 'STOP…' she screams out but he carries on. Gregori carries on because the boy will be told and shown what happens if they come. The boy will be given a lesson. 'STOP IT…' he ignores the woman screaming at him from the window. Why are they just watching? Why don't they run? Why are they standing dumb and stupid? 'STOP IT…GREGORI STOP IT…' she screams and releases the boy to unfasten the catch to open the window and scream again. 'RUN…STOP IT…' she sobs fresh tears with the boy at her side. His hands gripping her arm. His chest heaving as he cries ragged and hoarse. Why are they just standing there? Why don't they run or do something? Why don't they attack him? 'RUN…just just… don't just die…fight…do something…'

Still she doesn't notice as the boy's grip tightens or that he leans closer to the window. She sees only the sheer incomprehension of a man doing something that isn't right. People do not move like that. Every time she blinks he is somewhere else. Always moving, always weaving, leaning, ducking and twisting. It's almost beautiful. Like a dance. Like ballet.

She runs through the house and out to the heat and the stench of blood and innards. To the dull thuds as bodies fall. The infected pay her no heed. They don't look at her. They don't react to her. The boy watches from the window. His eyes taking it all in. She pushes through them. Touching them without thinking, without conscious thoughts telling her what she is doing. Such is the panic driven wildness of her actions that she doesn't notice when they draw back to open a path to Gregori.

Gregori turns to face her. His expression strangely serene and calm with barely a light sheen of sweat showing.

'Stop...please stop...' she runs into him, grabbing at his arm holding the knife. 'Please...stop it...'

He spots the boy in the window and sees the space around them growing larger by the second as the things draw back.

'Please,' she begs, sobbing harder, clinging to his arm. 'They're not doing anything...just...please...RUN...' she screams at the infected surrounding them. 'RUN...GET AWAY...GO...GO...' she waves her arm at them, sickened to the core at the senseless death given and the passivity of them to allow it.

Slowly, as the seconds tick by, as the sun shines down and the silence penetrates her mind, she realises they are moving away and the killing has stopped.

Slowly. As the seconds tick by, she realises Gregori is passive within her grip and has not killed her. The knife in his hand is lowered so the blood drips on the ground.

Slowly, as the seconds tick by, she realises the space around them is growing larger as the red eyed infected walk quietly away.

Slowly, as the seconds tick by, she understands this man, that child, these infected people and the world she is within is entirely and without doubt, not normal.

Not normal at all.

CHAPTER FIVE

D ay Eight

T he boy chatters on with an unrelenting stream of noise that never ends, skipping and moving between them. Holding hands with Gregori for a few minutes then going to Cassie to swing her hand instead.

The day is still early but it's already hot with a blazing sun beating down. She wishes she had sunglasses and a hat. She wishes she was somewhere else. She wishes many things but walks with them down the track towards the road.

They couldn't take the Skoda because of the sheer number of dead bodies littering the ground around it. There was no hope in hell the car would have gone over them and it would have taken hours to move them all. Gregori did find another car in the garage. A nice big Volvo that would have gone over the corpses with ease. The first problem was it already had two bodies inside it. An old man and woman lying entwined on the back seat surrounded by empty packets of sleeping pills and two wine glasses that fell from their hands as they succumbed to the fumes coming in from the hosepipe connected to the exhaust. The contrast from the violent death outside to the composed, almost serene appearance of the old couple was jarring and harsh.

The second problem was the fact the old couple had rather self-ishly used all the fuel while committing suicide. The third problem was that the Volvo and Skoda used different fuels.

'This fuel not same as other fuel,' Gregori said, explaining in his thick accent while surrounding by the ruined corpses of his kills. It was getting more surreal by the minute.

So now they walk. They walk down the track with rucksacks on backs. Cassie's filled with water. Gregori's filled with the weapons taken from the guards he killed in the house she was held captive in and not a single infected person is seen anywhere.

Gregori killed over a hundred of them. Maybe close to one hundred and fifty. The sight was something that will stay with her forever. Not just the bodies but the images of him killing them. The speed of him and the ease in which he did it. Now he looks entirely at ease. No, not at ease. Saying Gregori looks at ease is wrong. Completely wrong.

The boy kicked him in the leg when he finally came out the house. It was a hard kick too. A right belter in the shin that would have made Cassie scream and roll on the floor but Gregori didn't do a thing.

'Things not come,' Gregori said with a finality. The boy sulked for a bit but by the time they had found the Volvo, discussed fuels, found bags, loaded and made ready he was back to being normal.

'We're going to the Island of Wight,' the boy says, beaming at Cassie.

'What?' she asks.

'The Island of Wight. Can we go?'

'What this place?' Gregori asks.

'The Island of Wight,' the boy laughs.

'I think he means the Isle of Wight,' Cassie says. 'It's on the south coast.'

'We're going to the Island of Wight.'

'How know this place?'

'We're all going to the...' the boy sings the words, his voice high and happy.

'People go there on holiday,' Cassie says, 'maybe he went before...'

'Gregoreee, when will we get to the Island of...'

'Not go this place.'

'But...'

They bicker on while Cassie winces at the bruises on her shoulders and arms caused by the boy lashing out when she restrained him. Teeth marks too and tiny cuts from his nails. Little sod. Mind you, anyone would be upset at seeing something like that.

'I need to find a car,' she says once the other two stop arguing, which was more like the boy pleading and Gregori saying *no* a lot.

'Why?' the boy asks.

'To go home,' she says.

'Why?'

'Find my father.'

'Noooo,' the boy laughs, skipping over to grab her hand. 'All the mummies are dead and all the daddies are dead and all the homes are broked...'

'They might be okay,' she says tightly, half expecting Gregori to tell the boy off for being so rude. 'My father is an MP...'

'What's an M and P?' the boy asks.

'Politician,' she says, glancing to read the reaction on Gregori's face but seeing none. 'He's a cabinet minister actually...' still no response. 'He was chairing a select committee investigating the flow of illegal immigrants into the country.' Nothing. Gregori walks on. The boy swings her hand. 'That's why those men took me. To influence my father. The select committee were voting to decide if some report on drug trafficking should be released...and they wanted money too...' she trails off when he doesn't look or show interest. 'Anyway, they have bunkers and safe places,' she adds after a pause. 'For cabinet ministers...and their families...and er, people that er...that help them.'

'I no go London.'

'I never said that,' she says quickly. 'I just meant my father is probably alive and waiting for me in a bunker.'

'Is the Island of Wight in London?'

'No, no it's not,' Cassie says. She walks on, not knowing why she made that weird hinted suggestion at helpers of the families of ministers being looked after. She has no idea if that is the case. She has no idea if the Houses of Parliament even has bunkers but assumes they do. She hasn't even spoken to her father for five years since he left her mother after she caught him with a naked young man in their marital bed. That was bad enough on it's own but the other naked young man filming them made it worse and then the third naked young man in the bathroom chopping cocaine was the straw that broke the proverbial camel's back.

Now she is somewhere in the grim and grimy north with a freaky child that's probably possessed by a demon and an Albanian serial killer. Not that it looks that grim and grimy right now. It looks rather pleasant. There's even a heat shimmer hanging over the track.

Gregori listened to what she said and the hints dropped about her father but it makes no difference to anything. The only thing is the mission. The mission is the boy. Those things will stay away from him or they will die. It's that simple.

'Which way?' Cassie asks, looking up and down the tarmac road.

'This way,' Gregori says, setting off with a purposeful tread.

'Why that way?' she asks.

He doesn't reply. He doesn't want to reply. She walks after him as the boy skips out to the centre of the road to walk on the middle white lines as though on a balance beam.

Moorland on one side of the road. Woodland on the other side. Hills and peaks in the distance. A day like this would normally see the lands thronged with walkers and dogs. With day-trippers and school parties. With coaches winding through the twisting roads to see the picturesque north. Old stone walls constructed from large chunks of slate grey rock border both sides of the road. No cement or adhesive used. Just an eye for detail in the choice of rocks to make them fit like a never-ending puzzle.

They pass an old cottage. The door closed. The windows all shut and the curtains inside drawn together.

'No car,' Gregori says, ignoring it. Cassie stares at the cottage for a while then rushes to catch up as the boy calls her name. It feels wrong to just walk past but then Gregori is right, there's no point if there's no car so she walks on and the morning slowly passes. They drink water as faces grow red from the heat.

'Does he have suncream?' she asks, seeing the boy's flushed cheeks. Gregori stares blankly. 'The sun will burn him, does he have cream? Lotion? You know...stops the skin from...'

'No.'

She frowns, unsure of what he means. 'Sorry, did you mean no you don't have any or no you don't know what it is?'

'Not have this.'

'He needs some. Have you got a hat?'

'No.'

'He needs a hat.'

'I get this.'

'Right. Thanks...I mean, he's not my child but...'

'I get this.'

'Your nose is red too. You need lotion.'

No reply. They walk on.

'I need some too.'

'What?' he asks.

'Lotion. I'm burning. I'm fair-skinned. I'll burn then peel.'

No reply. They walk on.

'And he's blond which means he'll burn too.'

'I get these things.'

'Need a poo.'

They stop and look at the boy. 'I need a poo.'

'Go,' Gregori says.

'Where?' the boy asks, looking round.

'Anywhere.'

'But...' the boy screws his face up in deep thought. 'Can I poo on the road?'

'Yes.'

'Er,' Cassie cuts in, 'maybe go on the verge.'

'Go here. Go there. It no matter.'

'Go to the side of the road,' Cassie tells the boy.

'It no matter,' Gregori says, 'he go anywhere.'

'It does matter,' she says, ushering the boy towards the verge.

'Why this matter?'

'Because you can't…use the toilet in the road. You go at the side,' she stops at the edge of the grass as the boy walks over towards the wall. 'You okay?'

He nods sweetly, his face red and flushed. His blond hair wet against his scalp. She folds her arms and makes a point of turning away to see Gregori staring round at the road then over at the verge.

'He go anywhere,' Gregori says.

She shrugs, 'he's doing it now.'

'No cars.'

'He's doing it now.'

'Is no cars. No nothing.'

'Yes but it's not right. Not in front of…I mean, you can't do it on the road. It's not right.'

'Why this?'

'Just is.'

'Finished!'

'Wipe,' Gregori says.

'Have you wiped?' Cassie asks at the same time.

'Erm….yes?' the boy says.

'Have you got wipes?' Cassie asks, looking at Gregori.

'I have guns. You have wipes.'

'Right, hang on then,' she drops her back to start rifling the contents, finding a packet of wipes. 'These?'

'Yes.'

'These are for make-up.'

'What?'

'These wipes are for make-up, you know…lipstick, mascara…to rub it off…'

'Is wipes.'

'Yes for make-up not for bottoms.'

'Is same.'

'It's not the same. Have you got any others?'

'No.'

'Right. You'll have to use these,' she says, walking over to hand the wipes over and grimacing at the smell. She turns back to Gregori while the boy focusses on cleaning himself. 'You need to get proper wipes.'

'I get this.'

'Not make-up remover wipes.'

'I get this.'

'They have proper toilet wipes. In the shops.'

'Yes.'

'And sun cream...'

'Yes.'

'And a hat.'

'Yes.'

'Whatever. He's not my child.'

'Finished, Casseee.'

'Thanks,' she takes the wipes to put back in the bag. 'I'm not telling you what to do,' she adds with a glance up to Gregori with a sudden reminder that he is an Albanian serial killer that slaughtered over a hundred people before breakfast this morning. 'It's just advice and...'

'Ssshhh,' a harsh command hissed with a hand that rises quickly.

She flinches at the noise. Presuming offence has been given then hearing the engine in the distance. She packs the bag quickly, closing the flap then lifting it onto her back.

A van appears on the road. Big, red and going fast. A diesel engine roaring out. The boy moves to her side, leaning forward to peer down the road as Gregori stares intently.

'We take this,' he says bluntly, walking from the centre to join Cassie and the boy. He lifts an arm in greeting. Adopting the same nervous persona he used when he approached the house Cassie was in. A glance to Cassie, at her reddening nose and flushed cheeks. 'Look scared.'

'I am scared.'.

'You no look scared.'

She pulls a scared face, 'better?'

'Is too much.'

'Seriously?'

'Yes.'

She blinks and shakes her head while looking at the van then back to Gregori. 'Right,' she tries to look worried, frowning and nervous.

'No,' Gregori says. 'Is not scared face.'

'It is my scared face.'

'Do scare face or I shoot you.'

'What!?'

'Better. This is scare face.'

'You said you'll shoot me.'

'No speak now...' he steps out waving his arm, a tremble and falter in his step. His brow furrowed. A transformation that Cassie notices while processing what he just said.

The van starts slowing. A drop in the pitch and tone of the engine. Brakes applied.

'Are you stealing it?' she asks.

'Hallo!' Gregori calls out. The boy giggles at the sound. Gregori shushes him with a glare.

A man in the driver's seat of the van leans forward to stare. Two more men in the front passenger seats. Big men too. Shaved heads. Stubbled jaws. Hard eyes. A hundred metres to go and the driver says something out loud. The man in the middle of the front seats turns his head to say something. Gregori waves his arm. The van holds speed as though to drive past then anchors on at the last minute. The doors in the back slam open. Men run out. The sound of feet on the ground. The two men in the passenger seats jump down. Gregori backs away. His hand going for the pistol in the small of his back as he clocks the barrels of the shotguns.

'Grab the bird,' one of the men shouts in a deep northern accent. Cassie steps back, her hand instinctively grabbing the boy to pull him with her.

Gregori draws and fires as the air splits apart with the sound of howling and screeches that come from the wooded copse beyond the wall. The men coming from the van instantly turn and shout while looking round in panic at the figures running from the treeline to pour over the low stonebuilt wall. Red eyes. Hands clawed. Bodies pumped and charging. Wild and frenzied as they surge in towards the van. Gregori moves backwards, firing two more shots at the men who point shotguns at the infected coming at them and let rip with loud shots.

The whole thing is so quick. So sudden. Bodies fly back from the shots. Blood spraying out but the horde swarm in. Heedless to danger. Heedless to anything save the need to rake and bite and open flesh. The impact is harsh and brutal. The sound of meat against meat. Some of the men try and run but are ripped from their feet. Others run for the van but are taken down.

Cassie keeps going backwards with the boy. Shocked, stunned, horrified and rendered speechless at the sight. She sees the bites. She sees the things eating the men from the van. Sinking mouths into neck, arms, legs and stomachs. She hears the screams of those taken down and the snarling noises of the beasts. The same things that stood passive outside the cottage.

It's over so quickly. Gregori holds the pistol up. Still aiming and waiting for any threat but the infected draw back from the van with shiny red blood drooling down chins and spilling from mouths.

'Two minute,' Gregori says, still aiming. The boy stays quiet at Cassie's side. His eyes focussed 'It take two minute...' Gregori turns to make sure she is watching and not a flicker of emotion shows on his face.

She can't speak. She can't form coherent thoughts. Sounds filter through to her brain. The groans and whimpers of men dying in agony. She thought they were all dead. As the infected pull back she spots the men on the floor writhing in agony, clutching stomachs and calling for mothers, for wives, for each other, for the love of a God that was never given and now never will be.

As they fall silent, she holds the boy's hand and watches for long silent seconds until the first one sits up. No longer groaning or moaning in pain. When he opens his eyes, she sees the red bloodshot look of them. Another one sits up, another then more. Each with red eyes. Each with motion and manner of those that bit them. They rise slowly to stand and shuffle round to face towards the boy. The driver of the van struggles to get out, bitten in the thigh by an infected. Rather than opening his own door, he wriggles and crawls to drop from the other side and lands with a bone-jarring crunch on the road that breaks his nose. He pays no attention and rises to his feet to shuffle and face towards the boy. His face pouring with blood that soaks his top and his big gut straining against his filthy vest.

'This what they do...' his cold hard voice gets her attention, the words spoken so clearly in his thick accent. 'You get blood. Two minutes then you this.' He turns to glance at her. 'You see?' She swallows and nods. 'You see this now?'

'Yes,' her voice breaks with fear and tension.

'Good...hold boy...'

'NOOOO...' the boy screams out as Gregori opens fire.

'I say not bring them,' Gregori utters between shots. 'I say this, boy.'

CHAPTER SIX

The van would have been perfect if not for the blood all over the front seats and steering wheel. That's the problem with blood, it sprays everywhere and sticks to everything.

'Use wipes,' Gregori said while staring in at the blood-soaked front of the van. The boy was still sulking. He tried to kick Gregori in the shins again when she finally let go but the man was ready this time and placed a hand on his head to hold him away until he calmed.

They didn't use the wipes. The wipes are for make-up removal and not much good for destroying bacteria or diseases or viruses or whatever it is. They walked on instead, that was after Gregori examined the fallen weapons and chose one double barrelled shotgun. He broke the others apart and threw the bits over the walls. The shells he took in his bag. Cassie has never seen so many guns. She's never seen a dead body before yesterday either. Now she's seen a lot of both, and the insides of bodies too.

She plays the scene over in her mind as she walks. *Get the bird.* She would be in the back of that van now being passed around like a piece of meat. They didn't try and talk. They didn't try and help or ask anything. They just got out with guns to *get the bird.*

'I'm hot,' the boy complains.

'It is hot,' she says.

'Where are we going?'

'I don't know.'

'Gregoreeee?'

'We find place soon.'

'What place?'

'Place,' Gregori says, clearly not wishing to chat.

'He's too hot,' she says.

Gregori looks but stays quiet. The shotgun clasped in one hand at his side. His ears pricked and listening for sounds from the undergrowth. He knew the things were following before. They were quiet but his senses are tuned and sharp. Now there is nothing and no feel of being watched either.

The boy means something to them. The way they are drawn to him. The way they look at him. He remembers back to one of the houses he and the boy stayed in when he was teaching the boy to kill. The way the boy stabbed them without any regard. The way the boy made them sit down so he could reach the knife into their groins. It seems so wrong now. So bad. A terrible thing to have done. Not to them. Gregori has no regard for them at all. It was bad for the boy. Gregori was beaten and tortured to be what he is. He was brainwashed and moulded over many years. He was a payment to settle a debt and became a tool to be used and nothing more.

'He needs some shade,' the woman's voice penetrates his thoughts. He exhales and walks on. 'It's dangerous for children to get sunstroke...'

'Is town. Not far.'

'Where? I didn't see any signs or...'

Gregori points the shotgun at the field and the giant pylon structure looming like a cyborg alien.

'What about it?' she asks, looking at the huge metallic structure.

'Casseee? What bird did those people want?'

'They er...I mean they...I think they meant me.'

The boy goes silent. Clearly thinking. 'But...but...'

'Bird means woman sometimes. Like a bad word.'

'Why did they want to get you?'

'Er, to...they just did.'

'Maybe they wanted to go to the Island of Wight.'

'Yes...maybe'

She sees him thinking. The way his brow drops with concentration. Like he is trying to work something out. He goes silent for a few minutes. His hand hot in hers. His face red and shiny from the heat and sun. 'That man was called David.'

She blinks back at him having drifted off to her own thoughts and still looking round for a town that is apparently knocking about somewhere. 'Who was?'

'The man,' the boy say quietly.

'What man?' she asks.

'Man who said you are a bird lady. He was called David.'

'Christ, do you know him? Did he know you? How does he...' she stops to look back the way they came then back down at the boy. 'How do you know him?'

'And Gary.'

'What?'

'He fell over and hurt his nose.'

'What? You mean...the man driving the van? How...do you know them? Did they...Jesus Christ, Gregori, did you just kill people he knew?'

'He boy. Child. He has in head...the the...' Gregori twirls his finger by his head.

'Imagination? No. He knew them. Did you know them?'

'And Steve.'

'Jesus...look...how did they know you?'

'We go,' Gregori says, walking on.

'Come, we go,' the boy says, walking after Gregori and tugging on Cassie's hand to pull her along. 'Come, we go,' he says again, mimicking Gregori.

'But...no hang on. Listen, just....just wait!'

Gregori stops when she plants her feet and pushes a hand up over her face to rid the sweat.

'What is your name?' she demands. 'What's his name?' she asks Gregori.

'Boy,' Gregori says.

'It's not boy. He *is* a boy. He's not called boy. What's your name?'

'Come, we go...'

'No listen. How did you know those men? How do they know you? What's your proper name? Is your name Gary? Is it Steve or David or...'

'No!' the boy laughs, pulling hard enough to make her move forward a step.

'Boy, listen,' she snaps then curses at herself for calling him boy while the child laughs harder and even Gregori's lips twitch, only once though.

'He know them,' Gregori says bluntly.

'Knows who? Those men? How? They didn't act like they knew him and...'

'Not men. Things. The...the people with disease. He says names. His head. The magination. Yes?'

'Oh for fuck's sake,' she huffs and starts walking on. 'Like a game? He names them like a game? Is that what you mean?'

'You said a bad word,' the boy laughs, skipping at her side.

'I'll say another bad fucking word in a...' she stops talking at the glare from Gregori. 'I'm sorry,' she adds quickly. 'I'm just confused and...I don't know what's happening or...'

'Come, we go,' Gregori says. The boy mimics and they trudge on. There is nothing else to do. No other options. She could sit down and just refuse to walk but then what? She follows behind listening to the incessant chatter in the incessant heat and confusion.

'See,' Gregori's voice lifts her head. She moves out from behind him to the sight of rooftops nestled against the foot of a big sweeping hill. Church spires and towers. It looks so stereotypically northern. All grey with slate roofs, stonewalls and seemingly plonked in the middle of nowhere.

The details come clearer the closer they get. The size of the town is quite big and feels strange. Like eerily quiet. Cassie remembers walking into a village just after sunrise on a summer morning. It wasn't even five o'clock but it was broad daylight and the village was silent. She thought back then it was almost apocalyptic. It's like that now. Her mind expects cars and vehicles. People and noise but there isn't anything. Nothing. No planes overhead or background noise. Just the boy chatting on about new shoes, a new hat, new this and that and what car they should get.

With a jolt she realises she had forgotten she was only staying with them until she found a car. How could she forget that? Shock. It must be shock and stress at everything she has witnessed. Like post-traumatic stress disorder or something.

'Oh wow,' the boy near on bursts with excitement at the sight of the old humpback bridge with underside arches for the flowing water to pass through. A sign fixed to wall denies entry to vehicles over a certain weight. The boy runs ahead, laughing with glee at the sight of the water. Cassie looks over the wall to see a shallow river gurgling over stones and bloated corpses wedged between big rocks.

'Jesus,' she murmurs as Gregori grunts at the sight of the bodies.

'Can we splash?'

'No,' Gregori says.

'Casseee? Can I splash please, Casseee?'

Gregori blinks and shoots a look at the boy then at Cassie. 'I say no.'

'Oh but please, Casseeee,' the boy says, ignoring Gregori.

'Er, Gregori said no,' Cassie says.

'But but but…'

'You need shade,' she says, wincing inwardly at the child's attempt to play them off.

'Water is shade.'

'No water is water. Shade is shade.'

'But under the water is shade and…and water is cold and I'm thirsty and…'

'You can't drink that water.'

'Is people here,' Gregori cuts in, breaking the shotgun open to check the shells before snapping it shut.

'People?' Cassie asks in alarm at his actions. She spins in a circle expecting to see someone but seeing only the empty road ahead leading into the town.

'Smoke.'

'Pardon?'

'Cigarettes. Wood. Dead people.'

She sniffs the air, tilting her head back and turning this way and that. 'I can't smell anything.'

'Your smell stop you having other smell.'

'What?'

'Come. We find cars.'

'What did you say?'

'We find cars.'

'No about the...you said I smell?'

'Yes.'

'I don't smell.'

'Hair not clean. Smell bad. Is close to face.'

'What?'

'You smell. You not wash. I wash. I not smell. Come, we find cars.'

Cassie's mouth opens then closes in a stunned silence at the comment as fresh blooms of colour spread through her cheeks

'I was locked in a room for...'

'Quiet.'

She blinks at the rebuke. Her cheeks stinging even more. She grabs a clump of greasy hair to pull round to her nose and inhales deeply then fights to hide the grimace while Gregori stalks on with his senses at the fore.

They reach the first buildings. The end of a row of terraced cottages. The first one is boarded up with thick planks across the door and windows and a big red cross sprayed on the freshly cut wood. The next house is the same. The same on the other side of the road. Boards and planks over the doors and windows. Big red crosses sprayed on the wood. He spots a mound of sawdust in the ground and the marking of feet from a workbench that was propped there to cut the wood. The smell of death in the air. Old death. Putrid, rich and sickly.

'Eight days,' Cassie mutters. 'I was locked in a room for eight days...you know...after being kidnapped.

Five doors up on the right he spots the first tick spray painted on the wood. Not a cross but a tick. He looks harder, slowing his walk to stare.

'And held in a room and fed baked beans...and then...you know, everyone is pretty much dead and...' she almost voices her thoughts on the weird freak kid being infested with a demon and a serial killer but decides, on the balance of things, to leave those thoughts unvoiced. 'I mean they didn't let me wash and I didn't want to use the shower in that house,' she sniffs her hair again as though the second sniff won't be that bad. It is that bad. She sniffs at her armpits, recoiling at the stench of stale body odour. She rinsed this morning. Didn't she? Did she? She can't remember now. 'Whatever,' she adds, still smarting from the insult.

Gregori takes in the look of the street and the lack of corpses and debris strewn about that should mark the end of the world. Time and effort has been taken here, people have done something to these houses to mark them with crosses and ticks. He turns round slowly, viewing each house and in turn noticing there are far more crosses and ticks. A few strides to the closest door marked with a tick and he quickly realises the planks of wood nailed across the door are not actually connected to the door itself, but rather driven into the frame surrounding the door. On first appearance, it is the same as all the other doors and looks locked and sealed, barring easy access. Sudden understanding shows in his eyes. He reaches through a gap in the boards to the door handle and pushes down to swing the door in. A safe house. He steps back and looks round the street and houses marked with crosses, and spots the ones with ticks are few and far between. The method is crass and clumsy. The infected people have eyes and can see the difference between a cross and a tick. They track by smell and will move to the last destination seen. They are predators, with the instincts of predators.

At a push, in a rush, when chased at night in the hours of darkness when confusion is high he guesses it may offer a quick refuge. He turns again, still trying to detect where the stench of death is coming from.

'Seriously though,' Cassie says, 'it's not my fault I smell, I mean... It was eight days...'

Finally Cassie stops muttering to take in the sight. Her voice trailing off as she and the boy stare round at the view.

'What's with the crosses?' she asks.

'One with...the sign, this sign,' Gregori says, motioning a tick in the air, 'they not lock.

'Pardon?'

'Is open,' he says, striding over to the closest one bearing a tick. A gap in the boards that he shows to Cassie before reaching through to the door handle. He swings the door in and kicks at the space by his feet big enough for a person to crawl through.

She stares at his feet and the space below the boards then up and across to the next house and the others doors marked with crosses. A puzzled expression. A question forming. 'And it's hot.'

Gregori blinks.

'You do eight or nine days without washing in this heat and see if you smell.'

They move on along the deserted streets. Thankful of the shade cast by the houses. The boy stays quiet. Gregori scents the air. Lifting his head as though detecting trace elements within the thermals around them. Cassie huffs and tuts. Inspecting her filthy nails and grimy skin. Nobody has ever said she smells before. It's one thing seeing death and destruction but quite another to be told you smell.

The priorities in her mind start to jumble. The urgency to find a car and be away becomes secondary to being clean and wearing fresh clothes. The need to head for London is replaced by a need to rest in the shade and drink cold water. Even Gregori loses the great sense of fear and trepidation she had for him. He just told her she smells. She casts a loaded glance at him, half-wishing he would turn to look so she can look away sharply and show her displeasure. He doesn't look at her. He sniffs the air and stalks on like a crazy Albanian serial killer. 'Whatever.'

'What?' Gregori asks, hearing the mutter.

'Nothing. Where is everyone?'

'One place.'

'What place?'

'I not know. The people in one place.'

'I heard you. What place?'

'Together. One place.'

'I bet they smell too.'

'What?'

'Nothing,' she scowls round at the boarded houses and the lack of cars, vehicles, life, people, anything.

They come to a stop on turning the corner to see sheer sided walls made from large planks stacked side by side and held in place with carefully formed scaffold poles. Fifteen feet high and stretching out past the width of the junction sealing the street behind it. Bodies everywhere. Mangled corpses lying like a carpet across the expanse of road beside the high wall. Infected people cut down, shot down, killed and slaughtered then left where they died. The stench is over-whelming and finally pushes past Cassie's own odour to hit her nose, sending her reeling back with a retch.

Gregori spots the guard perched on a lookout tower on the inside of the wall lighting a cigarette and paying no attention to the newcom-ers. His gaze scans the surroundings, taking in the bloodstains on the ground. Spent bullet casings. Discarded shotgun cartridges. As they draw closer Gregori spots more blood spatters up the plank wall indi-cating shots fired at ground level. Nicks and chunks show where shotgun pellets struck the wooden wall.

'Blimey...'ere, we got t'people coming,' the guard shouts in a thick northern accent, scrabbling to grab his shotgun then cursing when the smoke from the cigarette held between his lips curls up into his eyes.. 'Fook it, can't bloody see nowt now...' he wipes at his eyes, blowing a cloud of smoke away while fumbling awkwardly with a heavy double barrelled shotgun. 'Pete! Got smoke in me eyes...can't see nowt...'

'Ye daft twat,' a voice shouts from the other side of the high wall. 'Someone coming is there?'

'Aye, family,' the man on the tower says.

'Tell 'em to go round.'

Gregori slows his pace, watching intently. His hand reaches out to the boy, steadying his pace and offering a paternal image for anyone watching them. Cassie stays quiet, seeing the swarms of flies that lift from the dried pools of blood with angry buzzing at the disturbance.

'He's got a shotgun,' the man on the tower shouts out, ''ere mate, you need to go round.'

'We need car,' Gregori shouts back, shielding his eyes with his hand against the glare of the sky.

'What's he saying?' the voice inside the wall shouts.

'Wants a car,' the man on the tower calls down. 'Go round...' he shouts to Gregori. 'Down t'road. Turn left. Go up t'alley to end then see Cliff but mind that shotgun now mate. Is it loaded is it? You can't be coming in with t'shotgun loaded.'

'You have car?' Gregori asks.

'Go round mate,' the man on the tower says again, leaning over the edge of the tower to look closer.

'I need a car too,' Cassie calls out.

'Aye, go round. Up t'alley and see Cliff.'

Sharing a look, Gregori and Cassie walk on with the boy between them. Taking a wide path round the corpses and swarms of flies. The boy stays quiet, plunging once again into the pensive reflection that he had yesterday. He stares up at the walls then round to the bodies and back up to the walls. A step to the left and his small hand reaches out for Cassie's.

They head down the road as instructed with frequent glances back to see the man on the tower waving them on then motioning for them to look left. Gregori acts the nervous survivor, showing a level of worry that hints at ineptitude. He spots the mouth of the alley early and notes the way rubbish and debris has been piled up as though to disguise it. Pallets of wood and old mattresses strewn with bodies rancid and decaying. Infected bodies writhing with maggots. Bloated stomachs. Mouths hanging open. Red eyes staring lifeless and dead.

'GO THROUGH,' the man on the tower bellows.

The three turn to look at him while Gregori makes a show of waving at the alley as though confirming that is the right direction. They start moving through the opening to find it doglegged in a zigzag fashion of a path set at right angles. A clever design of rubbish, litter, old broken furniture and bodies. Cassie covers her mouth, gagging at the stench. The boy moves closer to her, his eyes wide as he takes in the details. Gregori glances at him, unsure of the child's reaction. The boy has seen far worse than this. He normally claps and laughs at the brains, innards, and bodies ripped and torn. Why this reaction now?

Cassie heaves, unable to stop the stench pervading through her fingers clamped over her mouth. She pulls the boy in closer, tugging his hand up to cover his own mouth and nose with tears of disgust pricking her eyes.

Once through the initial dog leg section the alley widens. High brick walls on both sides covered in generations of graffiti and blackened exhaust fumes. Old stains of oil on the ground. A rusty engine block. Pallets. Fridges, microwaves and old goods no longer needed in houses dumped and forgotten about by lazy dwellers too ignorant or too poor to arrange disposal. Garages with buckled up and over doors faded with peeling paint. Some wide open with more bodies lying here and there giving a feast to the maggots and flies. The putrid stench hangs heavy on the hot air. The gruesome sight of it. Years of neglect now coupled with the degradation of society.

The three walk on. Glancing back to the mouth of the alley then to the sides and ahead without realising it, Cassie moves closer to Gregori as though clinging to his fearless aura.

'I don't like this,' she whispers, turning again to look down the alley.

'Bodies they smell. The people with disease they not smell the living...they not see this way.'

She doesn't reply but keeps her hand clasped firmly over her mouth and nose, glancing at the silent boy gawping at the bodies they pass.

Noise ahead. A man walks out from the left side with a shotgun clutched in his hands. 'How do,' he calls out with a single firm nod.

'Man say find Cliff,' Gregori says.

'Aye. That be me,' Cliff says, stoic and deep.

'We need car,' Gregori says. 'We look. No see car.'

'We got 'em all. That loaded is it?' Cliff asks, nodding at the shotgun held by Gregori.

'Yes. I take out?' Gregori breaks the weapon as he walks, turning the weapon to show the man the cartridges in the tubes.

'Aye.'

'I do this,' Gregori says, affecting his eager to please manner as he slides the shells out. 'You want gun? I keep gun?'

'I'll be taking that,' Cliff says, motioning for the weapon to be handed over. He takes the shotgun from Gregori while holding his own braced in his hip, aimed low but clearly ready for firing. His eyes show reaction as he looks to Gregori, to Cassie then to the boy. A second of confusion. Of seeing something he is unsure of. 'Your kid?'

'No,' Gregori says. 'His mother...she...' Gregori tails off, nodding sadly.

'Ah,' Cliff says.

'I find him,' Gregori adds. 'Look after.'

'You?' Cliff asks, looking at Cassie.

'She survivor too,' Gregori says, glancing nervously at Cassie with a wan smile. 'We meet these days.'

Cassie nods, finding it strange Gregori answered for her. 'I just met them. Have you got a spare car? I need to get to London.'

'Questions,' Cliff says, lifting his head while adding a level of force to his voice. A stiffening in his manner and countenance. His eyes harden. The shotgun in his grasp doesn't move but the way he holds it shows solidity and intent. 'Either of you Muslims?'

'What?' Cassie asks, casting a look at Gregori.

'Muslims.'

'I don't understand...'

'What this?' Gregori asks.

'Where you from?' Cliff asks, glaring at Gregori.

'Albania.'

Cliff spits to the side. A scowl on his face. The shotgun lifts a fraction. Gregori stays still and quiet. Nerves and worry pouring from his expression.

'Immigrant yeah? They Muslim in Albanian?'

'What this thing?' Gregori asks, looking to Cassie for support.

'Religion,' she says, 'like Christians and...you know...Islam? Islamic? Muslims?'

'I not this people,' Gregori says to Cassie. 'I not this peoples,' he adds to Cliff.

'I'm not either,' Cassie says quietly.

'No Muslims,' the man states. Still glaring as though expecting one of them to drop and start praying any second. 'Why you in our country?'

'What say?' Gregori asks, showing confusion.

'WHY. ARE. YOU. HERE?'

'I'm so sorry,' Cassie says politely, feeling jarred at Gregori's confusion and hesitancy. 'We just need a car...'

'Aye. Got cars,' Cliff says, not taking his eyes off Gregori. He shuffles a step closer. Menacing and tough. 'Ask you again. Why you here?'

'Jesus,' Cassie whispers. 'What's going on? Why are you asking him that? He saved the boy...the child...he saved him and helped me... we just want a car...two cars...well just one and...'

'You an immigrant?'

'I not this,' Gregori says weakly, widening at his eyes in fear of the tough man. 'I here business...when this happen...I no live in this place...'

Cliff nods, seemingly thinking deep and seriously with an obvious show of an advanced intellect at work. 'Fair do's,' he says with a nod. 'You been bitten?'

Again they look at each other. Shaking heads and every inch the scared survivors. 'No,' Cassie says.

'Scratched?'

'Er no, not scratched,' Cassie says.

'Skin broken?'

'Erm, no, nothing.'

'Got blood on yer? Their blood like. Not your blood.'

'I er...no,' she says.

'Had red eyes?'

'Pardon?'

'Them things have red eyes. You had red eyes?'

She shakes her head. 'No, no I...er...no red eyes here.'

'Alright nipper,' Cliff says, offering a humourless smile at the child.

The boy stares back then turns slowly to stare down to the mouth of the alley.

'He deaf is he?'

'He's hot,' Cassie says quickly. 'We've been walking for...'

'I said alright nipper!'

'Say hello,' Cassie says, nudging the boy while wondering why Gregori hasn't started serial killing already.

The boy stays quiet. Staring at the mouth of the alley.

'He's really hot,' Cassie says. 'He needs shade and some cold water.'

'What's your name then nipper?'

'Listen, I'm so sorry but he's so hot. His face is bright red and...'

'I asked your name,' Cliff barks, glaring angrily as the boy turns to look at him. 'Don't like rude kids.'

'Boy,' the boy says.

'What?' Cliff scowls.

'Sir, please he is just scared and terrified and...shock! He's in shock and...'

'Aye,' Cliff says, suddenly ending his advanced intellectual inter-rogation of a small child and switching his attention to Cassie. 'Where you from?'

'London. We just need a car. Please?'

'Southerner yeah? Why you up here?'

'I was taken...' Gregori shifts, a minute shuffle, a motion within his body. She stalls, detecting a message. 'I was er...visiting friends.'

'What friends?'

'From er...from university.'

'Muslim friends?'

'What?'

'Your friends Muslims? You university lot like them ragheads.'

'Oh my god. We just want a car.'

'Follow me,' Cliff says gruffly. 'Got to be careful.'

'Sure,' *What the fuck?* She mouths at Gregori as Cliff about turns to march back up the alley. Gregori motions with his head to follow the man.

'I reckon this was done by the ragheads you see,' Cliff explains, leading them past more bodies and filth strewn about. 'Bet they used a dirty bomb in the name of...whatever it is. I dunno. Anyway we got the bodies for the smell. The things don't come up here cos they don't smell us do they. Through here.'

A narrow walkway on the left. A long path between high brick walls topped with razor wire. They reach the end to another set of wooden planks seemingly sealing them in the alley. A tap on the wood from Cliff and it swings in easily. Cliff steps through, Gregori, Cassie and the boy traipsing after him into the street proper.

A sight to behold. A sight to see that will never be erased from either Cassie or Gregori's memories. In a weird way, and both from differing perspectives, they were expecting to see a place of structure and order. The cleanliness of the streets outside, the sheer sided wooden wall, the guard on the tower, the formation of the obstacles placed in the alley all led them to assume a thing that is clearly not so. What greets them is a commune of a long wide street sealed at both ends and therein ends the perception of order.

Filth everywhere. Worse than the alley save for the lack of bodies. Food wrappers, empty drink containers, papers, magazines, cardboard and crap strewn about the road and on the pavements. A central park area once given as a playpark now full of sagging tents. Front doors hang open, some busted, others propped to lean against the front walls of houses. A rich smell hangs in the air. Body odour, urine, faecal matter, stale food and cigarette smoke.

People everywhere. Men, women and children sitting sullen and quiet outside the tents in the small park. More slouching or standing by the houses. Bedraggled, forlorn and filthy with sunken eyes and heavy lines in faces. Lank greasy hair. Clothes stained and encrusted with dirt. They look beaten and ruined, like refugees from a warzone.

To each their own and while Gregori turns slowly to evaluate threat, risk and concern, so Cassie sees the desperation of this brave new world. Cliff walks off. Leaving them in the street while he heads towards a group of men with guns swaggering further up the road.

'Hi?'

Gregori and Cassie turn to see a man walking slowly towards them lifting a hand with a wan greeting. 'Saw you coming in, just arrived?'

'We just need a car,' Cassie says.

'May I come closer?' the man asks in a softly spoken educated voice, thin built, a crop of unruly dark hair, bags under his eyes that show a great and heavy sadness. Swelling to the side of his face with fresh bruising still coming out. A faint smile touches the corners of his lips with an effort to look friendly. 'My advice,' he says quietly, lowering his voice with a quick glance around. 'Is to go back out and head somewhere else.'

'Er,' Cassie says, looking to Gregori then back to the man. 'We really just need a car and...well it's hot and the boy needs shade and...' she winces at calling him *the boy*.

'Forgive me,' the man says, offering a hand. 'I'm Julian.'

'Cassie,' Cassie says, shaking his hand. 'This is Gregori and...' she hesitates, she can't call him *the boy* again.

'Honestly, you should go. Don't stay here...people are heading into the rurals,' he nods at them, desperation in his eyes, 'the Lake District...the peaks...some are going for Wales and the valleys...others said they'll try for the Dales and...'

'Why?' Cassie asks, looking round again at the abject squalor and filth and the sunken expressions of the people. 'What happened?'

'Happened?' Julian asks with evident confusion.

'I mean...the streets looked so clean and the houses have crosses and ticks so Gregori figured there was people here then we saw the big fence and the bodies but...'

'Ah I see, yes,' Julian says, nodding in understanding. 'My apologies. I haven't slept in days...the nights here are just terrible...but yes, yes we were lucky I guess.'

'Lucky?' Cassie asks.

'Did Cliff greet you?' Julian asks quickly. 'Did he do the whole Muslim racist thing? I am so sorry if he did. He's a tough man. Fearless. He's killed many and he seems happy to go out and meet people coming in and I tried saying he shouldn't say those things but as you can see there isn't exactly a local policeman to speak to him regarding his racist views.'

'Jesus,' Cassie mutters.

'I er, I saw he took your shotgun too,' Julian says with a sad wince. 'Last you'll see of it I'm afraid. Best not to ask him for it back either. He can get very hostile very quickly. Listen,' Julian moves a step closer, pleading in his eyes and tone. 'Just go. It might look safe with the walls but it's really not. I rather think there is a greater danger growing within than without...'

'I was heading for London.'

'Oh god no,' Julian says in real shock.

'I only became aware of this yesterday,' Cassie says. 'I was held cap...'

'We find in house,' Gregori cuts in quickly. 'No phone. She not know these things.'

'You are joking right?' Julian asks as Cassie glances at Gregori wondering why he jumped in like that. 'That's awful, so this is...this is new to you?'

'It is,' she says. 'Gregori has told me some bits but...is London affected?'

'The whole world is affected. This is everywhere.'

'The whole world?'

'I say the whole world but Europe definitely. I heard someone say they got a call from a relative in India as the phones went down and it was there so...this must be a terrible shock to you but...there's really nothing left and the big cities are...well...really bad. I was here on the night it happened...we were fortunate. We had workmen staying in the bed and breakfast over the pub. They were here to put scaffolding up round the church so...well, we managed to get the street sealed and...but they left the next day and since then people have come and gone but less each day now and...I am so sorry,' he says, softening his voice even more. He lifts a hand as though to rub her arm then falters weak and wan, shaky and trembling. 'I am really sorry.'

Cassie blows air out and sweeps her greasy hair back off her face while staring up at the sky. It's real. This is real. She half hoped it was somehow localised to here, to the north or wherever they are.

'We need car,' Gregori says bluntly.

'He needs to rest,' she says quietly, slowly looking down from the sky to Gregori. 'The boy needs a rest from the sun.'

'He rest in car.'

'He's exhausted. He's what? Five, six years old? He needs rest and shade.'

'You should go,' Julian says softly. 'It's not right here...'

'Pardon?' Cassie asks, struggling to process the sheer volume of change to her world.

'There's some men here. Armed...' Julian glances round overly casual as though merely glancing for the sake of it. 'They're getting worse...'

Gregori looks round and stares openly at the group of armed men now talking to Cliff while looking over at the new arrivals. All of them holding long barrelled rifles and shotguns. He already saw the swagger of them walking and the way everyone else was steering clear. Not that it mattered to him. His sole intent is to find a car to find a remote house to find peace so the boy can be a boy away from those things.

Cassie rests a hand on the boy's forehead. Wincing at the heat pouring off him and the flushed reddening of his cheeks. He's quiet too. Sullen and introverted. Like the spark has gone. She doesn't question her worry or care for him, only that she has been with him for a day now so he is the only familiarity of her life right now. That and the thing they shared this morning when Gregori slaughtered the things outside. There was a closeness. A connection. A protective energy even. 'Okay,' she says quietly. 'Where can we get some water for him? I'll cool him down for a bit.'

'Is bad?' Gregori asks, seeing her concern and her hand on the child's forehead.

'Feel him, he's red hot.'

He places his hand on the boy's cheek, feeling the heat radiating. 'Boy, you sick now?'

'I'm tired,' the boy says quietly.

'Please just go,' Julian whispers urgently, 'find somewhere else.'

'The houses with the ticks? Are they safe?' Cassie asks.

'No, no that was...we had an idea the first couple of days to try and make safe places but it all went wrong. We had some good people here. Ex-soldiers and military but...they died fighting then more people came and the ideas just stopped then those men got guns...they drink all night. Get drunk and fight. They make the other men fight them and then gang up if they start losing. They killed three men two nights ago. They raped a girl in the house next to me last night. I tried saying something but...' he fingers the bruise on his face, his features twisting up in abject misery. 'About a dozen people left this morning but that makes them angry. Now they're watching and shouting at people if they want to go...telling them they can't take anything with them. We're already low on food and we've got no medicines. We've got people dying but we can't do anything with the bodies. Please, just say this is not for you and leave now. Go before they see you. Before Cliff tells them you're...'

'Boy need rest,' Gregori says.

'It's not safe here,' Julian urges.

'Is safe. Where is water? You have house?'

'Listen, please just go...oh god this is awful and I am so very sorry but you are very pretty and I know how they'll react to you,' he says with a wretched look at Cassie.

'Let me take him,' Cassie says as Gregori goes to lift the boy up.

She bends to heft the child up, wincing at his weight and the heat of his body. His head instantly rests on her shoulder. His arm looping round her neck.

'Shit,' Julian whispers, 'they're coming over...Hi, Rod,' he blurts out with manic cheer. 'They're just going. They're looking for some people that left this morning. I said if they rush they can probably catch them up or...'

'Who?' Rod asks. Broad shoulders, thickset with heavy jowls covered in dark stubble. Receding hair, bloodshot eyes and pale despite the sun and heat. The nights of drinking and fighting show in his haggard appearance. The men with him match that drawn hungover look. Mean eyed, mean spirited and full of importance that shows in the hard glares they cast at anyone daring to look at them.

'Maybe we should go,' Cassie says quietly. 'We'll find somewhere...'

'I said who?' Rod asks, his voice rasping.

'The family that came yesterday,' Julian says quickly, 'Gordon I think the man was called...was it Gordon you were looking for?'

'Er yes, Gordon,' Cassie says.

'You from London?' Rod asks, giving Cassie a lingering look as he brings his group to a stop.

'Yes, er...I was visiting some...'

'You an immigrant?' Rod asks, switching his gaze to Gregori.

Julian coughs, taking a step forward closer to Cassie while offering a submissive smile to Rod and the men. 'Gordon only left a few hours ago. You can probably catch him up. They were heading for the Dales...north from here...I can show...' he falters at seeing more armed men sauntering towards them, drawn by the sight of Rod and the others and the pretty woman holding the child. 'I'll show them out,' Julian says, forcing some energy into his voice.

'Fed up with people coming n going,' Rod snaps. 'Not a fookin' holiday camp. You an immigrant? Cliff said you were immigrant.'

'Boy need rest,' Gregori says, his accent thick and guttural. 'We rest. We go.'

'We can go now,' Cassie says. 'We'll catch up with Gordon...'

'Boy hot. Boy rest.'

'I'll show you out,' Julian says again, 'er...perhaps ask your husband to...'

'Oh we're not together...'

'Eh? Wassat?' Rod asks, 'you not together? The fooking immigrant can bugger off then in that case...' a couple of the men snigger quietly. 'Ugly fucker too,' Rod says, scowling at Gregori.

'We'll go, thank you for your time,' Cassie says, offering a worried smile to Julian. 'Gregori, we'll go...'

'What's yer name?' Rod asks. 'Gregory?'

'Hi,' Cassie says, trying to sound polite while drawing Gregori's attention to the men walking up behind them. More guns held in hands. Hand weapons too. Machetes and bats with nails driven through the end. Macabre and sinister. A situation quickly escalating. 'Gregori? We really should go.'

'Boy need rest,' Gregori says, turning to look at the men walking behind them and the other men coming in from sides.

'Get him out,' Rod orders, turning away. 'The woman and kid can stay.'

'You heard him, out,' one of the men with Rod says, motioning at Gregori.

'We'll stay together,' Cassie says, still holding that polite tone. 'Thank you very much for the time today. We'll just go back out the same way.'

'Said you're staying love,' Rod says, half turned away. 'Gregory can fook off though.'

'That's very kind but we really need to stay together.'

'I'm not askin'' Rod says, his voice dropping.

'Is not Greg Rory...'

A change in tone. A change in manner. Cassie's eyes go wide. Her heart beating faster and harder. The scared foreign man vanishes instantly. The man she saw yesterday and this morning comes back with a dangerous energy pulsing out an aura that snaps heads up and over as the tension ramps.

The boy lifts his head from her shoulder. She can feel him breathing. The rise and fall of his chest and the pressure of his arms round her neck. Gregori moves out a step and continues to turn slowly, his hands at his sides. His head lowered. His eyes seemingly staring only forward. She swallows and opens her mouth, intending words to come out that stick in her throat.

The silence spreads, drawing the attention of every man, woman and child. People in the park rise to their feet to see better. People edge further out of doorways, glancing at each other full of fear and panic. They can see what will happen. Rod and his men will tear him apart.

A soft breath floats past Cassie ear. Words spoken in a whisper that make the hairs on the back of her neck stand up. 'I Gregori,' the boy whispers.

'I Gregori,' Gregori growls.

She can't breathe. She can't speak. She can't look away but watches the man turning that slow circle. Mesmerised and entranced. Captivated even. A hand touches her chin, turning her head gently. She looks into the blue angelic eyes of the boy so flushed and hot. 'Don't be scared,' the boy whispers with words only for her but yet they carry. They drift out to be heard by those standing close. 'Gregoree protects us...'

Time freezes. An eternal second of life stretching out. She turns to see Gregori staring at her. Their eyes lock. Her lips move to speak but still no words come out and there, right in that eternal second, she sees the power of the man. The absolute confidence to do a thing that must be done but within that power a great sadness shows in his eyes. Pain and suffering. Fleeting and hidden. It is a terrible thing to do. He is a terrible thing to be. She holds the child close and stares, entranced by the myriad of emotions flooding through her body.

'Hold boy,' soft words spoken that bring a resolve within her. Something else too. A hardening of her soul. A sudden rush of understanding that what he does, he does for the boy, for the child.

'I will,' she whispers.

The eternal second explodes. The foreverness of that shared thing detonates as the man she saw this morning comes alive with a fury glowing from his eyes and this time she doesn't flinch or squeeze her eyes closed. This time she watches him as he spins and draws with a blur of motion and suddenly the pistol is in his hand booming with the first shot fired and Rod's head bursts over his shotgun yielding mates who scream out and bring weapons to aim.

Gregori's placement was perfect. Gregori's placement is always perfect. The step he took was to draw the angle of fire. A single combatant against two groups of armed men. One group with Rod. The other behind Cassie. Gregori gained a central position between the two and in so doing he drew the aim away from the woman and the boy and knew when they returned fire, they did so at each other. While he took Rod with the first shot so they kill five of their own by a mistake designed to happen.

It's in the horror of that second that Gregori, already three steps away, goes to work properly. One pistol firing. One pistol booming to drop them one after the other. Headshots gained with each round fired. They fall with heads blown apart to thud on the floor instantly lifeless. Shotguns and rifles clatter on the road. Bats and knives tumble from hands. Some try and run but are gunned down as they flee. Some dive away but still the bullets find them.

Cassie watches him throughout it all and feels only the pressure of the boy in her arms and his warm breath on her cheek. The speed of Gregori. The intensity of his eyes. The dexterity of his body that flexes as he spins and whirls. The power in his legs that hold perfect balance.

She spots Cliff surging from the doorway of a house with his shotgun rising ready to be braced and fired. She thinks to yell and give warning but in the time it take to form that thought so the knife is in Gregori's hand and already flying through the air to embed in Cliff's eye with a power that sends him crashing back through the doorway as his fingers clutch the trigger that fire pellets into the air.

Then it's done and silence reigns. A silence of ringing ears and a man on the floor at her feet whimpering in fear. Cassie and the boy look round, seeing the slain then slowly peer down at Julian lying with his hands over his head. She becomes aware of the many people staring at them. Knowing they see a woman and child standing untouched amidst a sea of bodies.

'Is more?' Gregori calls out, turning a slow and deliberate circle. 'IS MORE?'

'No,' a woman's voice blurts from across the road.

'We rest,' Gregori says, addressing the street. 'We go.'

CHAPTER SEVEN

D ay Eight.

'Better?'

He nods with a big grin showing under the water pouring down his face. 'Where's Gregoreee?'

'Outside,' she says, holding the shower over his head to let the cool water spray down over his body. In his underpants in the bath. His golden hair plastered to his scalp and the flush of his face slowly easing as the waters cool his skin.

'Are we staying here?'

'No. Just to rest then we'll go,' she says, looking round at the bottles of shampoo and shower gel stacked at the end of the bath. 'Hold your hands out,' she reaches to grab a bottle of *Johnsons No More Tears* shampoo and squeezes a dollop into his palms. 'Wash your hair.'

'Okay, Cassee.'

The house was the closest one to the exit. The doorway still blocked by Cliff's body that was dragged out by Gregori holding his ankle. He even retrieved his knife and wiped the blade on Cliff's clothes before tucking it back in his belt.

'Out.'

That one word was enough for the people in the house to exit swiftly. A clattering of feet running, heads bowed, eyes averted. The street still in stunned silence. Gregori went in then came back out less than a minute later. 'I watch,' he said, turning to face out with the door at his back.

The boy didn't say a word but stayed in her arms as she carried him up the stairs to the bathroom then helped strip his clothes off before getting him under the shower.

'Has Gregori done that before?' she asks gently, using her spare hand to help massage the suds into his hair. He looks at her, blinking the water from his eyes. 'Killed people I mean?'

'Lots and lots and lots,' the boy says, somehow managing to get shampoo everywhere but on his head.

'Has Gregori ever hurt you?'

The boy gives up washing his hair to play with the mound of bubbles in his hands. Blowing at them then giggling when they blast away to coat the walls. Not a mark on his body. Not a bruise anywhere. Not a sign of ill-treatment. She didn't need to ask the question but somehow it felt right. So many thoughts in her head. So many things seen. Too many. Her mind struggles to find order within the chaos while she rinses the suds from his head.

'Clean under your arms... you feel cooler now? Not so hot? That was a big yawn. Are you sleepy?'

'Can we play in the park later?'

'We're not staying here.'

'Can we play in the park before we go to Island of Wight?'

'We're not going to the Island of...Isle of Wight.'

He yawns again as she leans over to switch the shower off and grab a towel. 'Come on, get dried.'

'Dry me.'

'No, you can do it.'

'My pants are wet now,' he says, staring down at himself.

'We'll find you some dry ones. Dry yourself off.'

'I'm sleepy, Casseeee. Dry me...'

'Stand still then.'

She rubs the towel quickly over his skin, patting him dry then tussling his hair to rid the excess moisture. 'Wait here. I'll look for some clean pants.' The bathroom had *No More Tears* shampoo so she figures a child lived here. She finds a small bedroom with bunkbeds. Half pink and half blue for a brother and sister to share. Drawers opened. Clean pants and socks found. She holds them up trying to gauge size then grabs a handful of shorts and tops before heading back to the bathroom to see him yawning again and looking exhausted. They've walked miles in the blistering heat today.

'Gregori?' she calls down the stairs, standing at the top with the boy swaddled in the towel in her arms. The Albanian surges in quickly, his face set and hard. He spots her holding him, seeing there is no threat or risk and lowers the pistol.

'Is boy okay?'

'He's exhausted. Are we staying here or...' she doesn't question the *we* of the subject. The inclusion of herself within their team. She came in with them. She held the boy while Gregori fought. She's washed him and now holds him.

'He need sleep?'

She looks down at the tired face snuggling down to rest against her chest, his eyes already closing and nods down to Gregori.

'He sleep,' Gregori says.

'Is it safe?'

'Is safe. He sleep. I watch.'

'There's a bedroom here,' she says, motioning to the room holding the bunkbeds but Gregori has already gone. Striding back outside the house to resume watching.

She takes him into the bedroom and lowers him down onto the bottom bunk. He rouses slightly, opening his eyes to smile at Cassie before yawning again. She waits with him, watching him sink down to sleep without a care or worry in the world. Mind you, with someone like Gregori taking care of him he has nothing to worry about. The speed of the man was staggering. Truly incredible. The sheer aggression he showed and the precision within it. With a jolt, she remembers she is meant to be finding a car and heading home then remembers what Julian said and everything she has seen. Questions form. Questions fade. So many thoughts and worries all jumbled together but a feeling inside invokes worry and care for the child now sleeping on the bed covered in a bath towel.

What now? What does she do? Does she head for home? She bites her lip and frets as the jumbled thoughts whirl and spin. Images in her head of Gregori just minutes ago killing everyone around them. The bullets must have flown past her by inches but strangely, she felt no real fear. One thing at a time. Worry about the now and decide what to do later.

She heads down the stairs to the front door and out into the bright sunshine and a street full of bodies. Cliff lies dead just metres away. Her gaze lingers on him as though drawn to the wound in his eyes with an unsettling feeling inside.

'He's asleep,' she says, folding her arms as forces herself to turn away. The people by the tents in the park haven't moved but stand watching quietly. A nervous tension in the air. Others gathered in small groups. Watching worried and scared. All eyes flicking to Gregori holding the pistol at his side. 'Stinks,' she mutters, grimacing at the stench of the place. She pushes her hands through her hair, feeling the grease and dirt clinging to the strands. The smell of the shampoo still on her fingers. Her clothes are filthy. Every pore of her body feels clogged.

Gregori watches the street. Scanning both sides. Not one person has made a move towards the bodies or the weapons still lying where they fell. No one cried out either or screamed at the violence. None of them ran away in terror and panic. This new life is already changing behaviours and instincts. The smell of the shampoo reaches his nose and he turns to see Cassie pushing her hair back from her face. She didn't flinch when he opened fire. Not a flicker of a reaction.

'Stop staring at me,' she huffs.

He looks away to resume scanning and watching. Always scanning. Always watching.

'Who are you?'

'Gregori.'

'No I mean...*who* are you?'

He glances at her then back to the street. No answer given.

'Are you a soldier?'

'No.'

'Policeman?'

'I not this.'

'What then?' she takes her turn to study him, seeing the pockmarks in his cheeks and the bulge of his eyes. His short brown hair and the light stubble on his jaw. He doesn't reply but stays watchful and silent. 'Why are you protecting him?'

'He child.'

She pauses, looking round. 'There's lots of children. Why him? Why don't those things attack him?' she waits already knowing he won't answer. 'What then? What will you do with him?'

A long pause but she senses this time he will speak. 'Find house.'

'And?'

'No talk now.'

'Why?'

Motion behind her. She turns to see the crowd easing back to let a man slowly walk through him. His head bowed. One arm clutched to his stomach, stooped and broken. Livid welts on his face. His eyes almost swollen closed. His legs weak and shaking but he walks on with purpose. A woman reaches out, grasping his arm to pull him back but he pulls it free with a snapped comment and trudges on with laboured breathing, snatching air into a body so obviously wracked with pain.

'Jesus,' Cassie recoils at the bruises on his bare arms and his swollen hands. She thought he was old but he's maybe fifty at the most.

'Christ, James. Come back now,' someone says.

James walks on. Heedless to the man calling him back. Seeing only the bodies fallen and dead. A glance to Gregori and Cassie. A look of utter agony on his face as he aims towards the corpses. His breathing coming harder and faster from the exertion of motion. finally reaches the first one to a hushed silence broken by a harsh coughing fit that sprays droplets of blood on his hands. No one says anything. No one rushes to his aid either and it takes seconds to compose himself and recover enough energy to move again and when he does he commences that slow pain-filled walk towards the remains of Rod and stares down long and hard before drawing bloodied phlegm that he spits down on the corpse.

Even that movement renders him weak and for a second it looks like he will topple and fall. The woman that replied to Gregori earlier stands at the edge of the crowd. Dark greying hair scraped back. She goes to move out but someone stops her. She grimaces, folds her arms and turns away with a look of disgust mingled with abject sorrow.

James starts to move again. Lowering himself inch by inch. The pain in his body sends blooms of colour through his vision that threatens to darken. His hand trembles as he starts reaching down. His whole body shaking as he fights to stay on his feet while stretching out.

'No touch gun,' Gregori's harsh voice breaks the silence. The accent thick and guttural. His tone hard.

James freezes with his hand but inches from the stock of the shot-gun. The woman with dark hair goes to speak but again the hand on her arm restrains her. Cassie can hear the man's laboured breathing. The rasp of fluid in his lungs. The tremble in his body that quivers from top to toe. He moves again. Stretching another inch as the dull click of Gregori thumbing the hammer back sounds in the air.

'No touch gun.'

'One left,' his voice rasps out. Broken and ruined. A whisper really but injected with force to make it carry. 'There's one left...'

'No,' Gregori says. 'We rest. We go.'

'You kill all these?' James asks, rushing the words out before being seized by another fit of coughing. A drool of bloodied saliva hangs from his mouth. He wipes it away. Either refusing or simply unable to stand upright. 'You,' James shouts the word with a force of power born of rage. 'You missed one...killed my son...raped my girl...'

Gregori stares on. Expressionless. Emotionless. Uncaring for the plight of another. The pistol at his side held firmly in his hand. James moves again, stretching for the shotgun.

'No...' Gregori says.

'KILL ME THEN,' James rages, forcing his head to turn as he looks at Gregori, showing the full brunt of his injuries. 'GO ON...'

'James,' the woman with dark hair says.

'JAMES NOWT,' James shouts, red spittle flying from his lips. 'KILLED ME SON, TRISH...'

'I know,' she says, her voice cracking.

'RAPED MY SUSIE...I'M NEY THREAT TO YOU,' he says, glaring through his ruined face to Gregori. 'One left...I'll kill him meself...'

Gregori stares on. Unreadable. Unflinching. 'You sick.'

'Sick? I'M DYING BUT I'LL TAKE THAT BASTARD WITH ME...I'M NEY THREAT to you...' he breaks off with a worse coughing fit that makes him stagger and fall to a knee. More blood sprays from his mouth. His whole body shaking violently.

'He tried to stop them,' Trish says.

'I failed,' James gasps. 'My son...my boy....they hurt my Susie...' he lunges to grab the shotgun, fumbling to lift the heavy weapon up and crying out when his body fails and he falls down. Gregori watches on. His awful terrible eyes so cold and empty. The whole street watches on. Too afraid of Gregori to move but too rooted by the abject misery to look away. James tries again. Pitiful and weak. His broken body desperately trying to summon the strength to stand with the shotgun. He slips down, falling onto his side but again starts to rise. Refusing to be beaten. Refusing to give in. The image of his son dying. The image of his girl so fresh in his mind. Trish moves towards him. Gregori takes a step. People move out to pull Trish back. Sobs sound clear in the street. With a roar, James tries surging up, righteous and strong, ignoring the searing agony but he can't do it. He cannot stand. He cannot rise so he sobs and tries again and weeps for the weakness of his limbs.

A whisper spreads in the crowd as the Albanian marches to James and in one smooth motion lifts the man to his feet and holds him steady.

'Please,' James whispers.

Gregori hefts the shotgun up and holds it out. James looks at it, swaying almost drunkenly. He reaches to take the gun but misses and staggers. He fights for composure to try again. Gregori turns the shotgun, placing the barrels down and the stock up. He guides it into the hand of James, forcing him to use the weapon as a crutch to hold steady.

'Where this man?'

'House,' James gasps, 'down street...twenty four...'

Gregori walks off. Veering towards Cassie as he slides the heavy rucksack from his back to land at her feet. He drops, unzips the main compartment and takes out a squat black pistol that he hands to Cassie. 'No touch guns,' he says clear and loud before walking off.

The crowd parts as he marches through. Men and women peeling away to open a path as he strides down, reading door numbers as he passes. Several men point to the house, to number twenty four.

'Got lads in with him,' one of them says.

'Got shotguns,' another says.

Gregori doesn't slow. He doesn't falter but walks to the door and boots it in with one solid kick. Then he's inside and the voices of those within scream out. Gunshots sound. One then another. A third. Seconds of silence then a young man with blond hair staggers from the door to sprawl in the street as Gregori comes out and boots him hard in the ribs then drops to grab a fistful of hair and walks on, dragging the screaming lad behind him.

'This man?' Gregori asks, showing no effort at all pulling the writhing body held by one hand.

'That's him,' Trish calls out.

Gregori takes him through the silent crowd. The screams and wails piercing and loud. James stares through his swollen eyes. His breathing ragged and hoarse. His whole body swaying with the effort of staying upright.

Gregori stops a few feet away and turns with frightening speed to pistol-whip the lad in the face, breaking his nose with a solid crunch of bone that sprays blood thick and fast down his chin and chest. Twenty years old. Muscular from steroid use. Acne scars on his back and face. The lad tries to rise but gets kicked hard in the back of his knees, forcing him down. The pistol jabs in his forehead. Rendering him silent with terror..

A step to James. Gregori grabs his right hand and presses the pistol into his palm. Angling his body to hold James upright. A click as the safety is turned off. Gregori holds him steady, taking his weight and keeping the barrel aimed across the short distance as Cassie watches on. Unable to tear her eyes from the sight. A growing feeling inside. Her heart booming faster and harder as she watches the final few seconds of the life of a young man weeping, bleeding and pissing himself.

'He kill your son,' Gregori says quietly. The pistol fires. James cries out as the lad slumps back, gargling and clutching his neck from the round sent through his throat. heads turn away in reaction. Men and women cry out at the execution but Cassie watches rapt and mesmerised at the blood spurting out between the lad's fingers. 'GOD FORGIVE ME,' James bellows and fires again. Sending rounds into the lad's chest and torso.

'Is done,' Gregori says, taking the pistol back. Trish breaks free, running across the road to grab James before he can fall. Others rush in, cradling and holding the sobbing man begging for forgiveness. They take him away, almost carrying him back across the road. 'You,' Gregori points at Julian, recognising him from when they first came in. 'Get guns.'

'Wh...wh...'

'Take guns to Cassie.'

'Cassie?' Julian whimpers.

'I can do it,' Cassie says, her voice tight and low. 'I'll do it. You go back to the door. Here,' she hands the pistol over.

She collects the shotguns and rifles with Julian, her eyes flicking to the bodies on the ground and the fresh corpse of the muscular lad. Her legs feel strangely heavy. Her heart still beating like the clappers.

Sensations and feeling inside. Blood on her hands from the fallen. Blood on her clothes. Sweat running down her face. Her hair matted and greasy.

'Thank you,' she says to Julian when they finish. She notices the crowds are still gathered and watching. More have come from houses. Muted conversations. Fear in eyes. People too afraid to move away and even more afraid to speak out.

Movement across the road. A small cluster of people. The woman Trish, Julian and a few others all whispering urgently while casting looks to Gregori and Cassie. A few seconds pass while Julian is talked into something. All of them urging him to go and speak. When he finally starts moving over he does so slowly with his hands out at his sides looking terrified.

'I don't think he wants to hurt us,' Cassie says quietly, earning a disdainful look from Gregori.

'Er...' Julian says, his voice trembling with fear. He stops midway and flounders, his mouth moving to speak but unable to find words.

'We're resting then we'll go,' Cassie calls out before realising what she is doing. Every head turns to look at her. 'Is that right?' she whispers to Gregori.

'Yes.'

She calls out again. 'The boy...the child I mean...he needs to sleep.'

'Right,' Julian says as though that's the best news he has ever heard while he tries to stop himself from dropping to his knees in thankful prayer at not being shot or having a knife thrown at him. 'Er...' he says again, puffing his cheeks out with a long exhalation of air. 'So...'

'We don't want to hurt anyone else,' Cassie says, speaking loud and clear. 'That okay?' she whispers just in case Gregori had desires to start serial killing again.

'Yes.'

'We just wanted somewhere to rest,' she adds.

'Great!' Julian says, nodding eagerly. The street stays silent. An awkwardness descends that begs for someone to speak.

'Er...sorry about the er...um...*that*,' she adds with a weak flick of her arm at the sea of bodies strewn about the road. 'Can I say that?' she whispers.

'Yes.'

'Is there anything I can't say?' Gregori looks at her. 'I'm new to this,' she whispers urgently.

'Is good.'

'Okay,' she blasts air out, puffing her cheeks while adding more things that need to be ignored to her ever growing list of *things-to-ignore*. Gregori just helped someone execute a man for murder and rape, *was that summary justice or another murder?* Gregori just killed over fifteen people within a few seconds, *was that murder or defence?* Gregori killed a dozen on the road today. *Was that defence?* Gregori killed more than a hundred this morning. It's hot. Dead bodies are everywhere. She was kidnapped. The boy is a weird freak that speaks in tongues but she can't deny the growing sense of responsibility for him. It's fucked up. Royally, massively, incredibly fucked up but inside there is a feeling. A something that makes her glance at Gregori then down to the pistol in his hand while she bites her bottom lip. She looks back to Julian, swallows and speaks out.

'Thank you for the warning about...about those men and er... trying to help us. We appreciate that.' She glances to Gregori again, tentatively trying to detect if she is saying the right things. The man remains passive and watchful, seemingly content to let her carry on.

'It's fine,' Julian blurts happily while looking like he wants to throw up. 'What do we do now?' he adds in a rush of words then looks more terrified.

'He a soldier?' Trish calls out.

'You from t'government?' a man asks from the park, his hands resting on the metal railings. Those questions spark murmurings and hushed conversations.

'Is help coming?' another woman asks.

'They were reet bastards,' Trish calls over, taking a step from her group to glare angrily at the corpses. 'Shouldn't speak ill of the dead mind but they had that comin' they did. I warned 'em. I said they'll have hell t'pay when help comes so I did. I said that.'

'You did,' someone says from the right.

'Aye, I did, pet,' Trish says. 'We all did.'

'Are you from the government?' Julian asks.

'No,' Cassie says. 'We're not are we?' she whispers to Gregori. 'I mean you...not me.'

'No.'

'No we're not,' she adds seeing people edging slowly forward. Trepidation in their manner but curiosity pulling them to hear and listen. She spots the glances they give to each other, seeking comfort that it's okay to go closer. Women slowly emerge from houses to look about in terror and fear to see the bodies of the men. They nudge each other to look over, nodding and whispering with unheard words. Some call back into houses, urging those inside to come out and look. Cassie swallows. Acutely aware of the attention being bestowed upon them.

'Er...' Julian looks round at the exhausted faces so drawn and tired. 'Is there anything we should do?'

Cassie blinks at the question and the silence that follows it. The tension in the air. The filth of the street. The stench of bodies, death and unclean people, herself included. A glimpse of a future so bleak and dire.

'Burn bodies,' Gregori mutters.

'Pardon?' she asks.

'Burn bodies.'

'Right,' she says slowly, 'so...you want me to tell them that?' he shrugs and resumes watching. She clears her throat and goes to speak then stops and looks at Gregori. 'You tell them.'

'I not.'

'Why not?'

'No English.'

'You bloody do speak English.'

'No English,' he says again, his accent thicker this time.

'Er...' Julian calls out politely.

'Burn the bodies,' Cassie calls out, surprised at the strength of her voice.

'Burn 'em?' Trish asks. 'What here?'

'Not here,' Gregori mutters.

'Not here,' Cassie calls out.

'Where then?' the woman asks.

'Other place.'

'Somewhere else,' Cassie says.

'Use the fuel from car.'

'Douse them in petrol.'

'All bodies together.'

'Pile them up, douse them in petrol.'

'Bodies make disease. Make people sick. Burn now.'

'You should do it quickly. Dead bodies spread diseases that make you sick.'

'Clean blood from ground.'

'And get some bleach on the street.'

'Clean hands. Like the surgeon.'

'Make sure you scrub your hands too. Use anti-bacterial spray and gel. You all look filthy.'

'Make clean. Is dirty.'

'I thought you said you didn't speak English? And you might want to get all this rubbish cleared away. You'll get rats and vermin in here.'

'Burn other bodies.'

'What other bodies?' she asks him quietly.

'Outside. We see before.'

'Oh those, and the bodies outside too. They need burning.'

'You wash. I watch. You smell.'

'Then go and have a wash while...' she stops to shoot a look at Gregori and the air of innocence portrayed while he scans the street. 'You mean me?'

'Yes.'

'Eight days.'

He shrugs.

'I was locked in for eight days.'

He shrugs. 'Smell bad.'

'Stop saying that.'

'Is coffee?'

'What?'

'In house? Is coffee?'

'You want me to make you coffee?'

'Yes.'

'You just said I smell.'

'I thirsty.'

'Sorry I don't speak Albanian.'

He glares. She pretends not to notice. A swift about turn and he marches into the house leaving her in the street being stared at by way too many people. He comes back within seconds, holding the pistol she had before out to her.

'I can't shoot that,' she says, staring at it.

'No bullets. People they see it.'

'Right,' she says, taking the pistol. 'Er...can I have coffee?'

'No English.'

CHAPTER EIGHT

She steps out holding two mugs. A glance from Gregori who takes in her freshly scrubbed face and towel dried hair pulled back into a simple ponytail. Clean clothes pilfered from a chest of drawers in one of the bedrooms. Simple jeans and a plain white t-shirt. The air around her scented with the fragrance of shampoo, shower gel and deodorant.

'Coffee,' she holds one of the mugs out. 'I didn't know if you took sugar. I figured probably not?'

He takes the mug without reaction. 'He sleep?'

'Out for the count,' she says. He frowns. Unsure of her words. 'Yes. He's asleep,' she adds.

The shower was lovely. So cold but nice and refreshing. She shivered pleasurably under the flow while scrubbing the filth from her hair that made the water run dark for a few seconds. The conditioner helped untangle the knots and clumps.

She frightened herself while showering. An act done that sickened her soul. She was washing and thinking about everything that happened. Soaking her body with a series of images flashing through her mind that culminated in the execution just metres from where she stood. A cold murderous act. Barbaric and truly awful. The snuffing of a life. James wailed and lamented for God's forgiveness but Gregori showed no reaction. Nothing. She thought back to the morning and the abject pain she felt when he slaughtered the people outside the house. Then she thought of the men from the van and the suddenness of it, and the same anguish she felt when Gregori killed them all.

What frightened her initially was more a sub-conscious, un-voiced reaction that Gregori killing the people in the street did not invoke the same reaction when she thought of him killing the infected people outside the house and then later by the red van. In fact, the thought of him killing Rod and his men invoked an altogether different reaction.

She was washing her stomach, working down to her groin, and as those images flashed through her mind so her hand moved between her legs to clean herself thoroughly and the realisation hit that she was turned on. Not just turned on but horny. Really fucking horny. Her breathing deepened, she swallowed and flicked her thumb over her clitoris that instantly enlarged in reaction to her own touch. Her nipples stiffened and the heat spread inside. A yearning to pleasure herself right there in the shower. A desire to orgasm as the mental images of Gregori killing fifteen or more armed men flashed through her mind.

It passed as quickly as it came on with the voice of her conscious screaming in abhorrence to invoke instant shame and guilt that flooded her body with hormones and chemicals. She burst into tears. Weeping in horror at her own reaction while internal reasoning worked to lessen the impact by convincing herself she was in a state of abject shock. It took several minutes to gain enough composure to leave the bathroom.

'Bodies are gone,' she remarks, looking over to the scene of slaughter. Men and women working with stiff brushes as others throw buckets of soapy water over the road. 'That was quick,' she adds, feeling a need to fill the silence.

Gregori grunts and sips his coffee. None of the people in the street came near him when Cassie went inside and even eye contact was avoided. He detected people staring at him but they soon looked away when he turned to face them. Not that it bothered him. The primary concern is the boy. The secondary concern is Cassie being near the boy but she hasn't showed the slightest threat to him in any regard. That was it. That was the finite list of things to worry about

'What happens now?'

He doesn't reply but drinks from the mug of coffee she made.

'Probably not much point heading for London,' she says by way of conversation. 'What do you think?' she asks trying to draw him out.

'No.'

'That's what I'm thinking,' she says. 'Julian said the cities have been hit hard. You said you were in Leeds or wherever...and he said about the call from India. Have you heard anything about it being in other countries?'

'Yes.'

'What then?' she asks when he doesn't elaborate.

'Television. I see news. Paris. Berlin...east Europe. Poland. All these places.'

'America?'

'I not know this.'

They drink coffee and guard the boy while all around them it seems the pace of life picks up as people start sweeping rubbish into piles and throw more buckets of soapy water about. A slight change to the atmosphere. A lessening of the tension.

'What do I do?' she asks after a lengthy silence. She knows he won't reply. He won't even acknowledge the question. She sighs deeply and leans back against the doorframe, resting the back of her head on the UPVC edge.

'We find house.'

'Pardon?'

'Find house. Away from people. Away from places.'

'You mean you and the boy or...'

'Boy no live in this place. Not be near these people,' a look of distaste shows on his features. 'Is not clean.'

She falters, unsure of how to voice the question in her mind. 'What should I do?' she asks again.

'Is your life.'

'Thanks,' she fires back curtly, earning a glance from him but at least it was a reaction. 'I could stay here I guess.' He shrugs. 'But like you said, it's not clean...I don't like it.'

'No stay then.'

'How can you do those things?'

He clams up without the need for words to show he doesn't like the question.

'I don't mean morally. I mean physically.' The look of uncertainty shows. 'Er...I mean how? Who taught you to do that? You must be a soldier or...a secret agent or something...no? Okay, Gregori. I won't pry. You don't like questions do you.'

'No questions.'

'No English?' she smiles at him, earning a hint of humour in his eyes. 'Then I shan't ask you questions. Agreed?'

He doesn't say yes but then he doesn't say no either.

'Listen. You've had a few more days then me to adjust to this. I only found out yesterday. Those men in that van would have taken me today and I didn't like the way the men here were looking at me either... what I'm trying to say is that it is safer with you...' she earns another look, this one with eye contact that holds for a second. 'So if it's okay can I stick with you and the boy for a little while? Just until I know what to do or...'

He looks away, turning to scan the street.

'No? Yes? Gregori? I'll help with the boy and...'

'Yes.'

'Yes? Sure?'

'I protect you,' he replies, still scanning the street.

A jolt inside. An instant pulse within her. She swallows and tries to blink it away. The way he said it. So cold. So fucking cold. Jesus.

'Er, thanks,' she says, her voice dropping an octave. She clears her throat, widening her eyes and huffing as though trying to think deep serious thoughts. 'Sorry,' she says quickly, 'what did you say? I don't think I heard...'

'I protect you,' he says, turning to look at her. 'I do this.'

'Oh right, er I er...I didn't know if I heard you properly.'

'Boy like you.'

'Yes! I mean...er yes, he seems to have er...taken to me quite well and...um...would you mind if...haha! I er...I need a wee...excuse me...'

'Is more coffee?'

'YEP!'

She runs up the stairs into the bathroom, closing the door behind her to finally release the gasp held within her throat. What the fuck? What the actual fuck? She has never been this turned on before. She wanted to hump his leg right there. Actually fuck him in the street with everyone watching. *I protect you.* Oh my god. He was so cold. The thought of it. The thought of him glaring at everyone, making them look away while she fucked him. Stop it. Instant revulsion surges through her. Sickened by her own mind she screws her face up, willing herself to get a grip and focus. It's just emotions. That's all. Gregori is strong. A protector. She was bundled into the back of a van eight days ago then locked in room in a house full of terrifying men that wanted to hurt her. Her senses have been battered. Her mind fractured from an overload of fear and anguish.

She splashes cold water on her face and neck. Shuddering at the sensation that makes her skin break out in goose bumps.

'Coffee?' she asks politely, once more descending the stairs ever so casually.

'Yes.'

She makes fresh drinks at the gas hob in the kitchen. Blithely ignorant to the fact this was someone else's house. People lived here. People with lives, with hopes and dreams. The things surrounding her were chosen, bought and gifted to make a house a home but she takes the cups and uses the pans and spoons without a single thought to who they were, only consumed by the need to master whatever sickening messed up emotional reaction she is experiencing.

'So,' she says, stepping back out to hand his mug over. 'Just wanted to say I appreciate your kindness and the care you have shown me already, so...yes...thank you, Gregori.'

He shrugs and sips the coffee while she clears her throat, widens her eyes and wonders if it would be weird to run to the bathroom again.

'Great,' she offers weakly. He turns to glare like a wolf detecting something he is unsure of. The change of tone in her voice. The flush in her cheeks. His predator eyes probing every inch of her, seemingly penetrating her soul.

'You sick?'

'Sick? No! Hot.'

'Is hot,' he says. The wolf relaxes, the threat negated. She slowly releases the breath she held while under his delicious scrutiny.

She doesn't speak for a long time. She can't for the multitude of emotions within her. She doesn't pay heed to the street in any capacity. She makes a show of looking but whatever is going on remains unseen while she battles to gain internal control.

'Take,' Gregori breaks the silence, holding out the unloaded pistol to her.

He goes inside, leaving her alone on guard. A pistol in her hand that she holds down at her side.

Finally, she looks round at the street that suddenly looks so much better. The rubbish now collected and loaded into wheelbarrows being pushed towards the end of the street. The tang of disinfectant hangs in the air from the detergent scrubbed into the road surface. The energy has changed too. The tension easing another few degrees. She spots Trish, Julian and a few others gathered on the other side of the street. A discussion underway. Arms folded. Heads nodding and low mutterings. She spots them looking over the same way they did before. Tentative and cautious.

'I'm telling you, he must be t'soldier,' Trish says. 'You see what he did? He were like that Keanu Reeves from movies he was.'

'Aye, saw it,' a tired looking man says, nodding rapidly. Days of growth on his jaw. Bags under his eyes.

'Where's our Tina?' Trish asks.

'Here mam,' a younger version of Trish pushes through the small gathering. Dark hair pulled back. Huge doe eyes giving her a timid, shy appearance.

'You saw him didn't you, pet?'

'I did mam, like that Jason Statham he were,' Tina says, nodding round at the assembled group.

'Jason who?' Trish asks.

'Statham, mam, he does t'movies too. British he is.'

'Oh aye,' the tired looking man says deeply. 'Shaved head, Cockney lad that were in that movie about the cars.'

'Transporter,' Tina says. 'My Derek saw it like hundred times.'

'Aw, pet,' Trish says tutting sadly at Derek being killed on the first night it happened. 'He were brave lad.'

'Reet,' another man asks, 'we goin' over then? That chap has gone in by looks of it. Lass is on her own.'

'Maybe we should wait for him to come back out,' Julian suggests. 'Might look threatening if we approach now...'

'What? Like we were waitin' for him to go indoors?' Trish asks.

'I can't believe he got James to kill that Barney lad,' Tina says.

'Had it comin',' Trish fires back. 'You know what he did to Susie and James's boy.'

'Aye but it were so...so...' Tina pauses, trying to think of the right word.

'Violent,' Julian says, 'and forgive me saying this but maybe it was needed?'

'Aye, you're right there, pet,' Trish says to a chorus of agreeable murmurs. 'This is first day our Tina has been out of t'house since...'

'My Carol said she feels safer,' the tired looking man cuts in.

'Did she say that, Pete?' Trish asks.

'Aye, said she were glad he done it. She been lockin' and boltin' door t'house every night...had knife in her hand and kids in same room. We've not slept for nigh on week now.'

Trish tuts. Tina pulls a sad face. Men and women make noises and nod with comments in the same vein about locking doors and staying silent during the night.

'He's back out,' Julian says as the crowd turn heads to see Gregori talking to Cassie before going back inside the house. 'Oh, nope, back in.'

'I say we go over and give 'em some thanks,' Trish says. 'They might hang on a bit if we show a welcome.'

'He said his son was resting,' Pete says.

'Lad sick is he?' someone asks.

'Just overheated I think,' Julian says.

'Mam? What about Elsie? She used to be midwife. We could ask if they want Elsie to check on their lad?'

'That's a good idea that is, Tina,' Pete says.

'Aye, good thinking,' Trish says, nodding round at the others.

'Sounds good,' Julian says, 'right, shall we? I would suggest we don't all crowd in or anything. Some hang back a bit and try and look friendly. Tina? You've got a lovely smile so come up front with your mum.'

'Aye lovely smile,' Pete says.

'Thank you,' Tina says with a shy blush.

They set off on mass. A solid crowd moving as one like a shoal of fish staying together for fear of the sharks circling.

'Christ, here comes the welcome party,' Cassie says then realises Gregori is inside making drinks. 'Gregori? There's some people coming over to talk by the...' she blanches at the speed he moves from the kitchen to the hallway to step out the front door so quickly it brings the shoal of fish to a sudden alarmed stop. 'Hi!' Cassie calls out quickly. 'Everything okay?'

'Fine, pet,' Trish calls back.

'I said don't crowd forward,' Julian whispers urgently to the group. 'Some go back a bit. Go on...a bit more...' he turns to face Gregori and Cassie, half wincing, half smiling. 'Sorry, everyone is on edge...we just wanted to say hello and...'

'Welcome t'street,' Pete says.

'Smile, Tina,' Trish says.

'Right,' Cassie says slowly, seeing a pretty doe eyed young lady offering a huge forced grin and the others trying to show teeth and look friendly through the haggard worn out exhausted expressions.

'Do you want Elsie to look at your lad?' Tina blurts.

'Pardon?' Cassie asks. 'Who?'

'She's a midwife,' Trish says.

'Retired now,' Pete adds.

'Right,' Cassie says again. 'Er I don't think he's pregnant or...er... anything,' she trails off as the joke falls flat and a scrub of tumbleweed blows past through the heavy silence.

'She's a nurse, pet,' Trish says.

'Of course. I know I was...I think he's fine but thanks so much for the offer.'

'Are ye staying then?' Pete asks.

'Pete,' Julian groans.

'I were just askin',' Pete grumbles.

'They had all the food,' Trish says.

'Took it all they did,' Tina adds.

'Only gave us a bit,' Pete says.

'Said were rationing us, said it were for our good,' another man says.

'Kids are starving,' a woman says, walking over from the park. 'Filthy too.'

'Can't they wash?' Cassie asks.

'With what? Where?' the woman demands. 'Living in t'tent for week now. Getting water from hose...'

'There's houses here,' Cassie says.

'Aye but not my house. My house is out there with bloody great big boards nailed over the door. Said to come in here they did. Said we'd share they did. Not bloody sharing. We're begging for food every day now.'

'Went bad quickly it did,' Pete says.

'Bloody vermin,' Trish mutters darkly.

'You need to share,' Cassie says as though the idea is obvious.

'Er that's one of the things I wanted to ask about,' Julian says, glancing round at the others. 'The men you killed…they put all the food in one house. That house Gregory went in to get…'

'Is Gregoreee, not Greg Rory.'

'Sorry. So sorry. Of course. Gregoree, yes of course. Er…the food is stored in that house.'

Cassie moves out to look down the street towards the house Gregori dragged the lad from and seeing a wide berth given as though no one dares go near it. 'I don't understand,' she says.

'We didn't want to just help ourselves,' Trish says.

'Thought we'd check first,' Pete says.

'Check?' Cassie asks. 'With us?'

'Aye,' Trish says.

'We didn't want you thinking we were looting or stealing,' Julian says.

'Oh I see,' Cassie says, somewhat shocked at the reactions. The pistol in her hand. Gregori standing so solid and cold in front of the door to the house. She stiffens to lift her chin, bringing some bearing and stature to her form. 'Well, the way I see it is the food belongs to all of you.'

'How we doing that then?' the woman who walked from the park asks. 'We say it's everyone's then every bugger will be getting in there. Needs to be shared out it does. Or rationed properly.'

'Rationed? We just had bloody rationing,' a woman at the back of the crowd says.

'We can't just help ourselves, be a riot there will,' the woman from the park says. 'And we need to wash our kids. We got no fuel for fires t'make hot water. You got gas in kitchens. We got nowt.'

'Why haven't the people with houses shared the gas?' Cassie asks, seeing a few heads drop guiltily. 'Bit bloody selfish isn't it. Seal the street off and trap people inside with armed men raping everyone then not helping each other. That's awful.' A few more heads drop, eyes averted as the woman from the park glowers round with her arms folded. 'So those people in the park,' Cassie asks. 'They've not washed or been allowed in the houses?'

'No,' the woman states.

'Rod didn't want people moving about,' Pete says. 'Everyone got scared and kept quiet. Some had bit of food hidden and didn't want anyone seeing it in case Rod got told.'

'Rod is dead,' Cassie says, her voice carrying clearly. 'Share the food. Make sure everyone eats. The people in the park should use the houses to wash and the gas too for hot water. You shouldn't even be living in the park. There's enough houses here. People will have to share what they have. Seems obvious to me.' She scans the faces looking at her, enjoying the feeling coursing through her. 'Has anyone looked how much food there is?'

'How do we choose that then?' the woman at the back of the crowd asks. 'Like who shares houses? I got a houseful I have. Only got two bedrooms. Me and Dell and our Billy in his room.'

'Oh my god,' Cassie says, lifting her eyebrows at the comment. 'Are you being serious? How old is your son?'

'Nine.'

'Nine years old? Can't he share a room with you? Do you have other rooms? Dining rooms? Living rooms? Attics? Basements? People are starving and living in tents while your nine year old child has his own room?'

'But...like...it weren't like that. It really weren't,' the woman protests at the glares suddenly sent her way. 'You all done the same. Don't be making me t'pariah now.'

'Right well listen. Gregori and I are not staying here so it's up to you what you do. Gregori and I are waiting for our boy to wake up then we'll be on our way but I suggest you organise yourselves properly. Get cleaned up for god's sake...'

'He your lad then is he?' Trish asks.

'Gregori and I do not like questions,' Cassie fires back before realising what she just said and the harsh tone she said it in. A glance to Gregori with an expectation he will say something or step in but he remains as passive and watchful as before.

'Sorry, pet,' Trish says quickly. 'Didn't mean no offence now. Just that Julian didn't think you were a couple like...'

'Pardon?' Julian says in alarm at being mentioned. 'Er, that's er... none of our business so...'

'Are you hungry?' Cassie asks, turning to look back at Gregori. A single nod. His eyes scanning the crowd and sides constantly. 'I'm famished. You okay here while I go down to get food?' A pause. His eyes lock on hers then flick down to the pistol in her hand before offering another single nod. 'Someone show me where this food is please,' she says.

'Sure, er...Trish? Me and you show Cassie the food?'

'I want to come,' the woman from the park demands. 'We haven't eaten properly for days.'

'Of course, yes, absolutely,' Julian says. 'Er, want to come with us?' he asks Cassie.

'Lead the way,' Cassie says. 'Be back in a minute,' she adds to Gregori.

'No touch Cassie,' Gregori says his tone so hard and flat. So deliciously cold and brutal. An extension of his aggressive aura that suddenly surrounds her, protecting her.

'God no, no no, we wouldn't dare...' Julian blurts, 'we're not bad people, really we're not. It just got bad with Rod and...but no, definitely no one will touch anyone.'

Cassie strides down the street. The tingle pulsing inside. The way he said her name. She glances back, offering him a smile and holding eye contact before he breaks it off to scan the area.

A second later and the revulsion sets in. An instant self-loathing that robs every shred of fragile confidence she felt but a moment ago. It's like the world slews to one side, distorting the reality around her. Julian says something. An earnest expression etched on his face but she can't hear or understand for the pure hatred she has for herself. Gregori is ugly. A violent ruinous man who has no regard for life. A man filled with vicious skills that he is only to happy to use to mould the world around him. No, that's not right. He's not moulding anything. There isn't a shred of tyranny about him. Just a singular mind-set to protect the boy. A flood of warmth rushes through her as her mind fills with the image of the child. His blond hair and angelic blue eyes. So small and vulnerable. They have to protect him and keep him safe. A second later the self-loathing abates. The revulsion is gone and she finds herself staring at the open door to a house with several people staring at her.

'You okay, pet?' Trish asks, 'look like you saw a ghost.'

'Fine,' she says. 'In here?' she goes through first, inhaling a deep lungful of air to soothe the emotional swings within her body. The house smells of death. A scent she is now familiar with. Blood and gore, metallic and distinct. A young man lies dead in the front room. His brains spattered on the wall, still glistening wet and crimson. Canned goods stacked everywhere. Tins of food. Packets, jars and boxes. An Aladdin's cave of treasure. She walks through the room to the small adjoining kitchen of the tiny house. More food everywhere. More packets and tins. Every shelf covered. The floor stacked deep. Every kitchen of every house emptied and the contents carried in.

'Bastards,' the woman from the park hisses. 'See all this food?'

'Aye love,' Trish says. 'Shameful.'

Cassie moves to the stairs and starts to rise, spotting the next body sprawled in the bathroom door. A single bullet entry wound in his forehead. The back of his skull now adding to the décor. Gregori did this. He came in and killed the lad downstairs then shot this one before grabbing Barney and dragging him out. She stares at the blood and gore, at the shards of bone and lumps of grey matter and wants to run outside and fuck Gregori in the street right now. She squeezes her eyes closed, desperately trying to cling to sense and reason but her mind fills with more images of Gregori killing. A soft groan escapes her lips as her tongue darts out to moisten the sudden dryness.

She opens her eyes, hoping and praying the sight will repulse her. It doesn't. It makes it worse. She forces herself to move away and look in the two bedrooms, finding more food stacked and stored. Bottles of booze, packets of cigarettes and pouches of tobacco. She doesn't care. She goes back to head downstairs and stops to linger at the bloodied mess again.

'Can we take some now?' the woman from the park calls up.

'Yeah,' Cassie says, her voice hoarse and deep.

'You okay?' the woman asks, starting up the stairs in concern.

'Fine. Er...another body here,' Cassie says, forcing herself to move away and show a pretence of horror at the sight.

The woman tuts, grimacing as Cassie descends. 'Awful,' the woman mutters.

'Awful,' Cassie echoes sadly, pausing for a suitable amount of time to pass. 'Right! Shall we get some food? I'm bloody starving.'

CHAPTER NINE

D ay Eight

I f someone had told Cassie she would one day spend an afternoon being taught how to strip and clean shotguns and rifles by an Albanian serial killer in a sealed street in the north during a zombie outbreak, she would never have believed them. Not only would Cassie not have believed them, she would have swiftly told the person they were talking rubbish and moved away. She would have given them a dismissive sneer. A look of daggers. She would have tutted and shaken her head.

Firstly, she had no interest whatsoever in guns. Secondly, the only Albanians she ever met were the workmen that sometimes came into her mother's house, but they may have been Polish. She could never tell the difference and wasn't interested enough to ask. Thirdly, zombies are fictional and part of the popular culture of the working classes and not a genre those within the Metropolitan elite chose to indulge in.

Fourthly, Cassie never liked the north, or people from the north. They speak funny and drop words in sentences. They are too common, too muddy and too earthy. Fifthly...she pauses to think of a fifth and decides four is probably enough to gain a suitable level of contrast from her former life to what appears to be this current one.

Mind you, she didn't expect to get kidnapped either. In a way, and although being kidnapped was truly frightening, she did look towards the end and the fame that would come with it. The girl who lived. The girl who defied the kidnappers. She'd make a fortune. She'd be on television and write a book.

'Pass the wipes please,' she says, reaching to take the packet from Gregori. She plucks a wipe from the packet and sets about cleaning the blood and gore from the stock of the shotgun.

If that person who said she would one day spend an afternoon being taught how to strip and clean shotguns and rifles by an Albanian serial killer in a sealed street in the north during a zombie outbreak, then said she would become the centre of attention and the sole focus for every single other survivor within said sealed street in the north, she would still not have believed them.

The people in the street had suffered lives ripped from normalcy. They saw it happen on the first night. They ran screaming or cowered in the shadows while outside a brave few made efforts to seal the ends and buy time.

That sealing of the street saved many lives. It gave a barrier behind which they could fight back. They found shotguns and rifles and once they realised the infected things were slow during the day, they set out to slaughter them.

They took back their town and worked fast to take supplies and get more people inside the barricade.

When night fell on the second day, the beasts once more turned into the wild creatures. Many people died but many survived. People left. People came. They fought back when they could and stayed quiet.

Then, as their town saw less and less attacks, and those few brave souls who took charge either left or died, so Rod took over and power corrupts. Absolute power corrupts absolutely and those inside the street, already weak in spirit, were brought under his rule of thumb.

Days was all it took. Just mere days for the whole of it to play out and now, on the eighth day, Rod and his abusers are dead, killed by one man and the word of what Gregori did spread down that street faster than the virus would have done so.

It was in the house with the food that it started. Cassie was feeling a weird thrum inside as she purveyed the food stacked inside. At that moment, her sole concern was to get food for her, Gregori and the boy.

'How do we do this?' the woman from the park asked.

'What's your name?' Cassie asked her.

'Kate. You're Cassie?'

'Cassie,' Cassie said.

'How do we do this?' Kate asked again.

Cassie was about to ask Kate to define exactly what she meant by *do this* when someone knocked on the open door, making them both turn to see a man standing meek and mild with a woman next to him and a teenage girl staring at the ground.

'Heard it we did,' the man blurted. 'Killed 'em?'

'Sorry?' Cassie asked, struggling with the clipped sentence and thick accent.

'John,' Kate said, 'they did...all of them.'

'Rod's dead?' John asked.

'They all are,' Kate said.

The change was palpable. The flood of relief on their faces. The way John looked at his wife and laid a hand on the girl's shoulder. 'That Barney...' John croaked the words out. 'Said he were comin' to see our Lucy tonight...we were bout to set fire to house to make distraction like...were gonna get out.'

'Barney's dead, John,' Kate said. 'Seen it with me own eyes I did.'

'Thank fook,' John gasped. 'You the one that did it?' he asked, eying the pistol in Cassie's hand.

'Her fella,' Kate replied before Cassie could say anything. 'Did the lot of 'em on his own he did. Never seen nowt like it.'

Cassie marvelled at the words *her fella*. Gregori is ugly. Ugly as anything but that tingle came back. The feeling inside that spread warmth through her belly.

'Got a kid, they have,' Kate said. 'Called him Boy. Right southern name.'

'Aye, tis,' the woman with John said. 'Listen, love. You saved our lives.'

'Oh I don't...' Cassie started to say.

'Your fella up there is he?' John asked. 'I'll pay my regards to him.'

'No! Er...I'll pass it on. He doesn't like talking to people.'

'Right you are, Miss. What's happening now? Them's people in the park need food. You said that, Kate?'

'I have, we're sorting it now, John. Give us few minutes eh, love. We'll get something out to you. Actually, John. You pass word we're working it out now. Tell everyone we'll get some food out but Cass and Greg want folks from the park in houses they do. No more livin' in t'tents. We need to wash and get our kids clean.'

'Aye, course,' John said. 'Whatever you need.'

Sometimes in the course of humanity, a single event can be noted as the turning point of change. That was it. Right there. *Greg and Cass want folks from the park in houses*.

John and his family moved away and that word spread. *Greg and Cass said to get folk out of the park. Greg and Cass said to get rid of bodies. Greg and Cass said to clean up. Kate's with Cass now sorting the food. Greg don't like talking. Speak to Cass.*

'Hi? Are you Cass?'

'Pardon?' Cassie said a few moments later, still looking round at the stacked goods and food. 'I'm Cassie yes.'

A woman at the door. Bags under her eyes but she smiled in, nodding in respect and greeting.

'Tilda,' Kate said. 'You alright, love?'

'John said Greg and Cass want folk out of t'park. We got room in our place. There's only me and Jerry. We can get our dining room and back bedroom used...'

'Good,' Cassie said when Kate and Tilda looked at her. Julian and Trish walked out from the kitchen at that point. All of them looking at Cassie. 'You should do that.'

'Aye, we will.'

'And er...anyone else with spare rooms should do the same,' Cassie said.

'Makes sense,' Kate said.

'Does,' Trish said.

Cass and Greg want folk with spare rooms to give them over to folk from t'park.

'Kate love? You in here are you, pet?'

'Aye,' Kate said, stepping back into the hallway again mere moments after Tilda went off.

'You got that Cass with you?'

'Right here,' Cassie said, moving out to look at the woman standing by the front door.

'Tilda said you want folk with spare rooms to let you know...'

'Right,' Cassie said. 'You have a spare room?'

'Aye,' the woman said sincerely.

'Sue? You talkin' to Cass and Kate in there are ye?' A man asked, looming behind Sue at the doorway. 'We got spare room in our place.'

'John said you're sorting the food,' Sue said.

'We will,' Kate said, 'give us few minutes eh.'

'Anyone with spare rooms should go into the park and offer them out,' Cassie said. 'Keep it simple.'

Cass said to go into park and offer the rooms. Said to keep it simple.

More people came to the door. A steady flow of questions asked by people wanting to see the woman for themselves. Fear within them. Pure terror and confusion of days spent waiting for the army or the police to arrive and do something. Waiting for the government to give instructions while all around them it only got worse and now, suddenly, there was someone here who wasn't afraid, someone who said to clear the bodies and clean the rubbish away.

Cassie rather enjoyed it. The novelty of suddenly being so popular and in demand. Her confidence grew quickly and with it a slightly scathing tone of voice that only seemed to enhance her perceived authority. The weight of the pistol in her hand and the assumption it was loaded and she knew what to do with it. The southern well-spoken accent. The cultured London tones. The lack of panic in her manner. The way she lifted an eyebrow and stood with a straight back. She looked healthy too. Her hair washed and clean. Her face scrubbed. Her green eyes so clear. Her red hair giving her a fiery countenance.

'I would suggest,' she said to Julian, Trish and Kate after fielding more questions from the steady flow at the door, 'that you ration this food out. Form a system and give it out from the door. Everyone gets enough to eat and pay attention to splitting nutritional requirements. Proteins, fats, carbs and vitamins. Can you do that?'

'Of course,' Julian said while the others nodded. 'Are you happy for us to...I mean...for us to actually do that?'

'I am,' she said firmly, selecting a few tins and a packet of pasta.

'Great,' Julian said, still consumed with frantic politeness. 'That's great...er...'

'You go and eat, pet,' Trish said. 'We'll shout if we need you.'

'Cassie?' Kate called as she stepped from the door. 'Are you staying?'

Cassie thought for a second, looking round at the already changing landscape then up to Gregori standing as watchful as before. A pulse inside. A desire to push for the hell of it. 'Gregori and I have yet to make a decision,' she said.

That was several hours ago. She heated food in the kitchen and took a bowl of pasta out to Gregori. She even took some care in preparing it. Adding a tin of tuna and the same brand of chopped tomatoes she saw him eating last night. He nodded with thanks, tucked the pistol in his waistband and tucked in. 'Boy still sleep?'

'He is, I just checked. He's fine.'

'He quiet.'

'Pardon?'

'Boy. He quiet. When we find you. He quiet then. He never quiet. Always talk.'

'It's hot. This heat...it saps energy and er, he didn't seem very quiet today.'

Gregori ate and watched the street, seeing the steady flow of people going into the park and the same steady flow of people packing up and leaving.

'Different,' he said after a long pause of eating and watching.

'Different?' Cassie asked. 'Different how?'

Gregori ate, spooning the food into his mouth while scanning everyone and everything.

'Quiet then not quiet...before was never quiet. Always noise.'

'We'll keep an eye on him then,' she watched him closely, scrutinising his reaction at her choice of words. 'If we get concerned we can find someone to check him. They said there's a retired nurse here.'

Gregori ate. Chewing while watching. Chewing while thinking.

'You have child?'

'Me? God no. Always hated kids...apart from the boy of course. Annoying as he is I'm already strangely attached to him.'

Gregori looked at her at that second. He even nodded. The boy is annoying. The boy is annoying as hell and god only knows the amount of times Gregori had tried to kill him but could never pull the trigger.

'We watch,' Gregori said. 'We do this.'

'Course, definitely.'

'You know guns?'

'Pardon?'

'Guns. You use before?'

'No, never.'

'I show. Shotgun easy.'

They ate then after finding suitable cleaning materials, they settled down in front of the house to clean the shotguns and rifles taken from Rod and his men. He showed her how to break the shotguns open. How to detach the barrels. Where to clean, how to clean. How the rifle works. Short words. Short sentences. More showing then watching her copying him. Nodding when right. Shaking his head when wrong and during all of it, the steady stream of people approached to tell Cassie they have a spare room, to say thank you for what they did, to say thank you for the food now clutched in their hands and to ask if they needed anything.

The afternoon faded out to evening that gradually ebbed with the sun dropping down through the sky. The park cleared and they learnt the bodies were all stacked outside the northern end barrier ready to be taken and burnt the next day.

Now, as the light of day starts to dwindle, Gregori takes one of the shotguns through the house and out into the small garden to a shed. He returns within minutes. A frown on his face.

'What's up?' Cassie asks.

'Cut,' Gregori says, touching the barrel. 'Here. Make small.'

'I don't understand.'

'Thing. Cut. I need this thing,' he says, sawing at the barrel with the edge of his hand.

'Saw?'

'Yes. This thing. Cut metal.'

'Okay, I can find someone... er excuse me...John is it?'

'Aye,' John says, striding over from his conversation with another man.

'Do you have a saw to cut metal?'

'Metal you say? Hacksaw will do job...'

'This. Make small,' Gregori says, showing the shotgun.

'Oh aye, sawn off eh? I can do that. Got saw in shed. Where you want it cut?'

'You have saw?'

'Aye, got saws.'

'You show.'

'Reet, can do.'

'What?'

'I say reet, can do.'

'What this?'

'What what?'

'Haha! Okay so John has a saw in his shed...and Gregori, he will go with you, John to cut the barrel.'

'Reet.'

'What?'

'Go with John.'

'I go?'

'Yep, he has a saw.'

'Aye, got reet load of saws.'

'I go.'

'Great.'

'You wait.'

'I'll stay right here.'

'No let people in.'

'I won't.'

'Shoot them. With gun.'

'I will.'

'Okay. I go.'

'Reet.'

'What?'

'Christ,' Cassie says as the men walk off stuck in a loop of words spoken in accents. At least he didn't serial kill him. So that's a good thing. Her mind instantly fills with the images of the bodies shot down by Gregori. The heat spreads. The yearning inside. The pulse of energy. She blows air from her puffed cheeks and looks round at a world she hardly recognises. A semblance of reality hits with a lurching jolt of abhorrence. Tears fill her eyes with a rush of emotions, of loss and mourning for her family, for her mother and friends and her life in London. Everything she knew is gone. The world is over. Death. Destruction. She's far from home with a crushing loneliness breaking her heart.

'CASSEEEEE!'

The sound of feet running down the stairs. The boy calling her name as he wakes and runs down full of glee to leap out into her arms. She catches him with an instant transition as every single negative emotion evaporates. A warmth rushes through her. She smiles at his mood, at his arms wrapping round her neck and the squeeze he gives while his legs wriggle to gain purchase round her mid-section.

'Where's Gregoreeee?'

'He'll be back in a minute, did you sleep okay?'

'I'm hungry. Can we go to the park now? Is it night-time? Do you have a nightie? Last night you fell asleep in the road and Gregori said you don't have a nightie…are we living here now? Are we going to the Island of Wight? There's a big fire and Marcy was bit on her bum and I'm hungry…'

'Whoa slow down,' she laughs at the words spewing from his mouth as he chatters at a hundred miles an hour.

'GREGOREEE,' the boy wriggles to get free, dropping to the road to run in his pants at seeing Gregori walking towards them. The Albanian shows no reaction. Not a smile or a greeting. He bends to scoop the boy up with ease, resting him in the crook of his arm while holding the now sawn off shotgun in his other hand.

'He just woke up,' Cassie says as Gregori stops next to her. 'Seems fine now,' she adds, smiling at the boy.

'What's that?' the boy asks, pointing at the weapon in Gregori's hand.

'Is gun, no touch.'

'Found a saw then.'

'Cut,' Gregori says, holding it up. 'Is small now.'

'Mind me asking why?'

'For you.'

'Pardon?'

'Is easy shoot this. The long one…is heavy. I show…' he lowers the boy and grabs a long barrelled shotgun. 'Is heavy. The shell is this,' he pulls a shotgun shell from his pocket. 'Inside many small bullets…in long gun they go far and go out…like this,' he swooshes out with his hands as the boy and Cassie watch with rapt interest. 'Is small,' Gregori holds the sawn off up. 'The bullets spread quickly but no go far…this very good weapon. Very good. You have this. I teach easy. Pistol I teach other day.'

'Crumbs I don't know what to say.'

'Yes. Is good weapon.'

'Gregori I…thank you, I really mean that.' She takes the sawn off carefully. 'It's very light,' she adds, hefting it up and down.

'Is good. Shoot close. Not far. Small bullets they no go far…' he looks round at the street, spotting a man on the other side of the road twenty metres away. 'This man too far. Hurt not kill this man…' he steps back a few times, judging the distance until he's only a few metres from her. 'This. This close. Is good this close. Kill this close.'

'Wow, that is close.'

'Yes. Close. Not far. No shoot far. Is loud...'

'I want one.'

'No. No touch.'

'But I want one.'

'No touch.'

'But but...I did it once and made the brains come out and the sausages...'

'You let him shoot one of them?' Cassie asks.

Gregori shrugs but with a hint of a sheepish look in his eyes. 'Is one time.'

'And I had the stick and the knife and...'

'Stick?' Cassie asks. 'Knife?'

'Is boy, is magination,' Gregori says, looking away a bit too quickly.

'Ow,' she steps away at being jabbed in her bum cheek by a small hand. 'What are you doing?'

'Darren bit Marcy on her bum.'

'What?'

'Bum bum bum...Marcy on the bum...Marcy on the bum...'

'What's...what are you singing? Who's Marcy?'

'On the Island of Wight!' the boy laughs, clapping his hands while dancing in the street in his pants. 'Can we go to the park now? Marcy on the bum Marcy on the bum...bum bum bum...'

'Sssh, stop saying that, don't run off...no, right...this isn't funny...'

'Bum bum bum...Marcy on the bum...'

'Stop it! Come back...stop running round you've only got pants on...no...no look you're making me laugh and it's not funny.'

'Casseeee on the bum...Casseeeee on the bum.'

'Boy, stop singing...' Cassie laughs, chasing him round Gregori who watches on as impassive as ever. The boy carries on. Singing as he skips away from Cassie.

People in the street watch on too. People with exhausted faces who feel weary to the bone and sick inside with panic and worry.

People who see a child laughing in his pants and a woman giggling as she chases him. They look to each other, unsure and afraid. No one says anything. None of them dare.

'CASSEEE ON THE BUM...'

'You monkey...take this,' she laughs, handing the sawn off to Gregori.

Gregori sees the looks coming over. People died here. People have suffered pain and anguish, loss, hunger and deep fear. He looks at the boy laughing as Cassie chases him and breaks the sawn off open to load two shells from his pocket. A flick of his wrist slams the gun closed with a loud clunk that carries far. A glare given. His head high. People look away quickly, rushing to be on about their business. Gregori turns, ensuring the same is happening all around.

The boy laughs and skips. Cassie chases him. Gregori glares and the street grows quiet and silent, emptying quickly as people head inside houses.

The boy will be a boy.

CHAPTER TEN

D ay Ten

A dull crack lost in the background noise. The window shatters into hundreds of small chunks. A bloodied hand reaches in to pull the handle of the driver's door.

None of them speak. He drops the bag on the back seat and works to reload his pistols while the other two get in and stare out the front to the mound of bodies stacked up at the far edge of the car park.

'No speak.'

'But...'

Gregori lifts his hand to adjust the rear-view mirror, framing Cassie in the middle of the back seats. Her hair sodden, her face smeared in blood, grime and sweat and the sawn off clutched tight across her chest.

He moves the mirror to see the flaming street behind them. Thick coils of smoke, flames licking the sky, the barrier now broken and lying in chunks.

He grunts. Shakes his head and pulls a small knife out to jam into the cowling under the steering wheel.

'But...' the boy says.

'No,' Gregori says. He opens the door, flings the cowling away and yanks the wires free.

The boy twists to look at Cassie, staring at her for several long seconds. 'But I didn't...'

'Later,' she croaks.

'But...'

'Later.'

A spark. A noise from the engine. Gregori grunts, tries again and nods in satisfaction when the car starts. He views the controls, adjusts his seat and looks over to the boy.

'Belt.'

'But...'

'Belt.'

The boy pulls his belt across, working to push the metal clip into the fastener. Gregori pulls out. Driving slowly away from the devastation behind them while Cassie winks at the boy who grins with sudden delight. She lifts a finger, pressing it to her lips then wincing at the sight of the filth on the digit. The boy giggles, watching as she wipes it on her top.

Gregori reaches up to tweak the mirror, bringing the angle down an inch to see Cassie who immediately pulls a mock poker face to act serious, which sets the boy off laughing.

'Is not funny,' Gregori mutters.

'No,' she says quickly, shaking her head, 'awful,' she adds, changing to an emphatic nod.

She stares back at him, eyes locked. 'Thank you though...for saving me I mean...'

The night they arrived in the enclosed street passed quietly and after the stress of the day she thought that was a good thing.

As darkness fell, so the people slowly drifted off to gain a sleep made at least partially less worrisome from Rod and his gang not roaming the street drunk on power and booze. The boy, having woken from his daytime slumber, was full of energy and wanted only to play. The strange thing, the weirdest thing, was that Cassie was happy to play too.

She hated children. They were small and made noise. They were dirty and needy. They couldn't use toilets properly or eat properly or do anything properly. They asked stupid questions and did stupid things. She figured one day in the future she would have to find a potentially suitable genetic match to produce off-spring and hoped that would bring forth the necessary maternal instincts. Until then, however, she really did not like children.

The boy was different. Something about him invoked an over-whelming sense of protection and although she only met him but a day or so ago, she was drawn into that aura. He was still annoying but the annoyance was off-set by the reaction within her. A bizarre part maternal, part bigger-sibling, part guardian mix of feelings and so organic and natural were those sub-conscious emotions that she didn't question it.

The boy grew hungry so they ate. They boy grew chatty and eventually, despite the weird protective instinct, even Cassie got a bit pissed off. The most loving of mothers eventually grow weary and say the dreaded words all children fear...*time for bed*. He went willingly. Brushing his teeth. Washing his hands and face and trotting, still chatting, to the bed he used before. Another hundred questions followed while he snuggled down and appeared to be wide awake and not the slightest bit tired. He then did that thing children do and just conked out within a few seconds. Cassie even stayed there for a few seconds and tried to punch through the fug in her head to question why she liked the boy but her mind suddenly found itself thinking of other things.

'Will you stay with us?' the boy grabbed her hand and asked the question as she rose to leave and such was his tone she looked back startled and somewhat shocked. That look was in his eyes. The older-than-his-years expression. An ageless essence, keen, smart and wise yet confused and scared with an intelligence beyond that of a child.

'I will,' she whispered.

'Promise?'

'I promise,' she said.

The ageless thing retracted and for a second just the boy was there who smiled sleepily and went back to sleep.

She felt jarred, unsettled even but it passed and a few seconds later she was walking down the narrow staircase in the tiny terraced house to join Gregori by the front door staring out to the deserted street. By the time she got to him, all trace of unsettled notions were gone. She felt buoyed up with a sense of excitement. The night was dark. Stars were shining high in the sky. The street was empty with just the faint flicker of the odd candle burning behind drawn curtains.

The weather was sultry too. Hot and close. Sexy and tropical. She had a light layer of sweat on her face and arms that glistened. It was romantic even. She breathed deeply, inhaling the night air filled with the scent of bleach and disinfectant poured liberally over the bloody ground.

One thought leads to two. The smell of the bleach made her think of the bodies and in turn to Gregori killing them, and, in turn again, to the brutal coldness and lack of emotional reaction. She wanted him to say *I protect you* again just to hear that deliciously thick accent, his voice so deep and hard, his awful pock-marked skin and the lack of beauty about him that only made him so much more fuckable. She grew horny. Turned on. Heat between her legs. The tip of her tongue darted out to wet her lips. Her heart beating with heavy booming thuds. The blood pounded through her skull.

'You watch.'

He went in without another word. Leaving her alone and stunned for a second. In her mind she imagined she would give him *a look*, and he would respond with *a look* and a second later they would rutting on the ground.

Christ. What was happening? She needed to get control. Get a grip. Focus and think properly. She sagged against the wall and looked over to the sagging tents left in the small play area.

He didn't come back for ages. She heard him in the bathroom.

Showering, washing, brushing his teeth. She even caught glimpse when he walked out of the bathroom with a towel wrapped round his waist and a pistol in his hand. She saw the muscles in his hard lean body. She glimpsed the scars too and fought to keep control.

When he did come back down he was dressed in clean blue jeans. Old style ones, the denim faded. It suited him. He was buttoning up a shirt as he descended the stairs. A soft cotton white and blue checked shirt. When he reached the bottom he started tucking the shirt in with his pistol wedged under one arm.

'You should leave it out,' she said.

He looked at her. His expression showing a hint of confusion.

'The shirt, looks better, leave it out.'

A frown and he carried on thrusting the tail ends into the waistband. 'I get pistol easy,' he said, shoving the gun in as though to show the lack of his shirt being out will aid his grabbing of it so much more.

'Shirt hides it though if it's out,' she said.

'I no hide.'

'Can I shove this down my jeans?' she asked, holding the sawn-off shotgun up.

'No.'

'I was joking.'

He stared.

'Nice shower?'

He shrugged. 'I clean.'

'Do you smell nice?' she leant forward to inhale the air around him.

'No smell.'

'Didn't you use deodorant?'

'No.'

'Not even shower gel?'

'What this?'

'Soap.'

'I use. I wash away. Others smell you. Know position.'

'Oh. So, don't you ever you use deodorant?'

'No.'

'Really? You didn't smell though...I mean, you didn't have BO.'

'Bee Oh?'

'BO...body odour. Stale sweat.'

'No.'

'Why not?'

'I fit. Not eat bad food.'

'That doesn't stop you having BO.'

He shrugged.

'I had BO and I'm not fat.'

'Little bit fat.'

'What?'

'Little bit fat.'

'I am not fat.'

'Here,' he pointed at her stomach. 'Is soft. Here,' he pointed at her backside, 'here,' he pointed at her thighs. 'Soft.'

'Fuck you.'

He shrugged.

'I am not fat.'

'Little bit fat.'

'Stop saying that.'

'Is fact.'

'Jesus, Gregory.'

'Gregoreee, not Greg Rory.'

'I know. I was being mean because you said I was fat.'

A pause. 'Little bit...'

'Okay thank you. Yes. I heard it. We're not all super fit serial killers, Gregory.'

'Is Gregoreee...'

'Fuck off.'

Another pause. 'What this thing?'

'What?' she huffed, realising that trying to fold her arms while holding a sawn-off shotgun wasn't easy.

'Seeeriel...this thing?'

'Serial killer.'

Another pause. 'I not this.'

An opening. A chance to score. She took it, looked away and shrugged. He can shrug, she can shrug.

'I not this.'

'I can't hear you, I'm too fat.'

'Little bit fat.'

'My fat ears have gone deaf.'

'Ear no have fat.'

'Are you a doctor?'

'Is not fat,' he said, reaching up to gently pinch the top of her ear. 'Is other thing...ear no have fat...' he moved down to take hold of her lobe. 'This skin. No fat,' he took his hand away, clearly pleased with himself at the educational lesson.

She huffed again while inside she tingled from his hands touching her. The hands of a killer. The hands of a cold ruthless bastard. 'I'm not fat. I'm not. I've got a nice body. I did Pilates and my Yoga instructor said I was in great shape.'

Silence.

'My Kapotasana is very good and my Chakrasana is exceptional.'

'What this?'

'See, you don't even know. Serial killers should know what Yoga is.'

'I not this...'

'Whatever. They should teach it in serial killer school. Can you do it? I bet you can't.'

'What?'

'Kapotasana?'

'What this...'

'I'm not showing you. I'm too fat.'

'Not fat. Little bit fat. Soft. I hard. I man. You woman. You soft.'

'That is so sexist. I know plenty of hard women...I could be hard too if I wanted...I just choose not to be.'

'I...'

'Plenty of men like women with curves.'

'I...'

'I don't even have curves. I'm just not toned like you with your...

your six pack and...I didn't see it though. I mean...I did but I didn't look. I didn't like look at it but I saw it and...fuck's sake wear clothes next time you come out the bathroom.'

'Is...'

'So the Kapotasana is when you bend your back to put your knees and elbows on the ground but the wrong way...like upside down. Like a crab but facing up. A facing up crab on his knees and elbows.'

'I...'

'The Chakrasana is kind of the same but you stay on your hands and feet like a bow. They call it a bow wheel...and a table top too. I can do that really well.'

She jabbered on much like the boy with words that spewed out, most of which he didn't understand. After several minutes she tutted, swore under her breath and thrust the shotgun at him to hold.

'Hold this while I warm up.'

He took the shotgun and watched as she started stretching. Pulling her foot into her backside then opening her legs while bending at the waist and all the time talking.

'...cos Yoga would really help with your serial killing you know. Stretching and turning so much and running about. Staying limber is essential for murderers. Not that I would know but...anyway. So, you're obviously very strong but flexibility is the key and it will only get worse as you get older. How old are you anyway?'

'I not know.'

'What?' she asked, standing up to look at him. 'How can you not know? Everyone knows how old they are.'

He shrugged.

'How many birthdays have you had?'

'Not have this thing.'

'That doesn't make any sense...' she said while lifting her foot to rest on the windowsill to stretch out some more. 'When is your birthday?'

'I not know this.'

'You don't know when your birthday is? What month? January? February?'

He stared blankly, expressionless.

'Wow. Shit life,' she said. 'How old do you think you are?'

'I...'

'Thirty five? Forty? It's hard because you're so fit. I mean, you know, like your body could be a man in his twenties but your face is older. Where did the scars come from? Was that acne? The marks on your face.'

The marks on his face came from a lack of nutrition given to his growing body as a form of punishment for not being fast or strong enough and failing in his lessons. They came from nearing starvation and being forced to sleep in the snow in the winter where he learnt to trap rats and eat them raw.

'Anyway, so you start like this, lie down on the ground and bend your knees then put your hands like this next to your head but see, they have to point down the body then...then you lift up and...so like a crab? Can you see? Then you shuffle in and move your hands towards your feet and...bloody hell I feel so stiff...'

He watched closely. He watched for form, extension, position, exertion and the points of stress going through her body. He knew which muscles were being taxed, stretched and which tendons were currently experiencing the most stress. She chatted on, explaining the position as if doing such a thing at such a time and place was the most natural thing in the world. Gregori knew she had a degree of fitness. She had walked all day without serious complaint and certainly shifted quickly when she needed to. He was slightly surprised at her suppleness though, and being a connoisseur of the human form and the many ways to kill, harm, hurt, injure and cause untold pain, he admired the balance and poise. Even if she did wobble a bit but that was more from a lack of warming up properly.

'Shit,' she said on losing balance and crumbling to a heap. She bounded back up onto her feet, grinning widely. 'Ooh, head rush,' she grabbed out at his arm, laughing at the dizziness rushing through her brain. 'Yep, so not bad for a fattie eh?'

'Little bit fat.'

'Wow, bring a girl back down why don't you. At least I have birthdays…oh no that was really mean. I take that back. Sorry. I feel awful now. I shouldn't have said that. Sorry, Gregori…do you like being called Greg?'

'No.'

'Cool, Gregori it is. Sorry about the birthday comment. Why don't you know your birthday though? Oh you said no questions. Right. Well, if you ever want to talk…I'm all ears…not fat ears though haha! Get it? You said ears don't have fat?'

'Ears no have fat.'

'Great! Coffee?'

'I watch. You sleep.'

'No, don't be silly. I'll keep you company and we can chat more.'

They didn't chat more. Cassie did. Not that Gregori appeared to mind. They stood in the street for a while, then perched on the doorstep then retreated into the hallway with Cassie on the bottom step and Gregori with his back against the wall side on to the open front door. He'd already checked the lock was intact but he liked being able to hear the world, especially in a place that had seen such turmoil. After a while, Cassie grew uncomfortable on the stairs and moved down to sit next to him with incremental surges coming and going.

Throughout the night, she felt urges to fuck him. Really strong overwhelming urges that made her voice go a bit croaky. Other times she felt so sorry that he didn't have birthdays and even got weepy at one point.

'I mean…that's just so sad,' she said, wiping her cheeks while resting a hand on his shoulder.

Other times she felt that she had to tell him everything ever that had ever happened in her life ever.

'And so I went on the date with Roger but Melissa said he was so arrogant but I was like you know what? I want to see for myself so I did. I really did. I actually went on the date. Can you believe I did that?'

Other times, fewer times, she was content to be silent and just listen to the night air and feel her heart beating in her chest.

She fell asleep at some point. Slowly leaning over to rest her head on his shoulder and half expecting him to tell her to get off, or shoot her, or both, or at least move away. Gregori remained where he was. He was not going to move for anything because she might start talking again, or worse, she might cry.

The dawn came as dawns do. The streaks of light pushing through the night to banish the darkness and move this part of the world into the ninth day of the apocalypse. It stayed quiet for a long time. Just the odd flush of a toilet here and there. Gregori had dozed on and off. His senses tuned enough and his reactions sharp enough to be confident to gain small chunks of sleep.

As more noise in the street signalled people up and about so he moved gently away from Cassie now sprawled across his lap having left a nice wet patch of drool on his leg. He found a pillow and blanket, propped her head, covered her body, made coffee and stepped outside before pulling the door to behind him.

Cassie slept on. The pillow was soft. The blanket comforting. The air warm and fragranced with the scent of coffee. She would have carried on sleeping too if not for the impact of the boy seeing the adhoc camp bed on the floor and deciding it would make a good crashmat.

'Bloody hell,' she yelped while the boy giggled and Gregori opened the door, looked in then closed it again. The boy snuggled down, pushing her over to gain pillow space. 'My bed,' she said sleepily.

'Move over,' he laughed.

'S'my bed,' she said again, allowing him to push her enough to gain space.

'Casseeeee,' he giggled.

'Shush, night time.'

He snuggled in and although giggling softly he drifted off for a while longer until she finally sat up, rubbed her eyes and proclaimed she needed a wee.

'Need a wee,' she rushed off up the stairs, missing her footing and falling back down as the boy laughed in delight and Gregori once again opened the door, looked in then closed it again.

By the time she had showered, finger-brushed her teeth while making a mental list of things-to-get, made food, eaten said food, got the boy washed and dressed the morning was fully underway and the steady flow of people and questions began.

It had been a peaceful night. There was no violence. No drunken shouting. No whimpers of pain from men beaten or women attacked. No swaggering lager filled armed thugs barging drunkenly into houses to urinate on people cowering in their beds.

Gregori was still there. Albeit washed and changed but he was still armed, still watchful and still just as frightening. They all knew he was watching to protect the boy, but in so doing, he vicariously gave protection to all of them. The house he stood outside of was right next to the entry point. That meant nothing could come in without going past Gregori first.

What they also saw was the boy. A cheeky golden haired, blue eyed child with a healthy glow and a constant laugh as he ran about. They saw the way the child interacted with Gregori. Sitting in his arms chatting away, running round his legs then sitting on the doorstep eating tinned fruit poured into a bowl.

They saw a happy child. The boy wasn't quiet or withdrawn like the children in the street had become.

That peacefulness of the night, the happy child and the start of another gloriously sunny day all combined to imbue a fresh sense of confidence within the people and when Cassie stepped out holding two fresh mugs of coffee so that confidence grew enough to walk over.

'Mornin', love,' Trish called out, strolling over with a mug of black tea held in her hands.

Cassie turned from watching the boy eat to see Trish heading towards them and felt a strange reaction. Like Trish was about to impose or disturb their space. For a second she felt like being cold and distant in the hope the woman would sod off.

'Sleep alright? We had a cracking good sleep. Oh aye, was lovely it was. Not slept like that since...well...not since it happened. Must have had five solid hours. Imagine that. Five hours of unbroken sleep. What a thing eh? See Boy looks all chirpy now then. Eating his fruit he is...'

'Hi, good morning,' Julian said, offering a tentative wave of his hand while walking over to join them. 'Hot one again by the looks of it.'

'Aye,' Trish said, glancing up at the sky. 'I were just saying I had five hours of sleep all in one go.'

'I should think the whole street did,' Julian said. 'What a difference...Rod and his er...you know...not being here and...'

'You're not wrong there, pet,' Trish said.

'Hi, Cassie?' Kate called out, coming from the side. 'Hey, alright? Sleep okay? It were so quiet last night.'

'Just sayin',' Trish said. 'Had five hours sleep I did. All in one go. Think our Tina had more.'

'It were amazing,' Kate said. 'We couldn't believe it. We had a proper bed, proper pillows with roof over our heads and a bathroom to use.'

'Mam? You want a cuppa?' Tina called over.

'Got one, pet,' Trish shouted back.

'Feels like a different place,' Kate said, looking round the street. 'All cleaned and swept like...we need t'get tents out of park...'

'And bodies need burning,' Trish cut in.

'We'll have to give more food out this morning,' Julian said.

'Aye, we doing it each day then?' Trish asked. 'We could give enough for the day if you get me meanin','

'Cass?' Kate asked. 'What do you reckon? Give it out each day or mornin' and evenin'?'

'Does it matter?' Cassie asked, slight taken aback at the question.

'Mam?' Tina asked, adding to the small group with a doe eyed look at Gregori and a meek smile offered to Cassie.

'Kate said she had a good sleep too she did,' Trish said. 'Julian said whole street did. Whole street had decent night. Cass just tellin' us what we should do with t'food. Give it out all in mornin' or twice a day but mind, that food not gonna last forever.'

Cassie didn't like the doe eyed look Tina gave Gregori. She didn't like the vulnerability of the girl either, the submissive way she dropped her eyes and gave only quick shy glances. Clearly an attention seeking whore.

'Once a day,' Cassie said firmly, lifting an eyebrow when Tina looked at her.

'Aye, grand idea that,' Trish said. 'Best way.'

'Best way,' Kate said. 'Saves bother.'

'Are we restricting all other access to the food?' Julian asked. 'What if someone doesn't take enough and needs to get more.'

'Control it strictly,' Cassie said. 'People are greedy and lie. They'll store it and use it for trade which will create more problems and put people in positions of power which in turn could lead to further disputes...' she made it up as she spoke but kept her voice hard and her head high. A pause followed when she finished. A pregnant silence that extended for a few seconds.

'Now that is smart,' Trish said in awe. 'You hear that? Smart that was. Smart as anything.'

'Very good point actually,' Julian said thoughtfully, taking a fresh interest in Cassie.

'But we don't want a...a...' Kate trailed off, clearly thinking of the right words to use.

'Dictatorship? Tyrannical rule?' Cassie asked.

'I were gonna say we don't want to be right bastards but aye, pretty much.'

'Up to you. Your street,' Cassie said, looking round nonchalantly. 'How did Rod get control again? How did that happen? I'm guessing he said he was going to sort things out? Protect you all? Something like that?'

'Aye, evil sod,' Trish said.

'Mornin', sawn-off okay is it?' John said, adding another number to the rapidly forming government of the street.

'Mornin', John,' Trish said. 'How'd you sleep? We heard whole street slept good they did. People sayin' they had best sleep since it happened.'

'Not bad,' John said.

'Cass said we're only to give food out in morning,' Trish said.

'Stops people stockpiling it to use for trade,' Kate added.

'Stops disputes,' Julian said.

'Good idea that,' John said.

'And keep people working too,' Cassie said, enjoying the feeling of having people actually listen to her. It was empowering and enjoyable. 'Keep them occupied.'

'No point bein' lazy,' John said.

'Stop 'em mithering and worryin',' Trish added.

'Did you empty all the food from the other houses?' Cassie asked.

'We got some,' Julian said with a shadow crossing his face in memory of those first few days.

'Get more. Organise people to clear it out and stock it here. Clothes. Bedding. Anything you can use...' she reeled off the instructions, looking round to gain eye contact and make sure the attention seeking whore knew she wasn't a push over. More people strolled over to join the group. More people to listen to Cassie while Gregori watched and scanned and the boy ate tinned fruit poured into a bowl. 'Use petrol from cars to burn the bodies but burn the clothes you use when you move the bodies too. Anti-bac everything. Disinfectant on everything. Get those tents down. Clean the park up...'

Her father must have felt like this. He was an MP and immersed fully into ministerial life, as well as rent boys and cocaine. He had power and influence. He chaired committees and made decisions that had direct influence on the lives of millions. Cassie always thought it was dull, boring and only for old men and ugly women but suddenly she felt the lure of it. To be in a position of authority and have people listening and nodding eagerly.

It was a novelty and one she relished. The boy finished eating and followed Cassie down to the house with the food. He was the same as ever. Running about noisily, chatting and getting in the way but where the boy went, so Gregori went and so not one person said or showed any negative reaction.

That day wore on and Cassie grew comfortable in her role. She enjoyed the attention and being able to carry a sawn off shotgun, even if it was unloaded. She gave orders. Organised groups to go and scavenge. Got work parties cleaning the park and more sent out to burn the bodies and timed it perfectly to make sure the doe eyed attention seeking whore Tina was one of them.

'Learn names, always pays dividends when you address someone by their name. Makes them think you actually give a shit about their miserable little lives.'

That's what her father told her once, before her mother found him with the men and drugs that is. Cassie didn't see much of her father after that. Not that she was really bothered by her father's indiscretion. She couldn't actually care who he fucked or who fucked him but the chance to be a wounded victim so dreadfully hurt by her callous father was too great a chance to pass up. Wise words though. Wise words indeed.

'Trish, there are four men over there not doing anything. Get them scrubbing that end of the street. John, you find me three groups with say...four or five people in each group. They can go out for food. Kate, count all the food, every single tin and packet so we know if anyone is stealing. Julian, make sure there is a rota of people to stand on those towers and keep watch and tell them no smoking or anything that will distract them. Colin, you get some people into the park. I want it cleaned with disinfectant. Children play in there. Tina, go with this group and burn the bodies. I don't care what your mother told you to do...'

She was smart too and made sure to play with the boy, giving him food and chatting with him. Holding his hands, swinging him round and carrying him on her back. Firstly, because she wanted Gregori to see how good she was with him, but secondly, and more strongly, she liked it. It gave real pleasure to hear him laugh.

'Are we staying here then?' she asked Gregori when they were alone.

He shrugged. 'Boy happy.'

That's all he said. Cassie thought about those words as the afternoon gave way to the evening. Gregori's sole purpose seemed to be the welfare of the boy. That meant that if the boy was happy here, then they would probably stay.

Problem was, Cassie was already starting to get bored. She was restless too and kept thinking back to Gregori killing. It was like she was missing it. She wanted to see it again. Just the thought of it made her tingle. The influence and position of power she was developing was good fun but it wasn't right. There was an urge. Like a voice deep down that was telling her staying here was the wrong thing.

Those thoughts carried on through the evening until the night descended. She hoped it would be like the previous night and that once the boy was asleep, she would be alone with Gregori. In her head, she would show him more Yoga moves and maybe, you know, lean over him a bit, to help him get it right, maybe push her boobs into him and accidently brush his groin at which point she would feel his erection and they would fuck. Like really fuck. Like go mad and he'd grip her arse from behind and push her head down.

Those thoughts kept coming as much as the others but as the night wore on, so the stupid bloody people in the street were suddenly all best friends with each other and wanting to hang around and drink tea and talk about how good it was now while that attention seeking whore scrubbed the dead body juice off her fat body then came back out to make doe eyes.

She tried suggesting to Gregori they go into the house.

'No. I watch.'

Fuck's sake. It was shit. Why didn't they all piss off and leave them alone. By the time they did piss off it was really late. She tried capturing the mood of the previous night but the time for it had gone. Instead, she managed to get next to Gregori on the landing at the bottom of the stairs and eventually fell asleep to dribble on his shoulder.

The next morning was even worse. The urge was so strong. The boy woke her up again by jumping on her bedding and that was fine. He snuggled in and they slept a bit more while Gregori stood outside.

She woke and left the boy in her bedding to use the bathroom.

That's when the urge came on. An incessant nagging thing. A will exerting the idea that staying in the street was wrong. She showered and touched herself for a few minutes while thinking of Gregori executing Barney. She even thought she would climax but the frustration was gnawing at her. She needed to do something but she didn't know what.

By the time she got downstairs bloody Trish and bloody Julian and the bloody rest were already well into another morning committee meeting. She felt a conflicting irritation of not being there to tell them what to do while feeling annoyed and wishing they would fuck off.

'Morning, Cass!'

Those were the words that greeted her the second she stepped out of the house. Seconds later they were surrounding her. All with steaming mugs held in hands. All with earnest expressions of *how to make everyones lives better*. It was sickening. It repulsed her while at the same time the lure of being in control and having the power of influence was still strong.

'Hey we cleaned street proper yesterday,' Trish said, looking round in admiration of the work. 'Gleamin' it is.'

'Bodies all stacked and ready,' Tina said as Cassie took pleasure in the look of distaste on the doe eyed bitch's face.

'Why didn't you burn them?' Cassie asked.

'Ran out of time we did,' Tina said. 'Only had two barrows to shift 'em down there. They stink something awful and we had to get ones from outside street too...all rotten they were...'

'Aw pet,' Trish said, tutting sadly.

'Not nice, love,' Kate said, rubbing Tina's arm. 'We'll get someone else to do it today. You done your bit so you have.'

'We put 'em in car park,' Tina said sadly. Now avoiding eye contact with Cassie who seemed to be constantly glaring at her. She even thought to tell her mam that Cassie didn't like her but she forgot and then got covered in dead body juices.

'Aw,' Trish said again.

'Got some good supplies though,' Julian said, clearly looking for some praise, the ingratiating smarmy twat.

'How much?' Cassie asked.

'Got list,' Kate said.

'Where?' Cassie asked.

'Indoors. Get it after I had me tea. Eh, can't do nowt in morning without a brew first.'

'And that's the truth that is,' Trish said with a cackle, nudging Kate with her elbow with an act that made Cassie want to throw her hot coffee in their faces.

The urge was strong then. So strong. A real thing. An absolute pressure driving her mad inside. She looked at Gregori who just stared about. She looked round for the boy then remembered he was getting himself washed and changed.

'What's today then?' Kate said. Everyone looked to Cass. John had walked over. More faces too. People with names she had memorised. Colin. Pete. Jane. Doe eyed whore. Suddenly the thought of another day here, trapped in this cesspit was too much but then the boy was happy and that was the important thing. As she thought of the boy, so some of the feelings of angst subsided.

'Cass? You alright there, pet?' Trish asked, suddenly full of concern at the wan look on Cassie's face.

'Fine,' Cassie snapped. 'I'll check on the boy.'

'Yeah course,' Kate said, casting an uncertain glance to the others. Cassie did this a few times yesterday too. Suddenly going all quiet and weird. Pushing her hands through her hair and looking either angry or like she wanted to cry. They asked if she was okay but then as Trish said, everyone had lost family and the *poor lass is suffering as much as us*.

Cassie went up to the boy in his room and again felt that repulsion of thinking of it as his room. She stopped in the doorway, smiling at him muttering away to himself while getting dressed.

'Who are you talking to?' she asked.

'Darren is dead,' he blurted, turning to show a face streaked with tears. He ran over as she dropped to a crouch. Her arms enveloping him as he sobbed hard. A sudden feeling of utter wretchedness inside her body as the boy repeated the same thing again and again. 'Darren is dead...Darren is dead...'

'It's okay, ssshhhh now, it's okay...' she rubbed his back and kissed the top of his head while he wept.

'FUCK YOU, HOWIE...'

'Jesus,' Cassie pulled back at the ferocity of the voice to see that same ageless thing back in his eyes that twisted his features to show pure rage.

'BOY?' Gregori roared as he charged up the stairs.

'He's fine, he's okay...' Cassie called out. Gregori still ran up. His whole manner changed. The man that killed Rod and the men suddenly back and ready to slaughter everything. 'What happen?'

'Darren is dead,' the boy sobbed again, the raw anger now gone.

'Who this man?'

Cassie shrugged, pulling a face to show she had no clue what the child was on about.

'Is dream,' Gregori said.

'He's awake,' she pointed out, still holding the boy.

'Is child. Have bad memory.'

'Boy?' Cassie asked. 'Who's Darren? You said his name before. Did you know him?'

'On the Island of White...but but...but Marcy isn't dead and...' he babbled on with most of his words lost to his sniffles and sobs.

She held him while Gregori watched. She rubbed his back, kissed his head and made soothing sounds until the boy pulled back, wiped his eyes and said he was hungry.

'Kids,' Cassie said, standing up. The urge came back. So strong too. So very strong. An undeniable thing. The glimpse she just had of Gregori charging up the stairs. She tried to hide it but it felt like her legs would give out. As she sought control, so she realised the boy was staring at her and the ageless thing was back. It stared at her. Stared through her.

'Can Gregori do my food?' the boy asked.

'Want me do food?' Gregori grunted.

'Yes please,' the boy said, still staring at Cassie.

'I've got to...' Cassie started to speak but the words dried up in her mouth. The boy's eyes were not his own. The expression within them.

It was pleading with her. It was telling her to do something. To follow the urge. To action it. 'I should...I'll er...I'll help them sort the food... from that house...'

'Yay,' the boy said, grinning at Gregori. 'Can we have choclit for breakfast, Gregoreeee?'

'No.'

'Oh but please...just one...'

'I'll go and...' Cassie moved out of the room towards the stairs.

The Albanian turned to look at Cassie. 'Go. Take gun. I come if trouble...'

She watched him for a second with composure coming fully into her mind. She smiled with a twinkle back in her eye as the boy stared past Gregori to her. 'Sure, make me something nice,' she said with a wink. 'Be back in a few minutes.'

She headed down the stairs, running his words through her mind. *Take gun. I come if trouble.* So good. So deliciously good. She did take a gun. She picked up her sawn-off, broke the barrel, found a single shell from the bag and slid it in.

'Boy okay is he, love?' Trish asked when Cassie stepped out.

'Oh fine, bad dream,' she said with a quick sad look. 'Now ladies finish your brews. Can't start the day without a proper cuppa now can we?' she grinned at the smiles and chuckles. 'John, Julian, you come with me down to the house and we'll make a start. Ladies, take your time. You all worked hard yesterday. Take it a bit easier today... oh and Tina, thanks for doing that awful job. I know it wasn't easy but...well, you saved someone else having to do it. Thank you. I mean that.'

The doe eyed whore almost floated off the ground at the praise and the earnest smile coming from Cassie, and the look of pride in Trish's face was vomit inducing.

'Gentlemen, follow me please.'

'Thanks, Cass,' Kate said with real feeling.

Go. Take gun. I come if trouble.

'No problem,' Cassie said, hearing the words in her mind while the tingle spread through her body. The way he said it. The coldness of him. The sheer brutality. The urge inside. Not just to leave but something else.

'Were good of you that were,' John said as they walked down the street.

'Oh it's nothing,' Cassie said.

'Not at all,' Julian said, smiling that sycophantic smile of his.

'Folk need work but folk need kind words too,' John said.

'Hmm, yeah sure.'

'Missus said last night she did. Said she's happy you and Greg are here. Said feels safe she does. My lass the same. Saw her smile last night. Not seen that in while now.'

'That's nice, John,' Julian said, looking past Cassie.

'Not given to speaking my feelings,' John said, his voice low, his expression one of being abashed and shy. 'But I'd agree. Good havin' you both here it is.' John glanced across when she didn't reply.

'Pardon? Oh...oh that's so sweet. Thank you. Sorry, miles away.'

'You okay, Cassie?' Julian asked.

'Me? Fine. Yep, er...totally fine...well, here we are. After you.'

She stepped back to let them go first through the door. The morning still early but plenty of people up and about. Mostly drinking tea in small groups. She took in the cleanliness of the street. The park cleared of tents and litter. The order gained and the smiles glimpsed on faces.

Inside the house was stacked with more goods taken from the nearby houses. Tins everywhere and all sorted in terms of contents and even with the labels facing out. She did that. She made that happen. She made them get the food and clean the street. She made it better.

She walked into the front room and down the narrow walkway between the piles of goods towards the small clear area in the dining room already filled with John and Julian.

'Tight squeeze,' Julian said with a smile trying to shuffle back from Cassie trapping them in such a confined space. No other way out. Only through her.

'Is,' Cassie said, staring at him.

'So er...' Julian said, dropping his gaze from her intense stare.

'Where we starting then?' John asked. Cassie turned that stare on him. Seeing the decency in his haggard washed out features. Taking in the bags under his eyes and remembering the emotion pouring off him yesterday when he thanked her for what they did.

'Er...Cassie?' Julian asked when she didn't reply. She turned that stare to him again. Relishing the uncomfortableness of the moment. The tingle growing. The heat spreading. The urge so strong. 'Do you want to fuck me?'

'What?' Julian gasped as John flinched in shock.

'Do you want to fuck me?' Cassie asked slowly, her voice low and husky.

'Good god,' Julian said.

'You what, love?' John asked.

She pushed her top up, grabbed the hem of her bra and yanked it down to expose her left breast. The nipple already hard. 'Yeah? Want to fuck me?'

'Fucking hell,' Julian said. 'I'm gay...'

'Eh now love, you put that away,' John said in alarm.

Cassie stared from one to the other. The urge now at least one step towards being satiated. An incredible feeling inside. John went to move but she stepped quickly, blocking his view while reaching over to uncup her right breast.

'Cassie, what the hell are you doing?' Julian asked in horror.

She smiled at them. Wolfish and hard. Her heart booming. Her blood pounding through her body. She raised the shotgun, pointing it up at the ceiling as the grin spread and the blood drained from John's face.

The boom was huge. The solid explosion of the shotgun shell detonating to send pellets into the ceiling. Plaster rained down and Cassie screamed. She screamed as loud as she could, pushing real terror into the pitch and tone.

Neither of the two men knew what hit them when Cassie lunged forward, dropping the shotgun to wrap her arms round their necks. For a second they stayed there. All three pressed together. Then she hooked her legs round theirs and let her weight go, pulling them down to the floor. Both men were strong and given space they could easily withstand the force, but they didn't have space. They had Cassie's legs wrapped round theirs and barging into each other with crates of food everywhere. The three fell with Cassie underneath and the ceiling raining plaster while the two men tried to push away without touching her naked breasts. John and Julian shouted. Cassie screamed. John and Julian scrabbled to get away. Cassie grabbed their hands to pull them on her breasts while she thrashed wild and crazed.

'GREGOREEEEE...GREGOREEEE,' she screamed the name over and again. Pure fear in her voice.

'Please stop it,' Julian gasped, fighting to break free. His head slammed into John's who grunted and tried to stand up. The poor man utterly confused at what was happening. His face already haggard and drawn from the last ten days. His whole life shattered from the fear of what Rod and his men would do to his daughter. He almost got onto his feet but Cassie grabbed hard, yanking him off balance. He struck out to steady himself, his hand lashing across her face. Her breasts still exposed. Her screams so loud in their ears.

Gregori heard the shot, grabbed the boy to swing on his back and was already running when she started screaming. His feet pounding the street. His hand clutching the pistol. He heard her screaming his name. He heard the fear and terror in her voice and burst into the house to stride into the front room to see them attacking her. Bits of ceiling over all three of them. Her face bleeding. Her breasts exposed.

Two shots. Two deaths given. Cassie saw it. She saw their heads blow out and felt the wonderfully hot sticky blood spurt over her face. She felt the bodies slump down dead across her but more than that, she saw the final second of fear in their eyes when Gregori came in.

'Did their brains come out?' the boy asked.

That's when it all went wrong. That's when the infected, the several hundred of them that had silently encircled the street during the night, came charging in response to the shotgun blast that startled the boy who was then wrenched off his feet onto Gregori's back.

A roar. A wild animalistic roar as Gregori heaved the bodies off

Cassie who, despite the awful appearance, was staring up in awe at the sight of Gregori looking so majestically brutal and trying to see if he looked at her breasts.

A hand on her wrist wrenched her up onto her feet.

'We go,' he said and she saw it. She saw him glance down to her chest. She saw his eyes take her in and the tingle became a fire and if not for the boy on his back she would have fucked him right there.

Instead, she was dragged in his wake but managed a glimpse to see the dead bodies of John and Julian.

'MOVE,' Gregori roared at Trish, Tina, Kate and more people already crowding the front door.

'My shotgun,' Cassie broke free to dart back and grab her weapon, sparing another lingering look to the shards of bone and the blood so red and wet.

'WE GO,' Gregori shouted. She ran back to join him as he barged through the crowd all confused at the gunshots and the wild roaring now coming from all around them.

Chaos ensued. The first infected broke through the side entrance accessed via the hidden path so carefully disguised. They came wild and frenzied, slamming into men and women as they ran for their lives.

Gregori ran for the house. His right hand holding the pistol out. His left holding Cassie stunned from the sight of the things running through the street. They were so fast. So wild. So incredible and not one of them even turned to look at Gregori, the boy or her.

Gregori still fired. He fired to clear his path to reach the house and barrelled in with Cassie right behind him. A few seconds to grab his bag of guns. Another few to reload Cassie's shotgun and push shells into her hands then back out into the street.

In those few seconds, dozens more infected had got into the sealed street sparking a massed charge from the residents running for the barrier at the far end. The residents screaming in fear. The residents dying in droves and the infected running round Gregori, the boy and Cassie on all sides without heed or interest.

In the maelstrom of disorder, Cassie spotted Trish and Tina

running across the street and in a reaction of pure instinct, she fired the shotgun. Tina went down screaming from the pellets striking her legs. Her mother stopped to help and desperately pulled to get Tina back up before the first infected swarmed them and the doe eyed little slut had teeth sinking into her legs.

It was the press of bodies ramming into it and trying to climb over that brought the barrier down, and that just allowed access for the infected on the other side. The two sides met. The residents, already either sprawled on the ground amongst the broken planks or trying to go over were simply overrun by the howling beasts moving so fast.

It was awful. Terrible. Just so very bad but Cassie snatched glances and felt the pulse and tingle grow each time she saw an infected bite into a person. She didn't care be they man, woman or child. She only cared for the sight of it and in those minutes that it took to get through, she saw the boy staring round with an almost comical expression of mild wonder.

The only way to break out was by going over the barrier but by then, Gregori had accepted the infected were not attacking them and so only shot those in his direct path, but in fairness, he also shot a few survivors too, which Cassie saw.

That's when they got covered in blood. It was spraying everywhere. There was no way to get though and *not* get covered in blood.

H e drives from the car park. His eyes flicking to the rear view mirror as Cassie turns to look out the back window. The sight is wild. So many human forms running, fighting and dying. She spots Kate sprinting hard and almost breaking free before being taken down from the side by a freshly turned Trisha.

'But I didn't make them...' the boy blurts as Gregori holds his finger up again. 'I didn't...I really didn't, Gregoreee.'

'It doesn't matter,' Cassie says. "I didn't like that street anyway.'

We had this day

CHAPTER ELEVEN

————————————

Darkness broken by the soft glow of the fire that fills the barn with the subtle scents of woodsmoke. Snores here and there. Soft breathing. Bodies rolling over and fidgeting. Blinky farts but she's on the other side of the wall made from hay bales that was formed to mark the boundary between the elders and the others.

Paula can't sleep. She sits up and looks round at the cubicles made by the bales. Heather and Paco at the end. Her form draped over him, loving and close despite the warmth of the night. Marcy and Howie curled up next to each other. She looks down at Roy on his side and the distance between them.

She needs a wee. The spider bites are itchy and the heat of the barn seems to be making them worse. The smell of Blinky's fart wafts over, mixing with the smoke from the fire and the smells of people sleeping. She needs air and to cool down. She grabs the tube of ointment and stands slowly, moving carefully so not to wake anyone else. She spots Reginald sleeping like a vampire flat on his back with his fingers entwined over his chest and snorts a quiet laugh at the sight as she threads a route towards the door.

Outside, the Second Watch Biscuit Club is underway. A giant, a dog and a horse gathered at the rear of the Saxon all munching noisily on digestives who all look over to see Paula coming out.

Meredith moves in a step towards Clarence. It's bad enough they have to share with the horse but the approach of another non-member of the Second Watch Biscuit Club is alarming. Jess takes advantage of his distraction to gently prise the biscuit from his hand. Meredith whines, spotting the theft and rises to plant her front feet on Clarence's legs as she stretches towards the open packet in his hand.

'You okay?' Clarence asks, whispering in the way of a dull rumble.

'Need a wee,' Paula says, twisting the lid from the tube. She squeezes a dollop out and starts rubbing it on her face with a sigh of relief.

'Itchy?'

'So itchy,' she says.

'Oi, get off,' Clarence leans back, trying to remove the dog's snout from the packet of digestives then finding a fresh attack coming in from the other side as the horse joins in with the attack.

Paula watches them with a gentle smile that forms in equal measure of the sight and the pleasant relief of the ointment. She strolls over, thankful for the cooler air not filled with bum gases.

'Second Watch Biscuit Club,' Clarence says, holding the packet of biscuits out behind him while fending the animals off.

'Oh,' she says. 'Am I intruding then?'

'No you're fine...look just bugger off,' Clarence says, falling backwards into the Saxon with Meredith and Jess surging at him. Snorts of hot air in his face. Paws on his chest. Tails swishing and wagging. Paula starts chuckling at the sight of Clarence almost dwarfed by the beasts on top of him. He holds the packet away, refusing to yield the goodies. Meredith goes over him, lithe and athletic. Jess whinnies and pushes more into the Saxon, stretching her neck over Clarence with her lips pulled back and her huge tongue waggling between the rows of solid square teeth.

'Oh my god,' Paula laughs, covering her mouth.

'No, sod off,' Clarence says, trying to roll on his side as Jess gets her front feet into the back and starts inching in. 'Wait...I said wait... Paula! Help...'

'No chance,' she laughs.

'Jess get off me...Meredith, just wait... Paula, take the packet.'

'How?' she asks, laughing harder as Jess crabs in with a very real risk of actually trying to squeeze in the back of the vehicle. A mess of limbs, tails, snorts, snuffles and the deep noises of big things moving in a confined space. Paula goes forward, aiming for a gap between Meredith and Jess and laughing more at Clarence's big legs dangling like a child's from the back. 'Meredith, come on... out....Jess, get out...' she tries grabbing to pull but she might as well try and push a house over. She starts laughing harder at her feeble attempts and Meredith's tail wagging in her face. 'Put your legs down.'

'I can't,' he rumbles, still refusing to yield the packet.

'Just drop your legs and...' she clambers up, the bites now forgotten as she laughs and giggles while climbing over him. She feels tiny, like a doll trapped between three enormous living things.

'Something on my legs...'

'That's me,' she giggles, 'give them the biscuits so they...'

'No! They have to wait their turn...'

'Clarence,' she laughs as Meredith backs up to try a new angle of attack. Jess snorts and turns her great head to view Paula with bulging rolling eyes and a fresh blast of horse breath.

'It's not funny,' Clarence says, breaking into a laugh halfway through speaking. 'Bloody animals...'

'Just give them a biscuit.'

'No they have...'

'Clarence,' she laughs as Meredith twists to lick her face with a quick whine. 'Give them a biscuit.'

'Right,' the big man says, chuckling as he stretches his right arm up to his left. The two animals spot his motion and snort, whine, blast air and fidget. 'Can't reach...'

'Give it here,' she says, stretching her hand out.

'They'll go for the packet if I pass it to you.'

'So?'

He looks down at her. 'Charlie said Jess can't have too many.'

'She's bigger than you...pass it down.'

'I can't. You're not an active member of The Second Watch Biscuit Club.'

'What?' she laughs.

'Only active members of The Second Watch Biscuit Club can handle the biscuits.'

'You've got...' she breaks off, laughing too hard to speak. 'You've got rules?'

'Yep.'

'Make me a member then.'

'It's not that easy, we have to admit you as a member...right, do all present agree to Paula being admitted to The Second Watch Biscuit Club?'

Meredith whines to say no, not at all. Jess snorts and whinnies in agreement that Paula should not be admitted. Unfortunately, those noises are translated badly.

'I hereby admit Paula to The Second Watch Biscuit Club,' Clarence says, passing the packet down over his body.

As the packet comes down, so the animals turn. The packet falls. The biscuits spill over his chest and stomach. Paula bursts out laughing at the sight as the two animals start eating the biscuits. She grabs a digestive and bites into it then realises eating and laughing don't go well together.

'Can I have one?' his hands flail about on his belly and chest.

'Here,' she says with a mouthful of digestive guiding his hand to the central pile.

'Ta,' he takes one up and starts munching as the back of the Saxon fills with the noises of four mouths chomping biscuits.

'Have you only got digestives?'

'Custard creams somewhere.'

'Where?' Paula asks, trying to look round while wedged between Jess and Meredith on Clarence's thighs.

'God knows,' he chuckles. 'How's the bites?'

'Itchy...I need a wee.'

'Thanks for that.'

'Sharing,' she eats a digestive, still chuckling softly. 'I'll get out.'

'Take the biscuits with you.'

'Yep,' she scoops the fallen digestives into her hands, earning hard glares from Meredith and Jess in the process. There follows a chorus of yelps, groans and huffs as a woman, dog and a horse climb back over Clarence to drop from the Saxon. 'You okay?' she laughs at him groaning as he rises and starts edging out of the vehicle.

'Fine,' he waves a hand, 'thanks for the rescue.'

'Welcome, do you want these?' she says, offering the mound of digestives in her hands to him.

'Not really,' he says.

'Fair enough, fill your boots,' she says, scattering the broken biscuits on the grass. Meredith and Jess move fast to sniff, snuffle and eat. She strides off, brushing her hands together to rid the crumbs, 'find the custard creams.'

'Bossy,' he mumbles.

'Heard that,' she says, moving round the side of the barn towards the back.

Paula tinkles in the grass and uses the cleansing wipes from the packet left for use. She tries reaching her hands round to scratch her back, wincing at the feel of the lumps and bumps. When she goes back she is greeted by the sight of Clarence holding the packet of custard creams.

'You do this every night?'

'Started a few nights ago at the golf hotel. Custard cream?' he says, holding the open packet towards her.

'Second on the lips,' she says, taking one.

'Pardon?'

'What?'

'A second on the lips?'

'It's a saying. A second on the lips a lifetime on the hips. It means it's easy to eat a biscuit but hard to rid the fat that comes with it.'

'But you're not fat.'

'I know...it's a saying, Clarence.'

'Oh.'

'I do have hips,' she says, looking down.

'Everyone has hips.'

'No I mean, like hips...like they poke out a bit.'

'They don't poke out.'

'They do a bit.'

'You mean the curve,' he says, pointing at her legs.

'Yeah here,' she says, patting the tops of her thighs where they sweep out ever so slightly. 'Marcy has gorgeous hips.'

'Oh. You have nice hips too.'

'She's got gorgeous everything.'

'Biscuit?'

'Thanks.' She eats and fidgets then tries reaching round to scratch the itchy bits on her back. 'You'll have to put cream on me in a minute.'

'Me?'

She chuckles at the look of alarm on his face, 'Bless, you fluster so easily.'

'Hmmm,' he rumbles, eating a biscuit that he almost sprays out when she turns round and starts tugging her t-shirt up. 'Now?'

'Really itchy.'

He tries to avert his eyes from her bare back and the material of her bra stretching across. His heart beating harder. The biscuits now forgotten. It feels wrong. Not because of the act of giving care but because of the other feeling he refuses to acknowledge, but then acknowledging it now and admitting it is wrong also gives voice to it.

'Cream,' she pulls the tube from her pocket and hands it back. 'Is this weirding you out?'

'No,' he says deeply, quickly. The sight of the bites are awful. Red and raised, livid and sore looking. He unscrews the cap, oozes a dollop out and hovers his hand over her skin, forcing himself to look only at the bites. 'Rub it in?'

'Yep,' she twists to look at him, her smile soft and warm. He touches the dollop to the first lump then pulls back when she shivers.

'Does it hurt?'

'No it's nice, cold...keep going.'

He rubs the cream into the first bite. Feeling the hard lump pushing through her skin. More cream goes onto his fingertips and he starts working it into the other bites, gently and slowly.

She groans softly at the relief it brings with a noise that makes him blink a few times. He works her lower back first then up her spine and out to the sides trying to ignore her bra strap as though even looking at it, let alone touching it is a step too far.

'Here,' she reaches back and unfastens the clasp, freeing the material as he swallows and blinks again.

'Thanks,' he carries on. Seeing the outline of the strap marking her skin with faint red lines.

'So nice,' she murmurs.

He nods and carries on working up to her neck, not just rubbing the cream into the bites but the soft skin between them too with an action bordering on massaging. She groans again, a soft noise of air escaping long and soft from her throat. She moves back an inch. Then another. Pressing further between his legs to make it easier for him to reach. She closes her eyes and breathes deep and slow at the gentle touch. A blush spreading across her chest and up her throat. She moves back again, an adjustment to position. She rests her right hand on his knee. Her left arm pressed gently to her breasts holding the bra in place. Her head lowered. Strands of hair spilling down her neck that Clarence moves aside with such a touch it makes her shiver. He can feel her hand on his leg, her thumb moving slowly back and forth. Just a fraction at first, then her fingers join in. Minutely opening and closing her hand to draw her fingertips over the material of his trousers. She shifts again, exhaling almost sensually. He loses focus to anything other than her. Seeing only her form so close to him. His heart booming. Her breathing growing faster. He moves on to the sides of her neck. She lifts her head so he can reach and he feels the motion of her throat as she swallows. He leans in a bit more, working the cream across the top of her shoulders then the front. Reaching round in an act that makes her feel enveloped. Their heads so close now. Too close. All sense vanishes. All thoughts other than this closeness dissipates. She moves again, pressing her body into his. A hardness detected. His hands freeze. Her heart booms.

She starts to turn, his face so close to hers. Leaning over her. Her hand on his leg squeezes hard. Both of them utterly caught in the moment.

'Bites itchy then?' Roy asks mildly from the doorway of the barn.

'Shit,' Paula lurches a step from Clarence, dropping her top and bending too quickly to grab it with her left hand that releases the bra that slides down her arms. 'Shit...just...I...'

'I'm just going for a pee. Back in a mo. Hey, Clarence, all quiet on watch is it?' Roy asks as he walks off down the side towards the rear.

'Yes,' Clarence booms, wincing at the volume of his own voice as he catches sight of Paula's breasts when she turns to look at him. He squeezes his eyes closed and looks up and away. His face flushed. His fingers covered in ointment.

Paula scrabbles to hold the top and get her bra back on. 'Thanks for that,' she blurts. 'I mean the...the cream not the...'

'It's fine,' Clarence booms. 'Anytime...the cream...for the cream and...'

'Yes. Thank you.'

'No problem. Thank you.'

'No, thank you. Very kind and...' She pulls her top down over the head and draws deep breaths to ease her heart threatening to boom from her chest. Her cheeks reddening. The crimson blush at the base of her neck and across the top of her chest so clear and evident.

'That's better,' Roy says, walking back. 'Bites okay?'

'Fine,' Paula says, her voice tight. She clears her throat, 'yes, er...fine.'

'That cream is good,' Roy says. 'What are they eating?'

'Biscuits.' Clarence and Paula say together.

'Ah, look like digestives,' Roy says.

'Er,' Paula says, looking at Clarence.

'Digestives,' Clarence says.

'Well,' Roy says. 'I'm going back to bed, you staying up for a bit?' he asks Paula.

'No, I'll er...I'll come and...'

'Night, mate.'

'Night,' Clarence booms, earning a look from Jess and Meredith at his excessive noise.

Paula walks behind her partner back to the bed space they share while Jess and Meredith formulate a new plan to get at the custard creams Clarence no longer wants, seeing as he just sank backwards into the Saxon with a long groan.

CHAPTER TWELVE

M o rises without being told. He heard Dave getting up from the other side of the hay bales and so starts dressing quickly.

Blinky rises too, pulling her trousers on while Mo glances over with a confused look. She fastens the belt, grabs her top and pulls it down over her head.

'What you doing?' Mo whispers.

'Training with you,' Blinky whispers back.

'Did Dave say?'

She shakes her head, casting him a quick almost nervous smile.

'Blinky? You asked Dave?'

She tugs a boot on and starts work on the laces. 'I want to be Dave trained.'

'You's got to ask him,' Mo whispers urgently as Dave walks in and stops on seeing Blinky getting dressed. She looks at him then over to Mo. An exceptionally rare show of worry on her face that she tries to hide.

'I want to train with you,' she says to Dave.

'Have you spoken to your section commander?' Dave asks.

'What Blowers?' Blinky asks. 'No but...I can fight. I'm good at it...'

'You must seek consent from your section commander.'

'Blowers? Can I train with Dave?'

'Corporal Blowers,' Dave says.

'I don't want to be called Corporal,' Blowers says, sitting up to scratch at the bandage round his head. 'Fucking thing...'

'Take it off then,' Cookey mumbles, peering over sleepily.

'It's grim though,' Blowers says.

'We kill people for a living dickhead. We see insides on the outsides everyday.'

Blowers thinks for a second, 'fair one,' he pushes the bandage up and away from his ruined eye. He seems older. Harder. An air about him now. A thing done that has toughened his soul and manner with a step closer to the aura Howie has. He scratches and rubs at his head where the bandage was. 'What's going on then?'

'I want to be Dave trained,' Blinky says, holding off from swearing or saying anything stupid.

'Er,' Blowers says, still rubbing his head. 'You can train with Dave but you stay in my team unless Mr Howie says. I lose Mo sometimes and I can't lose another one...unless we find another double hard hockey player...Dave? That okay?'

'You are Patricia's section commander, Corporal Blowers.'

'S'just Blowers,' Blowers says.

'Good luck with that,' Howie calls over. 'Corporal Blowers.'

'I don't want to be Corporal Blowers.'

'I didn't want to be Mr Howie but I am. How's the eye? And the finger?'

'Yeah neither have grown back.'

'That's shit.'

'It is boss, did you hear Blinky wants to be Dave trained?'

'Yup.'

'You okay with it?'

'Your team, Corporal Blowers...but I agree with what you said.'

'Which bit?'

'About not losing her from your team. Blinky?'

'Yes, Mr Howie, Sir?'

'You can train with Dave but you stay in Blowers' team. Fair one?'

'Fuck yes! I mean...Sir, Fuck yes, Mr Howie, Sir.'

'Dave?'

'Yes, Mr Howie.'

'You okay with that?'

'Permission to come round and speak, Mr Howie.'

'We're in a barn...'

'Permission to come round and speak, Mr Howie.'

'Fuck's sake...yes that's fine...I mean, your bed is right next to mine anyway so like, you were here a few minutes ago and...'

'Standby,' Dave says before marching smartly round the barrier of hay bales to stop next to Howie's bed. His feet shoulder width apart, his hands behind his back, his eyes fixed on a spot somewhere far away. 'Mr Howie.'

'Yes, Dave,' Howie groans, sitting up to see Paula already sitting up biting her nails.

'Shush,' Marcy mumbles, waving a hand in the air.

'I want to undertake training with another member of the team, Mr Howie.'

'Er yeah I heard,' Howie says. 'Um...Paula? You okay?'

'Huh?' she replies while trying to eat herself.

'I want to undertake training with another member of the team, Mr Howie.'

'Yes I heard. It's fine,' Howie says, looking up at Dave.

'Is it okay, Mr Howie?'

'Is what okay?'

'To train another member of the team?'

'Fuck me, yes it's fine. We just had this conversation. Paula, are you alright?'

'Huh?'

'I said are you alright?'

'What is?' she asks.

'Oh my god you are so loud,' Marcy huffs, sitting up to stare bleary eyed at Howie then Dave then over to Paula still chewing her digits. 'Are you biting your nails?'

'No,' Paula says, instantly dropping her hand. 'Night,' she adds, lying down flat.

'Okay,' Howie says, 'great. Glad we sorted that. Night then...'

'Thank fuck,' Marcy mumbles.

'Patricia is a female,' Dave says, standing at ease with his hands behind his back and his feet shoulder with apart.

'So?' Blinky says from behind the barrier.

'So?' Howie ask Dave.

'Shut up!' Marcy mumbles.

'Can't sleep,' Paula huffs, sitting back up.

'Nothing to report on my watch,' Clarence says, walking in.

'Night,' Paula says, lying flat again.

'Night, Paula,' Clarence says.

'Night, Clarence,' Paula says.

'What the actual fuck,' Marcy snaps.

'Why is Blinky female?' Howie asks Dave who finally drops his gaze to look at him.

'I think she born a female, Mr Howie.'

'What? No! I mean...why is that important.'

'My back is itchy now,' Marcy says, flipping over to lie on her back so she can wriggle and writhe in an attempt to soothe the itching. 'Is your back itchy?'

'Who me?' Howie asks.

'Paula not you. Paula?'

'What?'

'Is your back itchy?'

'No.'

'Night all,' Clarence booms.

'Alright foghorn,' Howie says with a wince at his voice.

'Why isn't your back itchy?' Marcy asks. 'Mine is driving me mad.'

'Dave?'

'Yes, Mr Howie.'

'Blinky?'

'Yes, Mr Howie.'

'No I mean, what's wrong with Blinky?'

'Nothing wrong with me,' Blinky says from the other side of the barrier.

'So itchy,' Marcy writhes.

'Put some cream on then,' Howie says. 'Dave?'

'Patricia is a female recruit, Mr Howie.'

'Yep, established that...and the point is what?'

'Why isn't your back itching,' Marcy says.

'S'not,' Paula says.

'Clarence put cream on her back,' Roy says.

Marcy stops writhing and freezes. A sudden silence on the other side of the barrier. Nick's head pops up to look over followed by Cookey, Charlie and Blowers. Clarence plays a statue. Paula sits up. 'I was itchy,' she says, staring round at everyone as Marcy lifts her head to look over. 'Really itchy.'

'Anyway,' Howie says slowly, looking back up at Dave still standing at ease. 'Blinky?'

'Patricia is a female recruit, Mr Howie.'

'Stuck in a loop now, Dave. What's the concern with Blinky being a girl?'

Dave stares ahead, holding position. A slight pause before he speaks in that flat voice. 'Close quarters combat training requires the instructor and the recruit to have close physical contact in order to develop the recruit's full potential, Mr Howie.'

Seconds pass. Marcy stares at Paula. Paula bites her fingernails. Clarence plays a statue.

'I don't mind,' Blinky's voice breaks the silence.

'She doesn't mind,' Howie tells Dave.

Dave stares ahead. 'There may be inadvertent touching of breasts and genitalia between the instructor and recruit. Regulations specify that should an instructor touch a recruit in an inappropriate manner that may or may not involve sexual touching then it should be reported immediately in accordance with the chain of command.'

'I don't mind,' Blinky says from behind the barrier.

'She doesn't mind,' Howie tells Dave.

'In order to achieve maximum efficiency situations may occur whereby I brush, graze, be in contact with or otherwise push against the female recruit's breast area.'

'You can touch my tits, Dave. I don't mind.'

'Right,' Howie says quickly as Paula finally blinks up at the last comment.

'Dave is not touching your ti...breasts,' Paula says.

'Unless she gets bites on them,' Marcy whispers.

'It was just my back,' Paula says.

'Just the back,' Clarence the statue says. 'Cookey, I can hear you sniggering. Go to sleep.'

'Yes, Clarence.'

'So,' Howie says to Dave. 'Seems fine then...er....carry on.'

Dave stares ahead. 'Mr Howie and Miss Paula. As commanding officers of this unit, do I have your consent to conduct training with the female recruit Patricia?'

'Yes,' Howie says.

'Yes,' Paula says.

'And should the female recruit Patricia need to report any contact, brushes, grazes or otherwise inadvertent touching of her breasts, vagina or any other parts of the body deemed to be sexual in nature then she can report such matters to her chain of command which in this instance is Corporal Blowers, who in turn, will report directly to Mr Howie or Miss Paula.'

'Blowers? You get that?' Howie calls out.

'Got it.'

'The same regulations also cover Mohammed and should any touching occur between Mohammed and Patricia they should be reported to the chain of command which in this instance...'

'Blowers?'

'Got it, Boss.'

'He's got it, Dave.'

'Dave said vagina...'

'Cookey!'

'Sorry, Clarence.'

'Do you people ever sleep?'

'Sorry, Heather,' Howie says.

'Sorry, Heather,' Paula says.

'Sorry, Heather,' Cookey says.

'Cookey! You'll be on brew duty for the rest of your life in a minute, son.'

'Cool,' Howie says. 'Er...that all makes sense to me. Paula?'

'It was just my back.'

'What?'

'What?'

'Fuck me, are we in a time warp? Are you alright with Blinky being Dave trained?'

'Yes. Why wouldn't I be?'

'Right. Awesome. Carry on then.'

'Mr Howie,' Dave says with a curt nod. 'Patricia. Full kit. Assemble outside with Mohammed.'

'I'm actually in love,' Blinky says, running for the door.

Howie sighs, looks round then starts to lower back into his bed. There's another couple of hours before Dave's watch ends. Plenty of time for a cuddle with Marcy. He goes for the snuggle, aiming to wrap his arm round Marcy only to find she is still sitting up and having a secret conversation of shared facial expressions with Paula. Frowns, scowls, eyebrows lifting, shoulders shrugging until eventually Marcy motions drinking from a cup and Paula nods. The two rise to stride off as Howie shakes his head, mutters under his breath and closes his eyes.

'Hey,' Mo Mo says as Blinky rushes over.

'Mr Howie said yes but I'm staying in Blowers' team.'

'I heard,' Mo says, handing her a bowl of fruit before lowering his voice to speak fast. 'Eat. Don't say yeah, say yes. Say *yes Dave.* If we break for water drink as much as you can. Be passive. Don't argue with him. If he hurts you just tell him...'

'What if I hurt him?'

Mo freezes while picking his own bowl of fruit up. 'You won't.'

Dave walks over to place his bag at his feet, his rifle resting on the top. He picks the third bowl of fruit up and eats.

'You have finished,' Dave says in his way of combining a question with a statement. He takes the bowls to the barn and marches back. 'Hydrate,' he says, picking his cup of water up. Mo nods at Blinky to keep going and drink it all. He knows what's coming.

Blinky blinks. This is the best day ever. This beats being selected for the England ladies hockey team. This beats everything. To be Dave Trained.

'We will warm up,' Dave says, going through the same motions as previously. Rotating his wrists and ankles. Mo and Blinky copy his actions. Swinging legs out that hinge from the knee joint. Doing slow kicks forward with sweeping legs.

'Hips.'

Mo widens his eyes and looks up at the sky. Doing this with Dave was one thing but doing it with Blinky here is something else. Blinky doesn't hesitate though. A warm up is a warm up and something she has done a thousand times before. They get through it with only the sound of them breathing harder breaking the silence.

Warm up complete and Dave draws the spatulas. One in each hand that he holds out for Mo and Blinky. Mo takes his without comment. Blinky takes hers almost reverently. Like she's being given a golden sword. She stares at it, blinking and silent then back up at Dave.

'I love this world,' she breathes. 'I actually do,' she adds emphatically to Mo.

'Mohammed. You will explain to Patricia the instructions I gave you. All of them.'

Mo Mo inclines his head with a second of hesitancy knowing that everything Dave does is for a reason. 'Blinky, we protect the boss from all threats. A threat is anything that's a risk to the boss. We negate that risk, you get me?'

'Yep,' Blinky nods. 'Yes, Dave.' she adds quickly.

Mo pauses with a look to Dave who nods for him to continue.

'If Marcy poses a threat to the boss we kill her, same with all of them. Blowers, Cookey, everyone. If they threaten the boss we kill 'em.'

'Got it. Kill everyone.'

'Yeah not everyone just anyone that has a risk to the boss.'

'Got it.'

'We er, we's watch the boss all the time. We's got to know where he is all the time and that means when we're fighting and…Dave called it the field of battle. We's watch the boss in battle.'

'Got it.'

'We's his eyes and ears yeah. We's got his back and the things he might not see,' Mo pauses again with another look to Dave who nods to keep going. 'The boss is hard as fuck, like braver than anything but he's got to survive so's we do that yeah. We's make sure he survives. We's go in first. We check the way is safe for the boss…'

Mo sees the brevity of the words sink in and Blinky hanging off every word he says. He checks Dave again who stares at him with that face so devoid of expression but again a nod to keep going. Mo feels something else too. Dave said he trusts Mo. No one other than Jagger ever trusted him before and this now, here, being allowed to impart these details to Blinky is an extension of that trust. The moment becomes special. A point in history he and Blinky will always remember. Blinky even stops blinking.

'Dave's autistic,' Mo continues, sensing and knowing he can say these things. 'He can't read people like I can…like we can…so's we do that for Dave too. Dave don't read faces like we can. He don't get the little shit people say and do like when they're joking or being serious. If you need Dave to know something then you's got to say it with words so he understands.'

'I will,' Blinky whispers, nodding at Mo then at Dave.

'If someone is fucking about and don't mean harm then we's say *safe Dave* but that means we gotta be switched on all the time. If Dave or Blowers tells us to protect Reggie then we do that. Reggie can't fight. He gets scared but he does what we say when it gets nasty. You get me? You need Reggie to move you tell him to move.'

Blinky nods. Firm and resolute. 'Yep…yes even. Yes, Dave.'

'Was that right?' Mo asks Dave.

'Yes,' Dave says, staring at Blinky for a long second before whipping a right jab at Mohammed who blocks and jumps back, instantly changing into the ready position. 'Fighting stance,' Dave says, pointing at Mo while still looking at Blinky. 'Make ready.'

———

W aiting for water to boil takes forever. Forever and ever and ever. Marcy even covers her hand with a top to hold the lid down on the pan in hope it will increase the heat inside and make the water boil faster because there is gossip and she wants it. A glance to Paula still trying to bite her own fingers off makes her push harder on the pan lid. Whatever has happened must be good. Like really juicy. It's the end of days but gossip is gossip. The instinctual interest in the lives of those close to you. The need to be part of the workings and doings. The desire to listen so she can nod and make noises and Paula is actually chomping with gusto so it must be good.

She looks over to see Charlie leaning out from behind a hay bale and motions quickly for her to come over.

Me? Charlie mouths. Marcy nods quickly. *Sure?* Charlie mouths. Marcy makes eyes and nods again as Charlie rushes silently from her bedroll then slows nonchalant and casual to the fire and Marcy almost sitting on the pan lid.

'Oh hi,' Marcy whispers in surprise. 'Fancy a cuppa?'

'I'd love one,' Charlie says, looking at Paula, ' as long as I am not imposing?'

'Huh?' Paula says with a mouthful of finger. 'No it's fine.'

'Water's boiling,' Marcy says, ignoring the distinct lack of bubbles in the non-boiling water. She pours quickly. Stirs quicker. Grabs quicker still and rises with three mugs clasped in her hands. 'Where we going? Roy's van? No! Not Roy's van...er...Saxon? Saxon. Yep. Right. To the Saxon...'

She takes the lead, resisting the urge to run. A chorus of grunts outside. A blur as Dave, Mo and Blinky try and beat the shit out of each other.

'She seems happy,' Marcy whispers to Charlie. Meredith bounds over, whining and snaking round legs as the three reach the Saxon. Jess spots the commotion and canters over in case a Third Watch Biscuit Club forms. They stop at the open back doors of the Saxon, Marcy using the back step as a shelf for the mugs before turning with excitement to Paula.

'Which one's mine?' Paula asks, reaching for the mugs after lighting a cigarette.

'All the same,' Marcy says.

'Didn't you sugar them?'

'No. So?'

'Christ, Marcy. You look positively happy.'

'Happy? I'm a pig in shit right now. What happened?'

'Nothing happened,' she says, handing Charlie a mug with a roll of her eyes. A thud behind them. Two yelps. The three women, the horse and the dog all turn to see Dave standing over Mo and Blinky flat on their arses.

'Centre of mass,' Dave says. 'Retain balance and do not over-reach...try again.'

'She seems happy,' Paula says to Charlie.

'I just said that,' Marcy says.

'Did you?' Paula asks.

'While you were shoving your hands in your mouth...so go on? What happened?'

'Marcy,' Paula groans, thereby commencing the dance of the gossip. Charlie sips from her lukewarm mug of coffee, blithely unaware of the tepid temperature as she waits with rapt attention.

Marcy huffs, tuts and sips her coffee, 'come on,' she urges, knowing it is her turn in the dance of the gossip to urge, plead and cajole in order to tease and extract said gossip.

'Well,' Paula says, adding her own deep sigh and another roll of her eyes. 'This coffee isn't hot.'

'Fuck the fucking coffee,' Marcy says, making Charlie snort with laughter. 'We want the info. Come on...get blabbing.'

'Can you believe her?' Paula asks Charlie while nodding at Marcy.

'Awful,' Charlie says seriously, 'er...so what happened?' she adds lightly.

'You pair,' Paula tuts.

'Spit it out before we get attacked or Reggie finds a cure or something,' Marcy pleads.

'Fine,' Paula says as though telling anyone what just happened is the very last thing she wants to do and is continuing against her wishes, which herein ends the *dance of the gossip* which in turn means *the actual gossip* can be given. 'So, I couldn't sleep. I was too hot, too itchy and Blinky farted and you lot were all snoring. I came out for some air and...you know...'

'What?' Marcy asks, leaning forward.

'Well he was outside on watch and...'

'Clarence?' Charlie asks.

'Oh yes,' Marcy says with relish, 'Paula's got a thing for him.'

'I do not,' Paula fires back indignantly offended and earning an arched eyebrow from Marcy. 'Well, just like a tiny thing,' Paula admits with a rueful look at Charlie.

'Bet it's not tiny.'

'Marcy!'

'Well he's bloody huge and I bet it's proportionate.'

'Oh my god you are so bad,' Paula says, trying not to laugh.

'Anyway, so go on,' Marcy says.

'Well,' Paula shrugs, sips her coffee and takes a drag of the cigarette, stalling for time with a mischievous glint in her eye at Marcy's impatience. 'We just sort of chatted for a bit. He was feeding the dog and Jess biscuits and got swamped in the back of the Saxon so I went in to help and...'

'Whoa, slow down. Helped how?' Marcy asks.

'I wondered why Jess kept sniffing round Clarence,' Charlie says.

'Don't tell him I told you for god's sake,' Paula says.

'No of course.'

'Oh this is all totally private,' Marcy says, waggling her hand at the other two women.

'Jess and Meredith were clambering on him to get biscuits so I went in, you know, for a laugh and tried to get them off but ended up on his lap and...'

'Oh yeah that happens to me all the time,' Marcy says. 'Just end up on someone's lap. *Oh sorry, am I on your lap again?* Don't you get that, Charles?'

'Daily.'

'Marce!'

'Sorry, go on. So what happened?'

'Nothing. It was just nice.'

'Oh,' Marcy says.

'Oh,' Charlie says.

'Then I went for a wee and he rubbed cream in my back.'

'While you were weeing?'

'No, Charlie! After I had a wee.'

'I thought you meant that too,' Marcy says. 'But whoa...go back... details. We need details.'

'That's it,' Paula says.

'So not it,' Marcy says.

'Fine,' Paula huffs. 'So I said my back was itchy and asked him to rub cream on. He was all like Clarence and polite and, you know what he's like...anyway I took my top off and...'

'I bet you did.'

'Have you turned into Cookey?'

'Yes,' Marcy says. 'It's the apocalypse. We see dead people every-day. Let me enjoy this sordid tale.'

'Don't say it's sordid.'

'Okay okay, not sordid.'

'Thank you, right...where was I?'

'More dirty but carry on.'

'Fuck's sake, Marcy.'

'I can't help it! This is the best gossip since some twat bit my arse three weeks ago.'

'Such an idiot,' Paula says, bursting out laughing.

'Took your top off and?' Marcy prompts, wide-eyed and eager.

'That was it. He rubbed cream into the bites and...you know...'

'I'll wake him up and ask him myself in a minute if you don't spit it out.'

'Fine! I took my bra off so he could get to the bites under the strap and he was rubbing the cream in so softly and oh my god it was so fucking nice.'

'Oh,' Marcy asks.

'Gosh,' Charlie says.

'His hands went up my spine and all over my shoulders then on my neck and I was like moving back, you know, so he could reach easier...'

'Yes,' Marcy says.

'Go on,' Charlie says.

'And er...yeah...my hand was on his knee and er...' she trails off, pursing her lips while lifting her eyebrows. 'Yeah and we almost kissed and er...I think he had an erection.'

'OH MY GOD!'

'Really?' Charlie blurts.

'Shush,' Paula says, waving her hand at both of them while glancing round to see Dave spinning Blinky and Mo about in wristlocks.

'Feet,' Dave says, 'leg sweep me...too slow...try again...'

She looks back at Marcy and Charlie while taking a swig of the lukewarm coffee that nearly gets sprayed out at the open mouthed gawping of the other two.

'An erection?' Marcy asks.

'Gosh,' Charlie says.

'Was it big? I bet it was big...'

'Marcy!'

'I bet it was big,' Marcy says to Charlie.

'He is a big man,' Charlie says.

'I don't like them too big,' Marcy says. 'Hurts too much.'

'Anyway,' Paula says quietly. 'So I was pressing back, just so, you know, he could reach easier...'

'With his short arms,' Marcy mutters.

'And er yeah, felt something at the exact same second we were about to kiss and the exact same second Roy came out and said hi...'

'OH MY GOD.'

'Really?'

'Shush! Yes. I almost shit myself. I ran forward, dropped my top, dropped my bra and was running about with my boobs bouncing about...stop laughing...it's not funny...oh you two sods. It's not bloody funny.'

'Is,' Marcy gasps, covering her mouth.

'Sorry,' Charlie says.

'What did Roy say?' Marcy asks, laughing and grimacing at the same time.

'Nothing. Not a word. Said hi, went and had a wee, came back and chatted for a second then we went in.'

'Oh,' Marcy says slowly, still chuckling. 'That's so good.'

'It is not good.'

'It is. That's the best gossip ever, thank you,' she nods sincerely and even darts forward to kiss Paula's cheek.

'Get off you daft sod,' Paula laughs, pushing her away.

'Seriously. I needed that,' Marcy says.

'What did Clarence do?' Charlie asks.

'Nothing, just went bright red and very loud for a few seconds. It was so awful. I mean...no seriously, Marcy! Listen...'

'Okay sorry, go on.'

'I was honestly itching. Those bites are evil. You know how bad they are. So I didn't think anything of it...just got a member of the team to put the cream on and...'

'Would you ask Dave to do it?' Marcy asks.

'Dave? No of course not but...'

'Blowers?' Charlie asks.

'Blowers? No...I mean Blowers is lovely and...but...'

'Nick?' Marcy asks.

'Who wouldn't want Nick rubbing cream on their back?' Paula asks with a laugh.

'Good point,' Marcy says.

'True,' Charlie adds.

'Lilly's a lucky girl,' Marcy says.

'She is,' Charlie says.

'Point is,' Marcy says, 'you would not ask anyone to rub the cream in.'

'I'd ask you or Charlie, or Blinky...Heather...'

'Men?' Marcy asks.

'Well,' Paula says tightly, 'I mean...Roy obviously and...oh fuck it.'

'Ha!' Marcy says.

'Has anything happened between you?' Charlie asks.

'Me and Clarence? God no. Nothing at all.'

'May I ask?' Charlie says politely, 'how long have you and Roy been together?'

'A week, maybe eight days and we're not really together. I mean... no shit, we are. We sleep together every night now and...oh I feel awful. I really do. Roy's so lovely but...'

'A week is not long,' Charlie says.

'Is in this world,' Marcy says quietly, the humour easing away.

'Christ,' Paula says. 'I feel so guilty now. We didn't do anything. I was genuinely itchy and it's Clarence for Christ's sake. Any of us could walk up to him stark naked and he'd look away...'

'Why feel guilty then?' Marcy asks.

'Because it would have happened,' Paula says instantly then frowns. 'Probably...maybe...I don't know. It was just nice. Really bloody nice.'

'Right, okay,' Marcy says, puffing her cheeks out. 'What you going to do?'

'Nothing.'

'Nothing?' Marcy asks.

'What can I do?'

'Talk to Roy?' Marcy says.

'Seriously?' Paula asks. 'This isn't someone I met online, Marcy. We're a...a....a fighting unit now. That's what Dave calls us. I'm in charge with Howie and no matter what I think we need Roy. None of us can do what he can. He's saved all of us. He's the bloody medic now.'

'If I may?'

'Of course, Charlie, we're talking openly,' Paula says warmly, smiling softly at her.

'Please don't think I am being disrespectful but none of us can do the things each other can. None can fight like Dave. None can match Clarence for his strength. Anyone other than Blowers would have been killed last night but he got back up stronger than when he went down. Marcy is unique. Reginald is. I am. Blinky is. We're all unique so, and please don't think I am speaking untoward but to use Roy's unique ability as a reason is perhaps not needed.'

'I'm unique?' Marcy asks, earning a smile from Paula.

'Narcissist,' Paula mutters.

'Totally. How am I unique? I think I'm the least unique person here.'

'I don't see that,' Charlie says seriously. 'I haven't been with you for very long but I even I can see how Mr Howie looks at you.'

Marcy smiles, grim and humourless. 'Looks *at* me. Not to me. Not for me but *at* me.'

'I didn't mean it that way, Marcy. Mr Howie is very clearly in love with you. If it wasn't for you he would have killed Reginald yesterday when he made Mr Howie get angry. None of us could stop him.'

'That's very true,' Paula says.

'Yeah maybe,' Marcy says, a flash of darkness crossing her face that she shakes off before giving the movie star smile. 'So? Roy?'

'You okay?' Paula asks her, reaching out to touch her arm.

'Fine! Of course I am. Why wouldn't I be? Stop changing the subject. Roy? Clarence? What you going to do?'

'I just said. Nothing. I can't do anything.'

'Charlie just said...'

'I know and it was a very good point but not a chance I'll do that to him. Finish with Roy and hop into Clarence's bed? How would that look? No. The team comes first.'

'Or,' Marcy says. 'Ease it off with Roy now. Be single and see what happens. You don't owe Roy anything.'

'Roy saved...'

'We've all saved each other so that argument doesn't count,' Marcy cuts in.

'Okay,' Paula says with a new point in mind. 'Would you do it to Howie? Let's say a new man was here or you fell for Nick or Blowers. Would you do that to him? I know nothing has happened between Charlie and Cookey. At least I don't think anything has happened between you...'

'It hasn't,' Charlie says.

'But how would Cookey react if Charlie suddenly said she fancied Howie? I can see why the army didn't want men and women fighting together now. Relationships are messy.'

Deep thinking follows. A loss of words and ideas to suggest and counter. A sudden seriousness to the closeness of their team. They watch Dave drill Mo and Blinky for long minutes while sipping the tepid coffee.

'It was a stupid thing to do,' Paula admits at length, dropping the cigarette butt to grind out under her boot. 'Clarence is lovely and in another time or another world then who knows but...' she trails off as Marcy and Charlie both nod slowly in agreement.

'Fair enough,' Marcy says.

'Come on. Get some more sleep,' Paula says, heading back across the grass towards the open barn door and the glow of the soft fire within. The first streak of grey already showing in the east. A new dawn of a new day in this brave new world.

'So?' Marcy says as they reach the door. She stops before they go. A serious expression etched on her exquisitely beautiful face. Charlie and Paula stop and wait. Sensing a troubled mind behind the beauty. 'Was it big?' Marcy asks, flashing the smile.

'Idiot,' Paula says, bursting out laughing as she walks in.

'Bet it was,' Marcy tells Charlie, making the girl laugh as she uses her charm to full effect that hides the sadness within so well. A sadness that grows too. She pauses to look back out at three extraordinary human beings moving in a way they have no right to move, with a speed they have no right to have. She looks in to see Blowers who should be dead. To Cookey and Nick so strong and capable and Charlie who can fight like them and ride Jess. Paula who can organise and plan so calmly. Reginald the genius. Roy the gifted archer and medic. Clarence the giant. Paco and his pure unfaltering aggression honed and made safe by Heather.

We're all unique.

'I was once,' she whispers. 'Not now...'

CHAPTER THIRTEEN

A new dawn of a new day in this brave new world.

Mo and Blinky stand drenched in sweat, chests heaving, eyes focussed. Mo spits to the side, clearing his throat. Blinky's face flushed deeply red. Her fitness is absurdly high but the last couple of hours have been the hardest physical work she has ever done. A relentless pace that increased minute by minute as Dave went at them. Giving them mere seconds to hydrate and recover.

Those few days of extra training show in Mo. His skill and abilities increasing with each session. He only has to be shown something once and then won't stop until he's mastered it.

They were both brought to anger. Both had ears tweaked, faces slapped, arses kicked, tripped up, pushed over, swung round and dumped on the ground. Mo held his anger in check a lot longer this time. Clinging to the coldness drilled into him. *Anger does not aid you. We are different. We see differently.* Mo applied it yesterday in the shopping centre and held his own against a horde many times their number and in so doing he saved the lives of Marcy and Paula.

Blinky however was brought to anger quickly. A different temper though and one Dave knew could be honed, focussed and used. When Blinky got angry she moved faster and hit harder.

Mo needs coldness of detachment to achieve his best. Blinky needs that rush. Mo must control his. Blinky must focus hers.

'End ex,' Dave says simply, not a drop of sweat on his face or a smidgen of exertion showing. 'Return to unit.'

'What's that mean?' Blinky asks.

'Go back to Blowers,' Mo says, turning away while wiping the sweat from his face as Dave walks off back to the barn. 'Hard innit,' he adds quietly.

'Fuck yeah,' she gasps, bending over to rest her hands on her knees.

'Good?'

'Good?' Blinky asks, looking up at him. 'You shitting me? That was fucking epic. You're so fast, Mo. Like a...like a fucking sneaky ninja fuckstick.'

'Dick,' Mo laughs, grabbing two bottles of water. 'Here.'

'Ta cockchops. So Blowers still our boss then?'

'Yep, we work in our team same as before but we get told to do other shit sometimes. Keep Reggie safe...go in places first...stuff like that.'

'So cool. It's different to what I thought it would be.'

'Yeah?'

'Yeah like more to it. Technical. All the places to cut and stab, the nerve endings and arteries and shit...like that move he did to break the wrist, elbow and dislocate the shoulder.'

'Works, did it yesterday outside that house when we got Paco.'

'Did you? Was it good? Did it work? What happened?'

'Exactly like Dave showed. Wrist, elbow and shoulder then cut his throat.'

'Fuck,' Blinky sighs dreamily.

'Sounds shit like,' Mo says quietly, almost sheepishly, 'but it makes you look at people differently.'

'Like what?'

'Like how they walk and move, always thinking what if they go bad now...how do I take them down. Legs, knees, throat, neck...heart stab or use the pistol, you get me? And like if we get out the Saxon then I'm looking to see where they can attack from and where the boss is and where Reggie is and how can I get to 'em...Blowers is brilliant at that shit. He's like the best soldier ever.'

'Fact,' Blinky says, looking at him intently. 'You stop that street talk when you're near Dave.'

'S'fucked innit,' Mo fires back, instantly back in the drawl.

'Innit blood,' Blinky says.

'Fuck off!' Mo laughs, 'that was shit.'

'You're shit.'

'Get fucked.'

'Fuck you,' she says, lunging at his legs.

'Fuck off!' he cries out, dancing back to fend off then trying for a leg sweep that she vaults. He spots the trailing hand and grabs for a wrist-lock that is countered and turned as she barges into his side and tries to flip him over. Both laughing and trading insults as they draw spatulas.

Pups learn through play. Meredith drops from her perch in the back of the Saxon having idly given her eyes and ears to Dave while he gave lessons. She circles off to the side, squats and pisses then trots past the warring pups to the barn door and the pack stirring within.

The first one she heads for is Blowers. The pressure of her feet on his bedroll bringing him awake as her nose blasts air over his face. He opens his one remaining eye and smiles. His hands reaching up to fuss and stroke. She whines softly, sniffing at his injury.

'Hey, Bear,' he whispers, earning a tail wag and soft whine. She twists her head to sniff at the dressing on his hand, sniffing the stump of his finger bitten away. He holds still, letting her sniff. He dreamt of the woman last night. Meredith.

'She your guide dog now?'

'Twat,' he bursts out laughing, turning to see Cookey grinning at him.

'Morning, Simon.'

'Morning, Alex.'

'Morning, Charlotte.'

'Morning, Alex.'

'MORNING EVERYONE!' Cookey calls out, rising up to grin over the barrier. 'We need to go shopping, Paula. Blowers needs a white stick and a disabled badge from the council.'

'Fuck off,' Blowers groans, sitting up as Meredith trots over to Charlie.

'And an eye patch.'

'Jesus, Cookey,' Paula says, rising from her bed. 'You still on brew duty?'

'He's always on brew duty,' Clarence says.

'Morning, Clarence.'

'Morning, Alex.'

'And a parrot. An inflatable one he can sellotape to his shoulder. Morning, Heather!'

'Morning.'

'Cookey?'

'Yes, Mr Howie? Coffee?'

'Aye.'

'On it like a car bonnet...can someone take Blowers for a wee please and help him wash. He might get piss on his feet.'

'Fuck off,' Blowers groans again.

'Seriously though, we can park anywhere when we get the disabled badge.'

'Such a twat.'

Meredith climbs the barrier to jump down and commence the morning greeting. Rushing to Paco who sits up grinning with delight as she pushes into him. Heather rises quickly, a hand on Paco's shoulder as she looks round at a room full of people. The nerves kick in instantly. The worry at being so close to other human beings. An instinct inside telling her to get dressed and leave right now. An instinct she pushes away and resolves to at least try. 'I'll help with the coffee,' she says, half suggesting, half-telling, suddenly full of worry that she said the wrong thing, and will look stupid.

'Ah cheers, Heather,' Cookey says, grinning at her. 'I'll tell you about my dream I had. Charlie was in it...'

'Er great,' Heather says, offering what she hopes is a genuine smile.

The morning starts. They rise to stretch and groan and pack bedding away. Boots on. Pistol belts on. Rifles checked. Clean tops found in bags. Wet wipes sourced and a steady flow commences to the designated toilet area round the back of the barn. The hose at the other end used to rinse faces and hair. Wipes used to clean armpits. Water boiling. Cups made ready.

Howie steps out to light a cigarette and spots Blinky and Mo fighting a few metres away. A score is gained. A trip given. They both go down, laughing hard as they wrestle and roll on the grass.

Charlie strolls out to feed and water Jess. Smiling at the sight of Blinky and Mo. Marcy walks back from the hose, sharing a smile with Charlie and a chuckle at Blinky calling Mo a barrage of names while he descends into a fit of giggles.

'Bloody hell,' Paula tuts, holding a cup of coffee out to Howie. 'You two, enough now. Get washed and ready. We'll be going soon.'

'Okay,' Mo says, rolling away from Blinky.

'Sir, Miss Paula, Sir,' Blinky shouts, surging to her feet.

'Hey,' Paula says, turning as Blowers comes out with a mug of coffee and an unlit cigarette in his mouth. 'How you feeling?'

'Fine...'

'Let me do that,' she says, taking the lighter from his injured hand.

'Thanks.'

'You in pain?'

'Bit. Not much.'

'Has Roy checked you yet?'

'Not yet but I'm fine...'

'Roy? You checking Blowers?'

'Coming.'

'I'm fine,' Blowers says again.

'How's the eye?' she asks.

'Which one?' he replies.

'The bad one.'

'Not there.'

'Blowers,' she says, giving him a look.

'Let him have a coffee and smoke,' Howie says.

'I am,' Paula says, stepping back. 'How's the hand?'

'Fine,' Blowers says, holding it up.

'Hmmm, we probably need to take it easy today,' she says, giving Howie a look. 'You can stay at the back with me and Marcy if we...'

'Not a chance.'

'Blowers, you've got serious injuries.'

'I'm fine.'

'Stay with me and Marcy. We'll make you coffee and ply you with food.'

'That is a very kind offer but I'll be fine.'

'I'll stay at the back and have coffee and food,' Howie says.

'You're not injured.'

'I am,' Howie says.

'He is,' Blowers says. 'Boss is more injured than all of us...'

'Yes because he keeps shoving his body in their mouths every day. I swear he actually enjoys it.'

'I do,' Howie says.

'Right, let me have a look,' Roy says, bustling out with his red medic's bag. 'How's the pain? You're up and walking so that's a good sign. Sleep okay?'

'Slept fine. I'm fine.'

'Great,' Roy says. 'You shouldn't take the dressing off...

'Was itchy.'

'Itchy is good. Shows healing, right let me have a close look...tell me if it hurts or...oh now. Oh wow. Now that is something,' he steps back to stare at the sunken eye socket.

'What?' Blowers asks.

'Bloody hell,' Howie says, stepping closer to look.

'What?'

'Jesus,' Paula says, grimacing at the sight.

'What!?'

'Is that a little arm growing out of his eye?' Howie asks, cocking his head over.

'Eh?'

'Looks like it, got a hand on the end,' Paula says, 'can see the fingers and everything.'

'What the fuck?' Blowers says, reaching up to touch his eye.

'Leave it alone they're pissing about,' Roy says, slapping his hand away. 'It's healing really well.'

'Fuck's sake,' Blowers groans. 'Sort of thing Cookey would do.'

'No, he'd say it was a willy,' Howie says. 'Looks good mate, considering.'

'Does,' Paula says.

'No sign of infection,' Roy murmurs, holding a small torch while gently probing the wound. 'Should be in agony. When did you last have pain relief?'

'What you gave me last night.'

Roy tuts, shaking his head. 'Unbelievable. Right, let me see the finger.' He cuts the dressing away and peels it back to stare at the tiny stump of the little finger. It looks raw and awful but already there is scab forming across the top. Not cauterized. Not stitched or treated but left entirely on its own to heal naturally. It looks like it's already days old. 'Hang on here a minute,' Roy says, walking off inside the barn, leaving Blowers, Howie and Paula to stare at the stump.

'How would I know?' Heather's voice floats out from inside barn.

'I just want you to look,' Roy's voice comes out, growing closer. A second later he walks out with Heather in tow.

'Look at what?' Heather asks.

'Look at his finger...'

'Hey, Heather.'

'Hey, Blowers...what am I looking at? I've not even done first aid or anything.'

'See the scab?' Roy says, holding Blowers' hand up.

'Yes,' Heather says, really not sure what she is meant to be looking at.

'Does that match the way Paco was healing? Have a look at his eye too.'

'I'm really not sure I can help...'

'It's fine,' Blowers says, pulling his hand back. 'Thanks, Heather.'

She winces internally at the blunt tone of her own voice. She doesn't like the fact Howie and Paula are both watching her, or that Roy is standing right there. Paco comes out, looming large and tuned in to Heather's discomfort. 'It's fine,' she says quickly, smiling at Paco. 'Can I see?'

'Sure,' Blowers lifts his hand, acutely aware of how uncomfortable she is.

She tries again, staring at the end of his finger then up to the closed sunken eye socket. She leans closer, examining the wounds then moves over to take Paco's hand and pulls him next to Blowers. 'You got any scissors please?'

'Right here,' Roy says, handing them over.

She reaches up to cut the dressing off Paco's neck, smiling into his eyes and gaining a big grin back. A look to Blowers' injuries then back to study Paco's neck and the awful wounds inflicted by the dog now meshed and knitting back together. At a glance it still looks terrible but the rate of healing is incredible. 'Same,' she says, nodding at Roy. 'As far as I can see anyway. Paco scabbed over but the scabs didn't come off. They were absorbed into the wound...he doesn't bleed much either. Clots really fast. He never reacts to pain. I don't think he even feels pain.'

'Very interesting,' Reginald says, having walked out unseen and unheard. 'The same you say?' he enquires politely, staring at Blowers' hand and eye then over to Paco.

'Not a doctor or anything,' Heather says, feeling the pressure of the growing audience.

'None of us are,' Reginald says. 'And I very much doubt even a GP could understand the process underway.'

'I was going to suggest we head back to the fort,' Roy says.

'To get Simon checked?' Reginald asks. 'I think not. He's healing. Are you in pain?'

'I'm fine,' Blowers says.

'He should be checked over,' Roy says.

'For what?' Reginald asks.

'Infection?'

'Bit late for that I rather fancy,' Reginald says.

'Not that infection,' Roy says stiffly. 'He might turn septic or something...'

'I think *that* infection is the thing preventing all *other* infections from inflicting harm. Of course, if Corporal Blowers takes a turn for the worse then we should seek medical assistance but at this time I see no reason for it and certainly we should not return to the fort.'

'I'm fine. We should keep going,' Blowers says, pulling his hand back.

'Indeed, that's the spirit,' Reginald says with a nod. 'I say, Heather. Whatever you did with Paco's injuries seems to have worked. I suggest we do the same.'

'Just cleaned and dressed them,' she says.

'There we go then. Clean and dress the wounds and all will be well,' Reginald announces. 'Now, Nick is requesting food for his seemingly unfillable stomach and I for one am famished. Do we have food here? I seem to recall during our battle of the arachnids we neglected the collecting of supplies. Shall we turn out and find somewhere to eat before we continue to harass and harry our enemy?'

'I said we should take it easy today,' Paula says.

'Of course,' Reginald says politely, 'it is not my place to lead but merely to advise...' he winks at Blowers, earning a shocked grin in response. 'Do you need a day of rest, Corporal?'

'Do I fu...no, no I don't.'

'There we go! Back at them I say. Just a mere flesh wound,' he adds quietly, a private joke shared between him and Blowers.

'Everyone inside. Reggie, word please,' Howie says. 'Paula, you hang back. Blowers, get them ready to leave.'

'On it.'

'I need to dress those wounds,' Roy says.

'Do it inside,' Blowers says.

A pause for them to go. Howie finishes his cigarette and waits. 'Why the rush?' he asks Reginald.

'We must press on,' Reginald replies, all trace of humour gone. All sense of joviality now vanished. 'Time is against us.'

'Explain,' Howie says.

'In brief, the other player is experiencing a rate of evolution far far greater than anything we can comprehend. I need time to think and plan. Keep them focussed on us and buy me time.'

'Done,' Howie says simply, glancing at Paula. 'Happy?'

She swallows her coffee before replying, 'we can go for the closest place on the list of immunes. Kill two birds with one stone. Help's Heather out. Keeps us together and we attack what we find on the way.'

A second to think. A second for Reginald to process the suggestion with every other idea, fact and opinion within his unceasing mind. *Subjective. Objective. Conjecture and opinion.* 'Agreed,' Reginald says.

'Awesome,' Howie says. 'We do that then.'

'Oh,' Reginald says as though suddenly thinking of something. 'May I borrow Paula for a second? I have some supplies I need and rather thought...'

'Yep, crack on. I'll get everyone moving,' Howie says, walking off into the barn.

'What do you need?' Paula asks, pulling out her notepad and pen.

'The unity of a team comes when every member holds their duty and undertakes no action to fracture that unity,' Reginald says, rushing the words out quietly. 'I have no experience in matters of the heart or romance but I am not stupid and if I can make an assumption based on your behaviour last night then others will also do so...'

'I beg your pardon?'

'What you and Clarence do is your business. But you lead this team with Howie. Your actions *have* to be exemplary. Your conduct *must* be exemplary. We need unity to achieve our objective and that unity comes from the top. Take your responsibility seriously. What we are doing is beyond mere fanciful yearnings. My advice, my very strong advice is to immediately cease any romantic connection to Clarence. Unity *will* be retained. Disharmony cannot be allowed to grow.'

She stares back, her mouth hanging open with a blush of shame spreading through her cheeks. An instant notion of immaturity. A loss of control and to be admonished like this is not only humiliating but, in her mind, is also rightly deserved.

'My upmost apologies for speaking out of turn. I have no wish to cause offence.'

'It's understood,' she whispers.

He nods slowly, 'I am sorry. Even I can see you rather suit one another but it cannot happen. The ripple effect of such a thing is too damaging and we have too much to lose.'

P ressure grows. Pressure builds. Pressure unrelenting. Reginald sits at his desk. His fingers drumming the table top. His papers, books and pads open in front of him. Deep worry reflected in his eyes. An impatience akin to that within Howie builds constantly but unlike Howie, Reginald also has to face his fear. Fear of conflict. Fear of harm. When the hive mind rage comes on it goes away but he is not now, nor ever will be, in his own mind at least, a brave man with courage.

A one-way conversation at the front. Roy chats while Paula nods and makes noises in return and refuses to think about Clarence's hands or his deep voice or the heat from his body and the pressure she felt when she moved back into him that sent a thrill surging through her that she hasn't felt for many years.

Howie drives the Saxon, deep in thought about what Reginald said. Harass and harry the enemy. Keep them focussed. Buy time. The rage inside held in check, waiting to be unleashed. The burning desire to inflict harm on them is stronger than ever and now given strength from a unit forming that has the beginnings of direction and focus.

Clarence sits in the front next to him, a distant almost pensive look in his face. Guilt inside at his actions. A breach of his honour. A loss of control. It won't happen again. He blinks slowly, refusing to think of the softness of her neck, the scent of her, the warmth of her body, the tone of her voice, the way she smiles at him, the image of her naked torso now seared in his mind. 'Hope we get a good scrap today,' he says quickly, gruffly, clearing his throat with a low growl.

'Same,' Howie says darkly.

Dave and Mo at the back doors. Blinky, Mo, Cookey, Nick, Blowers and Charlie talking happily, sharing jokes and comments about the training. The mood now so different to yesterday when they had Maddox with them.

Marcy listens in, smiling and laughing when appropriate while all the time thinking of Charlie's comment. *We are all unique.* An increasing sense inside her that she has no defined role within the team. They are all growing and developing with skills and confidence. She looks to Charlie, seeing the scar down the side of her cheek that somehow only adds to the woman's aura. The chunk of ear missing is the same. Marcy has a scar too. On her arse. She looks to the bruises on Charlie's arms and thinks *is this it?* She felt there was more. There was a power drawing her to Howie. A belief that together they would defeat the bad thing. That there was a stronger thing at work. There isn't. She has simply been absorbed into a team. Even Reginald now has more worth than her. Not worth, something else. She gains the perception that Blowers has held close for so many days. The two parts of the whole. Howie, Paula, Reginald, Clarence and even Roy in one section. Blowers and his team in another. Even Dave has a small unit now with Mo and Blinky. Where does she fit in? She can't plan. She can't fight that well. She feels lost somewhere in the middle.

Heather and Paco drive at the rear of the small convoy behind the horsebox towed by Roy's van. It's nice to be away from them all. They're all nice enough but still, the desire to just be with Paco is as strong as ever. She reaches over to hold his hand, marvelling at the instant grin he gives and seeing the spark of intelligence growing stronger in his eyes.

Pressure grows. Pressure builds. Pressure unrelenting. It's another hot day. Hotter than before. August. The height of summer. Scorching and glorious. A blue sky overhead so deep and high. Birds swooping to snag insects that buzz and chirrup as they feast on the life in the hedgerows as the world breathes air made cleaner and purer by the near extinction of humanity.

'That'll do,' Howie says, bringing Clarence back to focus as he points at the large green coloured signboard advertising *The Hungry Bird!* garden centre. *Try our new café! Fresh tea and coffee! Homemade cakes! Freshly cooked food! Disabled access! Cream teas! Pastry delights!*

'Someone likes exclamation marks,' Clarence says.

Howie snorts a dry laugh, reading the board back a second time. 'Bit much isn't it.'

'I could murder for a pastry delight,' Marcy says from behind Howie, leaning forward to read the sign. 'It's alright, Blowers. They've got disabled access...'

'Fuck's sake,' Blowers says to the laughs earned by a joke given with that movie star smile. 'Don't you start, Marcy.'

'I'm only playing...don't worry, I'll keep an eye on you.'

'BOOM!' Cookey exclaims, 'another point to Marcy...'

'What's got into you?' Nick laughs.

'Nothing, just being silly,' Marcy says, reaching for her radio, *'Marcy here, the hungry bird garden centre is ahead for a team breakfast.'*

'Thanks, Marce,' Paula's dull voice comes back.

A vast two-tier car park laid to gravel. Empty save for two white delivery vans parked at the far end next to a large rolled down metal shutter. Plants and cultivated shrubs adorn the front. Bushes cut into the shapes of animals growing from half wooden barrels and huge stone pots. Pagoda's and gazebos freshly lacquered with signs giving the prices complete *with delivery and installation arranged for an extra fee! Enquire within!*

Roy slows his van near the entrance, waiting for the Saxon to drive round the perimeter. Heather and Paco draw level in the four-wheel drive.

'Looks empty,' Roy says.

'Yep,' Paula murmurs.

'I do like garden centres,' he says. 'Always lots of little things, twine and brackets, bird feeders and ponds. I like that sort of thing.'

'Good.'

'Benches too.'

'Uh huh.'

'Can't beat a well-constructed bench. Look at that pagoda. Got a lovely tiered roof. Very nicely done. Well-crafted by the looks of it.'

'Is.'

'Did you like garden centres?'

'Not really.'

'Oh it looks clear, they're getting out. *'Boss, it's Roy. We clear to come forward?'*

'Did you just call me boss?'

'I did.'

'You never call me boss...yeah come forward. Heather, follow Roy in. We'll keep the vehicles close. It looks empty but keep eyes up and the noise down.'

'Should call him boss really,' Roy says, easing forward towards the Saxon. 'He is in charge. Should I call you Miss Paula?'

'If you want.'

'Really?'

'What?'

'You want me to call you Miss Paula?'

'Eh? No! Sorry, I was miles away...right we getting out?'

Weapons cocked and made ready. Blowers strides out from the rear, indicating placement for his team, pointing and motioning silently for the positions to be taken. Meredith runs out, nose to the ground tracking animal scents round in circles.

'Everyone ready?' Howie calls softly, turning to get a thumb's up from Blowers. 'Dave and Clarence up front with me...'

A huge atrium style entranceway complete with harshly angled panes of glass giving a jarring look completely out of keeping with the softly manicured parking area. A darker interior. A sensation of emptiness. A place like this would have been locked and sealed when the outbreak started.

Clarence tests the doors with his bulk then steps back with a frown. 'All glass,' he says. 'Can't boot it in.'

'Plant pot there, chuck that through,' Howie says, kicking a big stone empty planter.

Clarence turns to grab it, slinging his rifle and catching sight of Paula staring over at him. A falter in his step before he drops his head, ducks then rises with a heave and twist of his body to send the stone pot ten metres through the obliterated doorway that explodes with glass and the metal frame buckling inwards.

'Fuck mate,' Howie says, 'didn't like that door then?'

'It's open,' the big man says dully, booting the metal frame out of the way before crunching over the broken glass into the atrium. Dave and Howie follow in. All three sniffing the air for trace of people, infected or anything of risk. The air made fragrant and rich from plants growing within the huge warehouse style building. Wood, earth, scented candles and a dozen other smells so pleasant and different.

'Oh now that's a nice change,' Howie remarks, inhaling deeply.

'Boss?' Nick calls out. 'Meredith wants to come in...is that glass sharp?'

'Er...no, it's safety glass mate. She's fine.'

The furry missile launches to run flat out, desperate to be at the front. A leap through the broken doors and on into a glorious world of smells. Nose down and she runs forward as the three men watch her closely. 'Seems okay,' Howie says. 'Mo? You getting any weird vibes in your head?'

'Nah, Mr Howie. Nothing.'

'Pile in then, just stay ready until we've cleared it.'

Blowers holds his team back, waiting for everyone else to go through. He catches Mo's attention and points to Reginald. A nod back and Mo moves swiftly to Reginald's side.

'Ah, my guard is here. Just you or do I have the delights of Blinky guarding me also?'

'Just me,' Mo says.

'And I am eternally indebted to you, Mo Mo. Not a finer guard I could wish for. Gosh, this is a paradisiacal wonder and what a refreshing change from the ghastly smells we are normally exposed to. You know, Mo Mo. I was a terrible sufferer of hayfever before this. I loathed spring and summer. It was a veritable hell and not merely because of the overt expanses of flesh in display...'

'Prude,' Marcy says from ahead.

'Oh I should imagine you in the height of summer,' Reginald says.

'I bet you do you dirty sod.'

'Oh gosh no! Not in that manner you wanton woman. I meant I should imagine you paraded yourself most openly.'

'Yep, that's me, Reggie. Walked about with my tits out every single day.'

'Very coarse,' Reginald mutters, adding an indignant huff.

'Clear by the looks of it,' Howie calls out from the front. 'Dave is checking but Meredith seems happy and Mo isn't doing his freaky thing...'

'S'not freaky.'

'IT'S NOT FREAKY MR HOWIE...'

'S'not freaky, Mr Howie,' Mo says with a sheepish grin. 'Sorry, Dave.'

'You and Patricia to me. Room clearance drills. Pistols ready.'

'On it, Blinky...'

'Fuck you, ninja,' Blinky says, sprinting past as Mo runs after her.

An open plan café. Pleasantly designed with wide spaces between the solid wooden tables. A long counter fitted with glass display cabinets now filled with mouldy cakes and foodstuffs left to fester. An absence of flies and insects but then each serving dish is covered in cling film.

Marcy heads for the kitchen, striding behind the counter and heading for the heavy swing door. A hand on her shoulder easing her back as Nick sweeps past with his rifle braced in his shoulder.

'Not cleared yet,' he says softly. 'Blowers?'

'Behind you...go through...'

'I'm not useless,' Marcy says. 'I could have checked it.'

'It's okay, we're here now,' Blowers says, offering a grin before he pushes in behind Nick.

'But you're injured,' she says, going through the heavy door behind them. 'You've only got one eye.'

'I'm fine,' he calls back. 'Wait by the door for a second.'

'I'm not an idiot, Blowers.'

'I'd never say you were an idiot.'

'I am,' Cookey says, pushing into the room to sweep past Marcy with his rifle up and braced in his shoulder.

'Fact,' Nick says. 'Got storerooms at the back here.'

'Covering,' Blowers says.

'Fuck's sake. I am capable,' Marcy says, going after Cookey while lifting her rifle into her shoulder. She stops next to him, aiming at a wall.

'Safety's on, Marcy,' Cookey whispers.

'I know!' she says, flicking the switch. 'Right, where do I aim when you do this?'

'Eh?' Cookey asks.

'Teach me. Show me what to do.'

'Now?' Cookey asks.

'Shall I go with Nick and...'

'No! Just...go over to Blowers.'

'With me,' Blowers says, motioning her over. 'Nick's going forward to check those rooms so instead of all piling in to something we don't know we hang back and cover him. Look for any points of danger. Where could someone hide...'

'What like behind the work units?'

'Yep, anywhere really. Keep an eye on the door behind us. Make sure we can get out if it goes bent.'

'Right okay, why is Cookey a bit further back?'

'We're staggering so we're not on top of each other. If someone rushes Nick he can run back and I've got a clear line of fire. Same with Cookey. He's covering my back now. It's kinda what Dave is teaching Mo and Blinky now but he'll be showing them how to go in and clear rooms quickly and silently.'

'Okay, so...could someone hide in the cupboards?'

'Er yeah, yeah they could...'

'That was a stupid question. Sorry.'

'No, not at all. It's a good point. It's just awareness. Exactly that.'

'Marcy,' Cookey says, 'think of where you would hide if you were going to lie in wait...'

'Oh I get it...yep, so...wow, it could be anywhere then.'

'Absolutely,' Blowers says, 'that's why our positions are so important.'

'Clear,' Nick says, walking back with a wooden crate full of green apples. 'These are still good. Loads of stuff back there.'

'Nice,' Blowers says.

'Will you teach me properly?' Marcy asks suddenly.

'You want me to teach you?' Blowers asks.

She nods seriously, the idea already taking roots. 'Like you did with Charlie and Blinky...you did Heather and Maddox too. Show me like them.'

'Er sure, if that's what you want.'

'Marce? You okay?' Nick asks, 'apple?'

'Cheers,' she takes one from the crate.

'What's up?' Cookey asks, walking over.

'Nothing,' she says, rubbing the apple up and down the side of her top. 'I want to be useful. I should work more.'

'Er, you kinda do already,' Nick says.

'I don't really. I just...like...flounce about...'

'You don't,' Cookey says.

'I do! I don't do anything. I just follow everyone else and make jokes about hair and make-up.'

'That's you though,' Blowers says.

'It's not a bad thing,' Cookey says.

'It's cool, you're cool as fuck,' Nick says.

'I'm not just pretty,' she says quietly, staring at the apple. 'Oh god that sounds so vain but...I'm not *just* pretty...'

'You're awesome,' Cookey says.

'No I do. Right, listen. I want to work on your team. Teach me.'

'On my team?' Blowers asks.

'Yes,' she says firmly.

'Okay, fair enough,' Blowers says, glancing at the other two, 'er... does the boss know?'

'Howie? No I've not said anything but...oh,' she says with a flash of sadness. 'Does that put you off? You know...cos I'm with Howie and...'

'Nope, doesn't bother me at all,' Blowers says. 'You two alright with it?'

'Fine with me,' Nick says. 'It's fucking hard though, Marcy. Harder than it looks and you got to watch Blowers like the whole time for orders and to see where we should be. We can't argue or fuck about...'

'I saw it yesterday with Maddox,' she cuts in. 'I'll work.'

'Cookey?' Blowers asks.

'Yep, as long as Mr Howie says it's okay,' Cookey says.

'You alright with taking orders?' Blowers asks.

'I am. I will. I'll work. I promise.'

'Apple?' Nick says, holding one out to Blowers.

'Thanks bellend. We'll go out and see what they want. Er, you want to mention it now, Marcy or...'

'I'll tell him now.'

'Ask, don't tell. He's the boss,' Blowers says, effortlessly switching into his role of corporal.

She nods quickly, following behind him towards the doors as Nick and Cookey share glances.

'All clear,' Blowers calls out, pushing through the door to see tables being dragged together and chairs set. 'Power's off but Nick said there's plenty of food...we've got fresh apples too.'

'Howie, I want to work in Blowers team,' Marcy says. Blowers winces, closing his eye at the tone of her voice. 'I mean...I would like to work in Blowers team. If that is okay...Mr Howie,' she adds with a smile as Blowers groans and Cookey bursts out laughing.

'Smooth, Marcy,' Nick says.

'Do what?' Howie says. Feet planted. Rifle held low, his axe wedged down his back. Paula looks over, frozen mid organising while trying not to look at Clarence and Roy carrying tables and chairs.

'Marcy? What's up?' Clarence calls over.

'Nothing. I want Blowers to teach me like he did with Charlie and Blinky...'

'Toilets are clear,' Heather says, walking into a frozen atmosphere of everyone staring at Marcy.

'Thanks,' Howie says. 'Appreciate that.'

'So is that okay then?' Marcy asks.

'I don't mind him training you but I don't want you up front if it...'

'I want to work in his team doing what they do...'

'And I said fine but not up front if we get in a fight.'

'I'm not useless. I can fight.'

'What's this about?' Paula asks. 'Marcy? No offence love but neither of us can fight like they can.'

'I'll learn.'

'Let's eat then talk about it,' Howie says. 'Charlie, give the lads a hand bringing the food out. Roy, Clarence, you watch those windows. Heather, give the lads a hand please. Paula...'

'I'm helping them,' Marcy says, turning to go after the lads.

'Word please, Marcy.'

'I'm with Blowers team now so I'll do what they do...'

'Discipline,' Blowers whispers.

'On with it,' Howie calls out. 'We're eating then going.'

'Clear,' Dave says, leading his recruits into the café area.

'Blinky, Mo, give them a hand getting food. Dave, with Clarence and Roy watching the front.'

'Mr Howie,' Dave nods, marching past.

Marcy walks over as Heather and Paco walk past. Howie waits quietly for them to go before speaking.

'I'll sort the food out,' Paula says, only too glad to create distance between herself and Clarence and Roy.

'Right, what's going on?' Howie asks.

'Nothing. Honestly. I just want to do more. I feel so bloody useless. Everyone has a job...like a role. I don't do anything. I'm either following Paula or you or spend the day taking the piss out of Reggie.'

'Marcy, you turned then you turned back. That makes you unique as anything. We can't risk you in a scrap...'

'I've been in loads of fights now. The square? Remember? I was at your side nearly the whole time.'

'That was different. The lads do that all day every day. You can't fight like us. They'll be tripping over you.'

'Fuck's sake, Howie. You said you'll never try and own me. Don't do that...'

'Seriously? That was a cheap shot.'

'Sorry! I'm sorry...I just feel like a spare prick at a wedding. Let me work with Blowers team. Even for today. I'll get some training and you keep saying all skills are good skills.'

'I think I said that once.'

'Whatever. You still said it. I won't piss about or get in the way. I'll do what Blowers says and work...and I'll give you a blowjob tonight.'

'What!?' he bursts out laughing.

'Best blowjob ever.'

'Well, in that case...' he says, sharing the joke before softening his expression.

'I'm being serious, Howie. I want to work and do more.'

'Okay, if Blowers is okay with it then fine...but if I say to draw back then do it instantly.'

'Fine.'

'That means instantly. No arguing or...'

'I'm me, I'll always argue with you.'

'Yeah I get that but...'

'I'll always love you though...and you can still have the blowjob tonight. Oh, you're not saying yes just because I offered you a blowjob are you?'

'No, Marcy. I am not.'

'You'd get the blowjob anyway.'

'Thanks, but seriously. If I say to move back or whatever then do it. You can't always see everything when you're at the front. The lads are special. The way they move with each other and fight is so fast...'

'I've seen it enough times, Howie. Please don't patronise me. Not you...'

'I'm not...I'm sorry I didn't mean...'

'Okay listen,' she says before moving in to kiss him on the lips. A long slow lingering kiss full of love and tenderness. The same feeling hits them. The same lurch of time and space. Like the world is frozen and time ceases to be, that they are the only things in existence in a plane of living solely for them. She draws back with her eyes closed and breathing softly. 'That was from the me that loves you...' she says, opening her eyes while drawing composure into her manner and bearing. Her head lifting an inch. Her posture straightening. 'This is the me that works in your team. The two are separate. Okay?'

'Okay,' he says quietly.

'I want your permission to work in Blowers team please. I will follow the orders given and do what I am told. If it doesn't work then I will stop...I'd like this chance though...'

'That's fine,' Mr Howie says, matching the manner and bearing.

'That's so hot,' she whispers, making him burst out laughing. 'No be serious, back to boss and team member again...actually, can we role play this tonight? Right, stop it. Be serious. So I would like to work in...'

'I said yes,' Howie says curtly, 'get on with it please, we've got work to do.'

'So hot,' she whispers, 'thank you, Mr Howie. I won't let you down. Where do you want me, Mr Howie?'

'With Blowers. Help get the food sorted.'

'On it,' she about turns to rush off, 'so hot,' she calls back, turning to wink at him, making him laugh again. 'Sir, Mr Howie, Sir...on it... you wait till tonight...oh my god...I'll not let you down, Mr Howie,' she salutes as she strides behind the counter. 'Doing my duty, Sir...me and you tonight,' she adds in a whisper, nodding eagerly at him. 'Sir,' she pushes into the kitchen. 'Mr Howie said yes, Corporal Blowers and I didn't even have to hypnotise him with boobs...'

'Jesus,' Howie mutters, 'every fucking half hour...' he strolls over to the others. Dave, Clarence, Reginald and Roy and flops down at the tables pulled together.

'Overwatch on Marcy then is it?' Roy asks.

'Please mate but for fuck's sake don't tell her we discussed it.'

'It's not a bad thing,' Clarence says, easing his bulk down at the table. 'It's good she wants to do it really.'

'Oh of course,' Howie says.

'I must say I am rather surprised,' Reginald says, taking a seat opposite Clarence. 'But then one must consider that Marcy held great power so to now have no responsibility must be hard. As infuriating as she is I do not doubt her loyalty for one second, and as Clarence says, perhaps this will give greater focus...not that it will last given our fanciful Marcy.'

'On that note,' Roy says, looking over at the door to the kitchen before taking a seat. 'I wanted to say something.'

'Go on,' Howie says, hoping it's nothing bad.

'Er, well, this is not an easy thing for me to say so I'll try and be brief. I er...I don't gel with other people very well...you may have noticed...'

'Just a bit,' Howie laughs.

'It's true,' Roy says with a smile, 'I never liked people being around people. This end of the world thing didn't really bother me as I was so isolated anyway and I only stayed with you because of Paula. In truth, I didn't want to stay and would have been happier if we left...that said...' he pauses to think, looking from Dave to Reginald to Howie and finally to Clarence who shifts uncomfortably and clears his throat. 'That said,' Roy repeats. 'Yesterday changed things for me. I'm not going to gush with emotions but I felt an honour in fighting with you all. A kinship. As crass and cliché as that sounds. It was when Howie couldn't answer Blowers on the radio. I felt it then. Like a sudden inclusion...a sense of belonging...anyway. Enough said. We're chaps and British so any overt sense of emotion will have us all shifting about as uncomfortable as Clarence is...just wanted to say thanks and...and I give my service willingly from here.

Glad to be a part of it with er...with some good mates. In it to the end.'

'Bloody hell,' Howie says, genuinely surprised and more than a little touched. 'Cheers, Roy. Appreciated.'

'Roy,' Dave says, nodding his respect in an exceptionally rare show of a social situation, either that or taking a cue from the look given him by Howie.

'Well now, good words,' Reginald says, standing to offer his hand to Roy. 'Good chap, nicely said.'

'Thanks,' Roy says, shaking his hand.

'Same,' Howie says, standing to offer his hand.

'Mr Howie,' Roy says.

'Ah just Howie.'

Clarence stands, doing everything he can to hide the anguish and guilt he feels inside. He offers his enormous hand, stretching over the table with ease. 'Thanks, Roy.'

'Big man!' Roy laughs, shaking heartily. 'Us real ale lovers and cricket players have got to stick together eh?'

'Yes, sure...we do,' Clarence says deeply, offering a tight smile.

'Not my wish to create an awkward moment. Just had to be said. Right, so...discrete overwatch on Marcy. Got it. Mum's the word.'

CHAPTER FIFTEEN

A window broken. An extension cable stretching from Roy's van through the smashed pane to the coffee machine on the counter. A new skill learned yesterday in the shopping centre. All skills are good skills.

Three tables pulled together laden with food. Apple cores and empty tins of fruit, tuna and food litter the tops amongst the snack food wrappers. Muesli bars, fruit and nut bars. High-energy carbohydrate bars packed with sugary nutrition. Coffee cups stained and slowly emptying. A bowl of food on the floor refilled several times over rests next to Meredith lying content but alert.

'You gutsy fat shit.'

'What?' Nick asks, unwrapping another fruit and nut bar.

'Do you ever stop eating?' Cookey asks.

'Hungry.'

'You've had eight bars.'

'So?'

'And three apples, and a tin of tuna...and that tin of fruit...and those biscuits...and...'

'You actually counting what I eat, Cookey?'

'Fatty fat face.'

'Yep,' Nick says before shoving the next bar in his mouth.

'A little over thirty miles I would say,' Reginald says, looking up from the map spread open in front of him.

'Isthatfortheimmunepeoples?'

'What?' Cookey asks, laughing at Nick trying to talk with a mouthful of fruit and nut bar.

'Nick, don't speak with your mouthful.'

'ShorryPaula...I said...is that the immune person?'

'It is the geographically closest one listed within the documents,' Reginald says, studying the papers again.

'Yes,' Charlie says, translating when a few heads looks at her.

'I thought Heather was doing them,' Nick says, reaching for another fruit and nut bar.

'You fat bastard. You'll explode...'

'Fuck off, Cookey. I'm still hungry.'

'Doc, Nick needs worming,' Cookey says to Roy.

'We're staying together for a bit,' Howie says.

'Are we?' Heather asks, blurting the question out.

'Makes sense,' Paula says to her.

'Does,' Blowers says. 'You got us out the shit yesterday...'

'Stay with us, Heather,' Cookey says.

'Heather...shtaywivus...'

'Nick, don't speak with your mouthful.'

'ShorryPaula...'

'Stay with us, Heather,' Mo says.

'Go on, Heather,' Cookey says.

She can't help but smile at the comments and the mood so light and easy and she is rapidly learning that anything these people do outside of actually fighting is just chaos. Noisy messy chaos, but then that's not a bad thing. She can hide within chaos. Cookey is always making people laugh. Nick and the others make comments. The conversations roll round so quickly it's actually funny to watch and listen.

'Seriously, Nick. That is the tenth bar,' Charlie says in awe as he starts peeling the wrapper back.

'Sorry, Charlie. Did you want it?'

'No no, carry on. I'm just amazed you can eat so much. I thought Blinky could eat a lot but...'

'Bite me, Charles.'

'Lot of sugar in those bars,' Roy says.

'Not like we can diabetes or anything,' Nick says, shoving it in.

'Can we get diabetes?' Cookey asks. 'Marcy? Can we get...'

'No, Cookey.'

'What about fat? Can we get fat if we've got zombie?'

'Jesus, I have no idea.'

'Are you working with us then?'

'I am! Howie said it was okay and Blowers agreed,' she announces proudly.

'Cool, I get to ask zombie questions all day long then,' Cookey asks. 'Can I be paired with Marcy please, Corporal Blowers?'

'Twat.'

'So, plan?' Paula says. Clearly keen to be off and away as she and Clarence actively avoid looking at each other. 'Howie? Reggie?'

'What you said earlier,' Howie says. 'We go for the list of immune people and hit what we find on the way.'

'What?' Heather asks.

'Er, we're hitting what we find,' Howie says.

'It is imperative we draw the attention of the enemy to us,' Reginald says.

'Why?'

'Because...' Reginald says, pausing either for effect or to genuinely think of the answer. 'Because the other side are evolving at an alarming rate and I suspect they are massing to the north.'

'What's given you that idea?' Paula asks as everyone leans in to look down the table while Blowers reaches for an apple with a quick shared glance to Reginald. 'I know Blowers mentioned the north yesterday but...'

'It is what I would do,' Reginald says. 'While we are busy here I would draw forces ready to sweep down.'

'Shouldn't we go north now then?' Clarence asks.

'Indeed that would appear to be the most logical response, but alas, to do so would signify an awareness which in turn could provoke a reaction before we are ready. In short, we need to be seen so the other player believes us to be simply working through random places but our true objective is to use this time to secure the safety of as many immunes as we can.'

'Double bluff,' Cookey says.

'Don't start that again,' Blowers says.

'Yes, indeed, Cookey. A double bluff,' Reginald says.

'Fuck you,' Cookey says, showing a middle finger to Blowers.

'And furthermore, the double bluff will buy me time to plan and study so yes, there are many reasons why I believe this to be the correct course of action but I will stress, and this is very important, the rate of evolution means time is very much against us. We must move fast and we must keep moving. I can work the route but the actuality of exactly how you implement each strike is of course down to Mr Howie. One more thing I will stress, and again this equals the former point in terms of importance, is that your levels of confidence must remain high. To the other side we are recklessly hunting them down without apparent cohesive planning...oh good Lord don't stare blankly. That was not difficult to understand in any capacity...fine! Charlie, would you please?'

Chuckles and smiles as Charlie clears her throat and lifts her eyebrows. Heather watches them. Suspecting they all understood but that this is an extension of the humour and energy. Almost like a ritual and something that gives them the unity that holds the bond.

'One, find the immune people,' Charlie says, counting off on her fingers. 'Two, attack any infected groups we see. Three, do that as fast as possible. Four, Reginald will give us the route to take. Five, Reginald is concerned they are planning something evil and dastardly...'

'I never said...'

'You had your turn,' Marcy says, waving him down.

'Still five, so we need to show we are heroically attacking them with wild abandon...'

'Stop using big words, Charles.'

'Kill 'em all while laughing about it, Blinky.'

'Got it.'

'Six, don't let them know we're looking for immune people but rather, make a show of attacking them to draw attention on us so Reginald can study their behaviour and how they react so he can best plan what we do next. Seven...Reginald will tell us where to go but it is down to Mr Howie on what we do when we get there. Questions?'

'Brilliant,' Clarence laughs, 'love that girl.'

'Thank you, Clarence,' she beams with a blush in her cheeks.

'Very good,' Roy says. 'Such a nice way of speaking too.'

'Thank you, Roy.'

'Fit.'

'Thank you, Cookey.'

'And awesome,' he adds with a grin. 'Soooo, Marcy...can zombies get athletes foot?'

'Fuck's sake. I've changed my mind. I'm staying at the back.'

'Got the route?' Howie asks, looking over at Reginald folding the map.

'Indeed, Mr Howie. We are ready to go...that is if Nick can move after his sumptuous banquet.'

'Might have another one...and one for later, two for later...'

'Take the box, Nick.'

'Cheers, Paula.'

'Heather?' Howie asks, rising to his feet with the signal to make ready. 'Happy with all of that?'

'Guess so,' she says. 'What...when we get to the first place? What then?'

'We'll work each one out as we go. Stay armed. Stay alert and stay in contact...everyone ready? We're moving out.'

'I've got a question,' Cookey says while everyone else groans.

'What now?' Marcy asks. 'Can zombies get pregnant? Allergic to peanuts?'

'No but er...can they? No, so...Reggie, what happens if we don't do anything?'

'Eh?' Howie asks, lifting his axe and rifle.

'What if we do nothing? Like nothing at all…just let them crack on and do what they want.'

'They'll eat everyone, fuckstick,' Nick says.

'That's a good question actually,' Paula says.

'It is…for once,' Clarence says smiling at Paula through habit which she returns through habit until both suddenly remember and look away sharply.

'Reggie?' Cookey asks, thinking the small man hasn't heard him.

'Indeed, that is the question is it not,' Reginald says, packing his books away as Howie and Charlie clock the look on his face. Paula would normally see it to but she turns away to avoid looking at Clarence while Marcy compares her kit and clothing to Blowers.

'So?' Cookey asks, 'what then?'

Reginald doesn't reply but fastens the straps on his bag in an action designed to avoid answering. They're only going out to the vehicles. He doesn't need to strap his bag up. Charlie frowns lightly, glancing to Howie.

'Like Nick said,' Howie says. 'They'll eat everyone.'

'Indeed they will,' Reginald mutters.

'Apart from Nick,' Charlie says, deflecting the attention from Reginald. 'He'll be too big for them to swallow.'

'Boom!' Cookey laughs.

'Nicely done, Charlie,' Blowers says.

They file out. Marcy moving to fall in with Blowers and the lads. Paula rushing ahead to save any risk of being caught near Clarence. Clarence also rushing ahead but with Roy chatting away next to him. Heather and Paco slip out quietly, the big Hollywood actor forever at her side. Charlie falters with a pretence of gathering kit. Howie just waits until Reginald stands with his book bag clasped in his hands. A look from him to Charlie then to Howie.

'They wouldn't like the answer,' he says plainly.

'I see,' Charlie says, 'forgive me, this is not my place.'

'We can't win? Is that it?' Howie asks.

'It is somewhat more complicated than that,' Reginald says.

'We are too few?' Charlie asks, a quizzical look etched on her face.

'Do not try and guess,' Reginald says. 'Your intelligence may lead you to the correct answer and that is one you do not wish to know.'

'I think that's for us to decide,' Howie says.

'Us?' Reginald asks.

'I should go, excuse me,' Charlie says, turning to leave. She stops, turning back to look at Howie.

'Go on,' Howie says. Something about him hints that he knows the answer.

'The evolution will continue regardless of what we do, is that it?' she falls quiet, pensively staring at Reginald. 'We cannot stop them...'

'No. We cannot,' Reginald says. 'We can merely try and shape the destiny that I fear is already set.'

'Bollocks,' Howie scoffs, looking from Reginald to Charlie. 'Fuck 'em, we'll win.'

'Of course, Mr Howie,' Reginald says.

'Don't doubt me,' Howie says, the energy pouring from his dark eyes. 'We've got Dave on our side...and you, Reggie. We'll win.'

'We will,' Reginald says, his eyes locked on Howie as Charlie swallows from the sudden charge in the air. The way Mr Howie says it, the resonance within him, the sheer self-belief that refuses to even consider any notion other than that in his mind. A singular drive and focus so powerful it seems to suck the air from the room. She looks to Reginald, seeing the same look in the small man's eyes and that same energy of singular drive and focus. A thing witnessed. A thing she suspects not all of the others have fully seen. These two men will not stop. Not for anything. Not for anyone and right now, in this time and place, she would give her life for either of them because to be with people like this is a thing far greater than anything she could ever imagine.

CHAPTER SIXTEEN

'Do what you did to Maddox to me.'
        'Punch you in the face?'
'No!' Marcy laughs. 'Am I all kitted up properly?'

'You're fine,' Blowers says.

She reaches back to grab the handle of the brand new machete taken from the garden centre now wedged in her bag on her back.

'Don't draw it in here,' Blowers says quickly.

'I'm not, I'm just checking I can reach it.'

'It's really sharp,' Blowers says.

'I'm not an idiot, Blowers.'

'You said you'd take orders.'

'Fine. Okay, sorry, I'll be careful.'

'It's a longer blade than the knife you're used to. Watch where you swing it...don't over extend and slice your own leg off or, more importantly, don't chop my fucking leg off...I've already lost a finger and an eye and working on one leg might be quite hard.'

'Wouldn't stop you,' Nick says.

'What about my pistol? Do you need to check it?' Marcy asks.

'I don't know. Do I?'

'No, it's fine. My rifle is loaded and ready.'

'Great. Safety on?'

'Yep. What else do I need?'

'Knife?'

'On my belt and spare magazines in my bag and the flap is clear so I can open it quickly.'

'Water?' Nick asks.

'In my bag.'

'Make-up?'

'Piss off, Cookey...but yes, in my bag. Who am I pairing with?'

'With me,' Blowers says. 'You'll know most of it anyway, Marcy. You been doing this for days now.'

'Yeah but not properly, like trained. I hope I'm good at it...is it hard?' she asks Charlie sitting next to her in the Saxon.

'Can be,' Charlie says, pulling her bag out from under her seat.

'Stay on this side of me,' Blowers says, indicating his right side. 'Let Cookey cover my blind side. Same goes for everyone. Let Cookey stay on my left.'

'On it,' Cookey says seriously.

'Yep,' Nick says.

'I lose vision there,' Blowers says, holding his hand up a metre or so to the left of the centre of his face. 'So don't creep up on that side pissing about or anything.'

'Nobody will,' Clarence says from the front.

'Should you be doing this today?' Marcy asks, the new recruit changing into the concerned friend.

'It's cool. Doesn't hurt. Quicker I get used to it the better.'

'Can you hold the axe?' Howie calls out.

'Yep, tested it. Had Clarence trying to pull it out my hand while you were in the garden centre.'

'He was fine,' Clarence says.

'Mile warning.' Reginald's voice comes through the speakers and earpieces. *'Small town. We need the main road through the centre. Go past the pub to a junction then take the first road on the left. Heather, have you got your list to hand? Can you confirm the name and street number?'*

'Er...hang on...shit, no, Paco...no more zade...what? Pass me that

please...that one...on the floor...hey well done! That was so good, Paco. Er...right...yep got it, Sonya Harding. Number eighteen.'

'Marcy,' Charlie says, holding a large red checked bundle of material out.

'What's that?' Marcy asks.

'Just a big handkerchief, like a bandana... see?' she holds her wrist up showing a similar one tied and wrapped round. 'For your face if you start sweating.'

'Genius,' Nick says, 'when did you think of that? You got anymore?'

'I have,' Charlie says, smiling round as she pulls out a pile of different coloured checked cotton hankies from her bag. 'I grabbed them on the way out. Paula's already got one.'

'Clever and beautiful,' Marcy says, wrapping the material round her wrist.

'Mo? Blinky? Can you use these?' Charlie asks, looking at Dave.

'Yes,' Dave says. 'Well done, Charlotte.'

'Er, thanks,' she says quickly at the faces of the others showing surprise at the praise.

'Do not tie it too securely. If it gets tangled it needs to break away,' Dave says. 'Wrap it round and tuck it in...'

'How?' Mo asks. 'Is there a way to do it?'

'Yes.'

'Show me?' Mo says, holding his hand out to Dave.

'Wrap,' Dave says, winding the material round Mo's wrist several times, 'twist the ends and secure in.'

'Show that again, Dave,' Marcy says.

'Wrap, twist...secure...'

'We'll pull up at the edge of the town,' Howie calls back. 'Charlie, on Jess. You lead us in.'

'This is so exciting,' Marcy says, grabbing Charlie's leg to squeeze. A sense of purpose, of finally having something to do. A real excitement inside. A buzz even. She looks forward to the front of the Saxon, almost impatient to be there and working with the lads. She feels the Saxon slowing and the rustle of motion as everyone starts final checks of kit and weapons. She checks her rifle again, popping the magazine out then back in. Boot laces checked. Bandana on her wrist. Machete in her bag. She led thousands. She led an army and felt every single one of them within her hive mind connection. She had power. Real power. What she did with it initially was abhorrent and a sin that will mark her soul forever more but she tried to do the right thing at the end. She knows in her heart she did. She also knows she is vain and shallow and in her eyes has become a thing of beauty without depth. A trinket. A bauble of show. She bites down the urge to say stupid things and show her excitement with a real effort to be serious and work properly, to own her role in the team and pay for her place. That's how she sees it. To earn it like the others do. The seed was planted yesterday on seeing Maddox throw such a golden opportunity away. She wondered how she would react in his place and that thought process evolved to bubble up until she blurted the idea in the kitchen. Now she can't wait.

'Charlie...' Howie calls as the Saxon comes to a stop.

'On it,' Charlie says, bum shuffling down the Saxon to drop out the back doors opened by Dave and Mo. Marcy watches her run down past Roy's van and the clang of the trailer end dropping down. Meredith goes with her. Only too happy to be out and running. Hooves on metal. Hooves on the road. Jess skitters clear of the box as Charlie closes the ramp, grabs the reins and vaults up to settle in the saddle. Kit sorted and placed. A gee of her legs and Jess bursts to run on, cantering past the Saxon to take the front with the dog keeping pace. The engine rises in pitch as the Saxon pulls away to follow behind.

Marcy leans over to look down and out the back doors, seeing the glum look on Paula's face. She feels a stab of guilt for her friend being stuck in such a situation. There's no easy answer. Whatever Paula does someone will get hurt.

'You getting anything, Charlie?'

'Nothing, Mr Howie. Meredith isn't reacting.'

'Okay, straight on ahead...look for the pub.'

'Sir, will do.'

'Howie? I know I'm working with Blowers today but I'm not calling you sir.'

A chorus of chuckles. A well-timed joke said with just the right amount of humour and tone.

'Fair enough,' Howie says, humour in his voice.

'Thank you...Mr Howie...' A deft second touch. A good mood in the Saxon.

'Pub ahead...all clear...'

'Blowers, your team on foot. Eyes open, eyes up.'

'Roger, everyone out. The bum shuffle commences. Dave dropping out then jumping back in while Blowers gives his initial orders, 'Nick, Mo and Blinky take the other side. Marcy and Cookey this side with me. Range out...'

'Bloody hell,' Paula says at seeing Marcy run out to the left side of the Saxon with Blowers and Cookey. 'She meant it then.'

'Is that Marcy?' Reginald asks from the back.

'Yep, she's actually doing it.'

'I'll drop out and go with Blowers,' Roy says, 'you okay driving?'

'You're going out?' Paula asks.

'Howie asked me to keep overwatch on Marcy, but mum's the word,' he says, tapping the side of his nose.

'Bloody hell,' Heather says, having pulled out an angle to see ahead. 'She's doing it...good on her.'

'Ess.'

'Yep, good on her,' she says.

'There she goes,' Clarence says, watching as Marcy and Blowers go past the side of the Saxon.

'Good effort,' Howie says, 'Dave? You in?'

'Yes, Mr Howie,' Dave says as Howie ducks away from the voice coming right behind his head.

'Sneaky shit...'

'Why are we on foot?' Marcy asks, sweeping her rifle round to aim at any place she could hide in.

'So we can hear...get the feel,' Blowers says. 'Watch the windows and doors, that path at the side of those buildings...check behind...look up to the higher floors of the buildings...watch Meredith for reaction...'

The difference between yesterday and today is marked and distinct. A volunteer will always beat a forced worker and Marcy takes the instructions seriously, moving on at a brisk pace while Charlie leads and the vehicles follow.

'Junction ahead,' Charlie reports.

'Go ahead and check,' Blowers says, turning to get a nod from Howie to signify he is happy for Blowers to give commands.

They take the junction and move down the residential street. Ubiquitous and matching the signs of devastation now only so common. Doors hanging open. Windows smashed. Rotten corpses spotted in gardens. A burnt-out pair of semi-detached houses. A postal van rammed into a garden wall. All old and done days ago, but it serves to raise awareness and give reminder of the dangerous place they are in.

Charlie finds number eighteen and signals with an extended arm. The vehicles come to a stop. Howie, Clarence and Dave drop out to jog forward.

'You coming?' Paula asks Reginald, grabbing her rifle.

'Yes yes, I shall come and peruse the situation,' he says.

'Doesn't look good,' Charlie transmits.

'We'll move up to the other side of Charlie,' Blowers says, 'Cookey, hold back here.' Blowers sets off at a jog, veering wide to go past Charlie's position with Marcy running at his side. 'Don't rest your finger on the trigger...rest on the guard...like this see.'

'Okay, like this?' she asks.

'Yeah, switch sides...go on my blind side. We'll stop here.'

He drops down in the middle of the road, lowering to one knee. Marcy follows suit. Adopting the same pose with her rifle up and aimed. She hears the low voices of the others behind her and the clip clop of Jess moving about. She thinks to turn and look but holds position with her finger extended past the trigger.

Howie stares at the house. 'I reckon you might be right, Charlie.'

'Sorry,' she says as though it's her fault the door is busted in and every window is smashed with blood smeared just about everywhere.

'Ah well, Dave? Want Mo and Blinky to check it? I'll keep watch out here with Clarence.'

'Mohammed and Patricia to me. Double time. Pistols ready...'

Silence settles as they wait for Dave to use the house as a training exercise for Mo and Blinky. Pushing them through the rooms with instruction and guidance given of how to work in a pair and a team of three.

'Mohammed, report to Mr Howie.'

'Body in the garden, boss,' Mo says, walking out.

'Show me,' Howie says, following Mo back into the house and through to the garden and the body of a woman on the grass.

'Broken neck,' Dave says, waiting with Blinky.

'Broken neck?' Howie asks, looking up at the back of the house and seeing the upstairs window wide open.

He goes back inside as Reginald walks in. Damage to the front door shorn from the frame. The hinges snapped from a great weight forcing into it. Signs of disturbance everywhere. Side tables over-turned. Pictures on walls knocked down or skewed to the side. A crowd swarmed into the house. Too many people cramming and rushing through. Howie and Reginald go up the stairs to the bedroom at the back with the window open and the body of the woman lying on in the back-garden underneath it. Her head at a harsh angle. Debris everywhere. Dried blood spattered on the walls and bedding. Mo stands by the door, watching them take it all in.

'She jumped by the looks of it,' Howie says.

'I'd say so,' Reginald replies. 'Heard the attack. Knew they were in the house and leapt from the window as they came up.'

They head downstairs. Reginald's stops in the hallway going through letters scattered on the floor that must have been on the side table by the front door.

'Sonya Harding,' Reginald says, holding a utility bill up.

'She still lived here then,' Howie remarks, walking into the living room. He finds the thing he was looking for. Framed pictures of a middle-aged woman smiling with family. Dark hair, plump but not fat. An entirely average human being living a life. Reginald walks in, seeing Howie examining the pictures and does the same. Quickly scanning the prints and photos on display.

'Same woman in all of them,' Howie says.

'Ah here we go,' Reginald says, showing Howie an ornate framed picture with the same smiling woman and her name inscribed in golden flowing script at the bottom.

'Perfect,' Howie says. He leads through the kitchen to the back door and out to see Dave and Blinky still waiting by the body. 'Sorry love,' Howie says softly, using his foot to turn the corpse over. Squelches sound out. The hot weather already bringing advanced rot into the body. The skin streaked with dark patches of greens and purples. Flies buzz angrily at the disturbance. Howie and Reginald stare at the picture of Sonya Harding then down to the corpse on the grass.

'I'd say so,' Howie says.

'Indeed,' Reginald says. 'Hair colour and length is the same.'

'Same build,' Howie says.

'Ah, she wore that same top in another picture,' Reginald says.

'That's a shame.'

'Yes. A very great shame.'

'Righto, next one?'

'Indeed. Onward.'

CHAPTER SEVENTEEN

'*Phillip Kettering, apartment seventeen...Jubilee Place. The maps show a large building on a main intersection of four main roads. Buildings on all sides and a petrol station opposite occupying a large corner plot. The town is big and sprawling. I would expect a dense population resided there so we can expect opposition although as to what numbers I would not like to estimate. In short, and in brief...we are going into a hot zone, chaps.'*

'*Hot zone?'*

'*Yes, Cookey.'*

'*Hot zone.'*

'*Indeed, Cookey. Hot zone.'*

'*You said that. You said hot zone.'*

'*Indeed I did. Lock and load...'*

'*Haha!'*

'*Chinstraps on.'*

'*Everyone. It's Howie. We'll go straight to the target building this time and see what we've got when we arrive. Make ready. Less than a minute.'*

The hot zone is silent and empty with a tranquillity broken by three heavy diesel engines powering up a wide main road towards the intersection. Signs of affluence. Large Victorian and Georgian buildings with ornate metal railings, gates and tidy hedgerows.

'Garage,' Clarence says, pointing ahead.

'Nice,' Howie says, seeing the high-end motors parked on display surrounding the petrol pumps. BMW's, Mercedes and Range Rovers. All large and grand with prices displayed in understated signs.

The Saxon slows into the junction, Roy's van and Heather's four-wheel drive easing acceleration behind it. Four big roads feeding into the intersection. High brick walls in front of the buildings on three of the corners prevent line of sight to the doors or building names.

'Reggie, which building?'

'Corner opposite the garage, Mr Howie.'

'Which corner?'

'Oh I do apologise. Er let me see...diagonally across.'

'That one,' Clarence says, nodding at a huge brick building with white framed windows partially hidden behind a high brick wall.

Howie tuts at the lack of sight to the main door. There must be twenty metres of space inside the wall. A dangerous loss of sight and a greater distance to make up if those who go inside need help. 'Everyone hold on...'

'BRACE,' Clarence calls out as the engine roars from Howie powering it at the wall. A jolting impact as the heavy front end smashes through, obliterating a large chunk. He pulls back, turns and drives forward to take more out.

'Everyone out...'

They move quickly. Blowers ordering his team to cover Charlie as she gets Jess out and ready. Howie scans the area, turning quickly with Dave and Clarence at his sides. 'Big junction,' he murmurs. 'Roy, go high.'

'Yep,' Roy shouts back, throwing his kit on the roof of his van before clambering up.

'Heather, you and Paco stay by Reginald. I can't spare anyone else...We've got too many sides to cover. Blowers, your team covering the junctions. Nick, be ready to drop back on the GPMG and for fuck's sake don't anyone shoot the petrol station. Clarence, you and Paula go in. If it looks bad then shout and I'll send Dave in with you...'

'Me?' Clarence asks.

'Why me?' Paula asks, striding over.

'Clarence can open the doors and you can talk to people,' Howie says. 'Not that I need to fucking explain.'

'No course, sorry, boss,' Clarence says smartly.

'Bit harsh,' Paula says, lifting an eyebrow at Howie.

'Big junction,' Howie replies, still turning in that slow circle.

'North, east, south and west,' Blowers says, pointing to each junction in turn. 'Nick and Mo, north side. Cookey and Blinky, east. Charlie, west. Marcy with me on south...eyes up.'

They burst away to positions. Marcy running with Blowers past Howie and Dave.

'Hello, Mr Howie,' she says quietly, offering him a wink. He grins back at her then turns to check the lie of the land while Clarence and Paula run over the ruined brick wall to the front door of the building. Positions are gained. All sides covered. A glance to Clarence waiting by the door. A thumbs up given and the big man launches his boot to slam the door in. A single resounding crash. A pause. Everyone listening. Meredith runs to Clarence and Paula, pushing past them to get inside the building. Another nod from Howie. Clarence and Paula go in.

'Hopefully they'll clear the air a bit,' Howie says, looking at Dave.

'It's clear,' Dave says, looking up at the sky.

'No I...um...yep, no rain today then.'

'Doesn't look like it, Mr Howie.'

Reginald steps out of his van to smile at Heather and Paco. A glance up to Roy on the roof. A scan round to the others all in position. He spots Clarence and Paula going into the building and smiles wry and knowing. 'Kill or cure I do believe.'

'Pardon?'

'Thinking out loud,' Reginald says, beaming at Heather. 'So, you are my guard then. And a very fine guard too. I feel most safe.'

'Great,' Heather says, staring at the strange little man.

Inside Jubilee Place, Paula threads a careful route over and through the destruction of a doorway that thought it could stop Clarence coming in.

'Hand?' Clarence asks, offering a huge arm.

'I'm fine,' she says, offering a tight smile. 'Cooler in here.'

'Much cooler,' Clarence says.

'Right,' she says, getting clear before looking round. 'Flat seventeen?'

'Yes.'

'I'm guessing that's not on the ground floor.'

'Probably not.'

'Where's the fire plan?'

'Fire plan?' Clarence asks.

'They put them by the door so the fire service know the layout if they...is that it? On the floor? Must have been on the door.'

'This?' Clarence asks, picking a framed picture out of the debris. A schematic black and white drawing giving layout and flat numbers on levels.

'Top floor?' Paula asks, thinking initially to go closer and stand next to him then thinking better of it.

'Top floor,' Clarence says, handing her the frame.

She studies it for a second, the atmosphere heavy and strained. 'Top floor.'

'I doubt the lift is working,' Clarence says.

'Stairs?'

'Stairs it is...'

Meredith runs back to them having completed her initial assessment of the immediate environment and by deduction of her incredible sense of smell, she asserts a lack of zombies within the near vicinity, but then being a dog, she can't communicate that so she wags her tail instead.

'Seems happy,' Paula says.

'Me?'

'No. The dog.'

'Oh, yes. Yes she does,' Clarence says stiffly.

'Stairs,' Paula says.

'Yes. We should.'

'Er, they're behind you.'

'Right. Good. I'll go in front.'

'Okay.'

'Good. Not that you can't go in front but...'

'It's fine.'

'Sure? I'm not being weird by trying to protect you...but I would protect you...in the same way I would protect any er...member of the er...the team...'

She winces as he pushes the heavy fire open and steps into the concrete stairwell. 'It's fine.'

'Good,' he says, starting up the first flight. 'Good idea about the fire plan,' he says when they reach the first landing.

'Thanks.'

They climb the next flight to the first floor in silence. Feet trudging. Weapons and kit rustling. Clarence grimaces. Not knowing what to say. Paula rolls her eyes. The quietness between them is deafening. They didn't do anything. Why does it feel like they did? It shouldn't feel like that. Why isn't he saying anything?

'Next flight,' he says.

'Yep,' she says.

Feet trudging. Weapons and kit rustling. He goes to speak but stops himself. She lifts her head to say something but stays quiet and stares instead at the way his hand grips the railing. The same hand that rubbed cream in her neck and back.

'Fuck it.'

'What?' he turns quickly, instantly alarmed at her tone.

'Nothing,' she says quickly, dropping her eyes to his boots. 'Just thought of something.'

'Sure?'

'Yep,' she looks up from his boots over his legs to his groin then up over his massive chest to the concerned look etched on his face. 'We should...er...keep going?'

He turns to walk on. Feet trudging. Weapons and kit rustling. Up they go. Two flights of stairs between each floor. Meredith bounds up then back down as though urging them to move faster.

'How's the bites?' he asks, instantly wincing at himself.

'Much better.' *Why did he mention it?*

'Good.'

'Thanks.'

Up they go. A big building with many floors. A long trudge.

'Hot now,' she says.

'Is hot.'

Up they go. A big building with too many floors.

'At last,' he says, reaching the top landing.

'Clarence?' she asks, slightly breathless from the climb up. His hand on the door, he turns to look at her. A light sheen of sweat on his broad face. She swallows then laughs at herself and the stupidity of the situation. He smiles at her laughing. A slow grin that spreads with a deep chuckle rumbling from his chest. 'Bloody Howie,' she says.

'Bloody Howie,' he replies.

'We need to clear the air,' she says, still smiling at him. 'I think that's why we got sent in together anyway, kill or cure...something like that.'

He nods slowly, an earnest sincere expression reflecting his troubled mind. 'It is entirely my fault, Paula'

'For what?' she asks. 'We didn't do anything.'

'No,' he says slowly, choosing his words. 'But it was not appropriate of me to...'

'It was putting cream on my back. I had bites. You didn't do anything wrong. It was me that...that took it too far.'

'No. You were asking for help and...'

'And what? You gave it. You gave me help.'

'I did. That is true,' he says, with a frown showing and a look of helpless innocence flashing in his eyes.

'Jesus, Clarence,' the sudden vulnerability of him renders her almost weak at the knees. 'Listen, I er...so...nothing happened right?' he nods. 'So there's no issue.'

'No. No issue.'

'But,' she says, his dropped gaze lifts back to her in a way that makes her want to rush in right now and kiss him. She can't recall seeing the shade of his eyes before. The soft brown flecks in his irises. The crows feet at the corners. The heavy lines of his forehead that give him such gravitas and bearing. She swallows, drawing a breath. 'I might be wrong but...something *could* have happened...'

'I would never take advantage of a friend needing...'

'Me. Not you, Clarence! I would have made it happen. I was pushing back into you for god's sake. Your fingers on my neck were driving me mad. I felt your erection and I just wanted to...' she freezes at the look on his face. 'I am so sorry,' she breathes. 'I shouldn't have said that.'

He drops his eyes again. His hand still on the door. A deep unsettled feeling inside. A yearning. A desire. A need and a want and an urge but all which must be denied. A monstrous strength as he bends his will-power to hold the loyalty and honour embedded in his DNA.

'You are with Roy.'

'I am but...'

'I like Roy,' he cuts across her. His tone deeper, harder. 'I am not that man, Paula.'

'It's coming out wrong,' she says, lifting a hand to wipe the sweat from her forehead. 'What I meant is...'

'We need to get on,' he pushes through the door, finally giving access to Meredith who runs on with her nose to the ground.

'Clarence,' she strides after him as he paces down the long carpeted corridor. 'Slow down...I didn't mean that...' she rushes to catch after him. His long legs powering on too fast for her walking pace. She reaches to grab his arm, pulling him back. 'Hang on a second.'

'This is wrong,' Clarence says, turning to face her.

'Clarence...I wasn't asking you to have an affair with me.'

'I am not that man.'

'I know! I didn't mean it that way. The words just came out wrong and...'

'You are with Roy. Roy is a good chap.'

'He is. He is a great chap and wonderful and I didn't fucking mean I wanted an affair with you. Please, just hang on...let me...'

'Paula...'

'Let me speak...Clarence,' she grabs at his arm again as he walks on. Heedless to what doors they pass. Not seeing the numbers. Only wishing to create distance from her. From her tone of voice and the softness of her eyes and the way her skin shines from the sweat. 'Now just hold on!' she snaps, pulling him back round. She senses he allows her to turn him. 'I did not mean that. I meant I wanted it to happen... not now. I don't mean I want it to happen now...no I do... FUCK! It's coming out wrong again. I mean...yes I like you. Yes I wanted something to happen and...stop glowering at me.'

'I am not glowering.'

'You are. You're glowering.'

'You are with Roy.'

'I hardly know him! I met him a week ago but now I can't finish anything with him because we're trapped in this...this team together. Not trapped. I like being here. I love it. I've never felt so alive...I love the lads and Marcy and Howie and I love Roy but not that kind of love. I only just met him. The world was over. It was desperate and it was right at that moment but...Jesus...I am gabbling like a...I didn't mean *I* was desperate. I meant it was all chaos and death and I never expected to live more than a few days and meeting Howie and joining you...it was all so quick and...SHIT!' she boots the door next to her with a vent of frustrated anger that lapses one again into the strained silence she was so close to breaking.

That heavy charged silence settles between them. Both of them looking away. Both with hearts hammering. Both with chests heaving.

'We should get on,' she says, her voice as flat as Dave's.

He doesn't move. He can't. The raging battle going on inside him prevents any motion or movement. Will power against desire. Honour against desire and loyalty above all else. With an instinct born from the long days spent together and intrinsic connection of the hive mind brought on at times of great peril, she imagines the internal plight of him that only adds to the rush of guilt she feels.

'You're not that man,' she whispers. 'I'm not that woman either but we have to clear this air. It will affect the team.'

'Hello?'

They both turn slowly to look at the man standing in the doorway to number 17.

'Are you Phillip Kettering?' Paula asks bluntly.

'Er yes, yes I am. Are you the army?'

'No. Yes. Sort of. You're immune. Get ready to go.'

'What?'

'Immune. You're immune. Get ready to go.'

'Immune?'

'Yes immune. You are immune. Hurry up. We have to clear the air,' she adds, turning back to Clarence.'

'Immune?'

'Yes. I just said that. Get ready.'

'Contact south side...few running towards us.'

'How?' Clarence asks, staring into her eyes and ignoring the rifle shots outside.

'Contact north side. Only three.'

'I say. How do you know I am immune?'

'Got a list,' Paula says without breaking eye contact from Clarence. More shots outside.

'Blowers here, few more on the south side coming up but we're okay.'

'What list?' Mr Kettering asks.

'Tension is bad for the team,' Paula says. 'Reggie said we need unity and we can't be like this all day.'

'I say, about this immunity?'

'Cookey and Blinky to me on the south side. Mr Howie, can you watch their side. I'm going to do fire and manoeuvre with Marcy.'

'Unity is essential,' Clarence says, still locked on her eyes.

'Hello?' Mr Kettering asks.

'We can't carry that tension between us,' Paula says, staring up into his eyes.

'Immune eh? Well I never.'

'No. We can't,' Clarence says.

'So we have to clear it,' she says softly.

'Am I going to a government place?'

'Fort. Hurry up...' Paula says still without looking away from Clarence.

'We do but I can't be that man.'

'I'll never ask you to be that man.'

'Fort? What fort? Government got a fort has it?'

'I've always done the right thing, Paula.'

'Is that shooting outside? It sounds like shooting.'

'We're being attacked by zombies. Hurry up,' Paula says. 'I'd never ask you to do the wrong thing.'

'I've never stolen or taken anything that didn't belong to me.'

'Zombies? Here? Oh my god...what should I do?'

'No one is asking you to steal or take anything. We just need to clear the tension between us.'

'Sheesh, zombies eh? Still, apparently I'm immune so that's a good thing, right?'

'I'll stand by Howie to the end,' Clarence says.

'As will I.'

'Howie? Is he immune too? On the old list is he?'

'I'll not falter,' Clarence says.

'Nor will I,' she whispers.

'Wow, lots of shooting outside now. So about this fort...'

'You,' Clarence says sharply, extending an arm to point at Mr Kettering. 'Have precisely two minutes to get ready or I am carrying you out.'

'But...'

Clarence leans in, grabbing the door to slam it shut, sealing Mr Kettering inside. He straightens up to his full height. 'Paula, you are a very attractive woman and...and any man would be honoured to court you. I...if...other time and...I...I sometimes lose my thoughts when I am near you...' her breath catches in her throat at his words. 'I...I admire you. I respect you...as a man I...because you are beautiful and of course, yes, when I put the cream on and...the reaction...so yes very wrong but...but...I hope that helps to clear the air.'

'Sure,' she says softly having just fallen head over heels in love. 'Course, all clear.' She forces a bright smile and uses every ounce of resolve to force that smile into her eyes. 'Glad we sorted it out.'

'Me too,' he says deeply, the troubled look still so clear on his features.

'Hey, don't worry. We're all good...and anyway, any woman likes to be told she is beautiful. Especially when she looks at Marcy all day. It's fine. We're fine. I'm glad we spoke. You okay?' she pats him on the arm in the manner of a friend. 'For what it's worth...you're the most honourable man I have ever met and damned handsome to boot...even if you did poke your willy in my back.'

'I did not...'

'Joke! Okay sorry, too soon. Hanging round with Cookey too much.'

The smile forms slowly, spreading across his face as he looks at her. 'Yeah that lad does rub off on people.'

'And so many things I could say to that,' she says. 'Which I won't do. Come here,' she reaches up to kiss his cheek. He lowers to receive the kiss and for a fraction of time they both realise it was the worst thing she could have done. Not that she meant it badly or to try and lure him. She's Paula. She shows affection easily but right then, at that point, being so close again just sets them off and she freezes with her lips but a tiny distance from his cheek as his willpower once again starts to melt.

'Well, I am all ready. Got my essentials...'

'Shit!' Paula says, pulling away to turn again in a repeat of last night.

'GREAT,' Clarence booms. 'WE SHOULD GO THEN...'

'PRESS ON...'

She runs hard, keeping pace with the line. Her face flushed

and red. Sweat glistens and slides down her golden cheeks to be wiped away by the red checked cotton bandana secured to her wrist.

'FIRING LINE NOW...' Blowers booms. The line comes to a stop. Knees taken. Rifles aimed. 'SINGLE SHOT...COMMENCE FIRING...'

She aims and fires. Part of a unit. Part of a team. Part of a firing line that takes ground by pressing the attack against the horde. A glimpse of the structure and order needed to win these fights. Bodies lie gunned down all around them. The other three junctions behind them held safe by Dave and Roy while Howie watches on, walking behind the line as Blowers uses a live situation to train his team.

'HOLD,' Blowers shouts. 'CHARLIE...CLEAR THAT JUNC-TION,' he extends an arm out straight to the right, indicating the junction slightly ahead.

'ON JESS...ON GIRL...'

'HOLD...' Blowers repeats the command as the horse beats a drum of hooves, thundering a foot next to Marcy who feels the air displacement and gains the smell of horse and sweat. Charlie goes fast. Ploughing into the lines at the junction. Using the horses weight and power to decimate the ranks.

'FIRE ON THE LEFT SIDE AND AHEAD...DO NOT FIRE TOWARDS CHARLIE.'

Shots ring out. Bodies drop. The mini battle wages away.

'JUNCTION CLEAR,' Charlie roars as Jess rears up on her back legs.

'HOLD   POSITION...LINE   WILL   PRESS   THE ATTACK...MOVE ON...'

The time of her life. The pace of it. The fluidity but the structure held. Marcy hears Blowers giving the orders and copies what the others do. Running on. Stopping to fire. Covering the flanks. Protecting the integrity of the unit.

They run to meet the infected. Another firing line. More ground gained. Burst fire now. Aimed and direct. When they stop so Charlie is ordered to push through and clear space. Not an arrow is fired by

Roy. Not a shot taken by Dave although they watch carefully. The battle is won. The street gained and their foe slain with discipline.

'CEASEFIRE,' Blowers orders. He rises to his feet. Scanning round. Seeing the victory. 'STAND DOWN...It's over...'

'OH MY GOD,' Marcy flies up, rushing to hug Blowers who yelps at the sudden attack. 'That was so good.'

'Well done, Marce,' Nick calls over, pulling his battered packet of smokes out.

'Well done,' Charlie shouts over, trotting back on Jess.

'Yeah not bad,' Cookey grins, laughing when she runs to hug him.

'S'good innit,' Mo shouts, earning a huge smile in return.

'Can I go back to Howie?'

'Sure,' Blowers says, taking a smoke from Nick.

'Did you fucking see that?' Marcy calls out, rushing round and over the bodies shot down in their wake. She comes to a stop, beaming with real feeling. Her eyes so alive. 'Did you?'

'Brilliant,' Howie says.

'It was wasn't it? Not me. Blowers...all of them...and Charlie! Did you see that? The way we take ground then let Charlie push them back then she holds and we push on.'

'Spot on, nicely done, Blowers.'

'Cheers, boss,' he says easily, blowing smoke away. 'Check weapons, reload and move back to the vehicles. Load up with magazines and get water.'

'Better go,' Marcy says, winking at Howie. 'Corporal Blowers has given an order.' She goes to turn to walk and join the others then rushes back to plant a kiss on Howie's mouth before running back to her unit and the calls of the others all laughing and joking. She heads for the middle, immediately accepted into the fold.

'Well,' Howie says to himself. 'There it is,' he walks back to the vehicles as Clarence and Paula come from Jubilee Place with a small well-dressed man between them. 'Fuck me...' Howie murmurs. 'MR KETTERING?'

'Yep,' Paula shouts back. 'Safe and well.'

He waits as they clamber over the smashed down brick wall,

seeing the tension between Clarence and Paula. 'Everything all right?' he calls out.

'Yep,' Paula says, offering a tight smile. 'This is Mr Kettering. Mr Kettering, this is Mr Howie.'

'Wow,' Mr Kettering says, looking down his once immaculate street now strewn with bodies and bullet casings. 'Wow,' he says again, marvelling at the sight of Blowers leading his gun toting team back and the huge horse trotting next to them. 'Wow...this is...'

'Yep, not much time to chat,' Howie says. 'Can you drive?'

'Drive?'

'Can you drive?'

'I can drive.'

'Brilliant. Nick and Mo, pilfer a car from that garage for Mr Kettering. Do you know the way to the coast from here?'

'The coast?' Mr Kettering asks.

'The coast. Go for the coast. Find Fort Spitbank. Speak to Lilly. Tell them we sent you. They'll know what to.'

'Right. Well. Wow. Are you not taking me then?'

'Nope. Got more to find. Go with Nick and Mo and choose yourself a nice car. Do not tell anyone else you are immune. Tell only Lilly when you get to the fort. They will protect you. Best of luck, Mr Kettering. Everyone load up, we're moving out in five.'

CHAPTER EIGHTEEN

'You okay?' Howie asks, looking across to Clarence.
'Yep,' the big man says dully.

'Good,' Howie says slowly.

'But a fucking Volvo?' Nick says again from behind them. 'He took a Volvo. A fucking Volvo. There was a Porsche in the showroom. Mo Mo gave him the fucking keys to it.'

'Fact,' Mo says.

'Said he wanted the Volvo. Said he had seen it from his flat and always liked it,' Nick says. 'Fucking Range Rovers...M3 BMW's... Mercs...no taste. No taste at all.'

'I had a Volvo,' Clarence says.

'Volvo's are good cars,' Nick says quickly.

'Twat,' Cookey laughs.

'For big people anyway,' Nick says. 'For normal sized human beings who could choose...say a fucking Porsche...'

'Marcy?' Clarence asks, trying to rotate his shoulders to look back and join in with the conversations in an effort to clear his head. 'How was it?'

'Loved it,' she replies emphatically. 'We did fire and manoeuvre. Which is running at the baddies.'

'Baddies?'

'Fuck off, Cookey,' she laughs, leaning over to whack his leg. 'Anyway we did firing lines then holding position while Charlie went through to key points.'

'Worked alright did it?' Clarence asks.

'So far,' Blowers says.

'Buzzing my tits off,' Marcy says, grinning round.

'So coarse my dear Marcy,' Cookey says, mimicking Reginald.

'Do one,' she says, flicking a middle finger.

'I say! That is most not appropriate to the...fuck it, I don't know enough big words.'

'Most unseemly for such an exquisite young lady,' Charlie says, upping her cultured tones.

'Indeed it is most awful,' Mo joins in.

'Innit blood,' Charlie says, slipping into her street voice.

'So bad,' Mo laughs.

'Chaps, Reginald here. We are not far off the next one. We shall be looking for Sally Winthrope on Chestnut Avenue. Unfortunately, Chestnut Avenue is not listed on my maps so one can only assume it is a residential development constructed after the print edition of my maps. The house name is Puddleducks.'

'Reggie, it's Howie. Do we know where the road is?'

'Unfortunately not, Mr Howie. However, the town does not appear overly large so I would suggest we search for new housing developments.'

'Yep, cheers.'

The town is reached. A slumbering hamlet once gloriously tranquil and made bad by a direct rail connection to London placing it firmly within the outer reaches of the commuter belt. They pass new roads leading off the main highway. All of them bordered by modern executive style detached dwellings with once picture postcard lawns and shrubbery. Each road bears the name of a tree. Oak Avenue. Willow Avenue. Cedar Avenue. They slow at each junction, searching for the black and white street sign.

They can see the town was hit hard even from the snatched glimpses into those side streets. Corpses lie rotting. Houses open. Cars abandoned. Everywhere they go the same thing greets them. Every sight of it offensive. Every glimpse of the pain and suffering only fuels the desire to keep going and fight back.

They speed up then slow down. Another avenue named from a tree. Another view of death and pain. More suffering. The darkness starts to push up in Howie. The constant reminder of what those things have done. His breathing comes harder. His eyes brooding and dark.

'Easy,' fingers brush the back of his neck, a whisper in his ear. Marcy sees the white of his knuckles gripping the steering wheel. The energy radiating off him. She leans over to kiss his cheek while behind the laughs and jokes carry on. 'It's all good,' she says softly, easing the darkness away.

'Aye,' he reaches up to touch her arm.

'And you,' Marcy says, reaching over to kiss Clarence's cheek which just makes him think of Paula again. 'Bloody Volvo drivers.'

'Bugger off,' he chuckles as she drops back to the others.

They hit the town centre. A disgusting view of chaos. Howie slows, easing the Saxon round the burnt out cars and vehicles.

'Jesus,' Clarence mutters, leaning forward. The rear grows quiet as they cram forward or drop back to look out the front and rear.

A carpet of bodies on the left side of the road. A sea of corpses mangled and broken but not one of them looks to be infected. Dead hands still clutch weapons. Bats, knives, swords and sticks lie scattered amongst the ruined lives.

'*You seeing this?*' Paula's voice comes through the loudspeaker and earpieces.

'They went at each other,' Blowers says quietly. 'Two sides...see it...'

'Yeah,' Clarence says slowly. 'Fighting over the mini market by the looks of it.'

An attacking force angled in. A defensive force angled out in a slick wake running down the road and through the doors of the mini market now busted, looted and broken. Mild mannered executives. People who play golf and work in the city. Men and women raising children in a sleepy town where the streets are named from trees who took war on each other for the food held in a shop.

'Silly fucking bastards,' Howie says more to himself.

'*Er...you seen that kid on the right side...*' Paula's voice.

Heads snap over. A small filthy boy standing frozen in the entrance to an alley like a rabbit caught in the headlights on a dark road. Surprise and shock shows on his face at the sight of the vehicles in the road. A silence of seconds, of Howie reaching for the handle on his door and Paula doing the same. A silence of instinctual knowledge that he will run the second they move.

Heather shakes her head, staring at the child in disbelief. The suddenness of him appearing like that. She knows none of them can move. The look on the kid's face says it all. He'll leg it the second anyone does anything. She drops her hand to the door handle, easing the pressure to crack the door and catching motion in the rear-view mirror as she does so. Something behind them. Solid ranks running silently. Dozens of infected pouring from the store fronts, from doorways and out through broken windows to land in the street.

'Shit shit shit...' in her haste, she drops the radio in the footwell of the car. Paco reacts at her manner. His form tensing as he turns to see the horde coming towards them at frightening speed. She scrabbles for the handset. A glance to the mirror shows the infected are coming fast. So many of them too and all aiming towards the kid. A decision within a heartbeat. She wrenches the door open, surging out while thumping down on the steering wheel to sound the horn.

'ATTACK...' she bursts to run. Sprinting towards the pavement at an angle to get ahead of the ranks.

'FUCK,' Howie whips round at the sound of the horn, seeing Heather already running from her vehicle towards the pavement with dozens of infected just yards behind her. 'OUT NOW...'

Heather sprints hard. Gaining speed with each step taken. She sees Roy running from his van with sword in hand and a second later sees the blur of Meredith leaping from the Saxon to charge in with Paco.

Howie drops out, seeing how close they are to Heather. A tall female, rangy and thin with long arms so close behind, her hand already stretching out. Paco slams into the horde. Taking several off their feet. Meredith hits, taking another one down. Roy goes in, swinging his sword through a neck but the beasts run on. They don't stop and fight or try to take Paco, the dog or Roy. They see the child and go only for him.

Howie runs with his eyes fixed on the woman reaching out for Heather's hair. Heather sees him coming and the line of his vision going past her. She knows one is close and summons every ounce of strength but feels the floundering hand reaching into her hair. She leans forward, screaming for the small boy to run but he stands frozen with a look of mild interest etched on his face.

A millimetre between them as Howie goes bodily into the female infected, tearing her off her feet. She attacks instantly, raking and slicing with nails while biting into his shoulder as more infected stream past and through the team trying to stop them.

A change in behaviour. An instant show of evolution. The infected are ignoring Howie and his group but taking advantage of the chaos to slip through and run on. Some go wide, veering round the vehicles.

Heather reaches the boy with bare strides between her and the attackers behind. A hand on his arm grips and wrenches him up off his feet into her arms. She doesn't break stride but runs on and away.

Charlie slashes left and right with her knife while kicking the bolts from the back of the horse box. 'OUT JESS...'

The horse runs free. Whinnying loudly, her bulging eyes rolling at the sight and the smell of the things streaming all around her. She kicks out with her back legs, sending a heavy male metres through the air into a wall. She rears up, spinning round to drop and kill another but still they stream past. More coming from buildings and shops. More pouring from doors and side roads. Dozens and dozens.

Meredith streaks through the clamouring melee. Low to the ground and able to twist and turn to veer and dodge. She snakes at speed, whipping to sprint flat out through the chasing horde to Heather out in the front. The dog goes wide, opening her stride to power on past them then veering back in to take the lead one out, buying time for Heather to make ground with the child in her arms.

'GET ON JESS,' Howie roars, running hard with everyone else. A surreal second passes. A second of the team running with the infected. Of Cookey and Blowers side by side keeping pace with infected all around them. Of Nick grabbing a woman's hair to wrench her back then running on past infected who pay no heed to him.

Charlie runs to vault, landing hard with a grunt, her hand instantly finding the reins, her thighs clamping to hold her position. 'ON JESS...ON GIRL...'

Four legs beat two. Meredith saves Heather again and again. Whipping in and out to take out the ones closest. Ragging the throats then running on to do the same again.

Heather gasps for air. Her lungs burning from the long seconds of running at her absolute top speed. Paco cannot get to her. He tries. He runs harder than he has ever run before but the distance is too great and the dense numbers in front too many.

Four legs beat two and Jess gallops past with Charlie low in the saddle, bent forward with her eyes fixed on Heather. 'HEATHER...CHILD...'

Heather can't look. She can't afford the time to even glance. All she can do is run. They're so close. She can almost feel them behind her.

'CHILD...' Charlie shouts. 'LIFT HIM...NOW!'

Heather raises the kid, screaming out at the agony of doing such a thing while running so hard. A sensation of something massive swooshing past her. Charlie reaches for the child but the angle is too hard, the speed too great. She misses and goes past. Shouting in anger. Heather cries out too. The loss of power at having to lift the child slowing her a fraction, she stumbles, almost losing her footing as the dog takes the one lunging at her.

Jess turns on a dime. An almost impossible movement but holding her balance and poise beautifully before bursting back to Heather. Charlie leans, ready to grab the kid and this time Heather can see her coming. She lifts the child, crying out again at the force needed. At the last second she can't help but squeeze her eyes closed from the sight of the horse looming at her then the kid is gone and she runs several stone lighter with a sudden burst of power and speed.

'GOT HIM,' Charlie wraps an arm round the child's body, galloping Jess on to create distance away from the ranks. Four legs beat two and there isn't a hope in hell the infected will catch them now.

A flick of a switch and the infected turn on the team amongst them. A snarling twist of forms. Marcy grabs her machete, yanking it free to lay waste to those coming at her. Cookey and Blowers bare knuckle fighting side by side. Smashing them down with hard fists and harder boots. Dave spins in graceful combat, laying waste with poetic ease. His blades slicing fast and deep. Mo and Blinky work together, using the lessons learnt this morning. Both vicious. Both fast. Clarence and Paco devastate with raw power. Flinging the mere mortals aside that fly through the air with broken bodies. Roy slashes and stabs with his sword.

The compression is instant. The turning in and closing of the ranks around them but this is not new. This is a thing they are now versed in and within that chaos so the structure is gained.

The circle forms. The hallowed ground within that shall not be touched or breached.

Charlie gallops to Roy's van, lowering the shocked child to an even more shocked Reginald being guarded by Paula aiming an assault rifle. A squeeze of her legs sends the signal to Jess and she's off, cantering back into the fray with an axe grabbed that is heaved down left and right.

Victory gained. Victory gained with ease. Twenty one days of fighting for Howie. Less for others. A lifetime for Clarence and Dave. Chests heave. Hands drip blood. Faces spattered with crimson drops sprayed from arteries cut and opened. Bones showing through the joints of the fallen from the many breaks given by Mo and Blinky. Skulls dented, backs broken, legs at angles, necks snapped. A seething purity of violent form that stands righteous on the field of battle. Jess whinnies. Meredith growls, warning the crawlers she is coming to finish what was started. Paco stamps. Cookey drops to jab his knife into a throat. Nick draws his pistol and fires once into a head. The dull pop of the gun seemingly absorbed by the soft forms of humans carpeting the ground.

'I say, can someone take this child please...he's awfully heavy.'

The spell breaks. The hive mind eases to pull back as the connection between them recedes.

'Heather?' Howie says, turning to face her. His eyes still so dark and hard. 'That was awesome...'

'Amazing!' Marcy says.

'Jesus, Heather...you ran so fast,' Cookey adds.

'Good work,' Clarence says as they surround the woman who should balk at attention such as this, but right now, after that, it's okay. It's fine. She smiles back, the battle lust still strong but genuinely touched at the reactions. Pats on her shoulder that would normally make her snarl and tell the person to fuck off or worse, wilt back afraid and nervous. Now she laughs and grins round and feels the touch of other human beings as they tell her what an amazing thing she did.

'I thought I knocked him out of your hands the first time,' Charlie says.

'I saw that,' Cookey laughs. 'I was like...*fuck noooo don't drop the kid.*'

'That dog,' Heather says, looking round to see Meredith tearing an arm from a body.

'Good isn't she,' Nick says proudly. 'She's not my dog though.'

'Er, what's she doing?' Heather asks.

'Arming herself,' Cookey quips. 'Get it? Arming herself...eh my jokes are a bit handy...'

'Fuck's sake,' Blowers groans.

'HENRY? HENRY?' A female voice shouting in panic. 'HENRY...HENRY?' other voices shushing the woman shouting. Urging her to stay quiet. The group turn to move out, trying to detect the direction of the voice bouncing off the high fronted buildings. 'HENRY? HENRY WHERE ARE YOU?' an increase in panic within the voice. Desperation making the woman screech the words. The other voices with her shush and urge silence.

'HERE,' Howie calls back. 'TOWN CENTRE...'

'HENRY?' the voice comes louder, direction gained. They look over to a small junction further up from the centre and a woman running felt pelt into the road. Wild with panic and worry. She looks round frantic and too crazed with angst to see properly. She runs the wrong way as others edge slowly from the junction behind her and spot the people standing in the centre near the big vehicles.

Paula moves out, the child clasped in her arms. 'IS THIS HENRY?'

That does it. The sound of her child's name snaps the woman round who runs sobbing to Paula. Her eyes flitting to the group, to the bodies, to the horse and the vehicles but only seeing her child held in Paula's arms. She snatches him back, moving quickly away to grasp and hold the child close. Her sobs heaving thicker and faster. Her whole body trembling with emotion.

'Thought I lost you...thought I lost you...' she blurts the words over and over, crumbling to her knees with her arms wrapped so tight round her son. Any sense of joviality fades from the group. Smiles drop from faces as quickly as eyes turn to look away.

'My god,' a man gasps, striding towards them. Haggard and unkempt. Days of growth on his face. Several other men and women with him. All filthy and exhausted. 'Is he okay?'

'He's fine,' Paula calls back. 'He's not hurt.'

'Jesus,' the man says, pushing his hands through his hair. 'He ran off...he's autistic...keeps looking for his dad the silly idiot...what...my god, what happened here?'

'We were driving through,' Paula says, flinching at the child being called an idiot. 'We saw the kid, stopped...they attacked so...we er...'

'Killed them' Howie say, drawing their attention to him.

'Come on,' Clarence says to the others, 'we'll get cleaned up.'

'We're looking for Sally Winthrope,' Howie says, straight to business.

'She's Sally Winthrope,' the man says, pointing a shaking hand at the woman holding her son.

'Really?' Howie says, somewhat taken aback.

'She is. That's Sally...'

'Wow, doesn't normally go this well,' Howie says, scratching the side of his head. 'Means we're in for a shitter later then.'

'Pardon?'

'I said it means we're in for a shitter later. Doesn't matter. Er...so... you live near here?'

'Are you the army?'

'No. Yes...sort of,' Howie says, looking over at Paula.

'We knew they were here,' a woman says in a clipped posh voice, moving out from the small group to stand next to the man. Both middle aged. Both once professionals from the city who spent mornings and evenings on fast trains so they could enjoy larger gardens. 'Couldn't go anywhere...we've been hiding for days.'

'You knew who were here?' Howie asks.

'Those things,' she says with a look of sneering distaste that makes Paula groan inwardly.

'Oh. They were in those shops,' Howie says. 'They're out now though.'

'Howie,' Paula says, her voice soft but the warning evident. 'Want to get cleaned up?'

'So you live near here?' Howie asks.

'House up on Chestnut Avenue,' the man says. 'Sally has a room in our annexe. She's our cleaner and housemaid...'

'Housemaid?' Howie asks as Paula groans. 'Many of you?' Howie asks.

'Thirty or so.'

'Big house then is it?'

'Howie,' Paula says, walking over.

'See you've got a few shotguns there. What's that? That a rifle?'

'Rifle,' the man holding it says, his voice educated and cultured.

'Let a kid walk into a town centre then yeah?'

'Howie!'

'Could have taken them out,' Howie says. 'You've got guns.'

'Howie,' Marcy rushes over.

'Still, doesn't matter. We've done it now.'

'Okay okay,' Marcy says, grabbing his wrist, 'come on, leave it...leave it!'

'Sorry,' Paula says.

'I'm not sorry. Look at what they did. You killed each other for a fucking shop. Did you take part in this? Did you?'

Eyes drop. Heads turn away. Feet shuffle and fear grows in eyes at the hard words coming from the hard man dripping with blood that's smeared over his face.

'That is enough,' Marcy snaps, yanking him away. 'Not one more word, Howie.'

'Bye then,' Howie shouts.

'Leave it,' she walks faster, dragging him along.

'Is that Mr Howie?' the man asks, flicking his gaze from Paula to Howie.

'GO FUCK YOURsmmmm,' Howie shouts with his words muffled at the end by Marcy clamping a hand over his mouth.

'Jesus,' Paula mutters. 'Yes, yes it is.'

'My god,' the man says, his group all exchanging glances of shock. 'Are you Paula?'

'Eh?'

'Paula? We heard she's with Mr Howie and Dave...'

'I'm Paula.'

'My god,' the man says again. 'It's true? He's real? You're real?'

'I don't feel it sometimes.'

'I just hate people now,' Howie's voice sails over.

'Don't blame him one bit,' the man says firmly.

'Not one bit,' the woman with the clipped voice says. 'I must shake your hand. We heard about you. We heard about all of you,' she says, closing the gap to Paula with a business like hand ready for the shake. 'Absolute heroes. All of you. I mean that,' she says sincerely.

'DON'T BLAME YOU ONE BIT, MR HOWIE,' the man shouts.

'FUCK OFF.'

'YES! THAT'S THE SPIRIT. FUCK OFF I SAY TOO,' the man booms, 'that's Mr Howie,' he says to others all murmuring with excitement.

'We heard you've killed millions,' the woman says. 'We didn't believe it of course. I mean we're all educated people but well, seeing this, now I am not so sure.'

'S'not millions,' Paula says. 'A lot but...'

'We didn't take part in this,' the man says. 'Not one bit. They tried recruiting us to attack the mini-market but we had a committee meeting and said no...'

'FUCKING COMMITTEE MEETING?'

'Howie, shush, Nick, give him a cigarette for fuck's sake,' Marcy voice comes over.

'BLASTED COMMITTEE MEETINGS,' the man bellows back. 'Anyway, long and short of it, we said no. We had supplies and didn't see the point in it. We tried telling them it was the wrong thing to do and even offered to open a line of negotiation for a cut of the goods. You know, bartering and trade. I mean, we're all from the city so we know our way around a deal...'

'I'll fucking slap...'

'Sit down now!'

'UTTER WANKERS MR HOWIE,' the man shouts. 'So no, we did not take part in this.'

'I'll hypnotise you with boobs in a minute.'

'What did she say?' the man asks.

'Nothing,' Paula says.

'I feel a bit angry too come to think of it,' Cookey's voice comes over.

'I'm bit wound up too, Marcy,' Nick adds.

'Twats.'

'Anyway,' Paula says. 'I need to talk to Sally Winthrope. That's her is it?'

'Yes, that's Sally,' the woman says. 'Village girl. One of the locals,' she adds.

'Meaning what?' Paula asks, catching a tone in her voice and also feeling irritated but not for the same reasons as Howie, for other reasons, the main one being over six and a half feet in height and weighing over twenty stone.

'Oh nothing,' the woman says with a knowing wink at Paula. 'I'm not saying inbred but statistically speaking it is the children of villagers from small places that are more likely to suffer learning difficulties and...'

'Blinky, here now,' Paula snaps.

'Sir,' Blinky sprints out. Coming to attention smartly. 'Miss Paula, Sir.'

'Keep these people back while I talk to this woman.'

'Sir, will do Miss Paula...you lot fuck off before I dick punch you... my instructor is autistic and I'm having his babies...'

'My god, are you pregnant?'

They stop to stare as Meredith trots past with her head high and a human arm dangling from her mouth. She spots them staring at her and gives a low growl as she runs on with the hand dragging over the ground, slapping the dead bodies one after the other.

'That's our dog,' Blinky says.

'Sally?' Paula says, dropping to the side of the woman. 'Listen to me, you're immune from this virus. Sally? Are you listening? Good. We have a safe place you can go to but you cannot tell anyone you are immune. You can take your son with you. Now, can you drive? Yes? Good. Nick? Mo? Car please...now listen, you need to go straight there. Don't stop for anyone. Don't talk to anyone. It's not far. You can reach it in an hour or two. The motorways are clear. Okay? Good. Come with me. We'll take care of you. Are you hurt? We've got a medic...'

CHAPTER NINETEEN

H owie and Dave wait by the gate. Clarence poised at the front door. Charlie on Jess further up. Everyone else ranged out. A thumbs up from Blowers to Howie. A thumbs up from Howie to Clarence.

The door goes in with a single solid kick. Meredith goes first, nose to the ground. Clarence, Dave and Howie swiftly following.

'Looks empty,' Clarence says quietly. 'I'll check the back.'

'Dave, you go up,' Howie says. 'I'll do the front rooms.'

The house feels empty. Meredith isn't reacting, there's a layer of undisturbed dust on the floor and the air has that trapped stale odour but it's a big house so care is still taken. A detached cottage on the outskirts of a town down a quiet lane with a distinct lack of death or destruction showing anywhere.

Howie walks through the living room, feeling a sudden pang of homesickness at the sight of a house preserved so neat and tidy. The large leather sofa facing the flat screen television. An open fireplace. Rugs on the polished wooden floor. A dog bed off to one side covered in fine white hairs. He spots the coffee mug on the side table at the end of the sofa, half full too with a layer of mould growing on the surface of the once liquid contents.

An ornate curved doorway leads into a dining room filled with a gorgeous dark wood table and matching dining chairs. Display cabinets full of liquors, spirits and wines.

'Boss?' Clarence calls.

'In here mate,' Howie calls back, spotting the envelope propped against an empty vase on the table.

'Nothing,' Clarence says, walking through the living room. 'The electric box is switched off...'

'Clear, Mr Howie.'

'Thanks, Dave.'

'What's that?' Clarence asks, nodding at the envelope in Howie's hands.

'Just found it,' Howie says, he turns it over, noticing the flap is tucked in rather than glued down. A single sheet of paper inside that instantly takes him back twenty one days to the letter his mum and dad left in their house. A grunt, a frown and he unfolds the sheet to read the neat flowing script.

Northfield community centre

H owie turns the paper over, shaking his head before showing it to Clarence.

'That it? Northfield community centre?' Clarence asks.

'All it says,' Howie says, checking the envelope while reaching for the button on his radio. *'Reggie, is there a Northfield community centre on the maps?'*

Outside, Mo listens in while staring down his rifle at the peaceful country lane and the heat shimmer dancing over the road. Birds chirping in the trees and hedges.

'Sneaky ninja fuckstick.'

He grins at the whispered comments coming from Blinky kneeling next to him.

'Fuck you.'

'I don't do willies.'

'You ever?'

'What?'

'Shagged a man.'

'Fuck off! That's fucking gross...I'll puke on your boots.'

'Only asking.'

'You ever had sex with a man?'

'No,' he chuckles.

'I'd have sex with Dave though,' she muses.

'Yeah?'

'Fuck yes.'

'What about being gay?'

'Fist me.'

'Fair one.'

'You a Muslim?'

'Nah, family kinda was...we's didn't do religion on the estate. Mads was cool like that. Said religion sucked cock and we's look after each other.'

'You suck cock.'

He bites the laugh down, glancing round to see Dave coming out of the house and Paula smoking furiously at the side of the van. 'What's up with Paula?'

'Fancies Clarence.'

'Yeah?' Mo asks, risking another glance.

'Eyes forward, Mo,' Blowers says quietly as he walks past behind them.

Mo waits for Blowers to walk on, listening to his footfall moving away. 'How do you know?'

'It's fucking obvious,' Blinky whispers. 'Unless you're a blind gimp sneaky ninja.'

'It's not obvious.'

'Fucking is.'

'Fucking isn't. Does Roy know?'

'How would I know? Go and ask him.'

'You's go ask him,' Mo says, 'I take that back...you's would ask him.'

'Bite me.'

'Nah you taste of...'

'Of what?'

'Fuck you, can't think of anything,' Mo whispers.

'Good one. You been bit?'

'Bit?'

'By the drooly things.'

'Nah.'

'Has Dave?'

'You asking me if Dave has been bit? We's immune. Reggie said.'

'We'd be fucked if you and Dave turned.'

'We's immune.'

'Yeah but if you did...not even Mr Howie and Clarence could stop you.'

'I'd bite you first if I turned.'

'You could try,' Blinky says with a laugh.

'Then you'd be my bitch.'

'What you two sniggering about?' Blowers asks at the two trying to hide their laughing.

They fall back to the Saxon for a smoke and a drink. Jokes between some. Serious chats between others. An avoidance of eye contact by two.

'You's been bit?' Mo asks Dave quietly. 'By them, they bit you or cut you?'

'No,' Dave says in his way of ending a conversation.

They load up and once again the small flotilla moves off to snake from the tranquil lane to a country road that meanders past rolling fields to the town centre.

A deep sigh from Howie. The same from Clarence. Bodies. Damage. Devastation. The same thing everywhere and the contrast from the glorious countryside so abundant with life to the places of populace covered in the filth and shit of humanity grows weary in their souls.

They thread up the main road, taking in the smashed windows

and looted stores. The cars ditched at angles. The same thing as ever before.

'*I say, may I suggest we stop here,*' Reginald asks through the radio.

'*Where is it then?*' Howie asks, looking round for the community centre. 'You see it?'

'Wouldn't be here,' Clarence says.

'*No no, just an idea I have in mind, Mr Howie. If we could stop here and perhaps prepare for an assault?*'

Slowing the Saxon, Howie glances at the shop fronts, the darkened interiors, the recesses, small side streets, alleys and places to hide. '*They here then, Reggie?*'

'*It does make sense,*' Reginald says, staring intently at the monitor showing the live feed from the cameras fitted in the light clusters of the van. '*They were hiding yesterday in that town...and then again today. I would be interested to see if this is a standardising tactic currently being used. I would rather suggest it is another evolutionary step for a predator to hide and lie in wait.*'

Heather reaches back to check her machete is close. Her rifle already positioned to be taken up quickly. She looks round at the same things as everyone else. Staring hard at doorways and windows.

'Nothing,' Clarence says from the front of the Saxon.

'Same,' Howie says. '*Reggie? Want someone to call them out?*'

'*Now that is a grand idea, yes do that. Let's see if we have any here.*'

'This is so fucked up,' Howie says, pushing his door open to stand on the ledge. 'HELLO? ZOMBIES? ANY ZOMBIES?'

'Do you have to use that word?' Clarence asks, tutting loudly.

'Er...INFECTED PEOPLE WITH A BAD DISEASE? ANY INFECTED PEOPLE WITH A BAD DISEASE? Doesn't quite sound the sound mate.'

'Reginald called them living challenged before,' Marcy says.

'He did what?' Howie asks, ducking in to look down the back of the Saxon.

'Living challenged, he did...honestly.'

'*Reggie, did you use to call them living challenged?*'

'*Blasted Marcy and her blasted...yes, yes I did, Mr Howie.*'

'They's here,' Mo blurts, feeling that pressure in the back of his head. A sensation, an instinct, real and strong.

'Everyone out,' Howie snaps, grabbing his rifle before dropping down to aim round

Roy jumps out from his van as Paula grabs her rifle and moves through the hatch to Reginald in the rear, joining him to watch the monitor.

Meredith growls, her upper lip pulling back and the hackles down her back rising. Nick watches her closely, seeing her eyes fixed on one shop front further up. He motions for Howie and Blowers, pointing up to the store. Howie nods, walking up to join Nick. Both with rifles braced and aimed.

'Go on,' Nick whispers, giving the dog all the consent she needs to run off with a snarling growl. A leap over the windowsill. A split second then the sound of tearing flesh and a heavy body hitting the ground. A roar. A charge. They come out. All eleven of them.

'That it?' Cookey asks, looking round.

'Hold fire,' Dave orders, striding towards them. He takes the first one down with a flash of his arm slicing the blade across the throat. A quick step forward and he stabs both knives into the necks of a male and female then steps through and drives one blade into a chest and the other through an eye. He turns as he moves, going low and slicing to open arteries then turning on the spot to come up to drive the points into the fleshy underside of jaws. Two left. One has a throat cut. The other falls from hamstrings and Achilles tendons cut through to snarl and thrash on the ground.

The whole thing done in seconds and in one smooth motion. From start to finish like a choreographed dance. They've all seen it so many times but to see it now, without the heat of the battle is a reminder of just what Dave is, of what he can do. To kill ten people with the ease of walking down a street.

He places a foot on the one writhing on the ground, drops, wipes his blades and stands straight while holding it in place. 'Mr Howie. I have not been bitten or cut.'

'What?' Howie asks.

'Oh shit,' Mo says.

'I was only joking,' Blinky says.

'Joking? What joke?' Howie asks. 'Dave? What are you doing?'

'I have not been bit, Mr Howie.'

'You're Dave, they'll never bite you...'

'Mohammed to me,' Dave says.

'Shit...Mo I was joking,' Blinky says.

'What joke?' Howie asks.

'I asked Dave if he had been bit,' Mo says, stopping midway between Dave and the rest.

'Mohammed to me.'

'Mo, come back,' Howie says, wiping the sweat from his forehead as Mo about turns towards Dave. 'Dave, we're all immune. Just kill it and stop fucking about.'

'I am too dangerous, Mr Howie. Mohammed will return to me.'

'Pack it in. Mohammed will come back here...'

'Mr Howie. None of you can stop me and Mohammed if we retain use of skills.'

'We're immune. Mo, get back here...Dave, I'll shoot that thing if you don't kill it.'

'Mohammed will come to me, Mr Howie.'

'He bloody won't.'

'Argh dunno what to do,' Mo says, dancing on the spot halfway between them.

'Mo, come back here, honey,' Paula says. 'Dave, this is ridiculous. We're all immune.'

'What if we ain't?' Mo blurts, still trapped in the middle.

'But we are,' Howie says.

'He ain't been bit,' Mo says. 'I ain't.'

'We are immune,' Howie says firmly.

'We will test it now,' Dave says.

'We will not test anything,' Howie says.

'Mr Howie, if Mohammed turns and retains skills he will kill you all. If I turn I will kill everything.'

'Fuck,' Cookey mumbles at Dave's dull hard voice making such a statement. Not a boast but a fact. Not a threat but a reality.

'Mohammed skills are advanced,' Dave says. 'Mohammed, to me now.'

'Yes, Dave.'

'MY TEAM, Get back here now,' Howie orders.

'Yes, Mr Howie,' Mo says, about turning again.

'We will not risk harm or threat to Mr Howie,' Dave says.

'Enough,' Howie says.

'We will negate anything that poses threat to Mr Howie,' Mo says, walking to join Dave.

'Holy shit,' Paula says. 'Mo? We're not doing this.'

Mo stops next to Dave, waiting as Dave pulls his pistols and knives out, passing them one by one to Mo.

'Anything else?' Mo asks.

'More,' Dave says, plucking blades from all manner of places about his body to hand over.

'What the actual fuck?' Howie asks. 'Dave, this is...right, you two pack it in.'

'If we's a threat, Mr Howie, we's got to negate that threat.'

'Mo, you are immune. REGINALD?'

'Gosh, no need to shout I am right here.'

'Tell them they are both immune.'

'Have they been bitten?'

'No,' Dave says.

'No,' Mo says.

'What the fuck,' Howie says.

'Right,' Paula snaps. 'Enough of this...Jesus, Dave...how many knives have you got?'

'Eight...take them to Saxon,' Dave says to Mo. 'Disarm yourself.'

'Yes, Dave.'

'Reggie,' Howie growls, 'we are all immune.'

'Are we?'

'You fucking said it yesterday.'

'My apologies Mr Howie, I said we are infected. Not immune. We have a list of people with immunity. We are not on that list. We have something else.'

'CHARLIE!'

'Right here, Mr Howie.'

'Are we immune to the virus?'

'Did you not like my answer, Mr Howie?' Reginald asks mildly, watching with interest as Mo starts disarming himself at the back of the Saxon.

Charlie clears her throat with her precursor to voicing an opinion. 'I don't think we need to do this. We have said before about the sheer amount of blood in the air and...'

'Oh now,' Reginald cuts in, rocking on his heels, amiable, affable, benign and as fastidious as ever as he plucks lint off his top. 'I rather think we need to be certain,' he adds with a look to Charlie.

'Yes of course,' Charlie says, reading his body language. 'We should absolutely do this...*test*...if you can call it that.'

'Mo,' Paula says softly, walking over to him. 'Honey, you're sixteen years old. I am not going to let you get bitten in a filthy street.'

'We's got to,' he says simply.

'No you do not,' she says quietly.

Mo glances at Dave then over to everyone else before looking back to Paula, 'Dave's too fast. I can't touch him and I'm faster than everyone else. I ain't boastin' Paula...I'm disarmed, Dave.'

'Take a grenade from your pack and return to me.'

'Right no, not happening,' Paula says. 'Dave, this is wrong.'

'It's not, Paula,' Marcy says, bringing everyone's attention to her. 'You've not seen it like I have...imagine Dave in the fort instead of Lani...not the sex bit I mean. You know...when Howie had sex with Lani in the room while everyone else was listening...'

'You didn't need to say that bit,' Howie says.

'What bit? You and Lani having sex? That bit?'

'Sweetie, put that grenade back...'

Mo pauses as he takes the grenade from his bag, worry etched on his face as he looks up at her. 'I's gotta do what Dave says.'

'No, no you really do not. Dave is not god...' Paula says. 'If Dave told you jump off a cliff would you do it?'

'Yes,' the answer is instant.

'Wow...Mo...okay, listen to me. You're so strong and...and such a good fighter but...honey, you're sixteen.'

'He saved us yesterday, Paula,' Marcy says. 'You saw him. What if he does that *against* us...'

'He can't. We're immune,' Howie says.

'We are not immune, Mr Howie...'

'Infected then, Reginald. Same fucking thing.'

'Son,' Clarence says, walking over to join Paula at the back of the Saxon. 'Dave's good. I know he is...but this isn't right.'

'It is,' Mo says, staring up at Clarence. 'Honest, it is...we's got to protect Mr Howie and a risk is anything that...'

'I know what it is,' Clarence says easily.

'Gotta do it,' Mo says, looking from Clarence to Paula. 'Is that okay?' he adds so earnestly it makes Paula reach out to hug him.

'No, it's not bloody okay,' she says.

'Howie,' Marcy says, 'they need to know.'

'Not like this,' Howie says.

'When then? In a fight? You'd risk finding out then? I love Mo to bits. He's like a little brother but fuck me, he can fight. He's getting closer to Dave. Reggie is right, none of you are immune, you're something else...something different to me and Reggie. Don't all look at me like that...do it now where you can control it...Blowers?'

'It's shit,' Blowers mutters.

'It makes sense,' Marcy says.

'Does,' Blowers says reluctantly. 'Boss? Might as well know.'

'FUCK IT,' Howie shouts with a flash of the darkness pulsing through all of them. 'Right...Nick, GPMG...Blowers, get grenades, hand them out. Dave, drag that fucking thing into the road so we got space. Blinky, keep hold of that dog. Everyone else....and I mean everyone else will arm with a rifle, full magazines...'

Dave drags the gnashing body by the ankle over the pavement to the centre of the wide road. Faces drawn and tight. Tension thick and charged. Heather checks her rifle with the others, glancing round at the stress showing on their faces.

'This is messed up,' Paula says, hugging Mo. 'Nothing will happen, Mo. I promise,' she pulls back to kiss his forehead. 'I promise.'

'Come here,' Clarence says, grabbing the lad into a huge hug. 'You'll be fine. We're right here...'

'Cheers,' Mo says, feeling a rush of emotion inside that he fights to swallow down.

'Mo,' Marcy takes him from Clarence, pulling him in to kiss his head. Words said softly. Cookey jokes, grinning while showing the worry through his eyes. 'I'll have your kit if you turn.'

'Fair one,' Mo says, overwhelmed at the affection.

'Ninja fuckstick,' Blinky says, punching him on the arm, 'Mo, I'm such a cunt. I was joking...' she whispers urgently.

'S'cool, you's be my bitch if I turn.'

'You are being so brave,' Charlie says, kissing his cheek that makes him blush. She turns to walk back, sharing a look with Reginald.

'Why are we doing this?' she asks quietly, pausing at his side.

'Not everything is for the apparent result of the immediate action, and I did say to stop second guessing me. You are too intelligent for me to monitor all the time.'

'Fine,' she says curtly.

'Oh come now,' he says, casting a desultory look.

'Then why do this?' she whispers. 'For what? They are infected. We are all infected. Why waste time and cause worry. Look at Mo, he's terrified. Why do that to him?'

'You have just answered your own question.'

Charlie frowns, looking from Reginald to Mo and the way he tries to brave it out and hide the worry in his eyes. 'Rite of passage?'

'Do not guess. It is beneath you. Think, Charlie. Think clearly or perhaps you are spending too much time with Cookey discussing appendages and vacuous...'

'Without sadness there can be no happiness,' Charlie whispers with sudden understanding. 'Unity.'

'Indeed,' he says, the tutor to the student and without a hint of condescension.

'What happens if we lose unity?'

'Good lord, shoo woman. Go and brush your horse or flirt with Cookey.'

'Okay,' she says moving off before darting back. 'Tell me later.'

'I will do no such thing.'

'Fine. I'll work it out.'

'I am sure you will my dear.'

Dave waits, his foot pushing the squirming infected down into the road under the glaring sun.

'Dave? Do you want a hug?' Marcy asks, walking over to him.

'No.'

'I don't care, you're getting one.'

'I do not want...'

She moves in close, angling over the body held underfoot to pull him in. His face hardens at the act of being touched, at the invasion of his space. 'I'll make sure they kill you if it happens,' Marcy whispers.

'Take my head from my body.'

'I will. It won't happen but if it does I promise you.'

She pulls back, sighs with a long look at him and walks off as Howie and Mo move out from the others to walk the distance across the road.

'You's don't have to come, Mr Howie.'

'I know,' Howie says. 'Dave, you okay?'

'Yes, Mr Howie.'

The three stand together under the blazing sun of a silent street. Howie looks down at the infected that was once a person with a name and a life but is now just a thing to be stopped. He turns to look at the line facing them. Meredith held by Blinky. Charlie on Jess.

'Not seen it from this side before,' Howie says.

'Where is your sidearm, Mr Howie?' Dave asks, noticing Howie's empty holster.

'Sold it to buy drugs...'

'Howie? What are you doing?' Marcy calls over.

'Boss, you's going,' Mo says in alarm.

'Yeah in a minute,' Howie replies, pulling a small knife from his belt. He flips it over to offer the handle to Dave. 'Only needs a small cut, Dave. Back of your hands will do it.'

Dave takes the knife as Mo lifts his right hand. A swish and a nick of open skin shows on Mo's hand. A small well of blood oozing up. He does the same to himself, drawing a slight wound.

'Fuck me, you do bleed then,' Howie says at the sight of the blood on Dave's hand.

'Yes, Mr Howie.'

'Knife? Cheers, right, you'll need to stick your wounds in it's gob... let him have a suck and a nibble and get his blood and saliva in you. Got it?'

'Yeah,' Mo says.

'Yes not yeah,' Dave says.

'Not now, Dave,' Howie says. 'Tell you what, it's easy to get it wrong...' Howie cuts the back of his own hand, throws the knife away and drops to grab the back of the infected male's head before thrusting his hand into the mouth. He winces at the bite as Mo flinches and Dave glares. 'Like that...see?' Howie says, wrenching his hand away. 'Mo, you next...'

Mo drops to kneel, his hand shaking as he pushes at the mouth while looking with uncertainty at Howie. 'Dave, your turn,' Howie says, pulling Mo's hand away covered in blood and drool. Dave copies the action without a flicker showing. His hand bitten. Blood and saliva from the infected going into the wound.

'Done,' Howie says, standing up to slam his foot down on the back of the infected man's head causing a burst of blood and crunch of bone. 'BLOWERS.'

'MAKE READY,' Blowers orders.

The street fills with the sound of bolts yanking back and safety switches turning.

'AIM,' Blowers orders. The rifles lift to brace in shoulders. Meredith barks and Jess tosses her head at the tension rippling through everyone. 'LINE READY, MR HOWIE.'

'BLOWERS...IF THEY TURN YOU WILL OPEN FIRE.'

'YES, MR HOWIE.'

Mo glances at Dave with a sudden prickle of fear forming not from Howie's words but the look of worry on Dave's face.

'Mr Howie, you should go back to the line,' Dave says, his normally expressionless eyes now fixed on Howie.

'Give me that grenade, Mo,' Howie says.

'You will go back now, Mr Howie.' Dave says.

'We're in it together,' Howie says, pulling the pin from the grenade, looking from Dave to Mo.

Dave shifts, his head inclining. A hardening in his eyes. 'You will return to the line, Mr Howie.

'Nope.'

'You will return to the line, Mr Howie.'

'I said no.'

'You will go back, Mr Howie.'

'I promised you nothing will happen,' Howie says to them both. 'Mo, look at me...nothing will happen...'

'Yeah but...' Mo says, his voice choking off.

'You will go back *now*, Mr Howie.'

'Boss, this ain't right.'

'Now, Mr Howie.'

'We're a team,' Howie says simply.

'NOW, MR HOWIE.'

'Boss, go back...If we turn...'

'Then we die together,' Howie says.

'YOU WILL GO BACK, MR HOWIE,' Dave shouts, his face twisting with something halfway between anger and worry.

'ONE MINUTE,' Clarence calls out.

'Go back boss, you's got to go now...' Mo says.

'My team,' Howie whispers, taking Mo's hand to place over his own holding the grenade. 'To the end.' He takes Dave's hand, pulling it to join theirs on the explosive. 'Nothing will happen,' Howie says. 'Nothing will happen...I swear it...' He feels the fear from Dave. Not at the risk of his own demise but the danger placed to the man he protects.

'MINUTE AND A HALF.'

'Go back, boss,' Mo says, his voice trembling.

'I'll not,' Howie says. 'Not now, not ever...to the end yeah? Mo... you with me?'

'Yeah,' Mo whispers, the tears tracking down his cheeks.

'Dave? You with me?'

'Yes, Mr Howie,' Dave's voice, broken and low.

'To the end but not here. It won't happen. I swear it.'

'ONE MINUTE FORTY FIVE.'

'I swear it. Are you with me?'

'Yes.' Mo whispers.

'Yes, Mr Howie.'

'TO THE END. ARE YOU WITH ME?'

'YES, MR HOWIE,' Mo shouts.

'YES, MR HOWIE,' Dave bellows.

'ARE YOU WITH ME?'

'YES.'

'TO THE END.'

'TO THE END,' Mo roars.

'TO THE END,' Dave's voice booms.

Energy flowing through them. Energy coursing through their veins coming from Howie. Pure energy that makes their hearts boom and their muscles thrum. That fills their heads with hope and courage.

'TO THE END,' Howie roars.

'TO THE END,' Clarence's huge voice, others too. All of them shouting. All saying the words as the energy flows, the feeling pulsing from one to all. Jess rears, Meredith gives voice, telling the things they are pack and they are strong.

Reginald feels it but detaches his mind from the emotion to marvel at the unity created that is better than he could ever have hoped. He looks over to Charlie on Jess, seeing the animation on her face. *Told you* he mouths. She grins down at him, rising as Jess rears again before joining the others to cry out. This is good. Howie is learning to shape and use what he has. If the other player is evolving, so must they.

They roar words for the feeling of the fear in Mo and Dave. A unity gained. A whole made from the parts of many and the power of one at the core.

The two minutes come to pass and the legend of Howie grows that bit more.

The two minutes come to pass as Howie the legend realises he is holding a live grenade with the pin pulled out. 'Best get rid of this,' he says quietly, coolly. He steps away, dashing and roguish in manner and appearance. A born leader that pulls his arm back and launches the grenade across the road through a broken shop window. Everyone tracks it. Everyone sees Howie the legend throw the grenade through the window to the outdoors supplies store resplendent with adverts proclaiming it to hold the counties largest stock of camping gas stoves and bottles.

'Oh cock it,' Howie the legend mutters.

'DOWN NOW,' Dave roars, launching into Howie and Mo down as the rest starburst to run away.

The grenade bounces off the taut side of a display tent, sailing through the shop as gravity pulls it down to earth. It lands with a dull thud and rolls under a shelf through to the other side coming to rest, such is the way of fate, in the middle of the aisle holding all the small camping gas bottles.

The grenade blows. A supercharged explosion of heat that sends red-hot shards of shrapnel into the gas bottles, piercing the skin and igniting the contents that blow out one after the other. A domino effect occurs. One blows. The one next to it blows. The ones next to that blow and so on all in micro-seconds of explosions that appears to be long continuous boom of noise and flame.

The aisle detonates with flame and debris flying out. Flames roar, licking up the front of the building and that supercharged, super-heated shrapnel of the grenade and gas bottles hits the other, bigger gas bottles held at the rear of the store. The first one explodes, and as before, so the one next to it goes.

What was an explosion before becomes a deafening roar of bass filled booms that make the ground tremble. It blows the interior wall within the shop out. Flames and scorching hot metal ping through the offices and staff room, setting flame to anything they hit and touch. The door to the store room blows in from the pressure wave of air and heat, and such is the way of fate, the supercharged, superheated fragments reach the many, many more gas bottles in the store room because this store is, as the sign proclaimed, the counties best stockist of camping gas bottles.

Howie, the former legend that was, gets to his feet and starts running with Dave and Mo as the store room bottles go. The world shakes, trembles, rocks and heaves as the whole shop explodes in a solid whump of flying bricks, chunks of concrete, shop furniture and the contents of the flats above.

Roy runs for his van. Marcy for the Saxon. Heather and Paco for their vehicle. Everyone else just legs it. Sprinting down a street made dark from the plumes of thick black smoke billowing into the sky. They trip and fall from the earthquake like tremors as the explosions continue, getting faster and louder.

The shops either side of the outdoor place blow out. The interior floors break. The buildings crumple down with a reverse concertina effect that spreads down the whole terraced street. One after the other roofs simply crumple to drop with crashing twisting noises and flames searing out to lick the sky.

Such is the force generated, those supercharged, superheated burning fragments reach the stores on the other side of the street and gladly set flame to wood and combustibles. Such is that force, those fragments spew out on all sides to embed in houses, stores and anything within range.

Within a minute of Howie throwing the grenade, the town centre is fast on it's way to obliteration as three vehicles, one horse box trailer thing, one dog, one horse and eleven people run away.

CHAPTER TWENTY

The three vehicles, one horse box trailer thing, one dog, one horse and eleven people come to a stop. Marcy drops down from the Saxon. Paula from Roy's van. Heather and Paco from their four wheel drive as everyone else bends forward to rest hands on knees and gasp for air from sprinting so hard. All apart from Dave and Blinky who simply look about without hint of exertion showing.

'Now that,' Marcy says, striding over with a huge smile. 'Was very cool, Mr Howie.'

'Do one,' Howie gasps, waving a hand at her.

'Who throws a grenade in a gas bottle shop?'

'I do,' he says between breaths.

'Seriously, you looked so cool up until that point.'

'Did,' Paula says, smiling at him. 'I was impressed.'

'Oh me too,' Marcy says, the two women side by side with arms folded. 'The dashing hero standing by his men...'

'Holding a grenade,' Paula says.

'All brave and handsome,' Marcy adds.

'Brought a tear to my eye,' Paula says.

'Got everyone going,' Marcy says. 'Shouting and charged up.'

'Brilliant,' Paula says.

'Epic,' Marcy says.

'Do one,' Howie says again, still bent over.

'Even throwing the grenade looked cool,' Marcy says.

'Very cool,' Paula says.

'Fucked up a bit after that though,' Marcy says drily.

'Just a bit,' Paula says, the pair of them setting everyone off laughing.

'Have you seen it?' Marcy asks. They all turn to see the thick plumes of smoke growing bigger by the second and the sounds of the explosions still popping in the distance.

'Oh,' Howie says with a wince. 'Yeah that is quite bad.'

'Bad?' Marcy asks. 'Bad doesn't cover it.'

'Anyway,' Howie says, waving a dismissive hand, 'Mo and Dave are immune.'

'Oh no,' Paula says.

'No no no,' Marcy says. 'You never fuck up. We're enjoying this.'

'Piss off, well done Mo and Dave.'

'Infected not immune, Mr Howie.'

'Sod off, Reggie.'

'And might I add that when I said we need the other player to know where we are I did not mean blowing a town up...'

Howie bursts out laughing at the perfect delivery by Reginald. Glancing over to see the humour in the small man's face.

'Anyway, yes, Mo Mo, may I shake your hand and offer my heart-felt congratulations.'

'Cheers, Reggie.'

'And Dave, I know you don't like physical touching so I will keep my distance and offer you a respectful nod.'

'Well fuckity doo,' Howie says with a sigh. 'That was something else...anyone hurt?'

'Just your pride I think,' Marcy says, earning fresh laughs.

'With this lot?' Howie asks, 'I lost pride back in the first week I think. Fuck me that fire is huge...right, anyone need a break? Need a poo?'

'Er...' Cookey wriggles on the spot, 'I'm alright for a bit. Might need one later.'

'Okay, mate. Blinky? Need a poo?'

'No thank you, Mr Howie, Sir.'

'Roger that. So…anyway…pregnant then?'

'No, Sir, Mr Howie, Sir. Not pregnant, Sir…Mr Howie…Sir.'

'Ah, okay. Just thought I would ask…' Howie says, winking at Dave staring back as devoid of expression as ever. 'You'd be a great dad, Dave.'

'What?'

'Just saying.'

'I have not impregnated Patricia.'

'Yeah I know, Dave. I was…'

'There was only one inappropriate act of touching during training.'

'Eh?'

'I pushed the recruit Patricia to the chest area touching her left breast when she ran at me.'

'Right…I see…'

'There was no possibility of impregnation occurring, Mr Howie.'

'It was a joke, Dave.'

'Impregnation cannot occur in that way.'

'I know, Dave…I was…'

'There was no penetration of the penis, Mr Howie.'

'Yes, right! Okay, shall we go?'

'The penis has to penetrate the vagina for impregnation.'

'Yes, Dave. I know…right, load up…'

'And ejaculation.'

'Oh my god, yes I know.'

'There was no ejaculation, Mr Howie. Or penetration.'

'Haha, holy shit…right…so um…'

'Well, technically speaking,' Marcy says with a casual tone, 'doesn't have to be ejaculation. Pre-cum can do it.'

'What?' Howie asks.

'What?' Nick asks.

'Eh?' Cookey asks.

'Pre-cum,' Marcy says. 'Bit dribbles out before ejaculation. That can get someone pregnant as it's still semen.'

'Urgh, so gross,' Cookey says, pulling a face. 'Like premature ejaculation?'

'No, it's called pre-cum. Premature ejaculation is when the man shoots his load before...'

'Jesus Christ, can we go now?' Howie asks.

'You might not even know you had pre-cum,' Marcy says, nodding round at the rapt faces of the men. 'Pop it in, wiggle it about and boom, there she is...pregnant.'

'Are you being serious?' Howie asks. Horrified at the thought of his penis dribbling.

'No way,' Nick says, equally as horrified at the thought of his penis dribbling.

'Fucking gross,' Cookey says, truly disgusted at the thought of his penis dribbling while Mo stares down at his groin trying to detect if any dribbling is taking place.

'Seriously,' Marcy says. 'How do you not know about it?'

'No one ever told me my willy dribbles,' Cookey says.

'Twat,' Blowers laughs.

'I don't want a dribbly willy. Reggie? Is Marcy being honest? Where is he? Charlie...does my willy dribble?'

Charlie stops laughing to stare at him, open mouthed and stunned. 'How would I know that?'

'Marcy said every bloke has a dribbly willy...'

'Erm well yes...but not generally in day to day activities.'

'Doesn't even have to be erect,' Marcy says, grinning at Cookey's discomfort.

'So...so...' Cookey says, bereft in the knowledge. 'So when it's soft?'

'Yep,' Marcy says.

'What now? Is it dribbling now? My pants don't feel wet when I...'

'Oh my god,' Blowers gasps, leaning over to brace his hands on his knees.

'Do you get a dribbly willy?'

'No!' Blowers says, laughing even harder.

'But Marcy said we all get it. Nick? Do you...'

'You twat,' Nick laughs. 'She's winding you up.'

'I'm not,' Marcy says. 'I'm really not...Charlie, am I being honest?'

'Gosh please don't draw me into this.'

'No but...' Cookey asks, looking round in panic.

'Oh Cookey,' Charlie laughs at his puppy dog expression. 'It's true but only when you are sexually aroused.'

'Like when we danced?'

'What?' Blowers laughs, trying to see through his one eye now misted with tears as Charlie turns a deep shade of red.

'Fucking priceless,' Nick gasps.

'I mean...I didn't get a stiffy but...'

'I am going to turn around now,' Charlie says primly.

'Dribbler...'

'Fuck off, Blowers...seriously? Did it dribble? I don't think it dribbled...'

A gunshot. Clear and distinct. A snapping to awareness. Laughs dry instantly. Heads come up to look round.

'Shotgun,' Dave says, staring off into the distance. 'Twelve gauge.'

Another shot in the distance.

'Second barrel,' Dave says.

'How far?' Howie asks.

'Less than a mile, Mr Howie. That direction,' he adds, pointing off.

'Load up, get kitted. Charlie, stay on Jess but don't go too far ahead...line of sight.'

More gunshots come through the warm air. Shotguns and rifles as described by Dave after each shot. Tension within the vehicles. Rifles made ready. Faces sweating from running. Bags on. Hand weapons in position. Paula drives the van while Roy sorts his arrows and bow. Heather behind them. The rifle across her lap.

Charlie trots on, gaining distance from the vehicles to track the sounds. A solid flurry of shots all together. A fight clearly underway. Main road to a side junction. A residential street. She canters on, building speed.

'Charlie...do not charge in,' Howie's warning voice in her ear. She raises a hand, showing she heard him.

'Listen in,' Blowers says in the back of the Saxon. His words fast, his tone implying no joking now. 'This is different. That's multiple weapons being discharged. The things we fight don't shoot guns. Stay close and listen to the instructions...I fucking mean that...'

'Paula...it's Clarence. DO NOT charge in. Roy...the same. This is a live fire situation. Wait instructions. Heather, did you hear that?'

'Yep, heard it.'

'I'll follow your lead on this one,' Howie says, gripping the wheel with the pulse inside starting to thrum.

'See what we've got,' Clarence says.

The shots continue. Coming faster now. Louder. Another junction taken to follow the noise. Then it's there. The end of the road in sight that gives way to the vast open playing fields surrounding the squat brick building in the middle. A large sign erected at the entrance to the fields welcomes visitors to *Northfield Community Centre.*

With line of sight gained so the noises come clear and defined. A siege underway. A horde of many attacking the building. Figures on the roof firing down. A huge horde facing in, more pouring across the playing fields. Thick lines. Dense rows. The noise far off but a noise they know. The sound of hundreds of voices snarling together as they attack to feast and kill to spread the thing inside them.

'Building in the middle...' Charlie gasps the words out, the air rushing past her mouth, *'horde...horde attacking it...'*

'See it,' Howie's hard voice comes back.

'Charlie...it's Clarence...stop at the field...repeat...stop at the field...'

Jess lowers her head, seeing the things, smelling them, expecting the charge to happen then feels the reins pulling back and the voice of Charlie easing her back. For a second she ignores it, willing them to keep going.

'Easy...easy now...'

Tossing her head, Jess eases down from a gallop to a canter to a trot. Her feet on the grass now. Feeling the greater traction and the wide-open space around her.

'Shooters on the roof,' Clarence says. 'Dave? You said they're firing rifles?'

'Yes.'

'Range is high on a rifle...' Clarence says. 'Sound the horn, see if we can draw them back.'

Howie presses the horn, warbling long and loud to no effect. Even those infected still charging across the fields show no reaction but run on towards the fray.

'Cheeky fuckers,' Howie says. 'We're being ignored again.'

'We are,' Clarence says.

'It's not on,' Howie says.

'Not on,' Clarence says.

'Give me that handset...Hello! We're here to...' Howie says, expecting his voice to boom out but not hearing anything. 'It's not on.'

'It is on,' Clarence says.

'Testing? It's not.'

'It is,' Clarence says, flicking the switch off and back on.

'Testing...nope, not on.'

'Bloody hell,' Clarence huffs, flicking the switch to the off. 'Try it now.'

'That's off.'

'I know but it wasn't working when it was on was it?'

'Testing? Nope...er...it's off.'

'I know it's off. Can you see it?' Clarence asks, pointing at the switch.

'I'm looking right at it.'

'Now it's back on. See?'

'Testing? It's not on.'

'It is bloody on.'

'My willy doesn't dribble...'

They both look back at Cookey staring glumly at his groin.

'Nick?' Howie says.

'Isolation switch, Mr Howie.'

'Isolation switch,' Howie says to Clarence.

'I heard him,' Clarence says, turning to look at the electrical switches. 'Which one is that?'

'Nick? Which one is it?'

'We are so shit sometimes,' Marcy says.

'And we've got dribbly willies.'

'That one,' Nick says, bum shuffling to move up the front, stepping over Meredith and leaning over Marcy. 'That one,' he says again, pointing.

'Which one?' Clarence asks, trying to track his aiming finger. 'This one?'

'Next to it…other side.'

'This one? Got it. Try it now…'

'Testing…it's still not working,' Howie says.

'And I told Charlie I got turned on while we were dancing.'

'Try it now,' Clarence says.

'Why? Did you wave a magic wand at it?'

'No I flicked the switch again.'

'Testing…um…so…still not working.'

'Honestly, this is just embarrassing,' Marcy says. 'We just blew their town up…'

'Testing…still not working,' Howie says.

'Yes, Boss,' Clarence snaps. 'I can hear that.'

'Nick, fix your radio thing,' Howie says.

'It's not my radio thing and er…it's not a radio.'

'Don't argue with Mr Howie,' Clarence says gruffly. 'And fix your radio thing.'

'How?'

'How what?' Clarence asks.

'Don't punch me, you're massive…but how the fuck do I reach it?'

'Lean over,' Howie says.

'Lean over,' Clarence says.

'Fuck me,' Nick says, leaning over. 'I can't reach.'

'Lean over properly and stop pissing about,' Clarence says, helping the poor lad lean over properly by lifting his upper body over the back of the seat at the radio thing. 'Got it?'

'Jesus,' Nick yelps, 'yep, I need the wires at the back...'

'Everything okay?' Paula asks over the radio. *'Just that we're kinda sat here not doing anything.'*

'Nick's fixing his radio thing,' Howie replies.

'It's not my radio thing...and it's not a radio.'

'Why don't we just walk in?' Marcy asks.

'Because they are firing weapons,' Blowers says.

'What Blowers said,' Howie says. 'We might get shot.'

'Really? Is that what happens with guns?' Marcy asks. 'I never knew.'

'No need to be sarcastic,' Howie says.

'No need to blow towns up,' Marcy mutters.

'Might shoot my dribbly willy off.'

'Why does Nick need to fix his radio thing?' Paula asks.

'It's not my radio,' Nick says with a muffled voice as he tries to get at the wiring while head down in the footwell over the seat with his legs poking out making Marcy lean away.

'Trying to use the loudspeaker,' Howie says via the radio. *'But Clarence broke it.'*

'I did not break it.'

'Isolation switch?' Roy suggests over the radio.

'Good idea,' Howie says. 'Nick? Isolation switch?'

'We just tried that,' Nick says.

'I was being flippant.'

'No need to be flippant,' Marcy says with flippancy. 'But honestly...we're just sitting here. Nick! Your feet are in my face.'

'Move then...try it now.'

'Testing...nope,' Howie says.

'Do zombies have dribbly willies?'

'Why's don't we get Dave to shout?' Mo says. Nick freezes. Howie looks at Clarence who stares out the front. A few seconds pass before they all slowly turn to look at Mo Mo, apart from Nick who is wedged in the footwell. 'S'just an idea,' Mo mumbles.

'Mo should be in charge,' Marcy says.

'Fact,' Howie says. 'Dave?'

'Yes, Mr Howie.'

'Oh god not now,' Howie says, dropping his forehead on the back of the seat.

'Dave,' Mo says. 'We's need to get them people to stop shooting. Shout out to them.'

'Ask Dave to shout,' Paula suggests.

'Mo Mo just said that,' Marcy transmits back.

'Is he doing it then? We haven't heard him from here. Roy? Have you heard him? No, we haven't heard him.'

'He hasn't done it yet,' Marcy says as Dave moves to the hole in the roof with the GPMG fixed and ready. He goes up to purvey the world and all that is in it. A small man not given to expression and he stares flatly while sucking in air.

'Christ,' Howie says, pushing his fingers in his ears.

'*CEASE FIRRRRRRRRRRRRE.*'

The voice booms and rolls. Blades of grass bend from the onslaught. Trees sway. Birds give flight. The polar ice caps shudder. The moon wobbles. The spin of the earth on its axis slews off by a millionth of a millionth of a very small number. Jess startles, neighing as she lifts her front feet in fear. Meredith howls. Paco growls. Heather swears.

'That was loud,' Roy observes drily.

With the warm up over, Dave inhales to shout properly. Expanding his lungs properly with a suck of air that almost creates a vortex.

'Shit,' Clarence says, pushing his fingers in his ears.

'*CEEEAAASSSE FIRRRRRRRRRRRRRRRRRE...*'

Blades of grass snap. Trees die. Birds drop from the sky. The polar ice caps melt and the moon sods off to find another planet to orbit and the earth starts going back the other way for a nice change.

None of those things happen but Howie thinks they should. Instead, Jess runs off a few metres. Meredith howls again. Paco still growls and Heather swears some more.

'That was louder,' Roy observes, earning a look from Paula.

The field of battle comes to a silence. Every infected turns to look.

Every figure on the roof of the squat building in the middle of the playing fields stops shooting.

'Got it!' Nick says. 'Try it now.'

'TESTING...yep it's working now...cheers Nick... er...so...I THINK DAVE JUST SAID IT BUT CAN YOU STOP SHOOTING NOW PLEASE...'

'Just say ceasefire,' Clarence says.

'CEASEFIRE,' Howie's amplified voice says. **'ER...HAVE YOU CEASEDFIRED...CEASED THE FIRING...HAVE YOU STOPPED SHOOTING?'**

'Oh my god,' Marcy groans. 'We look so stupid.'

'WE DON'T LOOK STUPID...SHIT...FUCK IT... NOW WE DO...'

'Jesus wept,' Marcy says, shoving Nick's legs out of the way to lean over his arse. 'Give me that handset...'

'EH? WHY?'

'I'M BANNING YOU FROM TALKING TO PEOPLE...'

'WHAT? WHY?'

'YOU TOLD THAT MAN TO FUCK OFF EARLIER AND JUST BLEW A TOWN UP...GIVE ME THAT HAND-SET...IS IT ON? FUCK'S SAKE, HOWIE! MY VOICE IS COMING OUT...JUST...LET GO OF IT...'

'FINE...YOU DO IT.'

'I WILL, HONESTLY BLOODY HELL...RIGHT... HELLO? AS MUCH AS WE LOOK LIKE COMPLETE TWATS WE ARE HERE TO HELP... please do not fire at us so...is it still on? I don't think it's working...Nick? It's **NOT WORK-ING...NO IT'S BACK ON...ER...**please do not fire...**FUCK MY TITS THIS IS SHIT... RIGHT...WE'RE COMING IN TO KILL EVERYTHING...NOT YOU! THE BADDIES... THE THE...I GIVE UP...HOWIE, JUST DRIVE IN...'**

'We're awesome,' Blowers mumbles, moving his head for Marcy's arse to go past.

'Right, I'm back in your team,' Marcy says, beaming a pained smile at Blowers.

'My willy might dribble when we fight.'

'Why? Does it turn you on?' Blowers asks.

'No! I meant…'

'FOCUS,' Clarence says, 'we're going in…'

'We all going in?' Howie asks. 'What about Roy? We can't take his van into that lot. Hang on…*Roy? Come into the Saxon. Paula, you stay with Reggie. Heather, will Paco come with us without you?*'

'*Er…not sure. I can try? Hang on. I can come in with all of you.*'

'*No we need to keep you back guarding Reggie.*'

'*What about Mo and Blinky? I thought they guarded him?*'

'*Er yes, yes they do but we're taking on a big horde so I kinda might need both of them.*'

'*That makes sense…hang on, I'll try and get Paco to you.*'

'Really lost the mojo for a fight now,' Marcy says.

'Can you pull me back up please?' Nick asks.

'Who?' Marcy asks.

'Fucking anyone…all the blood has gone to my head…holy shit! Cheers Clarence…whoa…dizzy now.'

A knock on the back doors. Dave pushes them open. Roy nods politely, passing in his longbow before clambering up. 'Everyone okay? Bit tight in here isn't it.'

'Is Heather coming?' Howie asks.

'They'll all be dead of old age before we get there,' Marcy carries on muttering, adding a tut from being poked by the end of the longbow. 'That was my boob.'

'Er so,' Heather says, looking into the back of the Saxon with Paco standing large and growly at her side. His arms bulging. His fists clenched. His whole manner ready to kill for sight of the infected. 'Paco, you get in…you're going with them for a bit.'

Paco growls and bulges.

'Paco, go in there.'

Paco growls a bit more.

'Paco, go in…' she grabs his arm to push but his tensed stature prevents motion. 'I'll get in first...' she climbs up, squeezing them back into the tight space. 'Right, Paco...you come in. No seriously, Paco! You have to come in here...yay! Yay for Paco. Right. I'll get out...er, I can't get past now.'

'My boob again.'

'Does Paco have a dribbly willy?'

The bum shuffle commences again. Dave, Mo and Blinky all squeezing along the seats to give Heather room to go over them to get round Paco. Grunts and huffs. Feet trodden on. Nick's nose prodded by the end of an arrow while the longbow carries on squishing Marcy's boob.

'Got it,' Heather says, dropping from the back of the Saxon. 'No! You stay there...' Paco goes forward to follow her. His eyes fixed on her, the woman he will always stay with, the woman he will never leave and neither man nor beast will stop him. 'Not gonna work is it?' she says as he drops out to growl and bulge. 'Okay, so we'll both stay back?'

'Shame,' Howie says, 'he's good in scrap and there's a lot of them.'

'Well, do you want me to come too then?' Heather asks. 'I'm happy to.'

'What's going on?' Paula asks, walking over to the back of the Saxon.

'Paco won't stay in there without me,' Heather explains.

'I know,' Howie says. 'Get Reginald in here with us...then we can all go and Paula and Heather can stay inside the Saxon with Reggie while we get out.'

'Good idea,' Clarence says. 'Paula? Get Reggie.'

'I'll get Reggie,' Paula says.

'Are you being serious?' Marcy asks. 'Where the hell are they going to stand?'

'Hey now,' Howie says. 'Let's have a glass half full day.'

'Prick.'

'I heard that.'

'You were meant to.'

'Gosh, that is rather full,' Reginald says. Clutching his bag of books.

'Just get in,' Marcy snaps.

'Paco, come on...' Heather says, clambering back in. Paco follows, growling and bulging.

'That's a big step,' Reginald says. 'How do you chaps jump up so easily?'

'Just get in.'

'Yes, Marcy I am trying. Oh, Paco is picking me up...that's very kind of you. Gosh, this is a squeeze isn't it? I say, there is no room for Paula.'

'Go in the front,' Marcy shouts through the press.

'No,' Paula says flatly, trying to work out how to fit in.

'Paula, you'll never fit in,' Roy says. 'Go up the front with Clarence.'

'Everyone just budge up,' Clarence says.

'We fucking are,' Marcy snaps. 'That longbow is right on my tit.'

'Lucky longbow.'

'Who said that? Cookey? Was that you?' Marcy asks.

'No. I'm worried my willy will dribble.'

'Just go up the front,' Nick says. 'We'll be there in a minute.'

'Right,' Paula says, 'front then...er...am I closing these doors or leaving them open?'

'Close them,' Blowers says. 'Or we'll fall out when we move off.'

Doors slam and a muttering Paula stalks to the front as the passenger door opens to see a wincing Clarence staring down. She glares back, narrowing her eyes before clambering up while in the distance several hundred infected lay siege to a squat building.

She sinks down on his lap as he closes the door. Seconds of silence pass.

'Is Paula in?' Marcy asks.

'Yep,' she says tightly.

'Er...so are we going then?' Marcy asks.

'Yep,' Howie says brightly, 'isn't this nice? All of us together?'

'I fucking hate you,' Marcy says.

'Very nice,' Howie says, enjoying his spatial freedom.

'You're not getting that blowjob later.'

'Marcy!' Paula snaps to the giggles and sniggers in the Saxon, turning on Clarence's lap with an effort to look down the back and squashing a breast into his face in the process. 'Oh god, I am so sorry… was that my boob?'

'I wouldn't worry, Roy's bow is all over mine,' Marcy says. 'CAN WE GO PLEASE?'

'Charlie, we're going in now. Er…hold back till we get out then do that charging thing.'

'Will do.'

'Right well,' Howie says, pushing his foot down on the accelerator. 'In we go…'

Clarence plays a statue. Paula turns to face the front. Clarence wishes she wouldn't turn on his lap in that way.

'Mr Howie?'

'Yes, Blowers?'

'We're not fishtailing are we?'

'I was going to…do you not want to fishtail?'

Lots of replies come back with heartfelt and earnest requests not to fishtail.

'Seriously, you dare…you fucking dare…' is Marcy's response.

'We do get a lot when we fishtail,' Howie says. 'How about I drive through them? That always gets a few.'

'That's okay,' Blowers says.

'Straight line,' Nick says.

'No jolting, my willy will dribble.'

'No just stop and we'll get out and fight like normal people,' Marcy says.

'We need to make a bit of space,' Howie says. 'Otherwise we can't get out. I'll just do a few…er…so don't hate me but…BRACE!'

The juddering starts. The mighty Saxon, made heavier by the sheer weight of bodies within, ploughs a furrowed course through the outer ranks. A battering ram going deep then wide to create space. The Saxon rocks and jolts, bangs and sways making Paula almost slide off Clarence's lap onto Howie's. Clarence grabs out, his arms going round her waist in reaction to stop the slide. She feels the pull back into his body.

'I say, are they attacking us?' Reginald asks, unable to turn from facing the back doors.

'Not yet, Reggie,' Howie says.

'Very interesting.'

'I'll try again,' Howie says, turning the wheel to back in.

The jolting commences again. The shuddering lurch that rocks the heavy vehicle on its suspension and Paula on Clarence's lap. Her hands now on his arms still wrapped round her waist. Her fingers feeling the hairs on his arms.

'Any difference?' Reginald asks.

'Nope,' Howie says.

'A most interesting change of behaviour. I say, Mr Howie. Would you mind driving out of this gathering?'

'Out?' Howie shouts from the front, trying to hear over the bumps, bangs and squelchy noises.

'Yes. Out.'

'You want us to go out?' Howie asks. 'We only just got in.'

'Yes yes but I would like to see their reaction.'

'Can we stop fucking about please,' Marcy snaps, trying to push the longbow from her boob.'

'I guess we could aim in from the side and shoot them,' Howie says. 'Clarence? What do you think?'

Clarence swallows at the touch of Paula's fingertips on his arms. Her heart thudding so loud he can feel it through her back.

'Clarence?'

'WHAT?' Clarence booms, snapping his head to Howie. 'GET THE BASTARDS...'

Clarence, too caught up in the touch of Paula's fingers on his arm, and thinking he missed the cue to attack, pushes his door open and with a deft twist that belies his size drops out while depositing Paula carefully on the seat. Of course, with the Saxon still in motion he stumbles, trips, flails and goes down.

'SHIT!' Howie shouts, hitting the brakes to slew the Saxon as Paula cries out at seeing Clarence fall. Instinct kicks in. Pure blind instinct that has her wrenching the door open and jumping out to run back. A flick of a switch, the beat of a heart and the infected see Clarence out and down and as one, they switch to turn to snarl and charge. The big man starts to rise, shock etched on his face at the realisation of jumping from a moving vehicle. They engulf him. He swats a few away but the bodies hitting the back of his knees take him back down.

'OUT OUT OUT...' Howie dives over the seat to scrabble and drop from the open passenger door.

Paula hits first. Her knife in hand to stab down as she tries to yank a man from the pile. He turns snarling, wild eyed like a rabid beast. The point of her blade jabs his throat then rips out. A spray of arterial blood arcs, coating her face but she drives on, diving into the writhing mound stabbing frenzied and crazed as more infected pile in.

'*CHARLIE...IN NOW,*' Blowers orders through the radio as chaos and calamity ensue within the Saxon.

Blinky drops to crawls, pushing her hand between Reginald's thighs to reach the door handle he is pawing at.

'Oh I say,' Reginald says in alarm.

'I'm gay,' she grunts, groping for the handle, 'unless you're Dave.'

'Indeed,' Reginald says politely. She grasps the handle, twists and goes through his legs as the Saxon floods with daylight and a sea of infected faces charging at them. 'Ah,' Reginald says mildly. 'Got some angry chaps coming at the back doors...'

As Blinky goes out to charge, so Paco goes through Reginald, so Blowers, Cookey and Nick try to go over the front seats at the same time, wedging themselves with shouted curses as Meredith scrabbles over them.

'ON JESS,' Charlie roars the words. Jess explodes out, the power bunched in her muscles driving her on. Axe out and swinging. The tether on her wrist.

Dave goes up through the hole with Mo right behind them. Knives out, flicking to press against forearms as they run across the roof and land deftly by the mound. Meredith runs in, leaping to gain the top of the pile.

The lads fall from the Saxon, tangled limbs, legs everywhere but heads turned to see the mound and the more infected coming in.

'FORM A LINE,' Blowers bellows, desperately trying to get free from Nick and Cookey. He rolls away, springs up and instantly drops to the boxer stance at the lunging figures coming at him. Hard punches driven into noses, jaws and skulls. The pain in his hand from the missing finger hurts like hell and his vision is weird from the loss of an eye but years of skill and the thing inside work skilfully to buy his mates time to get up. A hand on the back of his belt. Pressure applied to pull him back. He goes willingly as Nick flies past swinging his axe round in a mighty heave as Cookey presses the axe into Blowers' hands.

'BLINKY...TO ME...' Blowers roars. 'HEATHER...GET OUR RIFLES READY...'

Blinky headbutts one down, grabs another by the arm and swings it into the others coming. She slams the back doors closed, securing Reggie inside then grabs Paco.

'HOLD THESE DOORS...HOLD THESE FUCKING DOORS...'

She runs off, fighting and battering her way through the chaos to reach Blowers and scoop the axe thrown from the Saxon by Heather.

'CAN'T GET 'EM OFF,' Howie shouts. 'GET PACO...'

'Fuck it,' Blinky mutters, she runs back, fighting and battering her way through the chaos to reach Paco busting a head open on the back step. 'WITH ME...' she grabs his wrist, heedless to the look of rage on his face. 'NEED YOU...' she goes back, dragging him in her wake. Heather drops out, a machete like Marcy's gripped in her hand. She runs to reach Paco, grabbing his wrist with Blinky to drag him through.

'GET 'EM PACO...' she shouts, pushing him at the mound. 'GET 'EM...'

Paco and Blinky go in. They go hard and fast with hands that grip legs, arms and anything grabbable to throw and discard. Bodies sail through the air. His monstrous strength working with ease. What was chaos before becomes wilder, harder, demented even and for a few glorious seconds the horde wilt from the combined ferocity of Blinky and Paco, from the utter viciousness of two people who have no voices in their heads telling them a thing cannot be done.

The sound of the horse reaches them before the sight is gained. A drumming of hooves that grows closer as Charlie aims for the back of the Saxon and veers to charge down the side mere feet in front of the line.

Instant space is gained. Jess's form and weight simply taking them away.

'FIGHT OUT...'

Blowers gives the commands, leading his team in a solid line to work towards the mound. His intent to circle it, to buy time for Paco to work.

'*COMING BACK*...' Charlie shouts.

'HOLD,' Blowers orders. Roy with his sword in his right hand shoots a hand out to pull Marcy back as Jess once again clears the compression in front of them.

'TAKE   GROUND...ADVANCE...Nick...help   Paco,' Blowers spits the words out.

A roar from the front of the building. Men and women run out clutching weapons, bats, sticks, knives and anything able to inflict harm.

'GO BACK...' Cookey shouts, seeing the folly of their actions. 'CHARLIE...'

'ON IT,' Charlie twists, sending the signal to Jess who rears to turn on the spot. 'GO BACK...GO BACK...' she cuts the survivors off, screaming at them to turn away. They falter and hesitate. Buoyed up to help and fight. Ready to kill and protect their ground. 'GO BACK,' Charlie screams again, charging the horse at them. They scream out, turning to flee.

Sensation at Blinky's side. Reginald in there with them. His hands covered in blood as the small man grabs an ankle and tries to pull. His hands slick and sliding over the flesh. He cries out, grips harder and pulls the body free with a long wet sucking sound as it pops out.

'RIFLES...' Blowers shouts. 'HEATHER...MARCY...GET OUR RIFLES...'

The two peel away, running for the Saxon to clamber up and in to grab rifles. Marcy takes two, gasping for air as she drops them down by the Saxon then goes back for more held out by Heather.

'MAGAZINES...' Blowers shouts.

'Grab a bag,' Marcy says. Heather snatches one from the back, flinging out it.

'CHARLIE...MOVE TO THE SIDE WHEN I SAY,' Blowers runs back, grabs two rifles and darts back into the line. Cookey takes his. Both dropping to knees as Marcy and Heather rush forward to join them. 'NOW CHARLIE...'

A jolt and Charlie rides Jess on towards the building. A pause. A count of three then four rifles open fire. Dave whips his pistols out, firing both one after the other. Mo the same, both standing side by side with arms extended. Blinky snatches a look round and sees the greater threat is to the majority. She moves quickly, leaping into the Saxon and up through the hole to detach the GPMG then drops down, boots the back doors open and hip fires the machine gun into the horde. Her body shuddering from the recoil as the spent casings spew out glittering and shiny.

Clarence, flat on his stomach and feeling somewhat ashamed at jumping from a moving vehicle and then getting taken down so easily, starts to get angry. Really very angry. Really really absurdly angry but the final touch is the sensation of teeth biting his backside. An actual infected biting his actual arse.

'SHIT!' Nick grabs Reggie to pull him away from the eruption of Mount Clarence sending bodies flying in all directions.

'MY ARSE,' Clarence roars, spinning round to try and see which one did it. He grabs a man, breaks him and throws him away. 'BIT MY ARSE...' he grabs and breaks, lifting human bodies with ease to send them slamming into the hard front corner of the Saxon. 'THEY BIT MY ARSE...' A flap of material hands open on his backside showing his bare cheeks and the neat imprints of teeth. 'WHO DID IT?' Clarence roars, stamping with Paco in a demented dance of giants breaking mere mortals underfoot. 'WHO BIT MY ARSE...'

With order gained, rifles firing, Blinky doing a *Rambo* at the back doors and Clarence enraged so the fight ends quickly and the tremendous noise eases down to the odd single shot fired, the dull pop of skulls busting from Jess and the snarls from Meredith as she hunts through to seek those still clinging to what they call life.

'I fucking love this gun,' Blinky says, jumping out to walk round with the machine gun braced in her hip.

'Suits you,' Blowers says casually, breathing hard from the fight.

'MY ARSE...BIT MY ARSE...'

'Cheeky,' Cookey quips.

'Howie, quick. Clarence has been bit,' Marcy says. 'Throw a grenade somewhere.'

'Seriously, best gun ever...oh shit...' Blinky burps, bends over and pukes.

'My arse,' Clarence mutters, turning in circles trying to look at his own bum.

'Why did you jump out?' Howie asks, smearing the back of a bloodied filthy hand across his filthy face.

'Thought we were here,' Clarence rumbles. 'That's not important...they bit my arse.'

'Cheeky,' Cookey quips again.

'Ha!' Nick bursts out laughing. 'I just got it.'

'Got what?' Blowers asks.

'Cheeky,' Nick says. 'Clarence's arse...cheeky?'

'Eh? Oh nicely done...' he says with a laugh.

'NOT FUNNY.'

'Yeah not funny,' Blowers says quickly at the glare from Clarence.

'Well you're not a zombie,' Howie says. 'That's a good thing isn't it.'

'I don't like that bloody word and I don't like being bitten on the bloody arse.'

'Don't jump from moving vehicles then.'

'I was flustered.'

'Flustered? At what?'

'Because...' Clarence fires back, suddenly aware of every face looking at him, apart from one who keeps her gaze averted. 'Just was...'

'Well done, Clarence,' Cookey says. 'Being immune I mean...'

'Well done, Clarence,' Nick says.

'Sod off,' Clarence rumbles.

'Infected not immune. I do keep saying that. I really do...'

'Who let you out of your office?' Marcy asks.

'He jumped in to help,' Nick says, 'cheers for that, Reggie.'

'Disgusting,' Reginald says, holding his dirty hands up. 'Urgh it smells. I say, does anyone have a tissue?'

'Hello?' a voice calls from the squat building.

'Not a word,' Marcy snaps at Howie, waggling a finger at him.

'Didn't say anything,' Howie says.

'Who are we looking for?' she asks.

'Ahmet Demir,' Heather says.

'I'll sort it. Paula, you coming with me?'

'Yep.'

'Good, everyone have a drink and...stuff,' Marcy says, flapping her hands about. 'Oh shit, sorry...er...Corporal Blowers. Is it okay if I...'

'S'fine, Marce,' Blowers says.

'Ask 'em if they got a disabled badge.'

'Will do, Cookey,' Marcy says, stopping to peer at Clarence's backside. 'Your arse is so hairy.'

'Thanks,' Clarence mutters.

'Skin's broken...that's you all sorted then...'

'Guess so,' he mutters, still smarting from it all.

'Oh give over,' Marcy says, reaching up to kiss his cheek, 'well done.'

'Thanks, Marcy,' he says, his voice a bit softer.

'Well done,' Paula says, half leaning in to kiss then pulling back as Clarence leans in then pulls back. 'Er so...that's good,' she says, wincing while hesitantly moving back in.

'GREAT,' Clarence booms when she offers him the briefest of

pecks on the cheek and as Blinky nudges Mo with a *told-you-so* expression.

'Not seeing it,' Mo whispers.

'So fucking blind.'

'HELLO, CAN YOU TELL US WHO YOU ARE PLEASE?'

'WE'RE FROM AVON...'

'Howie! Yes I'm just coming to talk to you,' Marcy calls out. 'Right, lovely...so, which one of you is Ahmet Demir?'

CHAPTER TWENTY-ONE

'I hate you.'

Cookey bends forward in the chair. His chest heaving. Tears streaming down his face.

'I fucking hate you,' Blowers says.

It's too much. It actually hurts. Cookey waves his hand, trying to speak but unable to draw sufficient air before setting himself off again. He turns to look at Nick on his knees with his head bent. Mo on the other side holding his stomach. Charlie braying. Blinky laughing so hard she can't see properly.

'Such a cock, Cookey.'

That just makes them worse. Marcy turns away. She can't watch anymore. She can't see it. She holds her hand over her mouth then glances back and almost squeals.

Even Heather can't stop laughing. The sight of it. The effort taken. Paula wipes her eyes. Roy tries to recover himself and blinks the tears away.

Blowers turns his head to look at Cookey through his one good eye. Cookey glances up at him and howls so hard he almost falls off his chair.

'Took all day,' Cookey gasps, flapping his hand in the air towards Blowers.

Blowers stands and lets the white stick unfold to full extension. The hinged joints pinging to a rigid structure. He reaches up to squeeze the inflatable parrot on his shoulder that gives a single miserable squawk that makes Meredith's head cock over and everyone else burst out laughing. He adjusts the black eye patch over his ruined eye and twitches the disabled parking badge hanging from string round his neck. Cookey cries. Charlie sinks down to her knees. Nick gasps.

Blowers walks over to stand next to Meredith in front of the Saxon and the visual image is complete. It's complete enough to even make Dave smile, albeit a twitch at the corner of his lips.

It's the dog that finishes it. Blowers, in his eye patch, with his parrot, wearing a disabled parking badge round his neck, with a white stick in his hand in front of the Saxon adorned in larger disabled parking badges are all good, but Meredith wearing sunglasses and a high visibility reflective yellow vest with *Guide Dog* written on the side in black marker and another disabled badge hanging from her neck is the final touch.

'All day,' Cookey gasps, trying to look at Blowers and Meredith before crumpling into a heap.

'You fucker,' Blowers says, finally spotting a new axe propped against the Saxon with the shaft spray painted white.

'I shall pee myself,' Charlie says breathlessly.

'A white axe? I'm not using a white axe...'

Mid-afternoon. A day of days. A morning spent seeking immunes from town to village. Skirmishes fought. Scraps won. Statements made with fire, smoke, death and victory to mark their presence. A day in which Cookey painstakingly sought each item while the others kept Blowers distracted with questions and conversations. Constantly asking him about tactics and strategy while Cookey grabbed disabled parking badges from cars, ran into houses and shops and even broke the window on a builders van to get the yellow tabard inside.

A day in which Marcy worked hard, fought well and took the lessons seriously, morphing with increasingly seamless effort from Blowers' trainee to an elder who stepped in to make sure Howie didn't speak to any survivors after having a scrap. He was fine at other times, but not right after a fight when his blood was still up.

Ahmet Demir was inside Northfield Community Centre. A man of Turkish origin who had worked fast to rally his neighbours and fortify the community centre. A man who lead to gather supplies and weapons and kept his small group safe. A man who fought back when the infected came sniffing and snarling. A man who was cut by a fingernail ten days ago but kept it to himself and a man who wept quietly when told he was immune. He refused to leave his group and it was clear his refusal was absolute. In the end, Paula and Marcy told them all to head for the fort but made it clear to Ahmet to tell no one until he spoke to Lilly.

After that it was hit and miss but far more successful than they ever imagined. Eight more immunes were found. A paltry figure given the populace before the outbreak but a stunning victory against the other player, and a victory gained quietly while attacking and killing any infected they found on the way.

A day in which Paula and Clarence found it harder and harder to be near each other while Blinky nudged Mo who kept saying he doesn't see it.

Now they rest outside a small café in the grounds of a gloriously lush green park with a cable running from the van to the coffee machine inside. Skin grimy, hair slick from sweat, boots filthy, clothes marked and the flap of material on Clarence's backside held together with a safety pin and a strip of duct tape over the top.

Assault rifles rest against chairs. Axes and hand weapons within reach. Knives in scabbards on belts, all used, all cleaned and made ready for the next fight.

As the laughing eases to chuckles, Charlie takes Jess from the horsebox to let her graze the lush grass while having bottles of spring water poured over her back and sides. The lads help, using brushes and bare hands to help sluice the sweat and gore away.

'Need a hand in there?' Roy calls out, twisting in his seat to look at the busted in door of the café.

'We're fine,' Paula shouts while laying the mugs out on the counter top.

'You've got to do something,' Marcy whispers, the two of them alone in small café.

'It'll pass,' Paula whispers back.

'I thought you were sorting it out.'

Paula shrugs while rearranging the mugs in order of sugar taken but really to give her hands something to do.

'When you went in that place together. That block of flats.'

'Tried,' Paula says bluntly.

'And?' Marcy asks.

'And nothing. We sorted it then...'

'Then what?'

'I messed up again,' she says glumly. 'We cleared the air then I made this terrible joke about his willy poking my back...'

'You didn't!'

'Shush, yes I did. Oh don't look at me like that. We were both tongue tied and being awkward...anyway he smiled and I thought it was okay so like a complete moron I went to kiss his cheek...'

'Paula,' Marcy groans, shaking her head.

'I know, I was flustered and not thinking straight...' Paula says, moving the mugs round without any clue to the order she gained a moment again. 'We almost kissed again...then Mr Kettering came out.'

Marcy tuts, her arms folded as she leans back on the counter and gives a sideways look to Paula. 'It's so obvious.'

'I know,' Paula says, still pushing the mugs about.

'You're acting like a teenager round him.'

'Maybe Roy and I should leave.'

'Don't be so bloody stupid,' Marcy huffs. 'Howie wouldn't let you and can you imagine Mo and Cookey if you left? They'd be heartbroken...everyone would be.'

'What then?' Paula asks. The day has been brilliant. Progressive, busy and constant but marred by her inability to think clearly when she is near Clarence.

'Finish it with Roy,' Marcy says. 'Do it later, tell him you rushed into it and all that stuff...if nothing else it buys you some time.'

'Reggie told me off this morning,' Paula says, her voice low and dour as she finally looks up from the mugs to Marcy. 'Said I had to stop anything and unity must come first.'

'Sod Reggie,' Marcy scoffs. 'You leave him to me if he says anything. Tell Roy tonight. It doesn't have to be weird, Christ you only just met him. That machine is ready. Which mug is which?'

'Fuck knows.'

'Jesus,' Marcy chuckles, holding the first mug under the spout, 'you have got it bad...I'm not taking over doing lists and stuff just so you know...hey, you should jump in with me working in Blowers' team...'

'No thanks.'

'No seriously, we could pair up and be all super soldiers, honestly, Paula. Try it. You don't have time to think and mope with Blowers being all bossy.'

'Nah,' Paula says. 'Wouldn't be fair on him.'

'On who? Blowers?'

'Yeah, telling me what to do...'

'He wouldn't give a shit. He's not like that. Think about it, even if you just do today...Blinky? Can you take Reggie's tea over?'

'On it,' Blinky says, running to take the cup held out by Marcy.

'I'll do it,' Charlie says, taking the mug from Blinky as she marches past.

'Why?' Blinky asks, holding the mug away.

'Because I want to ask Reginald something.'

'*Because I want to ask Reginald something,*' Blinky mimics, 'I'm Charles and I'm a clever fucker...did you see me on the GPMG?'

'Yes.'

'Did I look awesome?'

'You did, can I have that mug please.'

'You're a mug. Say I looked awesome.'

'You looked awesome, Blinky,' Charlie says, placing her hands on her hips.

'GAY,' Blinky shouts, 'I can say that cos I am,' she adds with a nod. 'Love that gun. Fucking awesome.'

'Great, can I have the mug now?'

'Fist me,' Blinky says, handing it over.

'Thank you.'

'Love you, Charles.'

'Love you, Blinky.'

'Coffee's ready,' Marcy shouts, earning an exodus from the tables and those cleaning Jess to start walking then running towards the café.

'Reginald?' Charlie asks, knocking on the open door while leaning in to show him the mug. 'Tea.'

'Ah now this is a pleasant surprise,' Reginald says, looking up from the papers and notepads open on his desk.

'Did you see Blowers?' Charlie asks, handing the mug over.

'I did yes, very humorous. Indeed, and if I am not mistaken I saw Dave smiling.'

'I didn't see that,' Charlie says. 'I was too busy crying.'

'Ah yes, yes the tears of laughter shall triumph over the tears of sadness, gosh this is nice tea,' Reginald says, peering at her over the rim of the mug held close to his lips before giving a theatrical sigh. 'I am beginning to learn that look.'

'What look?' she asks innocently.

'You are forever nipping at my heels my dear.'

'I didn't say anything.'

'Jolly good,' he states before taking a sip.

'Lani?'

'Good lord, can't a man enjoy his Darjeeling?'

'Am I right? Is that what happens if we lose unity?'

'Please stop second guessing.'

'I am right, aren't I. I don't see it though. I mean yes she was turned then turned back but I struggled with the idea that her reversal back to infected stems from breaking her connection with the group. Then I considered that you have Neal's books so of course you may have read something that takes it beyond mere conjecture. What does concern me though is the fact of the greater collective hive mind of the other side...'

'This is nice tea.'

'Lani was originally infected by Marcy. One might assume that if she then succumbed to the virus a second time that she would revert to being within Marcy's hive mind. That did not happen. From all accounts, it was clear that Lani became part of the infection. Now does that mean our hive mind is an inclusive separation *within* the greater hive mind?'

'I do like Darjeeling.'

'Now, Mr Howie and Lani had sex in that room. I wasn't there but, you know, everyone talks about and Marcy seems to take great pleasure in reminding Howie every chance she gets. So does that mean Lani retained some of her own character? I mean she must have done for Mr Howie to have sex with her. Anyway, my point is...you think that if the bond breaks then we can succumb to the infection. Am I right?'

'Earl Grey is also a very nice afternoon tea. Very refreshing.'

'But then what caused it?' Charlie asks, having given the matter great thought all day while riding Jess, fighting hordes, saving immunes, flirting with Cookey and joking in the back of the Saxon.

'Caused what?' Reginald asks, blinking at her.

'Lani reverting to infected. What caused it?'

'I am on a tea break,' Reginald says pointedly.

'Possibly her own perception was that she was rejected by the group. She heard a snatched conversation over the radio and that was enough. What else caused it? What else *could* have caused it? There is no medical history, no knowledge of pre-existing conditions or her mental state prior to all of this. Is there?' she asks.

'No.'

'Hmmm, I don't see it, Reginald. Emotions are the result of chemical reactions that *enable* us to think we feel certain things. The very act of procreation and sexual urges are from chemical reactions so Lani, given the fact she was badly injured only a short time before it all happened, was rendered weak initially which affected the chemicals within her body, then she suffered shock from hearing the radio transmission which continued to alter her chemical composition which enabled the infected to take hold.'

'Jolly good,' Reginald mumbles, sipping his tea.

'You cannot assume because one reverted or succumbed to the infection that we all will. Ah but then we are not immune. We *already are* infected so yes, possibly you are correct but then what is preventing us succumbing to it now? Is it the hive mind? Is it Mr Howie? Marcy? This is most perplexing.'

'Most perplexing,' Reginald mutters.

'For my own part, I don't see it.'

'See what?' Reginald asks, looking over the rim of his mug again.

'That we can succumb so easily and we're only held safe for want of a better word by the current hive mind. Are we part of the greater collective? Is that it? Why won't you tell me? I get very flustered not knowing things.'

'Indeed.'

'Does Mr Howie know?'

'No.'

'Why not?'

'Because I haven't told him.'

'Will you tell him?'

'Not yet.'

'Why not?'

'He is busy. As am I.'

'You should tell him and tell everyone else.'

'Why would I do that?'

'Because they have a right to know.'

'To know what exactly, Charlie?'

'That Lani is what might happen if they lose unity.'

'Not yet.'

'Why not?'

'Gracious you are most demanding today, Charlie.'

'Why not?'

'Because there are other factors at play here. A great many other factors. What you have deduced is but one strand of the tapestry and it has to be weighed against every other fact known, and not just facts but all of the objective, the subjective, the supposition and the conjecture. You are a remarkable young lady...gosh that was patronising. It is not my intent to patronise you but please, and I ask again, please stop nipping at my blasted heels.'

'Sorry, Reginald.'

'Don't be sorry. I am genuinely impressed that despite the hard work you have engaged in that you have had the capacity to process and lead to conclusion and to present your conclusion with a valid argument.'

'Thank you, that means a lot.'

'You are most welcome. How are things with Cookey?'

'Why do you ask that?'

'Good lord, woman! I am merely asking after your welfare as someone who has a great deal of respect and admiration for you.'

'Oh. Okay. Yeah fine. He's lovely.'

'He is indeed.'

'Do you like him?' she asks. Lips pursed and a light frown showing as she studies him closely.

Reginald sips his tea, his mind working far faster than even Charlie can imagine. Strands of thought all running together. A whole sequence of calculations within the time it takes to sip his tea and give a pleasurable sigh. Charlie is a young lady. Reginald is old enough to be her father. She respects Reginald. She admires him in the way of a student to a tutor. In the way of Mo to Dave. Reginald suspects there was discord in Charlie's home life before the outbreak. Comments made and observations gained. The question Charlie posed was not merely to seek Reginald's opinion but bordering on seeking his validation of her potential suitor. She is remarkable, intelligent, gifted even but still very young. He smiles warmly as he looks at her. 'I do like Cookey. I like him very much.' He spots the relief in her eyes and the smile that forms slowly. 'He is very annoying but a most endearing and genuine young man,' he studies for reaction, having no real experience of romance but knowing the great weight others place in it and their eternal wish for everyone else to *like* their partner choices. 'You suit each other,' he adds, wondering if that was a comment too far.

'Thank you,' she beams, suddenly all warm and gooey inside.

'You are most welcome, now may I enjoy my Darjeeling or shall we discuss the Greek onset of democracy and how it shaped the world?'

'It's fine,' she says with a laugh. 'You coming out?'

'In a moment…and Charlie,' he says as she jumps down from the van then leans in to look at him. 'Our conversations are private.'

'Yes of course,' she says, offering another smile.

His own smile fades as she walks off. The fret and worry showing clear as he exhales slowly. Charlie's guess means he has to work faster. Would Paula being with Clarence or ending her relationship with Roy cause a shock similar to that which Lani suffered? Does the strength of Roy's attachment to Paula equal that to Lani's emotional attachment to Howie? Roy's bond to the group is strengthening every day and the more his bond grows the greater emotional fall he could suffer when he realises Paula is in love with Clarence. Does he assume everyone knew? Does he assume everyone is laughing behind his back? Reginald cannot allow him to leave this group with a grudge knowing he could turn and pick them off at great range with his bow? But what if he stays? What if he puts a brave face on and says he is fine with it and all is well then in the night the chemicals released in his body take him into the same state as Lani and he tries to slit Clarence's throat or shoots Howie while Dave and Mo are outside on watch? They need Roy. They need his skill and it comes down to worth. Who is more worthy? Paula or Roy?

This morning was never about seeing if Dave and Mo were immune to the bite. It was to see how far they would go.

Now it comes down to Paula or Roy?

Which one does Reginald tell Dave and Mo poses a threat to Mr Howie. Which one is lost to a stray bullet, a broken neck or a knife across the throat in the confusion of battle to retain the unity of the group?

Which one is to be executed?

His hands tremble as he places the cup on the desk and starts gathering his papers together. His face reflected the worry. His whole manner consumed with what must be done.

Pressure grows. Pressure builds. Pressure unrelenting that accelerates the momentum gained and it won't stop now. It can't stop now. He has to bring the next stage forward. It must be done now.

With his papers safely back in his bag he takes a moment to compose himself. To steady his nerves and the knot of fear in his gut. The very idea of telling Dave to kill Paula is abhorrent. Reginald likes Paula. He likes Roy too but the atmosphere between Paula and Clarence is worsening with every passing hour, and Roy, as seemingly clueless as he is will soon see it.

His hands move to adjust the tie knot that isn't there. He mutters at the annoyance of not having a tie to adjust and takes his glasses off to clean the lenses. A moment later he steps out from the van and walks casually with his expression now one of affable politeness. Everyone else is at the tables. All drinking coffee, eating snacks and talking happily. He spots the distance between Clarence and Paula and detects the trace awkwardness in the air that only cements what must be done.

'I say, that was a most refreshing cup of tea,' he says by way of letting everyone know he is there.

'I made that,' Marcy says proudly.

'Gosh really?' Reginald says dourly, 'can I take my compliment back?'

'Cheeky sod,' she laughs.

'You okay?' Howie asks, seeing the flicker on Reginald's face that tells him the little man has something on his mind.

'Fine, yes fine,' Reginald says, 'are we all here? I have something I wish to say if I may?'

'Oh no,' Howie groans. 'Is it bad?'

'Gosh no, well, sad perhaps but not bad per se. I believe the time has come to part company you see,' he says while pulling a disappointed expression.

'Eh?' Howie asks as the café falls to silence.

'I am afraid so. The time has come for us to part company with Heather and Paco.'

'Eh?' Howie asks.

'Why?' Marcy asks.

'Don't go, Heather,' Cookey says.

'Don't go,' Blinky says.

'Stay, Heather,' Nick adds.

'Good lord,' Reginald tuts as Heather listens in with a sharp look.

'What's going on?' she asks.

'Indeed, well, to explain fully I would say that our objective today was to mark our presence in this area, which we have done, and to gather immunes to send on to Lilly, which we have done, and for me to gather intelligence as we moved along, which I have now done. They are not attacking us on sight so quickly. That shows a development in behaviour. The other side is learning to work round us, which is very alarming. Heather, I rather think you and Paco should continue to seek the immunes while we start moving north. Of course, Mr Howie is the leader of this team of ne'er do wells so he may choose differently, but as strategist and tactician, I would advise this to be the best course of action.'

'Charles? I need a shit.'

'You can go, Blinky,' Paula says with a groan.

'Thanks, Miss Paula, Sir. I think it's coming out.'

'And thank you for sharing,' Paula says.

'Sir,' Blinky says, rushing off.

'Heather?' Howie says. 'Makes sense but it's completely up to you. We love you being with us...oh hang on, you don't like everyone looking at you. Er...right, everyone sod off and let me and Paula speak to Heather.'

'No it's fine,' Heather says as everyone starts to rise. She hates it but swallows the discomfort down and looks at Howie. 'We'll do what Reggie says.'

'Sure?' Howie asks.

'Yeah er...you're all nice. Like er...so I don't like people but...you're nice people and...it's er...I hate this.'

'It's okay,' Paula says. 'Everyone can go.'

'No,' Heather snaps. 'Sorry, I'm not snapping at you I just...I hate people looking at me.'

'We like you,' Marcy says.

'We do,' Clarence says.

'I know and...I like you all...but...right so, the immune people are important. We can do that and...I mean...I never thought I could like people but I do and...fuck me backwards this is hard as shit...FUCK!'

'Go on,' Cookey urges with a laugh, 'let it out.'

'Twat,' she laughs, grinning at him.

'Fact,' Cookey says.

'I don't know how you do it,' she tells him, 'making jokes in front of everyone like that...scares the hell out of me, right okay...I'm going to look up at everyone...I will...okay...here goes...' she looks up with a rush of panic to see only easy smiles and friendly eyes looking back at her. 'Yeah I hate it,' she quips, dropping her eyes but earning a chorus of laughs. 'Cheers but Paco and I will go our own way. We like you, I like you but I prefer being on my own.'

'Fair enough,' Howie says.

'Can't argue with honesty,' Clarence says, wincing at his own choice of words.

'Er is it okay if we go back to the fort...never got a chance to see Subi and...'

'Might be a good thing actually,' Howie says. 'Let Lilly know we're all well and check she's okay.'

'Let Lilly know if Maddox turns up,' Paula says.

'Good point,' Howie says. 'And make sure the immunes are okay. Sorted. We'll do that.'

'Ah I'm gutted,' Cookey says. 'I like Heather and Paco being with us.'

'A very sad thing,' Reginald says seriously with a deep nod while he clasps his hands behind his back. 'But time is against us and we must do too many things at once. We need to go north *and* offer safety to the people on the list. Staying together means we cannot do both.'

It also means the impact of any action taken against Paula or Roy is lessened and contained within the immediate team. Reginald knows such a situation cannot be helped but still feels the irritation of having a personal relationship threaten the harmony and potential objective. He thinks for a second, wondering why he gave such a positive affirmation to Charlie about her feelings regarding Cookey. Surely another relationship could pose further issues but then he also considers he is somewhat crap at romantic things and even the very best of tacticians make mistakes from time to time. Perhaps he should have discouraged Charlie.

He tunes back into the group and smiles at the flow of words going from the others to Heather.

CHAPTER TWENTY-TWO

The screen reflects on the face of the young man operating the controls. His hands making small adjustments to the two sticks. He risks a glance to the other workstation.

'Get your eyes back on your screen you fucking prick.'

He snaps back to his monitor at the harsh tone of the corporal.

Ten minutes pass before he dares shift position. They never used to work this long before. It was only ever short stints done on rotation to ensure maximum awareness was maintained.

They found a town with recent kills a few hours ago. The blood on the infected was still wet and he heard the corp tell the posh officer that it matched the intel reports. Then, an hour or so later, they saw the plumes of smoke from a town on fire. The birds-eye view showed it was centred on the centre of the town and a circuit of the area revealed the fresh kills outside a small squat building in the middle of some playing fields.

Northfield Community Centre. Not that the young man on the controls of the drone cared where the fuck Northfield Community Centre was. He cared only that his extended shift still had hours to go.

He watches the landscape glide underneath. A never-ending view of green fields, green hedges, green trees and snaking black-topped roads. Villages here and there. Church spires and the roofs of houses and cottages. Boring. He can't keep doing this. Day after day. Fourteen hours a day, sometimes more. He is dreaming of drones now. Having nightmares in which his hands are glued to the controls.

The drones are top-spec military surveillance systems. Super quiet with extended power supplies enabling hours of flight. It's mind-numbing. It wasn't at first. It was exciting seeing the infected here and there, gathering and attacking, running and chasing. Spotting survivors in the countryside and seeing the odd glimpse of hiding places. Even a few communes rigged up and last stands fought against numbers too great. Now it's just dull. Painfully, awfully, dreadfully dull. He might kill himself. His family must be dead. The world is over and spending another day in this dark room is in this awful place is too much.

He jerks forward at a glimpse of something. A large park by the looks of it. Wide open spaces and huge old oak trees dotted about. He operates the zoom, panning down to focus on the top of an old Saxon APC, one of the old training vehicles they used in Salisbury. He's got them. He's actually got them. A dark blue van next to the Saxon, a horsebox on the back just as the intel said. Another vehicle, a four-wheel drive. He pans out with his heart booming to adjust the tilt of the camera and feels a lurch at the people gathered round a set of tables outside a small building.

He zooms in, panning down with his eyes widening at the sight of them. He spots the assault rifles on the table and propped against chairs. A small man with glasses standing as though holding court. A huge dog. Men and women. 'Fuck me,' he mutters, zooming in on a total fitty. She is gorgeous. Like just stunning. She looks like one of the porn stars he used to watch on the internet.

'Corp?'

'What?' the voice behind him snaps. 'If you need another shit I'll batter your head until...'

'I think I found them...'

'Show me,' the corporal demands, striding across the room. 'Get back to your screen,' he orders the other lad looking over.

'There,' the drone operator says, pointing at the screen as he deftly pans back on the camera. 'Saxon...blue van...horsebox...'

'I don't need the fucking commentary.'

'Sorry, Corp,' the young soldier says, lost in his eagerness to please. 'And er...there...drinking coffee by the looks of it.'

The corporal leans forward to glare at the screen. His eyes flicking from face to face and copying the young soldier by lingering on the beautiful woman with the big chest. He stands up swiftly, clapping the soldier on his back. 'Hold it there...do not fucking move it.'

'Okay.'

The corporal marches out, slamming the door open as the other drone operator risks standing up to see. 'You got them?' he asks.

'Yeah,' the young soldier says. 'All of 'em, right fucking there having a fucking tea break.'

'Fuck,' the other drone operator says before quickly dropping back to his screen and controls at the sound of feet coming up the corridor.

'In here, Sir,' the corporal says, his tone now polite as he walks back in leading another man into the dark room.

'Stinks in here,' the other man observes drily. 'Show me.'

'Sir,' the young soldier says as the corporal and the other man stop behind him to watch the screen. He pans and adjusts to glide the view over the whole of the group then zooms in to move from face to face.

The other man stiffens. His eyes dark and set. His face a mask of distaste. 'That's them alright. I'll tell the Major. I suggest you get your men ready to go and bring them in, Corporal.'

CHAPTER TWENTY-THREE

'ROAD TRIP!' Cookey exclaims once goodbyes have been said and Heather and Paco have driven off.

'Christ,' Howie says, rubbing his jaw. 'Gonna be a long trip. Paula. You taking Cookey with you?'

'Alex can come with us if he wants,' she says.

'Paula loves me,' Cookey states proudly. 'She called me Alex.'

'Reggie?'

'I am terribly sorry, Mr Howie but alas there is no room.'

'I wasn't going to ask that. I was going to ask where we're going.'

'Going? We are going north.'

'Er yeah but like, the *north* is a bit, you know...vague?'

'Oh I see, right yes. Dave? Can you help and point out which direction the north is?'

'That way,' Dave says, extending an arm towards the north.

'Ah, there we go,' Reginald says.

'You want me to follow Dave's arm?' Howie asks. 'Don't we have a specific destination?'

'Yes we do, Mr Howie,' Reginald says brightly, standing outside the open door to the van as everyone else slowly loads up. 'The north is our specific destination.'

'Where in the north?'

'I have no idea. We shall have to look and seek.'

'Fuck me, north east? North west? True north? Scotland north?'

'Yes, I think those will do fine to start with, tally ho,' Reginald says, clambering up the step into the back of Roy's van.

'Bloody buggering arse shit and...Jesus,' he stops at the sight of Blowers with his black eye patch, inflatable parrot and disabled badge round his neck. 'Is funny though,' he adds with a grin.

'The eye patch is better to be honest,' Blowers says, 'the bandage was driving me nuts.'

'Righto, onwards to *the north* then, wherever that is.'

'It's in the north, Mr Howie.'

'Thanks, Cookey.'

'Welcome.'

'I had a massive shit.'

'Cheers, Blinky,' Howie says, walking to the front of the Saxon.

'Paula?' Marcy calls out. 'Come with us for a bit, let Reggie go up front with Roy.'

'Er...' Paula hesitates, faltering again with that lack of quick decision making she is normally so good at.

'A grand idea,' Reginald shouts from the back of the van. 'Your seat is at least soft whereas mine does somewhat chafe the backs of my legs.'

'Yeah okay,' Paula says, clambering up.

Howie takes his seat, smiling as Clarence gets comfy with a sideways glance.

'Alright big fella?' Howie asks.

'Yep.'

'Good day so far.'

'So far.'

'Marcy's enjoying it.'

'Yep.'

'Said she loves working with Blowers team.'

'Good,' Clarence says.

'Heather and Paco have gone off to save people and spread the word of the baby Jesus.'

Clarence lifts an eyebrow, 'I know. I was there.'

'So all is good,' Howie says slowly, 'or not?' he asks, shaking his head.

'It's fine,' Clarence says.

'Awesome. We all in?'

'Yep,' Blowers calls.

'To the north then...' he starts the engine that sputters and roars to life with that solid thrum moving through the vehicle making quiet conversation harder. He pulls away slowly, checking the fuel gauge. 'We'll need fuel soon.'

'Okay,' Clarence says, leaning over to look at the gauge.

From the park, they gain the exit road that feeds through the small town past the infected they cut down earlier and on to the country road that Howie hopes leads to a motorway somewhere. Not that it matters. Motorway. Country road. Anything will do it given the ridiculously broad objective they now have.

'Fucking north,' Howie mutters.

The back doors stay open. The air hot. The sun still bright and blazing down. The fields they pass show the first tinges of brown from the intense heat killing the grass and the branches of trees offer dappled sections of shade as they pass under.

Paula, Marcy and Charlie sit together, heads bowed with an intense yet quiet conversation underway. Nick goes up top to smoke and watch the world glide by while thinking of Lilly. Blowers, Cookey and Blinky share jokes and take the piss while Mo smiles sitting opposite Dave at the back doors.

The young lad turns his head to watch the way the shadows and sunlight strobe the windscreen of the van behind and the verges either side swooshing past.

They've had a busy day and it's not long before the warmth, the digestion of the food they ate and the steady rumble of the vehicle start to lull a few eyes that droop as heads go back to rest against the sides.

Marcy stretches her arm out to rest her fingers against Howie's neck, stroking gently. Charlie leans to pinch Cookey's nose as he dozes off, making him smile and chuckle before he shifts a bit to lean against her. Blowers and Blinky stagger their positions to stretch legs over the midsection, giving more room for Meredith to lie down with her nose just outside the lip of the back step.

Mo's eyes start to go. The lure of sleep tugging him down. He blinks and shakes his head, fighting to remain alert and watchful. A few minutes pass and he drifts again. His head slowly sinking to rest against the side of the van. Again, he snaps awake and instantly checks to see if Dave spotted it.

'Sleep,' Dave says, having spotted it.

'Nah, s'good,' Mo says trying to stifle the yawn. 'I'm fine...wide awake innit.'

Ten seconds later he snores softly with his head bouncing to the rhythm of the van.

'Bless, you seen that,' Marcy says, nodding towards Mo.

'He's such a sweetie,' Paula says. 'I've got to stop mothering him.'

'I don't think he minds,' Marcy says, smiling at Charlie as Cookey shifts to lean against her a bit more.

On they go. A longer drive than normal. Going further from the coast and deeper into the countryside with no real clue as to location or direction. It's soothing and enjoyable. A nice end to a day of good work and good results.

Reginald joins the slumbering, dropping his head back after a thoroughly satisfying conversation with Roy about the books they have read.

All is well. All is good and the drone flying high above them remains unseen and unheard.

Time passes. Blowers drifts to dozing. Blinky the same, inadvertently slumping against Mo, not that the young lad minds or even notices, such is his pleasant slumber.

Clarence yawns with a deep stretch that Howie catches and repeats. His eyes momentarily misting from the moisture in his vision that he blinks away.

'Have to find somewhere for the night soon,' Howie says.

'Early yet,' Clarence replies. 'Need to get some biscuits.'

'Biscuits?'

'Can't tell you. Only members of the Second Watch Biscuit Club can know about the biscuits...'

A sudden silence behind him as Paula catches his words and thinks back to last night and Mo wakes up with a feeling in his stomach. A pressing sensation. An urge even. He ate a lot at the café and now shifts to squirm with the realisation he really needs the toilet. He looks up the Saxon at the same time as becoming aware of Blinky slumped into his side. Blowers is asleep. Cookey the same. Nick still up top. He waits for Paula to look round and lifts his head.

'What's up?' she asks, giving him that special smile she reserves just for him.

'I er,' he starts to say then coughs to clear his throat thick from his short nap. 'Need the toilet.'

'Okay, hun. Howie, find somewhere to pull over, Mo needs the toilet.'

'Could do with a leg stretch,' Clarence says.

'No worries,' Howie says with a yawn. 'Number one or number two?'

'What difference does that make?' Paula asks.

'Does he need a tree or a bush?'

'Oh, oh I see,' Paula says. 'Find him a bush just to be sure.'

'Ask him.'

'I am not asking the poor lad if he needs a poo.'

'Mo? Do you need a shit?' Blowers asks sleepily.

'Yeah.'

'Yes, not yeah,' Dave says.

'Yes, Blowers.'

'Yes, Corporal Blowers.'

'Yes, Corporal Blowers.'

'Needs a shit, boss,' Blowers calls up.

'Bush then,' Howie says. He leans forward as though to see better and examines the solid lines of high hedgerow on both sides that offer nothing in the way of privacy for a person to take a moment of reflection.

'There,' Clarence says, pointing at the old wooden five bar gate on the right side.

'Perfect,' Howie says, easing his foot off the accelerator. '*Stopping for a toilet break,*' he transmits through the radio.

'*Roger that,*' Roy replies as Reginald wakes up with heavy blinking eyes.

Howie glides right, bringing the vehicle to a gradual stop. Roy glides left, drawing his van alongside the Saxon.

'Mo, all yours,' Howie says, turning in his seat. 'Nick? Got a smoke mate?'

'Up top, boss.'

'Eh? Oh you're up there,' Howie says, dropping out to catch the battered packet thrown by Nick and once again wondering if it's the same battered packet or a new one that just looks like the others. He thinks to ask but decides, on reflection, that sometimes the mystery of life is better than the reality of knowledge.

Mo pulls his bag out from under his feet and roots round for a second before Paula passes a toilet roll down and a fresh packet of wet wipes.

'Thanks, Paula,' he says with a sheepish grin.

'Might have a smoke,' Blowers says. 'Fuckhead? You smoking?'

'Er...' Cookey says, snuggling even further into Charlie. 'Nah, I'm comfy as fuck.'

'Careful, your willy will dribble,' Blowers says making a sleepy Blinky snort and Charlie laugh.

'Twat,' Cookey says, sitting up to yawn. 'I'm going for a smoke,' he tells Charlie.

'Er, okay.'

'Don't move cos you're really comfy.'

'I shall come out but I shall also return for your leaning pleasure.'

'Shall you? That is most awesome,' Cookey says, bum shuffling down the seats before stopping with a sudden thought. 'You can lean on me if you want.'

'Thanks,' she says. 'I shall indeed.'

'Dribbly willy,' Cookey chuckles. 'The cheeky one eyed fucker.'

The road is wide with metres of space either side of the vehicles parked adjacent to each other. The hedges high. The air still hot. They all move sleepily, yawning and stretching to join Howie at the front. Reginald wanders over with Roy, both tutting at the plumes of dirty cigarette smoke wafting from the smokers.

Mo walks briskly back down the road, throwing the toilet roll up to catch as he goes. Humming softly to himself without any clue as to the tune. His rifle slung and his knives tucked in his belt.

Dave stands at the front while thinking to ask Mr Howie and Roy to switch the noisy diesel engines off so he can hear properly and staring at the apex of the corner just ahead and also wishing they hadn't stopped without clear view ahead.

Mo throws the toilet roll up and catches it deftly before turning at the noise of the claws on the tarmac that heralds the approach of Meredith deciding to join the pup as he wanders from the pack. She wags her tail and loops in front of him as though shepherding him back. He chuckles, rubbing her head and walking on to spot the old wooden five bar gate. He stops to stare it for a second, wondering if he should go through or over. He gives a tentative push with his foot and blinks when it promptly falls off the hinges with a dull whump.

'S'fucked innit,' he tells Meredith who rushes ahead to sniff the long grass within the field. He goes in and checks the view is clear before unfastening his belt and starting work on his trouser buckle and zipper. He gains a smell as he squats and laughs at the sight of Meredith taking a huge shit while staring at him intently. 'Fucked up,' he murmurs.

'Turn the engines off,' Dave snaps, turning with his eyes blazing at the detection of the noise barely discernible over the throaty rumbles of the Saxon and van.

'Eh?' Howie asks, 'do what mate?'

The chopper comes in from the left side. A small thing with a bubbled glass front flying low with the displacement and thud of the rotors suddenly so load as it roars overhead to turn and face towards them as it gains position to let rip with the single chaingun mounted on one side that decimates a section of the hedgerow.

'DOWN NOW,' Blowers screams, turning fast to drive Cookey and Nick towards the other side.

'COVER,' Clarence grabs Paula and Marcy, pulling them to the ground to cover with his body as the air around them fills with bits of hedge blown apart.

Dave whips his pistol out and fires shots, cracking the canopy that smears with blood from the passenger's head exploding. The chopper banks hard, slewing but feet overhead with an evasive movement as Dave tracks and readies to fire again, heedless to the noise, the chaingun and the bits of ruined hedge flying past him.

Reginald shouts in alarm having been pulled to the ground by Roy. He snaps to see ahead and the dozens of camouflaged figures running towards them.

'CEASEFIRE,' Clarence roars at Dave still firing at the chopper. He sees the men running at them and the front of the heavy tracked vehicle coming into view. 'DAVE...THAT'S A WARRIOR...CEASE-FIRE NOW...'

'The books...' Reginald shouts.

Dave spins from firing at the chopper to see the soldiers advancing at the double towards them and the tracked Warrior armoured vehicle mounted with a thirty millimetre cannon now aiming directly at them. Fury washes over his face at being so easily outgunned and outmanoeuvred. If on his own he would bust through the hedge and draw them away but to fire another shot will draw returning fire and place Mr Howie in harm and even he can't pick a fight with a chopper and a Warrior.

'GO,' he roars instead, grabbing Howie to push him down the road. 'RUN...I'LL COVER YOU...'

'THE BOOKS,' Reginald shouts, 'THEY HAVE TO BE DESTROYED...'

Howie takes it in, the chopper bobbing and swerving, the sound of it drowning nearly everything else out, the tracked army vehicle, the soldiers screaming as they move with order and discipline with rifles raised. 'WHICH ONES?' he shouts back, knowing they have bare seconds.

'ALL OF THEM,' Reginald shouts, on his stomach with his hands over his head, 'DESTROY THE BOOKS...'

'GO MR HOWIE...RUN...BLOWERS, COVERING FIRE NOW.'

'NO!' Howie shouts, 'Dave get a grenade in Roy's van...'

'JESS,' Charlie shouts, running past them as assault rifles from the soldiers fire warning shots and the chopper rises to follow her down. She boots the bolts out from the locks and jumps back as Jess charges out to receive a slap on her backside from Charlie sending her galloping down the road.

'*MOHAMMED...STAY THERE...STAY THERE...*' Dave bellows into his radio, walking towards Roy's van while pulling a grenade from his pocket.

'I SUGGEST YOU ALL GET DOWN BEFORE WE BLOW THE SHIT OUT OF YOU...' An amplified voice from the Warrior booms out.

'DESTROY THE BOOKS,' Reginald screams out.

'EVERYONE GET DOWN...' Clarence shouts, seeing they are already trapped. 'ARMS OUT TO THE SIDES...'

'No no no,' Reginald repeats the word in abject fear, not for the threat but for what it means, for the risk it poses to everything, for the timing of it.

'FIRE IN THE HOLE,' Dave lobs the grenade into the back of Roy's van and turns back to face down the dozens of camouflaged figures coming at them.

'HIM...THE SMALL ONE...HE MOVES SHOOT THE FUCKER,' the soldier in the front shouts. 'HE'S THE DANGEROUS ONE.'

Dave stands with his hands at his sides, seeing most of the rifles twitch to aim on him. He doesn't flinch when the grenade blows. The armoured panels of the van withstand the blast and send the force out through the windscreen, blowing it clear to sail through the air with a cloud of smoke and burning paper raining down.

'DOWN GET DOWN...' soldiers scream, all of them flinching at the explosion behind the small man. 'ON YOUR FUCKIN FACE... GET DOWN YOU CUNT...'

Dave's upper lip flicks once. His eyes taking in the positions as he calculates the order of fire while knowing he can't do a damned thing.

'SAID GET DOWN YOU FUCKING CUNT,' the soldier in the front screams the words, spittle flying from his mouth, his manner hinting at panic.

'My bloody van,' Roy mutters, seeing the burning chunks of paper and debris falling all around them.

Reginald thinks. He thinks fast as Dave lifts a hand to press the microphone under his shirt. *'Mohammed, radio off. They can track the signal. Go to ground. Track if safe.'*

'I's come to you.'

'Negative. Comply. Radio off now. Out.'

A click in Dave's ear tells him the radio turns off as the men advance and the Warrior rolls on the tracks towards them. Still he stands. Still he remains on his feet. 'Orders, Mr Howie?'

'Not a word,' Reginald says urgently. 'Not a word about what we are. We're idiots running around killing them for fun. They killed your families and we're just trying to get back at them...'

'GET ON YOUR FUCKING FACE OR I WILL SHOOT...'

'DOWN DOWN DOWN...'

'SHOOT THAT LITTLE CUNT...'

'We have no plan, we have nothing,' Reginald gets the words out before a rifle jabs in his head and the soldier holding it screaming at him to shut up while Roy shouts to leave him alone and chaos ensues. A chaos of the soldiers moving to jab rifle ends into each person on the ground, screaming they have them covered and will shoot. Brown combat boots. British Army desert fatigues. SA80 assault rifles. The army without doubt.

'DAVE...LIE DOWN,' Howie shouts.

'Yes, Mr Howie,' Dave says as flat and as dull as ever. He takes one last slow look round at the faces of the young men all flushed with adrenalin before slowly lowering to his knees then down onto his stomach.

'CUNT,' the lead soldier screams at him. 'SEE THAT? SEE WHAT PROFESSIONALS DO? FUCKING PRICKS...'

Mo tucks into the base of the hedge, his arms wrapped round Meredith preventing her from running off. His trousers still round his ankles and dogshit smeared on his face from a few rounds of the chain-guns hitting Meredith's deposit on the grass. He squirms deeper, whispering for Meredith to stay quiet. He reaches up to close her mouth, desperate that she doesn't bark. The chopper comes closer, hovering overhead as it scours the ground for sign of anyone else.

'Stay,' Mo whispers into her ear. She squirms to break free but he clamps harder, forcing the message across that she must stay. She doesn't want to stay. The pack is in danger. She must make noise and tell them who she is and how strong they are. 'Please,' Mo whispers. 'Don't bark...please...' but then the pup is on his own away from the pack. She settles into him, a low growl in her throat, her teeth showing, hackles raised but she stays still.

'CLEAR,' the lead soldier calls out, waving at the Warrior. The chopper flies low overhead before banking once more out to the side then turns and glides off. A silence starts to settle. A silence broken by the crackle of flames coming from Roy's van. The two engines now shut off by soldiers reaching in having checked and cleared them.

'BLACK BAG THEM.'

The amplified voice booms the words out, hiding the posh accent.

'You heard him,' the soldier shouts, 'black bag the fuckers.'

'My name is Howie...' Howie says. 'We're not...'

'SHUTTHEFUCKUPYOUCUNT,' the soldier screams, rushing to jab his rifle into Howie's head. 'YOU AIN'T A FUCKING SOLDIER...'

'I am,' Clarence says calmly. 'Parachute Regiment...'

'SHOOT THE NEXT ONE THAT TALKS...SHOOT 'EM THROUGH THE GUT AND LET 'EM BLEED OUT.'

Blowers grunts at his head being lifted by someone gripping a fistful of hair. He feels the soft material coming down and snatches one last glimpse at Cookey having the same done before the world grows dark.

One by one they have heads gripped roughly. Paula's hair yanked to lift her head. Blinky grim faced and holding the urge to fight back. Charlie, Roy, Reginald. All of them. Dave and Howie, heads lifted and black bags pulled down.

'WRISTS,' the soldier barks.

'Fuck,' Nick whispers as his hands are pulled behind his back to be bound by thick plastic cable ties cinched tight into his flesh.

'Hello darlin',' A soldier grins, pulling Marcy's head up. 'Fuck me...seen this one?'

'GET THAT FUCKING BACK ON HER HEAD.'

'I'll put something on your head alright,' the squaddie says, yanking the bag down. 'Hands behind your back...' he reaches under to grab her arm, giving one of her breasts a squeeze as he does so. She stays quiet. Her vision now gone from the material over her face. She grunts at the cable tie drawing tight.

'BAGS ALL ON, SIR' the soldier shouts. Howie listens intently. Hearing a door open and the sound of boots crunching on the road.

'Thank you, Sergeant,' a voice replies. Cultured and rich. A private education without doubt.

'I'm a corporal, Sir,' the soldier says.

'Of course you are,' the cultured voice says without a hint of acknowledging the mistake as Howie strains to listen. Blowers squeezes his eye closed, focussing on the voice.

'Er hi,' Paula calls out, forcing a neutral tone into her voice. 'My name is Paula...'

'I am sure you said you would kill the next one that speaks, Corporal.'

'Sir,' the corporal says. Howie stiffens at the sound of boots moving and a weapon being cocked.

'Shit,' Paula grunts at feeling the barrel pressing into the back of her head.

'Fire, Sir?' the corporal asks.

'If it speaks again then yes. Execute the next one who makes a sound.'

'Sir.'

'But do kick it now so it knows to stay quiet.'

'Kick, Sir?'

'Kick it, Corporal.'

'Sir.'

Paula cries out as the boot slams into her side. Instant pain in her ribs, she rolls onto her side, curling up while biting the agony down.

'It made a noise,' the cultured voice says.

'I kicked her, Sir.'

'Kick it again and if it squeaks then shoot it.'

'Sir.'

Paula clamps her jaw shut as the hard toe of the boot strikes her gut. She curls up tighter, breathing hard but refusing the urge to cry out as Mo's nostrils flare and his eyes grow hard while his arms stay wrapped round Meredith's neck.

'Load them up,' the cultured voice says. 'The Major wants to meet them.'

'Sir,' the corporal says. 'Get 'em up...shoot anyone that speaks. Use their vehicle. We'll take it back...destroy that van and leave it here.'

Hands grab to lift. Rough and without mercy. Breasts groped and squeezed. Giggles sounding out only to be silenced by the corporal screaming at them to move. Howie feels the hands on his arms dragging him up then the feet in his arse propelling him along. He trips from the lack of balance at having his hands bound only to be dragged up and booted along again.

One by one they are pushed into the back of the Saxon with shins striking the hard metal ledge. Kicked in, dragged, shouted at and dumped in seats. Clarence left on the floor as boots stamp down on his body and his mates are pulled over him.

The sound of doors closing. The engine starting, the sound of it a thing now so familiar to them and almost tinged with a sense of betrayal from the Saxon allowing herself to be driven by someone else.

A dull explosion outside. A grenade dropped into the engine compartment of the van as they move off to trundle down the road with rifles jabbing into their heads and bodies and a good day that has turned very bad very quickly.

CHAPTER TWENTY-FOUR

Mo waits. He forces himself to wait. The urge to get up and look is so strong but he must be sure they haven't left someone watching. Minutes pass. Long minutes of straining to hear anything above the crackle of flames coming from Roy's van.

Finally he starts to sit up but keeps hold of Meredith. Telling her to stay quiet and stay close. She growls on but remains at his side while he yanks his trousers up and works fast to fasten the buckle and belt without heed to the dogshit on his face.

He brings his rifle round and starts working slowly up the hedge line, staying inside the field. He listens and stops every few metres until reaching the edge of the section destroyed by the helicopter chaingun.

'Fuck,' he whispers, rising to his feet. The Saxon is gone but the road is littered with the rucksacks thrown from the back, the content rifled and strewn everywhere. Bullet casings from the chaingun lie amongst underwear, packets of wipes, bottles of anti-bac and the small things discarded and left behind.

He drops down to the road as Meredith runs on from item to item, inhaling the scent of the pack on each thing. He ventures closer to Roy's van, his arm up to protect from the heat of the flames now engulfing it. At least Jess got out. He looks round for her, hoping she will be close but seeing no sign.

'Fuck,' he says again. Meredith whines. The pack have gone without them. She rushes to Mo, snaking round his legs as he drops to rub her head with his rifle held ready.

She licks his face, scenting her own waste on his skin. Her ears down, her eyes huge and her tail tucked low. Mo spots the inflatable parrot on the road then the disabled badge that hung round Blowers neck. The folding white stick. Marcy's favourite hairbrush. Paula's notepad. The bandana Charlie tied round her wrist. The strip of gaffer tape that was across Clarence's backside. How did it happen so fast? Was it the army? It had to be the army. Why did they attack like that? Everyone has heard of Mr Howie now. Dave said to turn his radio off. He said they can track the signal. He feels an urge to turn it on to try and raise Heather but holds off, complying with the orders given. A sense of panic starts to grip. A sense of worry and sudden isolation at being in a place he doesn't know. Meredith pushes into him, sensing the pup's fear.

Track if safe. That's what Dave said. He closes his eyes, forcing the fear down and allowing the coldness to take over. The detachment that Dave taught him. *We are different. We see differently. We do not react like others.*

When he opens his eyes the worry is gone from his face. He rises to look round and immediately starts working to gather the things his team hold dear. He packs what he can, knowing it wastes time but also knowing the few things they keep are the things they value the most. Paula's notepad goes into his pocket. Charlie's bandana round his wrist. The rest goes into the bags that are hidden further down in the field.

He checks his kit. Two pistols, each with a magazine loaded. Four spare magazines. Four knives. An assault rifle. Two spare magazines. No water. No food.

'JESS?' he calls out, risking the noise. 'JESS?' he turns on the spot. Nothing. He calls again and waits. He looks to Meredith hoping she can hear or smell the horse but she stares up at him as though waiting to be off. He nods once, grim faced and feeling the pulse of rage at hearing Paula cry out and some toffee nosed cunt calling her an *it* and ordering her to be hurt.

'You's got legs?' he asks the dog quietly. 'We's running.'

He sets off down the road. He wants to sprint flat out but knows that is foolish. His energy will be wasted. He stays at a jog and only increases as his heart and muscles warm. Meredith at his side. A sixteen year old boy with a rifle slung to his back and his hands free to aid his motion.

He keeps hoping he will hear Jess behind them and that she will come cantering to catch up. He doesn't know how to ride a horse and doubts he can even do it but it's the idea of the separation he doesn't like. The idea of her being alone somewhere.

Sweat shines on his skin. His black hair glistening. The dog panting. Pressure builds and pressure grows. Pressure unrelenting.

CHAPTER TWENTY-FIVE

It grows hot in the packed Saxon. Sweat glides down faces contained with the hoods. Eyesight gone with no idea who is pressing into who.

Howie lies on the floor wedged between several others. It all happened so fast. One minute they were stopping for a leg stretch, the next they had a helicopter shooting at them and a tank pointing it's gun while soldiers charged.

It has to be the army but this is still south. They haven't ventured that far from the fort. How can an army unit be working here without them knowing? They are further than they have gone before but still not that far. They went to London of course but that was north-east whereas Howie knows his direction was steady north. He tries to calculate the direction he took and guesses they could have been anywhere between Winchester and Birmingham. Which is a vast area. They were on country roads too and not motorways. If they had taken a motorway he would have had a better idea. If nothing else it cements the reality of a world without instant accessible communication.

'Fuck's sake, leave her tits alone you fucking pervert,' the corporal snaps with a trace of humour that sets his men off laughing.

'Fucking nice rack though,' someone says.

Rage grows. Rage builds. Rage unrelenting but it has to be swallowed. To lose control now will see them executed or beaten. To the last they suspect it is Marcy being groped. Her chest bulges from her top and is obvious. The thought of it makes Howie's jaw clench. He keeps bunching his fists to try and pump blood into the them and to vent the anger inside.

Marcy thinks only of Howie. The hand kneading her breasts is getting steadily harder, gripping almost painfully. Tears spill from her eyes, lost within the hood. Her hands bunched to fists but she stays impotent, unable to speak or react. *Dave is here. Dave is here.* Dave only needs one tiny mistake and he'll kill the lot without blinking. She thinks of Howie and she thinks of Dave and gives a silent thanks when the groper gives one last painful squeeze and finally leaves her alone.

Reginald thinks while wedged into the last seat at the end of the Saxon. He forces his mind to work without panic. It must be the army or at least a section of it. Why the aggressive tactics? Why the brutality? It doesn't make sense. Thank god he told Kyle enough to keep it going.

Dave listens. He listens to everything and even without sight he gains an idea of the positions of those within the Saxon. His knives are gone. His pistols taken. The British Army teach their soldiers to search the enemy thoroughly. Fear prickles his gut. Fear that he cannot protect Mr Howie right now. Fear that he failed.

Marcy stiffens as the hand comes back and starts groping again.

'Fuck me,' the corporal laughs, 'you back on her tits?'

'Can't help it,' the groper says. 'Been three weeks without a shag...'

'Three weeks? You've never had a shag in your life you fucking virgin.'

'I fucking have!'

'Fuck off have you.'

'I fucking will later,' the groper quips, earning more laughs. 'Eh love, me and you...' he adds with a squeeze.

Different voices. All young. Clarence detects the youthfulness and the edge too. The hints of fear and worry masked with bravado.

Blowers hears it. The banter is coarse and almost forced. The laughs aren't genuine.

The Saxon starts to slow. They hear and feel the deceleration until it finally stops and one of the doors opens.

'You get 'em then?'

'Course we have you stupid cunt, hog tied and black bagged in the back.'

'No way!'

'You lifting the barrier then or what?'

'Nah, go round.'

'What did you say?'

'Soz, was a joke...ere' Corp. Send someone else up. I been on guard for eight straight hours.'

'So?'

'Well, it's a bit much.'

'Bit much? Bit much yeah? I'll ask the Major.'

'No! No it's...nah forget it. I'm fine.'

'Nah don't worry. I'll tell him Private Clarke said it was too much.'

'Ah now don't do that, Corp. I was only sayin'...I'm fine yeah. S'all good. I'll stay here.'

'Fucking pussy. Get that barrier up.'

The door closes. The Saxon pulls off as the men inside give those forced grating laughs.

Reginald takes it in. The Corporal is a bully. The soldier outside fears him but fears the Major more.

Clarence feels the worry increasing at the words he heard. Why is a Corporal leading such a large fighting unit? It should be a Sergeant at the very least, normally an officer.

The next drive takes a while. Indicating there is a significant distance from the perimeter guard to the place they are going. Blowers and Clarence try to think of bases in the area but it could be anywhere. It might not even be an operational one. The entire south is dotted with old Second World War airfields.

Again, the deceleration is felt and heard and the rustle of the few soldiers inside the cramped vehicle hint at the destination being reached. They come to a stop and hear a grinding metallic noise of heavy gates opening. A few seconds then they roll forward and stop. This time they hear two sets of heavy grinding and guess one set is closing while another opens. Voices from outside, the words missed over the noises. The Saxon moves slowly forward and keeps going for several seconds before finally coming to a complete stop with the engine switched off.

'YOU WANT THEM OUT, SIR? YEAH? Get those cunts out and lined up.'

The back doors open. Hands grab Howie's ankles, dragging him bodily out from the Saxon as he drops down hard onto a concrete surface. Hands on his arms yanking him up. The sounds of the others being moved forcefully. All of them trying desperately not to speak or make noise. He waits with a mixture of dread and rage in his gut.

'Corporal Jones, I'll take over from here,' an older voice says. Deeper.

'Hobbs,' Corporal Jones says.

'Sergeant Hobbs Corporal Jones. You will address me properly.'

'Whatever. You sure you can cope with this lot?'

'My name,' the sergeant says slowly. 'Is Sergeant Hobbs. You will address me as Sergeant Hobbs.'

'Sergeant Hobbs,' the Corporal says with a sneer evident in his voice. 'You okay with this lot or what?'

'Go away now before...'

'Blah fucking blah, come on boys...we'll leave them to these pussies. See ya later big tits.'

Marcy flinches at the Corporal's hands giving her a grope, followed by more doing the same.

'GET YOUR HANDS OFF HER NOW,' Sergeant Hobbs booms.

'Fucking homo.'

'Queer.'

'Such a cunt.'

The voices recede, drifting away with the crunch of boots on the ground. A sound of someone breathing hard and a tight voice, 'get those bags off,' Sergeant Hobbs orders. 'Do not speak. Do not eyeball my men. Do not do anything. You *will* be fired upon.'

'Shit,' Nick squints at the pain of the bright sunshine hitting his eyes.

'It's bright,' Sergeant Hobbs says. 'Close your eyes when the hoods are removed.'

'Where are we?' Howie asks.

'Please do not make me execute you here...'

Howie feels hands reaching round his neck and pulls back from instinct. 'Easy, just taking the hood off,' a voice says quietly. He closes his eyes as the material is pulled overhead. Instant relief and cooler air to breathe. His face slick from sweat. His hair plastered down. He blinks to see, wincing at the sunshine but forcing himself to look left and right. Nick, Blinky, Cookey and Blowers on one side blinking from the light. He looks the other side to see Clarence bending forward as a camouflage wearing soldier pulls the hood off. Three more soldiers stand further away with rifles aimed. Older men, still maybe late twenties or early thirties but not kids with guns.

'Marcy? You okay?' Howie asks.

'Don't,' Sergeant Hobbs says quickly. 'No talking. Trust me. They'll shoot you without thinking about it and if I don't do my job they'll shoot me and my men too. Don't put us in that position...few of us have got families here...' he adds with a quick look round. His men show no reaction to what he says but to the last they look grim faced, sullen and worried.

Sergeant Hobbs waits for the hoods to be removed and the soldier to return and dump the sweat soaked garments in a pile.

Howie looks over to the Saxon and beyond to the bigger vehicle on tracks like a tank with a big gun barrel. Beyond that he sees a proper tank. A huge think with a much larger gun and knows it to be a Challenger Battle tank. He turns round, wondering if he'll be told to stop looking. A high concrete wall behind them running off in both directions but Howie spots the curvature that speaks of a relatively small contained area and he blinks in surprise when he looks at the other direction further into the place they are. Large military tents erected.

Block metal containers with the end doors open. Mobile offices painted in army green or desert colours. What look like houses further up and bigger buildings.

'Listen in,' Sergeant Hobbs says. They all turn to look at him, all of them in pain from their wrists bound so tightly in the plastic cable ties. The sergeant looks down for a second, his assault rifle held ready but aimed low and away. 'There's no way out of here. It's open ground on three sides and a lot of razor wire. Don't even try it. I've got to take you up to see the Major and for god's sake don't do or say anything stupid no matter what you see...and if you do or say anything in front of me then I got to kill you too. We've got our kids here. Our wives...' his expression is clear. His meaning obvious. He's said it twice now. There is a risk to their families if he doesn't do his job properly. 'Walk in single file...'

'What's going on?' Howie asks.

'Single file,' the sergeant snaps, stepping away. 'No talking...'

They set off with Nick in the lead and the armed soldiers flanking on one side. A good tactical move that Clarence notes as it means they can fire easily without fire of hitting their own.

The place looks deserted. Quiet too but with a noise in the background slowly reaching their ears. A noise they all know and recognise.

A buzz overhead, they look up to see a military grade drone shooting over and dropping out of sight behind a container.

They walk on, unable to speak to each other, unable to do anything other than told. Paula's ribs hurt from the kicks but the thing inside her reduces the effects of the pain. Is that why they are here? Is it known they are infected? They would have been shot on sight if that was suspected.

They reach the first canvas tent and spot the blades of the chopper that attacked them further back behind it. A corpse on a wheeled medical trolley left outside the tent. The sheet covering the body blood stained and wet. Still no other people and no sign of the soldiers that brought them here.

They go past the containers and mobile offices. Doors open.

Chairs outside next to ashtrays and drinking mugs left in the open. They reach the houses. Thick net curtains inside the windows. Doors open again and still no people.

Howie stares ahead, sensing they are being taken to something. The air of trepidation is not contained to his own group.

'Not a word,' Sergeant Hobbs says as they reach the end of the small row of houses. A large open space on the left filled with hundreds of people crammed in all facing away towards a long flatbed truck fitted with a crane. A hushed silence hangs in the air and Howie spots the soldiers that attacked them grouped off to one side. All smoking, smirking and nodding as they nudge each other and look round to the single file prisoners. That observance catches on as the hundreds of people slowly turn to see what everyone else is looking at. Faces show instant shock at seeing Howie and his team all in single file with their hands bound. Some show instant recognition that shows hope then worry as they see the cable ties on wrists. A rushed whisper spreads through the crowd and more than once Howie hears his own name said in muted tones.

'Stop,' Sergeant Hobbs orders. Nick comes to a stop, turning to look back at everyone.

Movement in front of the crowd. Howie stares over to see a man walking up a set of stairs onto the back of the flatbed truck. Army fatigues and a smartness about him. His back ramrod straight. He comes to a stop and stands at ease with his hands behind his back. A pistol in a holster on his belt. He looks out across the expanse of faces and waits until an absolute silence descends, a silence only broken by that constant background noise.

'DESERTION IS AN OFFENCE UNDER MILITARY LAW,' the man's voice booms out, his tone clipped, his oration distinct and powerful. 'IT IS MORALLY REPREHENSIBLE AND IN TIMES OF WAR ONLY THE MOST SEVERE OF PUNISHMENTS WILL BE CONSIDERED.'

Howie listens, they all do, everyone crammed into that space listens. A huge screen flickers to life at the side of the area. Like something from a festival. The pixilation not as perfect as a television but the view it shows is clear enough. A soldier in camouflage uniform. His hands bound behind his back. His head bowed but covered with a black bag the same type Howie had on a few minutes ago.

'YOU HAVE WATER AND RATIONS. YOU HAVE SAFETY. DESERTION IS COWARDICE. THIS IS A LESSON TO YOU ALL…BEGIN.'

The head of the crane lifts with a faint whir of electric motors. A gasp in the crowd. Howie watches the screen, puzzled at what he is seeing until he spots the rope round the soldier's neck. He looks again to the crane on the back of the flatbed and the rope tied to the hook that goes taut as the soldier starts rising from the ground, his body thrashing as he lifts. Blood stains on his camouflage clothing and the crowd grows so hushed that even from this distance his gurgles can be heard.

Murmurs start rippling through the crowd. Eyes fill with tears that spill down cheeks. Men and women dressed in normal clothes look away. Sergeant Hobbs clenches his jaw but shows no other reaction.

It takes over two minutes for the man to die. Two minutes of frantic thrashing and kicking that gradually grows weaker as the oxygen is robbed from his brain and body. His legs stop kicking and his body gives one final spasm before he hangs still and dead and a woman at the edge of the crowd falls to the floor sobbing hard.

'DESERTION IS COWARDICE. WE ARE IN A TIME OF WAR. MARTIAL LAW WILL APPLY AND I EXPECT EVERY PERSON HERE TO DO THEIR BIT. DISPERSE NOW.'

The screen goes off and the crowd instantly starts moving back and away. Compliance given. The mood one of supplication and oppression. Scared people doing as told, watched by soldiers armed with rifles.

'Move,' Sergeant Hobbs orders.

Nick moves on, following the soldier in front as they traipse further into the area with last glances given to the crowd and the man hanging from the crane. Dread builds. Fear knots in stomachs.

They approach an old looking two-storey building. Squat and

solid looking with an institutional appearance and a flat roof one-storey section on one side.

'Old glasshouse?' Clarence asks.

'No talking,' Sergeant Hobbs responds quickly, dropping back to glare at Clarence. 'It was, decommissioned,' he whispers before moving away.

Howie knows what a glasshouse is. It's the term given to an old military prison. They were all decommissioned years ago. Maybe one or two remained but this place doesn't look like it has been in use for a long time.

They move down the side of the lower section to a large metal gate already hanging open admitting them to a high walled concrete yard. Broken chunks under of concrete under foot but the walls looks stout. Graffiti on some. The signs of old fires, scorch marks from where children came to play and tramps came to hide.

They are taken straight into another open door to a concrete corridor that smells of damp and piss. Cell doors line the walls. Solid metal things. Some hang from hinges at broken angles. Others on the floor covered in filth and litter.

'Women in here,' Sergeant Hobbs says, coming to a stop next to one of the cells with a functioning door. He pulls a knife from a pocket and waits while everyone hesitates. Blinky is prodded to move first. With a glance at Howie she walks to Sergeant Hobbs and the knife in his hand. 'Turn round...I'll cut the binds. Do a thing and we'll shoot everyone now.' She turns slowly, unsure and clearly very unhappy but winces as the knife cuts through the tie freeing her wrists. A glance to Howie who shakes his head. The men surrounding them are too well placed.

She goes inside. Charlie goes next. Silent and pensive. Paula after her then Marcy who earns a grim almost apologetic smile from Sergeant Hobbs. The doors slams, sealing them inside.

Further down the corridor Sergeant Hobbs stops them outside the next cell with a working door. Nick goes first. Blowers then Cookey and Howie. All wincing as the ties are cut as they rub wrists and feed into the large empty cell. Dave waits to go last. His eyes calculating the positions and how to take each down.

'Sorry,' Sergeant Hobbs says. 'Major said to be careful round you. Go in, drop to your knees and don't move.'

Dave goes in. There is no choice, every rifle is now aimed at him. He lowers to his knees and feels the barrel of the rifle pressed to the back of his head while the sergeant reaches down to cut the tie before walking backwards with his rifle still trained on Dave. He stops at the door about to say something. An expression of pure anguish fleeting then gone and he walks out to gently close the door.

CHAPTER TWENTY-SIX

M ajor Donaldson marches smartly through his base. His sleeves rolled perfectly above his elbows. His boots gleam. His moustache neatly trimmed. His brown hair short and tidy. His army fatigues ironed to perfection. Major Donaldson is a fastidious man. He does not like mess. He likes things to be tidy and just so. There has to be order and discipline. There is a right way of doing things and a wrong way and the right way is whatever he says it is.

Major Donaldson is also a man of conflicting virtues. A complex yet simple individual. Intelligent, articulate but obstinate to a fault. He loves the military and being an officer and adored being in conflict zones as long as he was nowhere near the front line. That's why he chose logistics. Not that all logistical soldiers and officers are cowards, far from it, some are very brave, just not Major Donaldson.

He liked being close enough to hear the bangs, whizzes and pops and the stories in the officers mess afterwards. He liked being able to order frontline troops about and tell them what to do. He liked the organisational structure and finite details. He liked discipline and held the record for the amount of soldiers reported for breaches of regulations.

What he didn't like was that by the age of fifty-one, his career had ground to a halt. The conflicts in Afghan, Iraq and numerous other shit-holes full of savages throwing bombs at each other had been wonderful. His services were in need and he suddenly he was at the epi-centre of it all. Then it fizzled out and he realised he was stuck at Major. He suspected he was not liked by the senior officers and also suspected, quite rightly, that it was his numerous character flaws and not the lack of war, that were preventing his career progression.

So, for the last two years he had pottered about being a complete bastard to anyone that crossed his path while growing increasingly hostile towards anyone senior to his rank. He even started thinking about retirement and had enquired with a few of those private military companies to see if they needed a complete bastard to help organise shipping, flights and the logistical planning that accompanied conflict.

Then the balloon went up and it was glorious. Wonderful. An absolute gem of a thing.

He was bored shitless in this very hellhole of a base, having been seconded to plan and organise the big military exercise at Salisbury Plains. It was his job to arrange space and facilities for the Drone Unit, the scout helicopter and space for the troops held in readiness to deploy. It was a big exercise and he spent a shitty few weeks planning to make sure it was all ready.

The large screen was erected for the command and control team to watch the live footage broadcast from the drones and they'd fitted the scout helicopter with a prototype chaingun. He even had to make room for a Challenger Battle Tank, the crews, the maintenance teams and all manner of personnel.

The night of the exercise, three weeks ago today, he was here in the base listening to the bangs in the distance when it all went wrong, or right depending on your view of the world.

Because of the exercise, they had first hand real live-time reports coming in and Major Donaldson was close enough to the Command and Control section to hear it all. It was awful and it got worse. They tried contacting Whitehall in London but comms dropped. Eventually, the senior officers in Command and Control made the decision to deploy and see the ground for themselves. Which was stupid. Major

Donaldson was about to tell them it was stupid when he was given command of the base until further notice.

Command of the base.

Major Donaldson had command of the base and not just logistics but all of it.

He said yes of course and then listened and watched as they went out and promptly died. Which was wonderful because he could continue to be in command of the base.

That was his moment. His time had come and he shone. He moved fast too. Securing the perimeter and getting the huge coils of razor wire outside the walls before ensuring the gates were locked and sealed.

'Sir,' he looks up at the sound of the lieutenant's voice to see the man holding the door open to the admin block.

'Are my detainees secured, Lieutenant?'

'They are, Sir. Sergeant Hobbs has seen to it.'

'Very good. We shall make a start soon.'

During that first frantic night and the day that followed it, Major Donaldson made two important observations:

One: Anyone that went out got killed.

Two: Anyone who tried to attack the things got killed.

As a result of his observations he established two rules:

One: Don't go out.

Two: Don't attack the things.

It was that simple and, as per Major Donaldson's obstinate manner, those two rules were adhered to. Mostly.

People could come into the base as that did not break rule one. People could not leave as that *did* break rule one.

Of course, Major Donaldson is not so rigid as to be unable to break his own rules when it suits him, hence Corporal Jones going out for supplies and set missions. Major Donaldson did not worry about Corporal Jones or his men deserting as Corporal Jones and his men were looked after, and it appeared to Major Donaldson that Corporal Jones was a man after his own heart. A vicious nasty complete bastard.

'Tea, Sir?' the Lieutenant asks, following the Major up the piss-smelling stairwell to the upper *senior officers' quarters*. The stairwell had been scrubbed many times over the last three weeks but the smell of piss seemed ingrained and if anything was only accentuated by the cleaning chemicals.

'Yes. Tea,' Major Donaldson says curtly, going into his office, this being the largest room in the admin block and befitting that of a senior officer. 'Tell Hobbs I want to speak to him.'

'Very good, Sir.'

The first few days of the outbreak passed and the Major was both heroic and amazing. Everyone loved him. He did not panic or flap but instead, he grew in stature and manner. He had his rules and it was those rules that kept everyone alive. Having Sergeant Hobbs also helped as Sergeant Hobbs was very widely respected in addition to being combat experienced. Major Donaldson even allowed a few of the men to go out and bring their families back. Which did break his rule but it suited him to break his rule as it meant his men would be more endeared to him and less likely to do stupid things if they had their families here to think about.

What he also realised was that something like this would kill lots of other officers and when the government got a grip on it they would need new senior personnel. Someone who kept a lid on things and stayed the course.

'Wanted to see me, Sir?' Sergeant Hobbs says, stopping just inside the door.

'How were they?'

'Compliant but confused,' the sergeant replies honestly, earning a sharp look that makes him stand straighter and avert eyes from the officer. 'Compliant but confused, *Sir*.'

'Do we have a problem, Sergeant?' the Major asks bluntly.

'No, Sir.'

'Are they secured?'

'Yes, Sir.'

'Separated?'

'By gender, Sir.'

'By gender?'

'Yes, Sir. Not enough cells, Sir. Only two are fit to be used.'

'Fit?'

'Others are not suitable, Sir. Broken bars on the windows. Doors not closing. Walls falling down...that kind of thing, Sir.'

'Bound?'

'Pardon, Sir?'

'Are they still bound?'

'No, Sir.'

'Why?'

'It er...they were cable ties, Sir. More than half hour cutting the blood off can kill the...'

'I do not like your tone, Sergeant.'

Sergeant Hobbs swallows, holding his expression as neutral as he can. 'Sorry, Sir.'

'Do you think I am a fool?'

'No, Sir.'

'I will be promoting Corporal Jones tomorrow.'

'Sir,' Sergeant Hobbs says, fighting harder to keep his voice level while knowing he is being studied closely for reaction.

'Do you have a problem with that?'

'No, Sir.'

'Good. You may go. Send Corporal Jones to me.'

'Yes, Sir.'

Snapping a salute, the Sergeant about turns and walks from the office as the lieutenant carries the tea tray up the corridor. The sergeant nods once, smart and formal then descends the stairs before finally releasing the breath held in his chest. It's getting worse. The Major is getting worse. Everything is getting worse.

After six days, Major Donaldson sent a scavenging party, led by Sergeant Hobbs before he was confined to barracks, to the main Salisbury base. They returned with food, equipment and supplies but also with a report that most of the infected things were dead. Sergeant Hobbs said there had been a rolling battle that was evident from the way the bodies had fallen and the spent casings strewn on the ground. Major Donaldson did not like the fact the infected had been killed but even more than that, he really did not like that Sergeant Hobbs was experienced enough to read the ground in that way. It undermined him.

'Tea, Sir,' the lieutenant says, bustling in with the tray. 'Sergeant Hobbs did not look happy. All well?'

'Did you get a look at them?'

'I did,' the lieutenant says, his light conversational tone dropping to a more suitably serious one full of gravitas. His cultured voice strong but so subservient.

'Is it them?' Major Donaldson asks.

'Without doubt,' Lieutenant Galloway-Gibbs says. 'Mr Howie, Dave...Simon Blowers was there. Alex Cooke and Nicholas Hewitt. The others I didn't recognise.'

2nd Lieutenant Officer-in-Training Charles Galloway-Gibbs screamed and pissed himself when Sergeant Hobbs found him, but later explained it was Post-Traumatic Stress Disorder brought on by fighting the infected for days on end. Heroically of course, and on his own too, seeing as his men all deserted their posts to go with someone pretending to be a British Army officer.

Sergeant Hobbs asked him how he had managed to kill so many infected on his own. Major Donaldson said he didn't like the infected being killed. Lieutenant Galloway-Gibbs said *oh dear, I think I have confused the situation. I did not kill them. That Howie chap did with his little friend.*

That was the first time Major Donaldson heard of Mr Howie, and since then, that name had become an obsession to him.

Mr Howie was fighting back.

Mr Howie had an army.

Killed millions they have.

Mr Howie is winning.

They killed tens of thousands in one battle.

That's what the refugees said when they got inside and we're debriefed. They said they were heading for a fort on the coast. It had order and law. Shops and doctors. Everyone was welcome and would be kept safe. *Mr Howie is a hero. His group are heroes.*

Major Donaldson hated it and as the days rolled on and more refugees came so the accounts became wilder and more outrageous. Some bastard pretending to be an officer was out there killing the infected and making it worse for everyone, but worse, he was making Major Donaldson look like a cowardly tit.

Mr Howie and his group use axes. Major Donaldson has a tank. Mr Howie and his group fight with bare hands. Major Donaldson has a helicopter and stores full of ordnance, explosive, mortars, heavy machine guns and more. Mr Howie and his team are saving children and women. They are fighting back and winning. Major Donaldson is hiding in a base full of soldiers. More refugees arrived and his cowardice became openly discussed. He saw the looks Sergeant Hobbs gave him and felt the pressure growing.

The mood inside the base worsened. More people arrived with fresh tales of Mr Howie. The oppression darkened. People said they wanted to leave. They grew louder with voiced opinions. A pressure cooker environment. A rapidly formed community displaced from homes and lives, bereft of loved ones with confusion and paranoia growing roots with every passing day. The people wanted to leave. The demanded it. They insisted on it. They gathered belongings and walked towards the gate. Corporal Jones formed a line of soldiers. Sergeant Hobbs intervened and said to let the people go. Major Donaldson demanded they all stand down and return to barracks. The people said they were not soldiers, they did not have barracks. The situation escalated and a man marched towards the line of soldiers with determination to leave.

Corporal Jones shot him in the chest and the silence that followed was only broken when the man's wife rushed to his side screaming in panic. The panic was such that she charged to attack Corporal Jones who broke her nose with the butt of his rifle, knocking her out. Corporal Jones then fired a warning shot over the heads of the crowd and made them all lie down in the dirt.

The line had been crossed. Martial law was imposed. The woman was hung an hour later for attacking troops of Her Majesty's Armed Forces. Two more tried to sneak out that night. Major Donaldson had them hung the following day and used the screen to make everyone watch.

Another two were shot as they dropped from the walls on the southern side two nights later and tried to run through the coiled razor wire. They weren't killed instantly and their cries could be heard through the camp for another day before they finally grew quiet. A man was hung for spreading dissent and trying to rally everyone else to join him and break out. His wife was hung with him but his children were spared death as an act of leniency by Major Donaldson. He had them beaten instead by Corporal Jones. That was ten days ago. Order had been achieved but the cost was evident. It was not a place of safety but an entrapment of tyrannical rule.

Lieutenant Galloway-Gibbs stands back from the desk. His tea cup in hand. His whole manner one of supplicated politeness. An officer through and through. Smart, neat, precise and more than happy to shove his head up the Major's arse at every given opportunity.

'We shall question them,' Major Donaldson says while sipping his tea. He sits back to show he is thinking deep and serious thoughts. 'Find out what they know. Corporal Jones heard one of them saying *'destroy the books'*. Do you know what that means?'

'No idea, Sir. None at all. I am just glad we have found the deserters. Truly awful business, deserters. Cannot abide them. Cowardice, Sir.'

T he only thing necessary for the triumph of evil is that good men do nothing. Sergeant Hobbs has always believed in those words. He has never stood by and allowed an injustice to take place.

Morals come with a cost though and whereas his values previously had the support of the entire military organisation, now he has nothing. His wife and kid are here. His three trusted men have their wives and kids here. Jonesy has nearly forty men, none of whom have wives or kids. Jonesy also has the Major's backing and that snivelling toady silver-spoon posh twat Galloway-Gibbs.

Sergeant Hobbs has led men into battle many a time. Firefights.

Insurgent attacks. He's seen legs blown off from mines and held his own troops as they died and he knows good men when he sees them.

Howie and those few were good people. It poured off them in buckets. They had dignity too and held their heads high.

Still, his wife is here. His kid too. So as much as the only thing necessary for triumph of evil is for good men to do nothing is a powerful influencer, so self-preservation is stronger.

'Jonesy, Major wants you,' he barks the order as he walks into the large canvas mess tent. Jeers come back. Catcalls and laughs. If this was three weeks and a day ago he would be busting jaws and wiping the floor with this lot.

'Having a coffee, Hobbs,' Corporal Jones replies with a big grin, his feet on the table in front of him.

There is nothing Sergeant Hobbs can do. He can't even summon the energy for a retort but simply turns and walks out as the jeers grow louder.

They've discussed it many times with his three men. Making a rush for the gates but they all know they don't stand a chance. The tank crews died on the first night and none of them know how to use it. They've got the Warrior and some other vehicles but they're kept under constant watch by Jonesy's men, same with the heavy weapons and explosives. All Hobbs and his men have are small arms, plus their wives and kids to protect.

If he could help Howie and his group, he would. If he could escape, he would. If he could do many things other than be here, he would.

Except he can't and he knows exactly what will happen to Howie, and worse, what will happen to the women with them.

CHAPTER TWENTY-SEVEN

The only time the police ever caught Mo was either with the helicopter or using a police dog to track. Dogs can smell everything. They can smell the placement of the foot on the ground and separate it from other footsteps. They can smell fingerprints that are days old. They can smell drugs hidden in coffee. They can smell a thousand things and discern all of them but what they can't do is speak. That was the loophole. Just because the dog caught you it didn't mean a conviction because they couldn't put a dog in court and ask it how it found the suspect.

It's like that now. Another junction. The third one since he set off. Wide too and there is no way of knowing which direction they took. He bends forward with his hands on his knees and sweat pouring from his face as Meredith sniffs around.

He knows Meredith can smell which way they went but she can't tell him. He wants to ask but knows the idea is stupid. All he can do is try and second guess without knowing if she is following the vehicles or chasing rabbits.

She stays on the main road and that's enough for Mo to start running again. He builds back up to the steady pace and holds the coldness inside that's keeping the panic suppressed. Miles pass. Long periods of nothing but hedgerows and fields and that nub of worry increases as the sun starts the glide down towards the horizon.

All he can do is run and hope for the best. That's it. That's all he has.

CHAPTER TWENTY-EIGHT

The door is solid. The bars on the windows are rusty but intact and don't move despite Clarence heaving on them. The walls are sound. The floor and ceiling the same. Dusty, dirty, stinky but the cell is as strong now as it was when first constructed.

Every inch scoured and inspected. Every section of the walls prodded to try and detect weaknesses.

'Nothing,' Howie says, 'okay, gather in, speak quietly...what do we know?'

'Old glasshouse,' Clarence says. 'Must have been a military prison back in the day but it's small. I'm guessing this building was the administration block with the discipline section built in.'

'So we're on an old military base, right?' Howie asks.

'Definitely,' Blowers says.

'They've got fucking tanks,' Nick says. 'And a bastard helicopter... why aren't they killing the...'

'How did they build those walls so quickly?' Cookey asks, cutting across Nick.

'Sectional,' Clarence says. 'They're easy to whack in place and by the look of them I'm guessing they were already here.'

'Grass was growing up at the bases, they've been in place for years,' Roy says.

'Right so they just took over an old army place then,' Howie says.

'Looks that way,' Clarence says. 'MOD still owns a lot of land.'

'Ministry of Defence?' Howie asks.

'Yep, and Salisbury isn't that far.'

'There was a big exercise running the weekend it happened,' Blowers says. 'At Salisbury I mean.'

'Maybe a unit was sectioned here ready to deploy into the exercise, or run the intel side or comms,' Clarence says. 'Only been three weeks but if they moved fast they could have secured kit, vehicles... that chopper...'

'Okay,' Howie says, nodding as he takes it in.

'Why aren't they killing the infected?' Nick asks.

'Fuck knows,' Howie says with a sigh. He rubs his jaw and thinks hard.

'And why be such cunts to us?' Cookey asks.

'That poor bloke they hung,' Nick says.

'Barbaric,' Roy says quietly.

'I think that was for our benefit,' Howie says, 'timed it to perfection with us arriving.'

'Probably right,' Clarence says. 'They said about the Major...a Major isn't that high a rank.'

'Does it make a difference?' Howie asks as Clarence and Blowers exchange looks. 'What?'

'That private was groping Marcy,' Blowers says.

'And the corporal called the sergeant a load of names,' Clarence says. 'Shows a decline in discipline...I'm guessing that's why they hung that lad...to scare everyone. The Major is hanging his soldiers but letting a corporal sexually assault women and abuse higher ranks.'

'Desertion,' Howie says. 'He said desertion. So he doesn't want people leaving. That explains why we haven't heard of them. If people aren't allowed out then they can't get to the fort or anywhere else... that's why they all looked so terrified.'

'Pressure cooker environment,' Roy says.

'Okay, does that help us? Sergeant Hobbs seemed quite decent. If he's seeing the others being dicks then maybe we try and get him on side.'

'Makes sense,' Clarence says. 'His lads seemed a bit older.'

'But he said they've got families here,' Roy says. 'And he kept control of Dave.'

'How did they know about Dave?' Nick asks.

'Must have heard of us,' Howie says. 'How the shit they knew where we were though...fuck me, what a mess. Okay, right...we stay passive and polite. Dave, you see a chance you go for it but only if you're sure. Tell us if you want us to do anything.'

'Just get down.'

'We'll do that. Everyone agreed? Stay passive. Stay polite and wait...thank fuck Mo got away. Did Charlie get Jess out?'

'She did, Mr Howie,' Dave says.

'Good, and Meredith's with Mo. Can he track us?'

'We went too far,' Dave says. 'Lots of turns. I haven't taught Mohammed any tracking skills.'

'Ah well, at least he can get back to Lilly...and er...Dave? That fucker that groped Marcy. He's mine if we get the chance.'

'Yes, Mr Howie.'

'If not then break every bone in his fucking body before you...

'Someone coming,' Nick cuts in at the sound of boots crunching on the dust and debris outside the door.

'Passive,' Howie says, pushing through to be closest to the door. He cocks his head to listen to the faint voices coming from the other side and frowns at the sound of a faint giggle.

'DOOR OPENING,' someone shouts but the voice is muffled. 'MOVE BACK...'

'We are,' Howie shouts. 'Listen we're not a threat to you...can we talk to whoever is in charge please...'

The sound of metal on metal as the locking bar is lifted. Howie shoots a glance to Dave rolling his wrists as though warming up.

The door opens a crack, the sound of giggling coming clearer. The lads frown at each other as Reginald closes his eyes and feels his heart sinking through his gut. The door opens a bit wider, enough for a hand to come through and throw the grenade in.

'DOWN,' Dave shouts. The men drop instantly, bursting away from the object hitting the concrete floor with a hard thud. A second later a hiss sounds out with a plume of gas jetting from the grenade.

'TEAR GAS,' Clarence shouts as the laughter from the other side of the door is heard clearer.

The gas fills the room quickly. A solid choking cloud that hits throats and eyes. They cover mouths and noses with hands and keeps eyes clamped shut but it matters not. It seeps through and hits the backs of throats that burn to invoke instant retching. Tears fill eyes that sting like hell. Reginald cries out, feeling a big hand on his arm that drags him across the ground then the sensation of being covered as Clarence goes over him. Nick joins him, Cookey and Blowers the same. Fighting through the coughing gagging pain to group together.

'STAY DOWN... STAY DOWN...'

A muffled voice booms the words as the door is kicked open. Through misted vision, Howie catches sight of camouflaged figures in gas masks striding in with rifles held aimed. Thick gloves on hands. Nato helmets fastened with chinstraps.

'STAY THE FUCK DOWN...' a boot goes into Roy's side.

'CUNT,' another one kicks Cookey.

'COVER THAT ONE,' Corporal Jones shouts, pointing at Dave as more men aim rifles at the small man seemingly not so affected by the tear gas.

'FAT CUNT,' a soldier shouts, standing on Clarence's outstretched hand as the big man stays over Reginald.

'GET THAT ONE OUT...'

Howie feels the hands grabbing to drag him over the rough floor. His body wracked with coughs and heaves as he tries to spew. His head hits the open door. His shoulder slams into the frame. Feet kick and batter him through into the corridor then further along. He curls into a ball, the rage flushing inside that pays no heed to the tear gas or the guns held by the soldiers. He goes to rise to fight and kill. A foot hits the back of his knees. A rifle butt slams into his head. Boots into his stomach and sides. Someone lands on him with hard knees driving into his back. A hand grips the back of his head, lifting it up then slamming it down into the ground. His arms held tight and pulled behind him. A cable tie applied and tightened. He rises to his feet from men gripping to lift. Punches to his head and stomach. He bends over, still gasping from the tear gas. The hand gripping his hair wrenches him upright as they propel him down the corridor.

The keep going as they drag him through the complex. Hits given. Cheap shots. Punches and slaps. He hears the laughing behind the gas masks. He hears angry voices venting rage and temper. They reach the base of an old concrete stairwell. He trips and stumbles to be kicked and battered for a few more seconds before dragged up the stairs. The rage inside surges up but the assault to his senses overwhelms his ability to fight back.

They go through hard wooden doors opened with Howie's head. Down another corridor, dragged and beaten. Into another room to a solid wooden chair in the middle that he is pushed into. Hands grab his ankles, forcing them against the chair legs. Cable ties wrapped and tightened, securing him to the chair while the hand gripping his hair yanks back hard and fists pummel his body.

'DONE,' someone shouts.

They all pull back. The macabre faceless soldiers all laughing at the sight of him tied to the chair with snot and blood dripping from his face. One of the soldiers grabs a bucket of water and launches the contents into Howie. He gasps at the sensation, coughing harder as it hits the back of his throat. Another one hits him. More water thrown.

'ENOUGH. Leave him...stupid little cunt...'

The room grows quiet. Silent even. Howie gasps and breathes hard. The rage there but held impotent and useless. The sting in his eyes lessons. The pain in his throat and mouth eases. He looks up slowly with his dark curly hair wet and dripping and his eyes flashing that darkness that makes the soldiers flinch and shift position from the intensity.

'CUNT...' Corporal Jones strides forward, slamming a hard fist into the side of Howie's head. He tips over in the chair. Boots kick his legs. He grunts from the hits then feels hands grab to lift the chair back up.

'Ain't so hard are you,' A voice whispers in his ear. 'You ain't a soldier...'

'Thank you, Corporal Jones.'

Howie looks up to see the same man from the flat bed truck standing at ease just inside the door. Neat and tidy. Brown greying hair cut short. A trimmed moustache. An immediate thought of Captain Mannering from Dad's Army that makes Howie snorts a dry laugh that earns another punch to the side of his head from Corporal Jones' gloved fist.

'Thank you, Corporal,' Major Donaldson says in his clipped tone.

'Sir,' the Corporal says, stepping away from Howie.

'Lieutenant?'

'Oh fuck,' Howie says as Lieutenant Galloway-Gibbs walks in.

'Is this man the one they call Mr Howie?'

'Why yes, yes it is,' Lieutenant Galloway-Gibbs drawls, only moving closer on seeing Howie's legs are tethered to the chair. He smiles a smug little grin as he leans forward from the waist to peer down. 'Remember me?'

'Yep,' Howie says, his voice ragged and hoarse. 'Crawled out from under the desk then?' He closes his eyes as the fist swings in that snaps his head over and the screaming Corporal Jones bellows in his ear and his own words of advice to stay passive remind him to stop being cocky. 'Sorry,' he whispers when the Corporal stops screaming abuse.

Major Donaldson rocks on his heels. His heart beating hard at the sight of a man held captive and being beaten. He felt the same thing when he had the people shot and hung. A thrill inside. A pleasure born from the power of it. He's never had a man beaten like this. Not someone tied to a chair. He forgets the questions he had ready as the room falls quiet with an air of expectation. A sudden worry that he will look stupid. The silence stretches. He needs to say something.

'May I?' Lieutenant Galloway-Gibbs asks.

'Carry on,' Major Donaldson replies tersely as though this silence is exactly what he wanted.

Howie lifts his head to look at the two officers. Both so immaculate and clean. Both staring with unabated pleasure showing in their eyes. 'What have we done?'

'Done?' Lieutenant Galloway-Gibbs asks.

'Impersonating an officer of Her Majesty's Armed Forces,' Major Donaldson says.

'Do what?' Howie asks.

'Beat him some more,' Major Donaldson says, flicking a hand out at Howie. 'I don't like his tone.'

'No wait...' Howie's head snaps over at the punch as he gives thanks the man punching him is wearing thick leather gloves.

'Go on, beat that man properly,' Major Donaldson barks, turning to look at the other soldiers behind him. 'Get in there, give him a damn good thrashing...that's it. Don't kill him now...don't kick his head. In the belly. Kick him in the belly. That's it...and his testicles...good kick in the bollocks always works wonders. Good man that man! My eyes are smarting somewhat, Lieutenant. Damned strong stuff that tear gas.'

'Here, Sir. I took the precaution of bringing us some surgical masks,' Lieutenant Galloway-Gibbs says, offering a tie back medical mouth cover to the Major. They take a few seconds fixing the coverings in place while Corporal Jones continues the beating.

'Enough,' Major Donaldson snaps. Relishing the power of having tough men abide his orders so promptly. 'Pick him now and let's see if he still wants to be cocky. Still cocky are you?' he asks, his voice a little muffled through the mask.

Blood pours from Howie's nose. His lips cut. His stomach hurts. His legs hurt. His bollocks hurt but there is a thing inside that lessens that pain. A thing that makes the effects of the beating not so bad but to show that now would be bad so he gasps for air and groans in pain. His head drooped and low. 'I'm sorry, Sir.'

'Better,' Major Donaldson says. 'Now, who are you?'

'Howie.'

'You will address me as sir. I am an officer of Her Majesties

Armed Forces. You are not an officer. You are an impersonator. Beat him again.'

'No please...'

Feet and fists rain into him. The chair goes over again. His skin is cut. His nose breaks. Blood spurts out thick and fast but clotting quickly.

'Try again shall we. Get him up. What's your name?'

'Howie, Sir,' Howie whispers.

'Better. Why are you killing the people with the disease?'

Howie gasps for air. The pain still not so bad. It hurts but nothing like it should. He drags the seconds out to buy time. 'Killed my sister, Sir...' Reggie said not to tell them anything. *Not a word about what we are. We're idiots running around killing them for fun. They killed your families and we're just trying to get back at them.*

'Ah yes, I remember now. Going to London to look for her. Yes,' the lieutenant says through his mask. His hands behind his back as he looks grandly upon the bleeding man tied to the chair. 'I say though, but you were on your way to London...which suggests you were killing them before you discovered she was dead.'

'Good observation, Lieutenant.'

'Thank you, Major.'

'What have you got to say about that? Hmm? Killing them before your sister was found dead.'

Sarah wasn't found dead. She was alive. She was alive and well but died later. Who the hell are these two idiots?

'Sorry,' Howie croaks.

'Sorry are you?' Major Donaldson asks. 'What about impersonating an officer? What about that? Denying that too? We've had people turning up here telling everyone that *Mr Howie* is an officer in the army. Saying he is leading the fight back. You, Sir. You are not an officer. Are you a soldier?'

'No, Sir.'

'What are you then?'

'Worked for Tesco.'

'What? Tesco? A supermarket?'

'Yes, Sir.'

'Major, we should ask him about the books, Sir.'

'What about these books? Hmm? What about them?'

'What books, Sir?' Howie whispers.

'DO NOT LIE TO ME...beat that man. Give him a thrashing.'

It starts again and the pain rises. The air is kicked from his chest. His face bloodied and bruised. Hard hits given that render him unable to think or focus. He can't even curl up into a ball but can only wait for it to end. He holds Marcy in his mind. Cookey's smile and laugh. Blowers died and came back. His group in his heart that he holds close while the feet and fists rain down.

'Books?' Major Donaldson asks, his lips wet from licking too many times at the sight of the beating. He wants them to kill him. He wants to see it but also wants to draw it out for the pleasure of the delay.

Howie's head swims. His mind closing down from the abusing but coming back slowly as the thing inside works to numb the pain and bring him back. Blood pours from his mouth and in that minute he worries they will see his rate of recovery and form a connection.

'What books did you destroy?' Major Donaldson asks.

'She died,' Howie slurs the words out. A separation within his mind and enough guile left to act dumb and hurt. 'Killed her...'

'Sorry, Sir,' Corporal Jones says, breathing hard from the exertion. 'Coward can't take a little beating by the looks of it.'

'S'dead,' Howie whispers. 'Sarah...she...hurts...'

'Damn wimp. Eh lads? See that? An officer my backside. That is not a brave man. Not a man with courage and virtue. That is a cowardly shelf-stacker. Take him away and bring me another one.'

'I'm fine,' Howie says quickly, lifting his head to look at the two officers. 'I impersonated an officer...they didn't know I wasn't...I lied... my fault...' a soldier bends to cut the ties on his legs as others yank him up out of the chair. 'IT'S MY FAULT...I LIED TO THEM...' he goes screaming through the door, thrashing while shouting he did it all and it's all his fault.

CHAPTER TWENTY-NINE

'I T'S MY FAULT...' Howie goes down hard. The beating becomes dangerous. The blows to his head threaten to knock him out but he clings to consciousness to scream the words to tell the others. 'I LIED TO THEM...IT'S MY FAULT...'

He's thrown down the stairs to more laughing. Landing hard on his right shoulder and screaming out in pain. Dragged and kicked. Pulled and hit. Gas masks on.

'I LIED...I LIED...I L...'

His words cut off as a boot slams into his head. The impacts and blows too many to withstand. He swims out of consciousness, rallying to shout but the hits keep coming until his body shuts down completely but still they keep going.

'HOWIE?' Marcy's voice screams out at hearing the soldiers going past her cell down the corridor. 'HOWIE?'

'DOOR OPENING...MOVE AND WE'LL SHOOT HIM...

The tear gas goes in. They wait for the coughing and hacking to start before booting the door open and storming the cell.

'STAY THE FUCK DOWN...DOWN NOW...GET THAT ONE...HIM...'

'No!' Roy cries out as Reginald is dragged away. He reaches out to pull Reginald back. Rifle butts slam down on his head and back.

Cookey rolls while coughing to reach for Reginald as a hard boot snaps his head over. The severity increases. The application of force is harder. Howie is dumped on the floor.

Reginald flies down the corridor. His hands cable tied behind his back. Terrified beyond compare. Fists hit his head. His glasses fall to be broken under a heavy foot. The little man goes faster than Howie. His body lighter. He saw the state of Howie through tear misted eyes. His guts cramp up. His whole body shakes with fear. This is not meant to happen. This is wrong. They are meant to go north and fight the other player. This is not in the game. This is not a move either side have taken. He didn't see this or plan for it. He never even thought about it. Tears stream his face. His whimpers so awful. This cannot happen. It cannot.

He goes into the room, propelled into the chair. His ankles secured. Water thrown in his face. He cries out and tries to turn his head. He has never been so scared, so terrified. He isn't brave like Howie. He cannot take a beating like Howie. He cannot take pain or torture. He isn't strong or courageous. He chokes on the tear gas in his throat and the water filling his mouth. A leather gloved fist punches the side of his head. He feels his body dropping as the chair topples over and the laughing of men muffled behind the gas masks.

'Pick him up.'

Reginald feels himself rising as the chair is righted. The voice from the flat bed trucking speaking. He sobs in fear. Shaking so hard, so scared. He won't last a beating. He cannot do it. He isn't brave.

'Name?'

Reginald opens his eyes, expecting his vision to be blurred from the loss of his glasses but of course the infection has corrected his eyesight. He only wears the glasses now for the comfort of it. That one thing gives him a tiny bit of courage. He is infected. The pain will be less. The damage they do will be less.

'Beat him again...'

'No please...'

His pleading makes no difference and Major Donaldson watches with an expression akin to lust as the small man is thrashed.

'Try again...name?'

'Reginald,' Reginald blurts. He can taste blood in his mouth. His body hurts. They hurt him. Kicking and punching, slamming his head into the concrete. The fear rises. The panic that he cannot do this. He cannot be tortured. He tries to summon courage but finds only terror. He looks to see two men immaculate in uniforms staring at him through surgical masks. Do they know he is infected? 'Please don't hurt me...'

'Coward,' Lieutenant Galloway-Gibbs remarks with a sad shake of his head.

'My men heard you ordering the books be destroyed. What books?' Major Donaldson asks. He wants them to beat him more. He wants them to hurt him so he screams and cries and begs.

Reginald thinks fast. He thinks through the pain and terror. They heard him telling Howie to destroy the books. An angle to play. Leverage to be gained. Sudden hope dawns but he has to play it right. 'We didn't know who you were,' he says quickly, blood spraying from his mouth as he speaks. If he does this right he might be able to save them. 'I am so dreadfully sorry, truly I am, we didn't know you were the army...'

'Books. What about them?' Major Donaldson asks, not really listening.

'Oh gosh, thank god it's you,' Reginald gasps, he looks to the two officers with hope etched on his face. 'Thank god we found you...'

'What?' Major Donaldson sneers.

'We were looking and...we had to fight as we went but...I am so thankful we found you. The army is functioning.'

'BOOKS,' the Major roars. 'Beat him again...bloody idiot blathering on.'

'No!'

Reginald head is hit from behind, from the side, from the front. Solid whacks that knock him senseless. Boots kick his shins. A hard fist in his stomach.

'Got an idea,' Corporal Jones says, rushing off to the side of the room. 'Hold his head back...Sir, can I use your hankie please, Sir?'

'My hankie?' Lieutenant Galloway-Gibbs asks, pulling it out to hand over with a bemused look at the Major who smiles like a father watching his children play.

The hankie goes over Reginald's face. His head held tight and forcing him to look up.

'Please no...I beg you....' He sputters as the water hits the material over his mouth that soaks through to pour into his throat. His body instantly believes he is drowning. He convulses to vomit as more water pours in.

'Oh I say, well done chaps,' the lieutenant says in admiration. 'Old water boarding eh?'

'Saw it on youtube, Sir,' the corporal says, 'and might have done it once or twice if you get my meaning.'

This is new. This is wonderful. Major Donaldson watches with fascination at a man trying not to drown.

Reginald chokes. He can't breathe. Panic sets in. Images of life should flash through but his mind fills with Marcy and Paula. He hears Cookey's laugh and Clarence's deep voice. He sees Mo Mo's sheepish smile and Blinky grinning. Memories of the last few days. Good memories. Strong memories. He thinks of Blowers with the inflatable parrot as the water pours into his mouth and suddenly the hands let go and the material is taken away. He gasps to draw air, spewing water out across the room and earning a punch from drops hitting the Major's shiny boots. He has to think. He has to use the one weapon he has and let his intellect work. 'We have...' he tries to speak but retches and heaves instead. He must get the words out and save everyone. 'Have a cure...' he retches on the last word that goes unheard.

'Corporal, I rather think he needs another round,' Major Donaldson orders.

'NO! WE HAVE A C...'

Head back. Material over. Water poured and while his senses shut down so he understands this is sadistic pleasure at play and it matters not what they say. That's when the true fear hits. The worst fear. The very essence of horror because Reginald knows you cannot reason, deal or barter with depravity and madness.

The little man so brave and courageous is not given a chance to speak. His body is battered. His hands stamped on. His head punched until he feels drunk. The little man who took his swatter into battle yesterday and leapt terrified from the van but hours ago to pull the infected from Clarence is rendered helpless. Time becomes meaningless. He has no clue if the torture lasts minutes or hours. He hears laughing and the voices of the officers asking questions but each time he gets close to the word *cure* so they start again.

He blacks out and comes back while being dragged down a corridor. His body in agony. His head swimming as it slips between layers of consciousness. 'We have a cure…have a cure…a cure…' his whimpers and words go unheard. The only chance they had to buy time and get through this. The one word he could have said that might have made them listen.

'Wrong door you twat…that's the women's cell.'

'Who gives a fuck…chuck a tear gas in…'

Reginald hears the screams followed by the coughing and slips away for a few seconds. He comes back as he is dumped on the ground and another boot slams into his stomach then the boots go away.

He cries out when the hands touch him. He flinches to crawl away from the beating and boots and punches. He cries and weeps as the hands find his face and turn him softly.

Marcy's tears fall on his face. Charlie and Paula holding him close. Blinky staring in abject misery. All of their eyes streaming from the tear gas and the pain of seeing him so hurt. His eyes swollen, his nose broken, fingers snapped, blood coming from his ears. His body ruined.

'Oh Reggie,' Marcy's voice breaks. 'I am so sorry…'

Reginald sinks down into darkness that's so warm and safe. A void of anything. A place of eternal rest but the infection within him forces his heart to work. It forces blood to pump and sends him surging back to agony and life.

Marcy's voice. Soft and soothing. Her hands on his cheek. Paula's hands cradling his head.

He has to speak. He has to say it. It is the only hope now. His mouth moves but no sound comes out. The darkness tugs to pull him down. His body weakened and broken. So much water went into his lungs. His brain went without oxygen for too long. The infection fights to hold on, to keep him clinging to life. He surges up to the surface, to the place where the living dwell. His hand, broken and bent, reaches for Marcy. He speaks but the words are lost, a faint whisper of breath.

'Sssshhh, rest now, Reggie...rest now...'

His heart booms to give energy to grip her hand and pull her closer. She bends forward until his mouth is next to her ear. It has to happen now. There is no other way. It's all they have. Four words are whispered then he is gone. Sucked down into the darkness where there is no pain and only a void.

He lives but barely. His heart beats but weakly. His life force hardly remaining in this world as Marcy stares at his near lifeless form.

CHAPTER THIRTY

Pressure builds. Pressure grows. Pressure unrelenting.

He has run for miles. His body is exhausted. His legs heavy. He keeps slowing down but finds the strength within to keep going. Meredith is panting hard too. Her mouth wide and her tongue swollen from thirst.

Pain everywhere. Pain in his head and chest but it doesn't matter. He has to find them so Mo Mo runs and Meredith stays close to the pup.

They gave Mo something. They gave him family and love. He keeps thinking of all of them. Of all their unique traits but most of all he thinks of Paula. When she calls him sweetie and hun. When she hugs him and kisses his head like a hundred times a day. When she stands next to him and gives him that smile. He'd die for Paula. He'd die for the love she has given that has changed his life.

Night now. Stars overhead. Roof tops ahead glinting the reflection of the bright moon from grey slates. Water. They both need water. He runs on with Meredith at his side. His mouth is so dry. His throat parched. He kept thinking to switch his radio on and call out but Dave gives orders for a reason.

A side junction ahead. A signpost indicating the direction to the village. He has to find the others but they must hydrate. Dave would order it. Dave would tell him to stop and drink.

He takes the junction with Meredith rushing ahead a few metres. On they go. Trapped in a nightmare of running where his steps don't take him forward. They pass thickets of trees full of creatures of the night that screech and make noise but are ignored.

They pass fields that burst to life with white tailed rabbits running helter skelter but they too are ignored.

He sees the rooftops glimpsed through the trees and keeps going. Every step now hurts. A stitch in his side. The pain in the back of his skull getting worse. Dehydration taking its toll.

He tries to think of what the others would do. Reginald and Charlie would come up with a clever plan to find everyone. Dave would just find them by pure instinct alone. Blowers and Clarence would know all the military places and work out the closest one. Paula would think smart. Mo doesn't know how to read a map. He doesn't know where he is. He doesn't know which way to go and suddenly there is nobody to ask.

He runs through a corner to a straight road opening up leading into the village. More rooftops than he initially saw. A bigger place than he was expecting. Drink water. Keep going. That's it. Does he go back to the side junction or go through the village? Has he messed up any hope of Meredith tracking? Was she tracking anyway?

The pulse hits as he nears the turning into the village proper. The feeling in the back of his head that is never wrong. Meredith growls, she can smell them.

'No,' he mutters, 'not now...'

The sound reaches him. The snarls and growls. The banging of bodies throwing themselves at hard surfaces. Fuck. He doesn't have time for this.

They reach the junction and stop to stare. The road leads on past the village. He can keep going and find water from somewhere else. Meredith growls but doesn't bark. Her hackles up as she presses into the pup's side as though shielding him from the horde laying siege to the boarded-up shop in the middle of the village. Infected all throwing themselves at the windows and door. The air thick with the sound of their impacts. Glass breaks to shatter. The main door rattles as they slam into it. Twenty, maybe thirty of them. Mo looks to the road leading on past the turning into the village. He's far enough back for them not to see him if he keeps running. This isn't his fight. His team have been taken. He has to find them. There is a threat to Mr Howie and Mo's job is to negate anything that poses threat or risk. This now does not pose threat to Mr Howie.

Meredith pushes harder into his side. Her teeth bared. She is thirsty and hot. She can't sweat to cool down. She needs water but the pup is on his own and they are pack. Pack fight the things and there is another smell here. A trace of it hanging between the layers of shit, piss and blood covering the things. A smell she knows. A smell she has followed for the last few miles.

'We's gotta go,' Mo whispers. 'Not our fight...' he moves away to run on, patting his leg to get Meredith to come with him. She growls and stares down the street to the horde. 'Not our fight,' he whispers. She turns and follows him. She has to stay with the pup. He is pack. They run on away from the village into the night. They run to find their pack.

The woman exhales at the sight of the boy running away. For a second it looked like he was going to run at the zombies with his dog. She flicks her eyes back to the horde attacking the store and knows there is nothing she can do. There are too many. It would need an army to take them down.

Mo runs on. 'Not our fight,' he tells Meredith. She glances up at the sound of his voice. Her eyes so big and brown, so expressive. 'S'not our fight,' he says again. She looks ahead then back at him. 'No. We's find the others.'

Meredith pants hard. Her tongue hanging from the side of her mouth. Sweat on his face, he lifts a hand to wipe it away and catches scent of Charlie on the bandana on his wrist.

The woman eases back from the window, stepping deeper into the shadows as she listens in horror to the sound of the things charging at the shop.

'YOU'S FUCKED INNIT.'

She stops going back, her eyes wide, her heart booming in fright at the voice shouting outside. She goes back to the window to see the boy and the dog stopped midway from the junction to the horde.

'YEAH BITCHES...' the boy shouts, clearly trying to get their attention. She sees the rifle strapped to his back. The pistols on his body. The combat boots and black clothes. His dark hair shiny. His skin Arabic or mixed race. His hands draw two knives from his belt that he holds down at his sides. What the hell is he doing? He's so young too. Seventeen? Eighteen?

'IN A RUSH YEAH,' Mo says, holding his hands out.

A snarl. A turn. The horde charge.

The woman's heart quickens at the sight of the boy just standing there with the dog at his side. She expects them to run, to draw the horde away. She wills them to run. She wills them to flee but the bloody idiots just look at each other. She blanches when the dog barks and such a bark it is too. So loud. So powerful. So aggressive. She watches the boy slide his right foot back and his left foot forward. She watches the boy pull his right arm back and bring his left arm across his body. 'S'MY FIGHTING STANCE INNIT...'

Holy cow. He's done for. The horde speed up. Charging straight at him. Why isn't he running? Run you bloody fool. She presses closer to the window, grimacing with horror at what she about to see, but what she does see is not what she expected at all.

At the last second the dog bursts forward to leap into the first one coming. A deep throaty growl as the dog clamps jaws on the neck of the man and simply drops while thrashing her head. Blood sprays out but the boy. Oh my god the boy. He pauses in that position. His eyes staring fixed then he moves to dance and weave. His blades cutting jugulars open. He spins and takes another one down and jumps back to let two more come on. The dog takes one down as the boy goes low and cuts the back of the infected woman's leg then flashes round to cut her throat as she falls. After that is a blur. A mirage of a boy and a dog slaughtering them one after the other and each time she thinks he is done for so he moves to counter. The speed of him. The speed of both of them. The way they seem to move together that is near on impossible to track with the naked eye.

Grunts reach her ears. The dull whumps of bodies hitting the ground. She sees the dark blood spilling and spurting. She sees his blades flashing in the moonlight and the dog that leaps so high.

The fight goes down past the front of the boarded up store with the boy using the high kerb and litter bins to his advantage. He leads them past a metal post with multiple ornate solid iron signs pointing off to different tourist spots within the village. He ducks and weaves, spins and kills and then it's done and the street is covered with bodies.

She stares wide eyed as the boy turns to view his kills and the dog moves as a predator to snap jaws on those still moving. Oh my. That was something else. It really was. To see such a thing.

'Do the right thing innit,' the boy says as cool as you like. Clearly very impressed with himself, as he should be too. He drops to wipe his blades on the clothes of a body and looks round again. 'Blinky'll be jealous,' he tells the dog. The woman watches him wipe the back of his arm across his shining face while he stays crouched. 'We's ready yeah?' he asks. The dog looks at him. 'Water then we go...' he surges up fast. His legs strong. His muscles thrumming from the fight. His situational awareness profound and his skills advancing closer to Dave all the time. Dave, however, would have noticed the solid iron sign above his head and not stood so fast to headbutt and knock himself out with a metallic thonk rolling down the otherwise silent street.

'Ooh,' the woman winces and turns away at the thud. The silly sod. That will hurt. She watches with a grimace as the dog walks over to stare down at his unconscious form. The woman leans forward to look up and down the street. She should go and help. She really should. 'Right...I'll do that,' she says softly, her voice tinged with accent. She hefts the hand axe by the door, slides the bolts back and steps out into the alley running at the side of her house.

Meredith stares at Mo. Her head cocked to one side. The pup has hurt himself. She lowers down at his side and whines softly. She can hear his heart beating. She pants hard with her tongue swollen and so thirsty.

The woman eases out of the alley with her axe held ready to use. A vicious looking thing with a nasty curved head holding a gleaming sharp edge. She smells the blood in the air mixed with other body fluids. All stinky and gross. She starts to cross the road, gently, slowly.

Meredith detects the movement and snaps attention to her. Her ears pricked. Her eyes fixed.

The woman walks slowly, stepping over and round dead bodies and the pools of hot blood.

Meredith watches her intently. A low growl sounds to warn the woman the pup is her pack.

'Good doggy,' the woman says. 'Yes yes, good doggy...' she tuts at the sight of the boy flat on his back with a welt across his forehead where he hit the sign. 'That will bruise,' she tells Meredith. 'I won't hurt him...I promise,' Deep blue eyes, long blond hair held back in braids, her voice so soft and lilting. Her face so open and friendly. An aura of soothing calmness that has no hint of threat.

The woman lowers next to Mo with another sad tut and a shake of her head. 'Well now, what a truly cuntish thing to happen.'

A click behind her. The hammer of a pistol being pulled back. The woman instantly becomes aware of the dog staring past her while slowly wagging her tail.

'And all our lives forever more will be entwined...'

A deep voice whispering with clear pronunciation. Eloquent even. The woman turns slowly, pivoting on her haunches to look at the broad-shouldered young man aiming a pistol at her head. A rifle slung on his back. A baby swathed in blue blankets held in the crook of his left arm. The door to the store behind him now hanging open. She heard the baby crying today and knew someone had taken refuge in the flat above the shop. The dog moves past her to push into the man's legs, whining with her tail still swishing slowly.

'He's not dead,' she says quietly with that soft accented voice.

The man treads carefully to the side of the boy and stares down while slowly lowering the pistol. 'You's fucked up innit bruv,' the eloquence vanishes to a harsh grating street drawl as he lowers to a knee. 'Little Mo Mo...' Maddox whispers. 'Little Mo Mo all alone...'

CHAPTER THIRTY-ONE

B oots crunching in the corridor. They make ready. Tops pulled up to cover mouths and noses. Pure aggression ready to vent. Howie at the back, his body battered, his face a mess but he rises on shaky legs ready to fight.

'DOOR OPENING...STAY DOWN OR WE'LL SHOOT SOME FUCKER...'

The muffled voice screams the order but they are ready this time. Some of them might die. They know that. The soldiers have rifles and will open up but it only needs Dave to get amongst them and they will win.

The door opens slowly, an inch at first. Low voices arguing outside. Giggling and laughing.

They wait for the tear gas to come in knowing the tops over their mouths and noses will buy them a few seconds.

The grenade comes in. Different. Smaller. Another one behind it, then another.

'FLASHBANGS...' Blowers screams as the first one blows with a deafening boom and an explosion of pure white light. They reel away, blind and deafened. The second and third go in quick succession. More noise and light. Senses overwhelmed. Pain in ears. They don't hear or see the tear gas coming in but feel the gas hitting their throats a few seconds later and drop to gag and retch the same as before.

The soldiers swarm in. Rifle butts into heads. Boots lash out. Several aim at Dave, not giving him an inch of movement.

There is tough, then there's Simon Blowers. They start dragging him towards the door and despite the pain, the burning in his throat, the blindness in his one good eye and the nauseous disorientation he fights like a bastard. He gains his feet and for one glorious second his fists can work. Giving a barrage of blows to gas mask wearing heads and sending young soldiers reeling back. For one glorious second he gains the advantage and roars to fight because he does not fear death.

Then they swarm and take him down. Rifle butts hit his head. Boots kick his knees. Someone grabs him round the neck in a choke-hold. Others punch his mid-section. Held down and cable tied. Grabbed by the ankles and dragged with his head bouncing on the rough concrete. Still he tries to fight. Still he writhes and bucks and still they beat him.

In the room upstairs he uses every ounce of his strength to resist going into the chair that gets kicked over and sent flying again and again. They beat him harder. They beat him until he can't think straight but always in his mind is the woman who said she will wait for him so fuck you, fuck you and bring more because they'll have to kill him before he gives in.

They do bring more and those more add boots and fists and as tough as Simon Blowers is, he is still a mortal man and eventually he is bound to the chair with blood pouring from many wounds and a great wave of sickness pulsing through him.

All around him stand the soldiers. Chests heaving. Gas masks dislodged and knocked askew.

'He's a lively one,' Major Donaldson remarks.

'Simon Blowers, Sir,' Lieutenant Galloway-Gibbs drawls.

Blowers knows who he is. He heard the voice when they were captured but couldn't place it until now.

'CUNT...' he roars out, thrashing to break free and fight. His chairs tips over to the side, he writhes impotent and useless as the soldiers laugh at his pathetic plight. 'YOU'RE A COWARD GALLOWAY...YOU HID...YOU HID WHEN WE FOUGHT THEM...'

'I say,' Lieutenant Galloway-Gibbs says in offence at the comments.

'Are you going to take that insult, Charles?'

'No I am bloody not, Sir.'

'Give him a kick if you want. Go on, right in the belly...kick him in the belly...'

'I will,' the lieutenant says, striding over to give a desultory weak kick.

'Put some effort into it,' the Major booms. 'Draw your foot back.'

'I will,' the lieutenant kicks again as Blowers thrashes and strains to break his binds. Blood pours down his hands from the ties slicing his skin open. He feels the boot hitting his stomach and laughs hard and forced. 'PUSSY...FUCKING PUSSY...COWARD GALLOWAY... FUCKING COWARD...'

'KICK HIM,' the Major orders.

'HE'S A COWARD...HE LET US FIGHT ON OUR OWN... HE HID AND CRIED...'

'Impudent little deserting bastard,' the Major snaps the words out as he strides to join the lieutenant in kicking Blowers. Both of them laying boots in with weak kicks that build up harder and faster as they get into the swing of it.

'GO ON SIRS...' Corporal Jones shouts. His men join in, urging the officers to kick more and kick harder.

Blowers doesn't feel them for the first moment or so, such is the rage within him, but they get harder and aimed better. They hit his stomach, his bollocks and then his head. He stops screaming to choke on his own blood pouring in his mouth from biting his tongue. His body starts to shut down. Diverting energy to protect the vital organs. The infection keeps him alive. Clotting wounds. Rushing to numb nerve endings screaming in pain. He goes still and silent. His body a mere thing that rocks and jolts as the officers keep kicking. They hold onto each other for support, both flushed with hair poking up but still with face masks in place to prevent the tear gas residue hitting their throats.

He comes to while being dragged down the stairs and fights again. His efforts are weaker and less violent but he tries nonetheless. The girl with the golden hair touched his hands, she touched his face and said she will wait for him.

'THEY'RE PUSSIES,' he roars out, knowing the others can hear him. 'FUCKING COWARDS...'

The soldiers drop him in the corridor to beat him again. Paula's voice screaming for them to stop. Charlie pleading. 'FIGHT ME... COME ON...' Blinky roars.

The door opens, the flashbangs and tear gas go in. The soldiers swarm fast to aim rifles at Dave as Blowers is dumped and the next is dragged screaming and fighting.

CHAPTER THIRTY-TWO

'Little Mo Mo,' Paula gives him that motherly smile. 'Little Mo Mo all alone...' it doesn't sound like her voice but it doesn't matter. She carries him somewhere quiet and warm. He wants to tell her not to call him *little Mo Mo* in front of the lads but then it is funny. Cookey will rip the piss. Nick will use it for a few hours and grab him in a headlock to rub his knuckles in his head. Blowers will laugh and Blinky will punch him on the arm. It's cool though. He likes it. Nick is never too rough or pushy and it feels like a thing a big brother would do. Like he and Jagger used to do. He fights back sometimes when they grab and tussle him but he never uses the skills Dave taught him. That would be wrong. Those skills are for work, not for play. It was different this morning with Blinky. They were play-fighting and using the skills but that was okay because they'd just finished Dave Training. The best time was the water fight in the house in the beach. All of them together. Even Charlie was joining in.

'How do you know him?'

Mo doesn't understand why Paula asked him that. He doesn't know who she talking about. A worry starts to build. A sense of dread that tells him something is wrong. The dream becomes a nightmare. Paula is crying. Marcy and Charlie are crying. Reginald is hurt. Blinky is telling someone to fight her. The boss. The boss is hurt. His heart races. His body twitching. He cries out and flinches when a cool wet cloth is rubbed gently over his face. Words spoken but he doesn't understand the language. He feels Meredith licking his face and the pressure of her next to him. He hears her lapping water and that's good because she was thirsty. She needed to drink. Hydrate. Dave tells him to hydrate. Dave tells him they think differently. They are different.

'Sssshhhh,' the cool wet cloth comes back. Soothing and nice. A cup pressed to his lips. He drinks deep and wonders if he is asleep or awake.

'Rest.'

He rests because Paula tells him.

CHAPTER THIRTY-THREE

'We had this day,' Marcy whispers in the darkness of the cell illuminated only by weak moonlight coming through the grimy barred window.

'What?' Paula asks, her voice low.

Marcy smiles sadly at Reginald and feels the tears roll down her cheeks. He's so badly hurt. His face all pulped and broken. They can't even wash him or give him water. Her hand rests on his chest, feeling his heart beating weakly. His breathing shallow. She knows Howie has been beaten, Blowers too but Reginald is different. He's never lifted a hand against anyone. Even when he was turned. His intelligence somehow deflected the awfulness around him and now he is barely clinging to life. An awful desperation hangs over them. A silence deep and terrible but if it ends now then they had this day.

'Dribbly willy...' Marcy whispers.

Paula and Charlie smile at the memory. 'Blowers was funny,' Charlie says.

'He was,' Paula says, reaching out to rest her hand on Charlie's arm. 'At least he fought back by the sounds of it.'

'I bet he hurt a few,' Marcy says.

'Wait till they take Clarence or Dave,' Paula says.

'I'd rather not.'

'Marcy I didn't mean that.'

'I know, I'm sorry.'

'Why ain't they coming for us?' Blinky asks.

The other three stay silent. Unwilling to voice the fears inside.

Charlie swallows and winces at the soreness in her throat from the tear gas. 'I can take a beating but...'

'Ssshhh,' Marcy says, pulling Charlie in to hold. 'It might not happen.'

'I don't think I can do that...I really don't. I'd rather die,' Charlie says.

'It's only pain, Charles. We've had worse on the pitch.'

'Christ,' Paula whispers.

Marcy holds Charlie close, feeling the tremble running through the younger woman's body. 'I'll go first...' she whispers. She takes Paula's hand, holding it tightly in her own. 'Hopefully they'll leave you three alone.'

'Jesus, Marcy.'

'Shush, Paula.'

'Fuck that,' Blinky scoffs. 'No offence, Marcy but I can fight better than you and I've had more beatings than...'

'I've sinned remember,' Marcy cuts in, holding the other two women while Blinky stands by the door. 'The things I did...I took life, thousands of lives...I'll try and keep them away...'

'Stop it,' Paula snaps.

'What the fuck?' Blinky asks. 'What you on about?'

'There's dozens of them,' Charlie whispers.

'Maybe it'll pay back for what I did. If it doesn't work then just stay passive...'

'I can't...I won't...' Charlie says. 'Not that...'

'They can't hurt what's inside. It's just the body they'll use. Not what we are. They can't have that and what we have will lessen the pain. We can get through it. I'll try, I swear I will try and keep them away from you...'

'Marcy, fucking stop it,' Paula says.

'Said I'm going first,' Blinky says obstinately.

Marcy closes her eyes at the innocence of someone so brutally capable. Paula's cheeks grow wet as she lowers her head.

'Blinky, Marcy means they might not beat us,' Charlie says.

'Eh? What cos we're women? Fuck that. I'll fuck 'em up and...'

'Jesus, Blinky. Yes because we are women,' Charlie snaps.

'Shush,' Marcy says quickly. 'Blinky, they're probably going to rape us.'

'What?' Blinky asks. 'Like...like sex? I'm gay...I don't...' she reels at the concept that has never once entered her mind. Not once. Not ever.

'Blinky, come over here and stay close to Charlie and Paula. Look after Reggie...we'll get through this...'

CHAPTER THIRTY-FOUR

They lay into him the second the door closes. Blowers dumped in the cell and Cookey now curled up in a ball as they set about with kicks and stamps. The soldiers are tired and sore from handling Blowers. The gas masks are making them hot. The humour of it all now drying up so they become vicious and mean with nasty digs to vent anger.

They go fast. Up the stairs and through the door to the waiting chair and the room now soaked with water and sprays of blood. His ankles are secured. The re-filled buckets of water thrown in his face. He coughs and turns his head, yacking water up but at least it clears some of the tear gas from his eyes.

'Alex Cooke,' Lieutenant Galloway-Gibbs says. 'A deserter with Simon Blowers, Nicholas Hewitt, Darren Smith, Jamie...'

'Hiya,' Cookey says, looking up at the face mask wearing lieutenant. 'Heard you were here. How's your mum? Still a crack whore?'

The punch comes hard. His head snaps over. Blood sprays and he sags for a second before slowly turning back to look at the man who punched him. 'His mum give you the clap did she?' Blood sprays again. The pain is intense. Stars behind his eyes but he turns back and smiles with bloodied teeth. 'Okay okay...' he says quickly, 'no more mum jokes...s'bad taste...well, I mean she does leave a bad taste...holy fuck that one hurt...haha! Jesus, you lot got no sense of humour...okay stop now. Sorry. No more I promise...'

'He always was a card,' the lieutenant says.

'Your mum takes cards...OW! Stop punching me for fuck's sake...' Cookey gasps as he tries to open his eyes and spots the Major standing smartly with his hands behind his back and promptly bursts out laughing. 'No way...no fucking way...'

Major Donaldson frowns quizzically and rocks on his heels that just sets Cookey off even more.

'Best day ever...oh my god...'

'Corporal Jones, will you please beat this man...'

'Corporal Jones! Oh my days...' Cookey howls, tears streaming down his face. His whole body heaving with laughs and such is Cookey's infectious laugh that several of the soldiers start chuckling at the sight. 'He said...oh my god...he said Corporal Jones...did you hear him?' he asks a soldier wearing a gasmask who giggles a bit louder. 'WE'RE DOOMED...' Cookey booms in a Scottish brogue before erupting again.

'I don't understand,' Major Donaldson says stiffly, his face twitching as Cookey starts rocking the chair from laughing so hard.

'S'not funny,' Corporal Jones mutters.

'Fucking is...' Cookey gasps. 'WE'RE DOOMED...DOOMED I TELL YA...' more soldiers laugh, trying to hide it from the stern and slightly confused expressions on Major Donaldson's and Lieutenant Galloway-Gibbs' faces. '*Don't tell 'em your name, Pike,*' Cookey quips between laughs, his voice a near perfect impersonation.

'Shut up cunt,' Corporal Jones hisses.

'*Don't panic Mr Mannering...*'

'Beat that man, Corporal Jones.'

'OH MY GOD...stop...please stop...my stomach hurts...'

'Corporal Jones. I said beat that man...'

'I think some wee is coming out...*don't panic Mr Mannering*...go on...please...say it...' he glances to Corporal Jones while laughing. 'Oh mate...so funny...go on...just once...'

'Say what?' Corporal Jones sneers before scowling round at his men still trying not to laugh.

'*Don't panic Mr Mannering,*' Cookey quips again.

'Right enough of this. Do the water thing, Corporal Jones...' he cuts off at Cookey squealing from laughing so hard. 'That boy has a mental issue I would say...fetch the water, Corporal Jones.'

'Stop, don't...please...too funny...*fetch the water, Corporal Jones... don't panic Mr Mannering...*go on, say it...'

'You men, stop laughing,' Major Donaldson barks. 'This is not funny.'

'Go on, Jonesy,' one of the men urges.

'Shut the fuck up,' Corporal Jones snaps at the man. 'GET THE WATER...'

'*Don't tell 'em your name, Pike...*'

'Think this is funny? Corporal Jones asks, yanking Cookey's head back.

'Yes!' Cookey laughs. 'Funny as fuck...'

The cotton hanky goes over his mouth and nose. The bucket of water is poured slowly, the drips soaking through the material into Cookey's mouth. He drinks the first few mouthfuls, gulping the liquid down to ease his thirst.

'POUR THAT BLOODY WATER,' Major Donaldson orders. Cookey bursts out laughing at the voice which makes the liquid pour into his windpipe. He tries to cough but more comes down. He gags and heaves, thrashing from being unable to breathe. His body tries to purge the liquid but more comes in faster than he can cough it out. The humour vanishes in a second. Fear and terror grip. He tries turning his head side to side but strong hands grip and hold.

'Ain't funny now is it,' Corporal Jones says into his ear. 'Who's laughing now?'

Cookey starts drowning. Water in his lungs. Pain in his head. Images flashing. The material is taken away and the fists come hard and fast. He spews while they beat him. The chair topples backwards. He can't breathe, he cannot draw air but still the feet come. Corporal Jones drops to land hard punches in Cookey's face. His thick leather gloves battering his eyes. Breaking his nose. Words shouted. The material comes back over his face. Cookey panics and tries to get away but the water pours again.

Still they go at him. Still they kick his legs and arms. Major Donaldson and the lieutenant join in then take over. The two in obvious sadistic lust for the pain they cause until they render the lad unconscious.

Finally they drop back. Both officers trying to draw composure from such a crazed attack in front of what they see as enlisted men. They smooth hair down, straighten clothes and heave for air.

'He's almost dead,' Corporal Jones says, pushing at Cookey with his foot. 'Want me to shoot him?'

'No,' Major Donaldson replies breathlessly. 'They'll all be hung tomorrow. Let everyone see Mr Howie and his men be strung up. Damn hard work this interrogating, wouldn't you say, Lieutenant?'

'I would, Sir. Hot work interrogating detainees.'

'Hot work it is. You men, take a break. Come back in an hour and we'll carry on.'

'Sir, you heard the officer, get him out...er Sir? You said about the women?'

'Haven't forgotten, Corporal,' Major Donaldson says. 'All yours once we've completed the interrogations.'

'Thank you, Sir. Very kind. Three weeks without a woman for some of my lads is a bit long and a couple of them are fit as anything. Are the officers partaking in er...the enjoyment of the women, Sir?'

'I might have a go yes,' Major Donaldson says. 'Not that slutty one though. Big tits never did it for me. The older one. Might have a go on her. Lieutenant?'

'Oh I don't see why not. Cowards and deserters. Get what's coming to them and yes, I rather agree with you, Sir. The older one is certainly very attractive.'

'Agreed then,' Major Donaldson snaps. 'Your men can have the three sluts and the lieutenant and I will take some company with the older one.'

CHAPTER THIRTY-FIVE

Flashbangs, tear gas. Lots of them. There is no hope in hell in fighting back. All they can do is scream from ears hurting so much and the retina burns of the bright flashes while heaving and retching from the constant exposure to the noxious fumes.

Cookey is dumped but another is not taken. The soldiers withdraw, slamming the door behind them and it takes minutes before anyone can see or hear enough to start looking for Cookey.

'Got him,' Clarence's ragged voice spits the words as he lifts Cookey into his arms and slumps back against the end wall. Clarence can't see properly. His eyes hurt from the flashbangs. He can't breathe properly or hear fully but he holds Cookey tight and feels the lad breathing in his arms. Roy crawls over, groping out until he feels Clarence's legs then working up to find Cookey's head. His fingers run over his skull and down his face. Gently, so gently. His lips purse at what he feels. The nose broken. Blood wet and sticky. His eyes swollen. His skin puffing out.

It's as bad as it can be and getting worse. Nick or Roy will be next. The soldiers are obviously holding off trying to drag Clarence out and are clearly scared of Dave. The two most likely to break free are not being touched. Blowers drifts in and out of consciousness. Howie the same. The two side by side. Dave's hands rest on their chests the same way Marcy's does on Reginald's, to feel their hearts beating.

Nick closes his eyes and thinks of Lilly. Roy and Clarence hold Cookey. An awful sense of finality settles mixed with confusion at why they have been taken and what they have done to cause such a reaction. They would charge if they could. They would fight and risk death to save the others, but sometimes a thing just cannot be done. Their captors are still British Army trained soldiers and know their business well. The only hope left, the only tiny hope is if they take Dave or Clarence. Dave for his skills. Clarence for his sheer strength but from the way the soldiers are conducting themselves they will take all necessary steps to lessen those risks.

'It's just pain,' Clarence whispers. 'Remember that...it's just pain...' Nick nods in the shadows. Roy stays silent and Dave stares into the darkness, unblinking, unflinching, waiting.

CHAPTER THIRTY-SIX

An awkward silence in the room. Maddox stands by the window, turning and leaning to see up and down the street. He expected the Saxon to arrive or see the others charging in but nothing. Mo really is on his own. Something has happened. How did Mo find him? Maddox fled north and stayed quiet after running. He didn't speak to anyone. He didn't see anyone. He found baby books in a chemist and grabbed formula, bottles, nappies and everything else needed. He bathed the boy, cleaning the birthing liquids away and worked out how to put the diaper on. He fed him too and made sure the bottles were cleaned in sterilising solution. He thought to go south for the fort but knew it would be a mistake. Lenski wouldn't go with him. The cold sex they had in that dingy room told him the connection between them was broken.

He found the village and made his way through the shop to the flat above. The windows had already been boarded up. Whoever lived there had obviously fled days ago and it crossed his mind the former occupants could now be in the fort being cared for by his girlfriend. Lives entwined and the world had suddenly shrunk to a very small place.

They came in the evening. Just two at first and Maddox stayed quiet. He had the rifle and pistol and was confident to deal with them.

Then more came and the baby cried and that sound carried to bring more. He fortified the stairs up the flat and hunkered down to wait for sunrise. He thought of Howie and Blowers. He thought of what Blowers did and what he saw when Blowers got up. It wasn't human. Nobody can take that punishment and get back up, but then they're not immune are they, they're infected. Same as Mo now.

He hears the dog growl and turns to see the woman edging closer with a look of profound distaste on her face.

'I wouldn't,' Maddox whispers.

The woman stops, the braids of her golden hair shining in the moonlight. Mid-thirties, maybe forty but the Scandinavian genes show in her unblemished complexion and the startling blue shade of her eyes. 'It is disgusting,' she says softly, her English so clear but lilting and accented. 'I am not going to hurt him,' she adds into the silence leaving Maddox unsure if she is talking to him or the dog. 'I just washed his face a moment ago...'

'She's guarding the arm not Mo.'

The woman stares again at the severed arm laying across Mo's chest underneath Meredith's head. The end a bloodied stump of raw flesh. A watch on the wrist. Gold rings on the fingers.

'She does that,' Maddox says.

'It's bleeding on him.'

'He's immune.'

'What?'

'Immune. So am I,' Maddox says, bending the truth for want of a long explanation.

'Oh,' she says mildly as though hearing the most normal thing ever said.

'What's your name?'

'Anja.'

'Swedish?'

'Danish. You?'

'British.'

'No, your name, I know you are British.'

'Maddox.'

'Nice to meet you, Maddox.'

'And you, Anja.'

'Good. We have made formal introductions, which is always important. So perhaps you can now tell me what the fuckity fuck is going on and what you mean by immune?'

'The what?' Maddox asks at the perfectly pronounced swear words.

'I swear when I am perplexed.'

'Perplexed?'

'Confused.'

'I know what perplexed means. It was the way you said it.'

'Did I say it wrong?'

'No.'

Silence falls. Anja stares at the arm on Mo's chest. The dog stares at her. Maddox stares out the window.

'Are you saying I can touch the boy?'

'Yes. Don't touch the arm.'

'And she will not bite me?'

'No,' Maddox says crossing over the room to drop at Mo's side. Meredith switches her gaze to him. Her tail offering a single wag but the low growl is there. She doesn't show teeth and her hackles stay down. A grumble more than a growl. Maddox presses the back of his hand to Mo's forehead. 'See?'

'I see yes,' Anja says, now staring at the baby cradled in Maddox's arm. The blue blanket pulled down showing the baby's head and arms.

Maddox looks up at her and spots the direction of her gaze. He glances to the baby then back to Anja and reads the expression on her face.

'I didn't steal him.'

'I never said anything.'

'His mum died giving birth...I was there,' Maddox says, gently sliding one of Mo's pistols from the holster.

'What are you doing?'

'Taking his guns.'

'Why?'

'So he doesn't shoot me when he wakes up.'

'Oh,' Anja says as though that is also the most normal thing she has ever heard. 'I thought you were friends.'

'We were.'

'But not now?'

'Not now.'

'Oh. What a confusing situation this is.'

'Do you have a car?' Maddox asks, carrying Mo's pistols to the other side of the small lounge.

'A car?'

'Yes. A car.'

'I have a car.'

'Good.'

'Do you want my car?'

'No. I want you to take him south.'

'South?'

'South. To the fort.'

'The fort.'

'Yes.'

'In the south.'

'Yes, the fort is on the south coast.'

'I see,' Anja says. 'Now?'

'Sunrise. It's safer in the day,' Maddox says, back at the window rocking the baby in his arms.

Anja nods. This is all very strange.

'How are you immune?'

'Not sure,' Maddox says.

'Are many people immune?'

'No.'

'Am I immune?'

'Probably not. How long have you been in the UK?'

'Six months.'

'Have you been arrested here? Had blood taken? DNA? Had an operation?'

'No.'

'They wouldn't know then.'

'Who wouldn't know?'

'The people with the list.'

'What list?'

'The list of people with immunity.'

'There is a list?'

'Yes.'

'Are you on the list?'

'Yes.'

'And this boy?'

Maddox looks down to Mo and again avoids the long explanation, 'yes.' He then remembers Reginald said they were never to mention the list. It has to be kept quiet. What if the woman turns? The infection would know about the list.

'Don't tell anyone about the list.'

'Right.'

'Forget I said anything about it.'

'I will.'

Another long silence. Awkward and heavy. Mo lies on his back in the middle of the floor. Anja on one side near the door to the kitchen. Maddox by the window.

Mo starts to stir. A change in his breathing. Images in his mind of Howie hurt. Cookey hurt. Blowers hurt. Reginald almost dead. Feelings of pain and confusion. His heart beats faster. Meredith stares at him, her head cocked to one side. Her tail starting to swish. Maddox turns from the window with a heavy sigh. Anja sees the look of a great sadness in his face as he walks over and holds the baby out. She stares at it then back to Maddox.

'What?' she asks.

'Take the baby.'

She stares at it again. 'Why?'

'Because Mo'll go nuts when he wakes up.'

'Nuts?'

'Angry.'

'He'll be angry?'

'Yes.'

'Oh.'

'Take the baby.'

'I see,' she takes the baby, instantly cradling it into her arms with a natural motion that Maddox notices.

'Nieces,' she says.

'Oh.'

'And nephews.'

'Sure. Might want to move back a bit.'

'Move back?'

'Just a bit.'

'I shall move back.'

Mo's eyes snap open. A weight on his chest. A dead hand in his face. Meredith staring at him, her mouth open, her tongue hanging out, her tail beating a drum against the side of the sofa. His heart still booming. His mouth dry. A woman, tall with blonde hair held back in braids edging back into another room while holding a baby wrapped in a blue blanket. Meredith staring at him. A dead hand in his face. A weight on his chest. He blinks to look at the watch on the wrist resting near his chin. Nice watch. Looks expensive. 'Rolex?'

'Cartier...'

Mo's head snatches over to see Maddox standing easy a few feet away. 'YOU'S FUCKED...'

'NO, MO...STOP...oh fuck...'

Mo surges up, springing to his feet to charge into Maddox who takes the incoming force with a turn designed to flip Mo but the lad has been Dave Trained and instead gets a hand under Maddox's chin to rip him off his feet. They go down hard into a shelf of glass Viking ornaments that scatter across the floor as Anja takes another step away into the kitchen.

'Wasn't me...fuck's sake, Mo...listen!'

'I's fuck you up...' Mo seethes, pawing at the empty holster on his right side.

'Mo! Listen...you got knocked out...' Mo spins over to get on top of

Maddox, his face furious. Maddox goes limp, pushing his hands above his head in a show of supplication. 'You knocked yourself out...'

'Fuck you...' Mo says pulling his fist back.

'The fucking dog you idiot...'

'What?'

'The dog...she's right there...she would've killed me if I hurt you...'

'He's right,' a voice says, soft and female. Not Paula. Not Marcy either. An accent. Mo snatches a view to see Meredith now growling with teeth showing and the woman holding the baby leaning through the doorway. 'You knocked yourself out.'

'What?'

'You gone deaf?' Maddox asks.

'Fuck you...' Mo says, gripping Maddox's chin harder to hold him in place.

'You stood up,' Anja says. 'I saw it. Your head...it hit the...oh what's the cunting word...'

'What?' Mo asks.

'Sign,' Maddox says.

'Sign,' Anja says, clicking her fingers. 'You hit your head on the sign...right there,' she says, touching the top of her head.

Mo's eyes narrow as something about what he is being told penetrates the confusion in his mind. He gently pats the top of his forehead to find it sore and tender. 'What you doing here?' he asks Maddox.

'Me? What the fuck you doing here? Get off me...Mo, fuck's sake...'

'Where's my guns?'

'I hid them so you wouldn't shoot me.'

'Where?'

'Get the fuck off me.'

'I got knives you...'

'Jesus, Mo Mo. I didn't do you...you took out thirty infected then stood up and knocked yourself out you fucking idiot.'

'You did,' Anja says, leaning through the door to speak before pulling back.

Mo pulls back quickly, rising to his feet as Meredith lowers her top lip. The pup was fighting and she is pack so she will fight with him but the pup is also stupid sometimes, besides, she has an arm to look at.

Maddox exhales slowly but stays still. 'Mo? Where is everyone? Why you alone?'

'What you doing here?' Mo asks.

'Hiding from you, how did you find me?'

'Ain't looking for you.'

'Mo, what are you doing here? Anja? Can you get Mo some water please?'

'Who's Anja?' Mo asks.

'I'm Anja,' Anja says. 'Er...would you like some water?'

'Yeah...I mean yes, yes please...some for the dog too.'

'She had some,' Maddox says. 'I made sure. Mo, what you doing here? Where's Howie?'

'I's got to go, where are my guns?'

'Mo, slow down...'

'Ain't got time, Mads. Not here for you...where's my guns?'

'Behind the sofa, what's going on?'

'Get fucked. What's that ladies name again?'

'Anja,' Maddox says.

'Anja,' Anja says.

'Is there an army place here?' Mo asks her.

'A what now?' Anja asks.

'A what?' Maddox asks.

'Army place. Where the army are...'

'Mo, slow down.'

'How long I been out?' Mo asks, rushing behind the sofa to find his pistols and assault rifle. 'You fucked with these, Mads?'

'No,' Maddox says with as much patience as he can muster.

'How long was I knocked out for?'

'Half hour,' Maddox says with a shrug, sitting up slowly.

'Perhaps forty five minutes?' Anja suggests.

'Fuck,' Mo mutters, his hands working fast to eject the magazines in the pistols and check both before reloading. 'Where's the army place?'

'What army place?' Maddox asks.

'Fuck,' Mo gasps in frustration, the images in his mind when he was waking up now gone but the feeling of dread is still there. An ominous portentous brick twisting his guts up. 'Gots to find them...'

Maddox watches him for a few seconds. He knows Mo Mo. He's known him since he was running round with snot on his face bunking off primary school and shoplifting from the local spar and right now he can see Mo is terrified of something. 'Mo, take it easy yeah,' Maddox says softly, his voice deep beyond his years.

'Ain't got time, Mads,' Mo mumbles, holstering the guns. 'Anna? Where's the army place?'

'Anja, her name is Anja.'

'Here,' Anja says, carrying a glass of water from the kitchen. 'Drink some water, sweetie.'

That hurts. That's the the name Paula calls him. His hand shakes when he takes the glass and suddenly he is a sixteen year old boy and not the killer they saw outside.

'Where are they, Mo?'

'Army took 'em,' Mo replies, his voice stronger from draining the glass of water in one long gulp.

'More?' Anja asks.

'Please,' Mo says, 'if I may, ma'am.'

'Of course,' she says, offering a tight smile at the show of manners.

'Do you know where the army place is please?'

'Mo?' Maddox asks slowly.

'They took them.'

'Slower, Mo. Take a breath and tell me the whole thing.'

Mo looks at him sharply, at the old Maddox and the thing he used to say when one of his crews got in trouble. *Take a breath and tell me the whole thing*. Pressure grows. Pressure builds. Pressure unrelenting. Tears fill his eyes. His lip quavers as he fights to stay composed.

'We were going north,' Mo starts to explain, the street slang easing as he speaks. He tells the whole thing. From the day of looking for immunes to Heather and Paco leaving then driving north. They were on a wide country road. Mo needed the toilet. He went down to a gate with Meredith. That's when the helicopter came. Not a police helicopter. A small army one. It had a chaingun. Soldiers came with a tank thing. He thinks Dave got a grenade into Roy's van. The soldiers were kicking Paula and Mr Howie told Dave to lie down. Maddox's face hardens at hearing Paula was kicked. The soldiers tied their wrists up and put black bags over their heads then took them away in the Saxon.

Anja lowers midway through the explanation to perch on the arm of the sofa. The baby asleep in her arms. Maddox listens closely, knowing to let Mo get it all out in one go without interrupting him with questions.

'That's it,' Mo tails off. 'I ran...got no idea if Meredith was following them or...she could have smelled you...'

'Can't ask her,' Maddox says, more to himself.

'Loophole,' Mo whispers.

'We're not far from Salisbury,' Maddox says. 'Could be anywhere, Mo.'

'There is an army er...base,' Anja says, bringing both of their attention to her. 'Old...I think from the big war. Second World War. Maybe later, the cold war I think you call it.'

'Hang on,' Maddox says seeing the look of focus on Mo's face. 'How many soldiers?'

'Dunno, Mads. I was down the road...maybe twenty? Could be more.'

'They had a tank?'

'Yeah and a chopper.'

'Mo, that's some serious ordnance.'

'How far is it? Which way?' Mo asks, looking back at Anja.

'Mo, that's the army.'

'How far?' Mo asks.

'Forty kilometres, maybe more...' Anja says. 'I don't know. I drive past the sign. It says Ministry of Defence...is that an army place?'

'Mo, listen. They could be anywhere and it's the army. They had a tank and a...'

'Show me,' Mo says. 'Please...tell me the way and I'll go...I'll get a car and...'

'Mo, you's got to listen bruv.'

'You's get fucked, bruv,' Mo fires back, slipping into the harsh slang to match Maddox.

'S'army, Mo. You don't fuck with the army.'

'I ain't leavin' 'em, Mads. Dave said to track if...'

'Don't be a fool. What you going to do against a tank? Against a chopper?'

'Blowers stood for you,' Mo says, his face hardening. 'He said you were alright. Mr Howie asked him if they should find you. Blowers said no. He said your heart was in the right place...he could have killed you, Mads...'

'Mo, this isn't about...'

'He lost a fucking eye for you, Mads. He lost a finger and got back up to fight so you'd get away. He took them on. He fucking died and got back up for you...so fuck you...fuck you coward...where's the crews, Mads? Where are they? They's dead. They's all dead. Jagger's dead. Darius is dead. They's dead because you made bad decisions but Blowers still stood for you so fuck the army and everyone else...' His words end quickly. His face flushed with rage. His chest heaving. Seconds pass. The air charged. 'Ma'am, where's the army place?'

'At least wait till daylight,' Maddox says.

'Nah,' Mo says, his voice lower, the anger abating as he tries to think what to do. He finally takes notice of the baby in Anja's arms. 'That the kid?'

'Yeah.'

'He okay?'

'Think so,' Maddox says. 'He eats, shits, cries and sleeps a lot.'

'That kid would be dead if it weren't for...'

'I get it, Mo. I understand but it is the army.'

Mo shrugs with the weight of the world on his shoulders. 'Done it before.'

'What?'

'Said done it before.'

'What the fuck you on about?'

'That navy place...Portsmouth.'

'Fuck, Mo. That was a burglary,' Maddox says with a laugh.

'Same thing. Still did it.'

'Did what?' Anja asks, drawn fully into the lives of these two strange young men slipping in and out of slang.

'We broke into a naval base,' Maddox says, shaking his head and smiling at the memory. 'We heard some ship had seized a ton of weed from the English Channel. So we broke in and took it. Difference was it was Ministry of Defence police guarding it and not soldiers with a tank and a chopper on an army base.'

'Oh,' Anja says mildly, nodding to herself. 'And what did you do with the er…the weed?'

'Sold it,' they both say together. Maddox grins. Mo shakes his head.

'Mads, I ain't waiting. You didn't see it. They kicked Paula…put black bags on their heads.'

Maddox sighs, seeing the determination on Mo's face. 'We'll go to the fort. Lilly has got some men…'

'Ain't got time.'

'You don't know that, Mo. You're panicking.'

'Mads,' Mo says quietly, shooting a glance to Anja. 'You ain't got what I got. I got to go now.'

'Immunity?' Anja asks.

'Yeah,' Maddox says before Mo can answer.

'You stay here,' Mo says. 'You got that kid…just tell me the way. I can drive…have you got a car, Anna?'

'Anja,' Maddox says. 'Mo, what if you go steaming in and get taken? What then?'

'I ain't steaming in. Fuck, Mads. How many burglaries I done? Give me some credit.'

'Yeah and you always had Jagger with you.'

'Don't matter. Please,' Mo says, looking at the woman. 'Just drop me near it…go to the fort after…I ain't good at speaking nice like Maddox and…but my friends…if you's knew them you'd help me…'

'I can show you,' Anja says, offering a shrug. 'Sure.'

CHAPTER THIRTY-SEVEN

Sergeant Hobbs lights the cigarette and stares over at the four privates walking slowly up the central road. Four more down by the gate. Another four at the top of the road by the glasshouse. More on the walls. More in the section between the two gates. More sleeping and that's not even counting Corporal Jones's inner circle in the admin block.

Too many. It's just too many. Some of these lads have seen combat too. Some were fresh out of basic training but all of them are too scared or too dumb to do anything other than what they are told.

'Can't fucking wait,' one of the privates says as the patrolling four walk by. 'Did you see her? See the tits on her? Can't fucking wait.'

'That other one was fit, had the scar on her face,' another one says.

'When we going then?' another asks.

'Jonesy said he'll call us up,' the fourth one says, clearly the leader of the small group. 'I wanted that older one but the Major's having her...'

The voices recede as the lads walk on. Rifles held low but ready. Sergeant Hobbs drags on the cigarette. Inhaling the hot smoke that burns his throat. His guts in pieces from acid reflux, too much coffee, too many cigarettes, not enough food. He grinds the cigarette out and goes into the small house. It's taken twenty-one days for them to become rapists, murderers and tyrants. Three weeks. What will it be like in three months? Cannibalism? Slavery? How much worse can it get?

The four on the main road patrol stop to chat with the four coming down. News and gossip shared. Jonesy is going to be a sergeant. Four have been interrogated so far and royally fucked up, like pulped to a mess. They're all going to be hung tomorrow so everyone can see what happens to deserters and cowards. Smiles given, laughs too but a sense of unease growing. They all saw the people coming in. They all saw Howie and Dave and the big one Clarence. They saw the marks and injuries on and the aura surrounding them. The soldiers also know that Blowers was a Marine before but left when he broke his leg and only came back in the reserves with the others to get enhanced benefits and it was their first weekend training exercise so how are they deserters? They also heard that Galloway-Gibbs pissed himself when he was found and that hundreds of the infected were killed in Salisbury. Not that they can voice those thoughts, so they smile and laugh instead and call them cunts for being cowards and deserters. Rape is wrong. Murder is wrong. Holding people captive is wrong. Taking food away is also wrong. It's all wrong but the Major is a bastard and Jonesy is twice as worse.

In the old glasshouse, through the door behind the stairwell down a graffiti covered litter strewn corridor the air is thick with smoke and the sound of harsh laughing. Jonesy holds court in the room given over *for the lads to relax in.* Plastic chairs line the walls. A big table covered in high energy drinks and chocolate bars. Squaddies smoking with eyes red from the tear gas particles clinging to their clothes. Faces flushed from the exertion of beating and carrying people.

A few, a very few relish what they are doing. Strong characters with forceful natures who are quick to single anyone out not taking pleasure in the things they do. The others laugh on cue. They crack jokes and gulp sugary drinks laden with energy that make them bounce knees and tap feet. The worry and stress shows in their eyes. The nerves show in their trembling hands as they smoke. Rape is wrong. Murder is wrong. What they are doing is wrong. Voices scream in heads to stop doing it but they can't. Too much momentum has been gained now.

Some of them blink rapidly to rid the images of the blond lad laughing before he was beaten. The little chap with the glasses who couldn't punch his way out of a paper bag. The hard one with the missing eye. All of them covered in wounds that speak of fights but beaten while tied to chairs. They think of the way Howie looked at them. That darkness in his eyes that was taking names and remembering faces.

Such is humanity. Such is the way of life so they smoke and laugh and think of their sisters and mothers while bragging about who they will fuck first, the one with big tits or the one with the scar. A few joke about the other one, the stocky one and how she should be grateful for anything she can get.

They feel sick to the core and many know they won't be able to get erections when the time comes, such is the fear and guilt inside. One of them is gay and feels even more wretched that Jonesy will somehow find out, he looks at his rifle and once again thinks to put the barrel in his mouth and pull the trigger. Another nurses a fat lip from being punched by Jonesy for cracking a joke about Dad's Army. Jonesy doesn't like jokes made at his expense.

'I make that an hour,' Corporal Jones says, checking his watch.

'Who's next?' a big lad asks as he starts putting his gas mask on. The rest follow suit. Stubbing cigarettes out and swallowing the last of their drinks before grabbing the masks that they can hide behind as though it's not really them doing these things.

'Pretty boy,' Corporal Jones says. 'We'll see if we can improve his looks...eh? That's funny that is...'

Laughs come back. Chuckles and guffaws muffled by masks over mouths.

Jonesy isn't a fool. He knows an hour has passed since the last one.

Time enough for the detainees to come up with a plan. He silences his men before leading them out. They tread carefully, softly. Creeping like naughty children down the corridor and through the door to head into the walkway between the cells. Near silent movement. A few scuffs. Jonesy stops by the cell door and motions for the next lad to lift the locking bar. It goes quietly, hefted off and held away. Jonesy and his chosen few pull the pins and crack the door. A roar on the other side. The door wrenched open by Clarence waiting. The soldiers pull back quickly, laughing as the flashbangs detonate in the threshold and watching as the big man reels back with his hands over his eyes. They go fast. Slamming rifle butts and feet into his body. Clarence crumples to the ground, he can't do anything else. His hearing and sight gone. Roy and Nick were behind him, ready to fight but they too scream out in agony. The tear gas goes next. Hissing to fill the room still thick with the ones done before. Rifles aimed at Dave crouched at the back with his hands on Howie's chest. Nick dragged, kicked and battered into the corridor. Pinned down. Binds applied. Beaten more. Dragged through the corridor and up the stairs with fresh energy served from sugary drinks.

Nick thrashes like Blowers. Fighting every inch of the way. His body strong, his form heavier and it takes hard work to get him into the chair.

Jonesy goes for him. Jonesy hates good looking men. They make him feel insecure. He rains punches into Nick as the Major and Lieutenant stroll in fixing surgical masks to faces now refreshed from a pot of tea.

Not a single question is asked. They call it interrogation but it's purely the sadistic pleasure of it and the Major's eyes light up at seeing Nick's face swell and bruise from the punches laid in by Corporal Jones.

It's just pain. Nick holds those words in his mind. He thinks of Lilly and the night they had together. He hears her voice and laugh and the feel of her hands on his skin as his heads snaps side to side from the constant punches. He consumes himself with being back at the house on the beach and such is his detachment he hardly notices when the bone in his nose crunches and thick blood pours down over his mouth.

Corporal Jones pulls away, heaving for air through his respirator and feeling the smarting on his knuckles despite the thick leather gloves.

Nick's head drops forward. Blood pouring from his nose but it clots fast, faster than it should. He should be dead or unconscious too but he isn't. All those signs penetrate the minds of the soldiers who feel that unease growing but the momentum is too great for anyone to stop and think and the officers are too drunk on power to notice.

The water comes next. Snapping Nick back from the house on the beach to the present reality of drowning and staring up at stained ceiling tiles through misted swollen eyes. A beating starts. Enough to knock him from the chair. Feet land on his legs, driving into his back and stomach then a step is taken. A gloriously wonderful idea that pops in Corporal Jones's mind who fumbles at his flies to grab his cock and aims a jet of piss At Nick's head. A stunned silence follows. The lads all recoiling until the Major bursts out laughing.

'Well done, Corporal Jones. Initiative in the field of battle eh?'

'Thank you, Sir,' Corporal Jones says, adding a sway to his waist. 'Don't just fucking stand there lads...piss on him...'

Major Donaldson feels the thrill increasing. The sight of it, the act of it. Utter dominance over another human. Something an animal would do. A complete lack of regard that makes him want to take his cock out and join in, excepting of course that he is an officer and will not urinate in front of enlisted men.

A few don't piss on Nick. Stage fright cripples them. The thought of exposing themselves in front of the others. They laugh though and say they don't need a piss and wish they'd drunk more.

Nick feels it. He feels each spray hitting his face, burning the cuts and wounds. He smells it, tastes it but knows there isn't a damn thing he can do to stop it. Mo will get to Lilly and she'll come here. He'll be dead by then. They all will but it doesn't matter. Lilly and Mo will kill them all. They'll tear this place apart.

In the cell, Clarence waits with an aggression growing with every passing minute. His time will come. He judges that Roy will be next then either him or Dave. That's when it ends because there is no squad formed that can contain either of them. He doesn't even say anything to Dave. He doesn't need to. Dave stays by Howie. Unflinching, unspeaking, waiting.

The boots come down the corridor. The voices with them. Clarence reaches to lay a huge hand on Roy's shoulder. Words are not needed. Roy's hand comes up to cover Clarence's. He'll take the beating. 'In it to the end,' Roy croaks.

'It's just pain. Cover your ears.'

They hunker down and wait. Charging the door failed. The soldiers are planning ahead too well.

The first flashbangs drop inside the door the second it opens. The tear gas comes and the soldiers barrel in, dragging Nick to dump at the sides.

Dave waits at the back. His eyes closed and his head dipped to protect from the light. His hand still on Howie's chest, feeling his heart beating.

They lay into Roy but he knew it was coming and curls up. A barrel presses into Clarence's head. Pushing hard. 'DO HIS HANDS...ONE MOVE YOU FAT FUCK AND I'LL BLOW YOUR BRAINS OUT...'

Clarence's heart lurches as he and Roy are bound with cable ties. Several going on Clarence's wrists and cinched tight. Roy is dragged, kicks and punches given as he goes through the door.

'Get up...' Corporal Jones demands.

'No,' Clarence growls.

'SHOOT THAT CUNT OUT THERE...'

'Okay...' Clarence tries to shout but his voice breaks as he coughs and retches. He rises up slowly, getting to his knees then onto his feet to tower over the soldiers aiming rifles at him.

'HE TRIES ANYTHING SHOOT THE OTHER ONE.'

Desperation hits. Clarence cannot do a thing. He walks from the cell to see Roy pinned down with a rifle pressed in the back of his skull, his hands secured.

'You were waiting for your turn weren't you?' Corporal Jones sneers. Clarence's lack of reaction infuriates the corporal who slams his rifle butt into Clarence's head. The big man takes the blow and leans over a few inches but otherwise remains nonplussed.

Roy is dragged. Clarence walks. He walks seething and ready with aggression pouring off him that quietens the soldiers tracking his every move.

The Major waits in the room with a buzz of excitement pulsing through him. This is like big game hunting. Taking a beast down. He even widens his eyes when Clarence walks in. The size of him. The height. The width of his shoulders. The thickness of his arms and legs. The complete lack of fear in his face that shows the barely restrained fury.

Clarence looks at the chair and the blood and water spattered over the floor. Blood on the walls. Blood everywhere and smeared in a wake to the door. His head turns to take in the Major who visibly quivers with anticipation while Lieutenant Galloway-Gibbs takes an involuntary step back.

Roy is dragged past to the chair and forced to sit while his ankles are secured. His face bleeding but his eyes alert and watchful. Clarence tenses his arms, testing the strength of the binds. Gently at first, discreetly. A feeling he can break them. It'll hurt. It might even cut deep enough to the veins but he only needs a couple of seconds.

The SA80 assault rifle bolt going back brings Clarence's attention to Corporal Jones who aims the barrel at Roy.

'Stop tensing your arms you fat cunt.'

'On your knees,' someone says from behind Clarence. He holds still, refusing to comply but they lay into Roy with vicious glee. He goes down, one knee at a time. Eyes fixed ahead.

'Soldiers do not do this,' he says simply.

'BEAT THAT MAN,' Major Donaldson roars. The soldiers hold off, too afraid of Clarence's aura to strike him. 'BEAT THAT MAN NOW...' Clarence turns his head to face the Major as the first kick comes but he doesn't flinch. More come and he stares hard and impassive. Feet slam into his arms and sides. Rifle butts strike his back but still he stares. The Major's face grows red with embarrassment at being bested by a man on his knees. 'Water board them both...' he growls. 'We'll see how long that stare holds...'

CHAPTER THIRTY-EIGHT

They move fast but not fast enough. Maddox is an adoptive father now after all.

'I got to get the nappy bag.'

'The what?' Mo asks.

'Nappy bag.'

'What the fuck is a nappy bag?'

'A bag for nappies.'

'Diapers,' Anja says.

'And he needs a feed soon. I need to get the sterilised bottle...and he's got this little blue babygrow and matching hat and...' Maddox tails off, nodding at Mo. 'Be two mins...'

Mo watches him go across the street to the store while Meredith holds he arm in her mouth and Anja rocks the baby side to side in this strange new world.

'How old are you, Mo?'

'Sixteen, Ma'am.'

'It's very nice you say ma'am.'

'Clarence said we should call older women ma'am if we don't know them...shit I didn't mean you's old...cos...you's not old...like you's fit and...er...'

'Thank you, you may turn away and blush if it helps.'

'Got it,' Maddox calls out, running back over the road, jumping dead bodies with his blue polka dot nappy bag in his hand.

'Nice bag,' Mo says.

'Yeah blue for a...fuck you, Mo.'

'Well gentlemen, my car is this way.'

'We should go for the fort,' Maddox says as they walk down the dark silent side street.

'Drop me off then go.'

'You's fucked bro takin' on an army.'

Mo sucks his teeth in a natural response to show his disdain.

'Don't suck your teeth,' Maddox says.

'Don't tell me what to do.'

'Little Mo Mo all grown up.'

'Fuck you, Mads...carry your bag.'

'Sikke et par klaphatte...har de tabt sutten eller hvad?' Anja mutters softly.

'What?' Mo asks.

'Pardon?' Maddox asks.

'Pardon?' Mo asks, shooting a look at Maddox.

'My car,' she says, clicking the bleeper to unlock the car.

'Volvo,' Mo says.

'Yes it is,' Anja says, opening the driver's door then stopping at remembering she is holding a baby. 'We don't have a baby seat.'

'A what?' Mo asks.

'Baby seat,' Anja says.

'We need a baby seat,' Maddox says, looking round for another car.

'Just hold it.'

'Him' Maddox says.

'Whatever...we's got to go.'

'Look for a baby seat,' Maddox says, walking over to the only other car in the street.

'Where?' Mo asks, the frustration growing inside.

'Any good?' Anja calls.

'Booster seat in the back but I think that's for toddlers.'

'You need a baby seat for a baby,' Anja says.

'What the fuck,' Mo mutters. 'Hold the baby...*I'll* hold the baby... we's got to go. Just give me the keys, you two stay here and look for a high chair.'

'Baby seat,' Anja says. 'You're not taking my car.'

'I got to go.'

'Have you passed your test?'

'Fuck me,' Mo growls, itching to pull a gun and just take the car.

'I'll drive, you hold the baby,' Maddox says, walking towards Anja.

'But it's my car. I just paid the finance on it...fine. You drive.'

'Thank fuck,' Mo says, climbing into the back with Meredith then cursing when Maddox opens the other back door to put his rifle and nappy bag in. 'MADS!'

'We're going,' Maddox says, dropping into the driver's seat. 'Nice car.'

'Thanks,' Anja says.

'Danish?'

'Volvo is Swedish.'

'No I mean did you get it in Denmark?'

'MADS!'

'Yes, Mo. We're going,' Maddox snaps, starting the car. 'Is he okay?'

'Oh he's fine,' Anja says, looking down at the baby.

'He's due a feed.'

'He's asleep.'

'Do you wake them up to feed them or wait till they wake up? The books say different things.'

'I think it's best to let them wake up'

'MADS I WILL FUCKING SHOOT YOU...'

'Shush,' Anja says, 'you'll wake the baby.'

'Wake the baby,' Mo mumbles, earning a look from Meredith. 'Fuck's sake,' he groans at the human arm still clamped in her mouth.

'We are not going anywhere with that in here,' Anja says firmly.

'Mo, get the arm out...the baby is right there.'

The back door opens. Mo surges out. His face furious, he ducks back in to grab the hand and tugs. Meredith tugs back. A low growl in her throat. 'Give me the arm...Meredith...give me...give...' he tugs, she tugs. He pulls harder. She pushes her front paws into the leather seat. He yanks. She yanks. 'NOW...' she lets go, he throws the arm away, gets back in and slams the door. Anja and Maddox both turned watching him. 'What?' Mo asks.

'Nothing,' Anja says, turning to face the front.

Maddox finally pulls away, driving a few feet before stopping, 'which way we going?'

CHAPTER THIRTY-NINE

'Fiver he won't.'

'Money don't mean shit now.'

'Pack of smokes then...'

'You're on.'

Clarence used to hate forced marches over great distance. His body is built for power not endurance events. Chris and Malc got him through it. Always at his side. Always in his ear and through them, Clarence learnt that pain is just a mindset and something that can be overcome. He does that now. He does it to protect Roy because it's become a thing in the room to see how much abuse the big man will take before he gives in, and for every minute they are focussed on him so they are leaving Roy alone.

So he rises again. His hands still bound behind his back but he pushes his head into the floor and shifts so his knees can find the ground and heaves to rise and lean back to hold his head high.

The soldiers have never seen anything like it. Jonesy has battered him senseless but he keeps getting back up. Jonesy even took a break and let two others have a go but still he got back up.

They still laugh, despite the sickening repulsion of it. They jeer weakly and make jokes to invoke harsh forced laughter. They cover his face with a cloth and pour water over it and watch as he gurgles and drowns. They beat his body with rifle butts because fists don't seem to have any impact and all the time being watched by Major Donaldson and Lieutenant Galloway-Gibbs held entranced at the spectacle. Like watching a gladiator in the arenas of ancient Rome. Like watching a freak being taken apart piecemeal. A thing they will talk about for years to come because no matter what they do to him, he still rises.

Roy lies unconscious and Clarence knows they are going to die here. He knows that now. Only Dave remains before the soldiers start on the women and the diligence shown tells Clarence they won't give Dave an inch of room. Weirdly, the most horrifying thought of all is the concept of Dave being tortured. Dave is untouchable. Unstoppable. The only time they ever saw him bleed was today and he did that to himself. Maybe Dave will break free or fight back. Clarence hopes so. Even if Dave only takes one with him it'll be worth it. Behind those thoughts, and while he takes the batterings to rise again, he thinks of Paula and Marcy and of Charlie and Blinky and what these men will do to them. It gives him the strength to keep rising. The more these lads exhaust themselves maybe the less harm they'll do to the women. They can all fight. Clarence knows that. Especially Blinky. She'd tear this lot apart in minutes on a level playing field, but there is no way in the world she can do what the others have failed in. She'll try of course, they all will but the torture they'll be given will be different to this.

Jets of piss hit his face but that's okay and he rises. The water pours down his throat again, filling his lungs until he is sure he will die but that's okay and he rises. He rises until the joke becomes flat. He rises until the Major grows angry and demands Clarence be beaten so he stays down.

It's an affront is what it is. Impudence done on purpose to undermine him in front of his men. The Major won't stand for it. Not one jot of it. No Sir.

The final beating wins the day and Clarence cannot rise. The darkness takes him. Pulling him under to a place of nothing where there is only a void and a fleeting memory of Paula kissing his cheek outside Mr Kettering's apartment.

'There you go,' Major Donaldson booms, somewhat relieved that it's over. Not for the disgust of seeing it but the bizarre worry that the giant would just never go down and they'd be forced to shoot him.

CHAPTER FORTY

Sixteen hours. Sixteen fucking hours. Private Clarke looks at the radio and thinks again to call up and ask for someone to replace him but the fear of invoking Jonesy's wrath far exceeds the discomfort at being on barrier guard for sixteen hours.

He has food, water and plenty of cigarettes. He even has some magazines and books to read. The temptation is there of course. The urge to just go. Run off. Simply leg it into the darkness of the night and make his way south to the fort. That was before Jonesy said they'd found *that cunt Howie.* Then they came back with them. Now private Clarke does not know what to do. He could still run off but is too scared Jonesy would find him. Jonesy told all the perimeter guards they are being watched and will be followed by one of the drones if they even think about going anywhere. Private Clarke doesn't believe that is true but he still doesn't run away. He's seen what happens to deserters.

He lights another smoke for want of anything else to do and stares up at the night sky so full of stars. He could serious thought to existentialism or ponder that imprisoning people, hanging people and shooting people is wrong. He doesn't do that. He huffs and smokes and feel a myriad of conflicting emotions that all become fuddled and muddled.

'Fuck this,' he grunts, rising stiffly to his feet to grab the radio handset.

'You there?'

He pauses, listening for the response.

'What the fuck was that?' A voice crackles from the radio.

'S'me, Clarkey...'

'I know who it is you bellend, I was questioning your radio use and terminology.'

'Fuck you, Jacko. I been out here for sixteen fucking hours.'

'I'll play a violin for your discomfort. What do you want?'

'Can someone swap with me?'

'Er let me think...no. Fuck off. Jonesy is calling us up in a bit to shag those women he brought in.'

'Eh? That ain't fair...'

'Bye Clarkey...dumb cunt.'

Private Clarke slams the radio down fuming at the unfairness of life while free as a bird to run and escape but his mind confines itself to the here and now and being denied the chance to have sex with a woman. Private Clarke only had sex once before and that was with a prostitute in Berlin. She was nice though. He went back the next day with some flowers but her pimp smacked him in the mouth and told him to fuck off.

'Bollocks,' he huffs and flicks the cigarette away and watches the glowing tip while hating everyone and everything.

CHAPTER FORTY-ONE

L ogistics are the Major's trade. The ability to achieve multiple simultaneous objectives with a combination of resources. He's good at it too. One might even say he has a gift, especially when he is supported by damn good chaps like Corporal Jones and Lieutenant Galloway-Gibbs.

Only Dave remains alert in the cell. Clarence and Roy were brought back through a haze of tear gas and the after effects of flash-bangs. Dave was ready to go but they didn't take him. They withdrew and closed the door.

Now he hunkers down at the back of the cell with his hand on Howie's chest and he waits. They'll come soon. He blinks several times but resists the urge to rub his eyes that will only agitate the particles of tear gas on his eyelashes. It is what it is. All things have an end. All things must come to a close. This now invokes no greater or lesser emotions than anything else and the only thing he feels is worry at seeing Howie hurt. To be angry now will not aid anything.

Across the filth strewn corridor and up a short distance the four women stay huddled in the far corner with Reginald. Everything that can be said has been said. Everything that should be said has been spoken. Now there are no words to give. They heard Clarence and Roy being taken. They heard them coming back too. They heard the heavy drag of Clarence's body and the soldiers grunting and swearing from the exertion of pulling him. They also heard the soldiers bang on their door and call out *not long* and *be back in a minute* as they laughed and traipsed away.

This is it. They can fight as best they can but if Clarence has been taken down what hope do they have? It isn't defeatism. It isn't anything other than the reality of the situation. Howie has been beaten. Blowers, Roy, Cookey and Nick. The only one they haven't heard is Dave and that is the only glimmer of hope but a weak paltry hope it is. Dave might kill one, maybe two but that's it. Even Dave, as gifted and dangerous as he is, cannot win against trained soldiers with assault rifles.

What they have left is dignity. To face mortality with heads held high. To give thanks for the extra days of life and the honour of knowing each other. Special days. Wonderful days. Days they would never take away or do differently.

Marcy found something today. She finally found a place in the team. The disjointed detachment she felt before was gone. She found her role and she liked it, she loved it. Working with Blowers and the others pulled them closer together. She bantered with the lads. Laughed and joked and not just because she was Marcy who was once turned, or Marcy who is with Mr Howie, or even Marcy with a big chest or Marcy the beautiful but because of Marcy the person. She put real effort in too. It was good and she gives thanks for having this day and the honour of knowing these people.

Charlie thinks of Cookey. She wishes she had kissed him. She wishes they had spent the night together and made love. She wishes she had told him she loves him and she thinks of the night they danced together in the garden of the house on the beach. She thinks of all of them and feels the resolve harden to see it through and show her dignity in death for the honour of a man called Howie who refused to be cowed when everyone else hid and ran.

Paula thinks of Clarence and Roy. Guilt tearing her apart inside. Guilt that she should have been a better person. Guilt that she is a leader of this team and she was so fucking pre-occupied she didn't take notice of anything around them. She would never have let them stop in a lane before a corner. She would have mentioned it. Said something. Made a remark that Howie and Clarence would have joked about and called her bossy for making, but they would have moved position. That's what leaders do. They work together to see the issues and make sure the gaps are covered.

Blinky feels abject terror. She has never been so scared. The prospect of a beating didn't bother her one bit. Not the thought of it or what it means. She always saw herself as one of the lads and not once did it ever cross her mind that her gender would be used as a weapon against her. Now, suddenly, she is fearing something far worse than a beating. Even if they knock her out they'll still do it. It can't happen. It won't happen. No.

All things must end. All things must come to a close. It's life. It's what being alive means. To have death always in front of you. To know mortality and see it for what it is.

All things must end. All things must come to a close. They did well. They fought back against an enemy far greater than they. They won too and if nothing else they gave hope where there was none. They gave light to the darkest of days but this is it and all things must end. All things must come to a close.

L ogistics are what he does and it takes but a few minutes to make the plan. The night is getting on. Everyone needs sleep. They need to be alert and ready for the mass hanging tomorrow.

Three teams assembled and chosen by Jonesy. Three objectives to achieve simultaneously.

'Listen up,' the corporal barks, stepping up after getting the nod from the Major in the smoke-filled room on the ground floor. 'Three teams, three objectives. Team one with me. We get big tits and scarface in here for us. Team two, you get the little bloke and take him up for interrogation. Don't give him an inch. Dangerous little cunt from what everyone says. Team three, you take the older bird upstairs for the officers pleasure. If the officers stand you down you return to help them fuck up the little bloke. When my team have finished with big tits and scarface we'll swap over. Got it? Questions?'

'Yeah er...Corp? What about the other one?'

'What other one?'

'The other bird.'

'You want her?'

'Yeah, she's er...'

'Right, the stocky bitch comes in here with big tits and scarface then. Might have a go on her actually, something about her...right, questions? No? Sirs, we're ready?'

'Well gentlemen. I must say in all my years I have never served with a finer troop of soldiers. You are a credit to your country. Wouldn't you say, Lieutenant?'

'Oh without doubt, sublime, Sir.'

'I'm proud of you boys. Not one for emotional outpouring. We're soldiers. We're men. We face the danger while the civilians cower and call us murderers but if not for us they wouldn't be alive. You deserve this night. Enjoy it. All yours, Corporal Jones...or perhaps I should say *Sergeant* Jones...'

The lads cheer because that is what is expected for them to do. Corporal Jones grins and accepts the handshake given by the officers and the sick feeling in guts ramps to make legs weak and those voices inside heads scream out that this is wrong, but they cheer and they applaud because that is what is expected.

Dave lifts his head at hearing them come. He slowly stands up and moves away from Howie to the middle of the room. His hands at his sides. Unflinching, unrelenting, waiting.

'Fuck,' Marcy whispers. She grabs the others, pulling them in as the boots crunch down the corridor towards them. They might be coming for Dave or them. She won't take the risk. 'I love you... remember that...don't cry now. We're in to the end, remember? Stay here.'

She rises on legs that feel weak and shaky. Her hands tremble as she smooths her hair back. She has sinned. She took life. Her head drops to draw composure. She gives thanks for this day and feeling what it's like to belong. She prays for Howie and asks God to take him peacefully. She prays for all of them and asks God to let her take any sins they may have done. She is Marcy and she has sinned. She is Marcy and all men ever wanted was to fuck her. Her head lifts. Cocky. Brazen. Sultry. Fearless and ready. She is Marcy.

The door opens. Flashbangs detonate. Tear gas comes in to fill the room. Team Two charge with rifles raised. Lieutenant Galloway-Gibbs said Dave is dangerous. Special Forces. Everyone that comes here talks about him. Nothing can hurt him. They'll see about that. Dave waits in the middle of the room. Tears on his cheeks from the gas. Pain in his head from the flashbangs. The soldiers scream at him. He sees fingers on triggers and lowers to his knees. He lies down and feels the barrels pushing into his head and body and does nothing when they bind his hands with thick cable ties. He does nothing when they bind his legs together and does nothing when they lift him up ready to carry out. He's heavier than expected with a solidity to his form that belies his size.

As Team Two breach their cell to take Dave, so Team One and Team Three open the door to the other cell and Marcy stands ready with a slow grin forming and a single eyebrow ready to lift as they walk in. Hands on hips, a push of her lips to form a sexy pout. She is Marcy and all men ever want to do is fuck her.

The flashbangs detonate. She screams in pain at her eyes burning and the deafening boom in her ears. All composure vanishes. She reels away with her hands to her face. More come. More flashbangs that boom and shake the room. Paula and Charlie drop over Reginald, protecting him while they scream from the noise and sight. Tear gas comes. Hissing to fill the room. Choking and acrid. It hits throats, inducing gagging and retching. Blinky screams out. She can't do it. She won't do it. She's one of the lads. She roars and charges through the bangs and lights of the flashbangs, through the cloud of tear gas that burns so bad but pain is a mindset. She gains the door, wrenches it open and storms out.

Fast, hard and devastating in her delivery. Shock given to the soldiers who had no expectation of an attack. Their complacency is her advantage to use. She grabs the front of a gas mask and headbutts the wearer with that roar of defiance that echoes through the building. She throat punches another away who reels back gargling from the impact. She grabs another and breaks the wrist, elbow and shoulder with three distinct crunches of bones. As that one drops she pivots and slams her fist into the head of another one. A rifle butt slams into her but she feels no pain now, such is the rage unleashed. She turns to boot the soldier in the guts and grabs his rifle as he bends double. Her strength is greater than his and she pivots the rifle to slam the butt in the side of his head then yanks down so hard the coupling on the sling snaps. She gains the weapon in the chaos of the dark confined space. She aims and fires. The corridor fills with gunshots. Men scream out. She kills one instantly and twitches to shoot the one writhing on the floor with his arm and shoulder broken. Two dead. She is unstoppable. She is violence incarnate and she will win. She veers to the right to strafe the corridor as Sergeant Jones shoots her through the head from behind.

Marcy screams. Paula's mouth falls open as Charlie feels the same gut-wrenching severing of an essence they didn't know was there. Instant loss. Instant pain and shock. Blinky is dead. They feel it. They feel the instant void within the connection they have. In the other cell, dreams and images strobe minds as they lie battered and unconscious with limbs tensing. Blinky is dead. Blinky is dead.

'GET IN THERE,' Sergeant Jones bellows. He pushes his shocked men into the cell without a single thought to whoever was just killed. Only rage. Pure spite filled sadistic rage. The soldiers flounder in shock, unable to compute or process what is happening but Sergeant Jones screams with orders and orders are easy to follow. They grab fistfuls of hair and yank the woman apart from each other. Marcy, Charlie and Paula try and fight back but the fists and feet beat them across the room. Blinky is dead. They feel it. The loss of her within their minds that renders them sickened in horror. Blinky is dead.

———

Team Two carry Dave past. All of them stunned at the sight of the dead bodies. Blood everywhere. Anger and shock inside. Twisting thoughts that magnify the wrongness of what they are doing while another thought tells them these fuckers have killed two of theirs. Terror and rage mixed together. A dangerous combination that robs the ability to think straight or clear. The immorality abates because they have something to seize on and use. Two of their mates have been shot. Two of their own are dead.

Dave sees Blinky's body and shows no reaction. He hears the beatings underway in the other cell and shows no reaction. Anger does not aid when there is nothing he can do. Emotionless, unflinching and detached from everything around him.

———

'GET HER UPSTAIRS,' Sergeant Jones roars. His hands full of Marcy's hair. Team Three take Paula. They take her while she kicks and thrashes and screams. Cable ties on her wrists, dragged through the door over Blinky's body to the stairwell. She screams out at the sight and fights with everything she has to get to Blinky. To be with her. To hold her and believe she isn't dead. The pain inside is searing. A maddening rush that denies all other thoughts and renders her mind frenzied with panic. Blinky is dead. Blinky is dead.

Marcy and Charlie are held back. The same as Paula and they both fight to break away. Not to escape. Not to fight but to be with Blinky. Both are ragged and beaten but the pain and suffering is nothing to the surging agonising trauma of feeling Blinky's essence wrenched away so violently. Blinky is dead. It consumes them. The fact of it. The pain of it.

Marcy goes through the door first. She fights, oh she fights but the application of force against her is greater than that which she can give back. Charlie comes out behind her. Fit, strong, athletic and smart but seeing her best friend dead drives her mad. She loses all reason. She screams and goes wild but is still half dragged half carried past the concrete stairwell smeared with a wake of blood down the middle. They go through the doors into the dingy corridor lit with bulbs running from a generator outside and into the smoke-filled room lined with chairs and the big table cleared and made ready in the middle.

D ave lies on the floor while the soldiers get the chair ready. He can see the blood of the others. He can smell it. He saw the water buckets and wet cloth and knows what is coming. It is what it is. Blinky is dead. Anger does not aid us.

He turns to see Paula going past the door. Her screams carrying through the building and beyond. Men, women and children in the main base here it. They hear the screams of pain and lie in beds, on mattresses or soft materials scavenged and coveted. Sergeant Hobbs smokes. His wife weeps behind him for here there is only misery.

The two officers wait with barely controlled excitement for Paula to be delivered. The Major will go first of course and be given privacy in his taking of pleasure. The Lieutenant will wait in the anteroom next to the Major's office and take his pleasure second. They both take a step back as the five men struggle to get Paula through the door.

Marcy slams into wall. Her hands tied behind her back. Jonesy surges after her, his gas mask now off. His hands bare. He grabs her hair and throws her down the side of the next well. His face twisted with manic lust. Charlie is pinned on the table and held in place while the others watch Jonesy take his time.

Dave goes into the chair. Rifle barrels pushed into his head while his ankles are bound to the chair legs with cable ties. Thirteen men in gas masks and wearing leather gloves. Thirteen rifles. Dave has his hands secured behind his back and his ankles tied to the chair. He cannot move. He cannot do anything. He looks from one to the next, devoid of expression, he looks down at his ankles then up at the stained and sagging ceiling tiles and the skylight further back. There is nothing he can do. He sees the men lower their rifles. He is trapped and secured. There is no way out.

They manhandle Paula onto the campbed prepared and made ready in the Major's office but she won't go, such is her wild demented fighting. They try and pin her down. They shout and make threats but she screams and fights and her voice carries into the base.

'Make her be quiet,' the Major barks, 'I cannot stand that bloody noise.'

M arcy backs away from Jonesy, her face bleeding and bruised. She lifts her head and gulps for air. 'Listen...you want me? Yeah? You want me?' the words come low and broken, her throat hurts from the gas, her nose and eyes hurt. Everything hurts but the pain inside is the worst of all.

'Oh I fucking want you,' Jonesy says, his face flushed with lust.

'I can...we'll...nicely...we can have a good time? Want that? I can give you a good time.' She tries to brazen it out and be the Marcy that men want to fuck but Blinky is dead.

'Shut the fuck up,' Jonesy sneers. 'Stupid bitch.'

'Do you want me? I'll take all of you...'

'What the fuck is wrong with you?' Jonesy asks, bursting out laughing.

'Marcy no...please...' Charlie whispers.

It's coming out wrong. Marcy can't summon the feeling again. The confidence to tell them they can have her and leave the others alone. Blinky is dead. She swallows, her throat hurts so much. She sways on the spot and tries desperately to think. 'All of...all of...I can... you don't need...' she tails off. Blinky is dead. Dave has been taken. Paula has been taken. This is it. There's no way out now. She lifts her head, tears streaming over her cheeks. She tries to speak, to summon words and thinks of Howie. 'I'll fuck all of you,' she blurts the words out knowing it's all wrong.

Jonesy smiles. Wolfish and the delight in his eyes is evident. 'Yeah you will...'

M ajor Donaldson watches Paula. His skin flushing from the sight of a woman being beaten. He licks his lips, wetting them as he starts breathing harder. 'Not her face...that's it...in the body a bit more...kick her in the belly, in the belly...'

The pain of the blows robs the fight from Paula. Shock kicks in.

Blinky is dead. The others will die but to go like this isn't right. The finality hits her. There is no saviour coming. There is no sudden surge from the power of the hive mind to see them through. Howie is not at the centre now. These are men with guns, not infected. If she fights now they will beat her unconscious and it will still happen. Calm spreads. An icy calm that stills her body and quietens her voice.

'That's it,' the Major booms. 'Eh? Good thrashing has taken the fight out of her.'

Downstairs Marcy backs away from Jonesy. Jeers egg him on. Chants and shouts. A sick energy in the room. A twisted grotesque display of the very worst of humanity. Of good people reduced to barbarism within three weeks. Two of their mates are dead. Killed not minutes ago. They feel disgusted, angry, repulsed and shocked to the core but they can't show those emotions so they channel them into a thing nearing hysterical rage because this is the only vent they can give. They cheer Jonesy when he makes a fake lunge at Marcy who backs away with horror in her heart. The world is skewed. This isn't right. Not like this. Marcy can't process what is happening. They are the good guys. They are the light. They'll fight the infected and take death on the field in glory but not like this. A wrong turn has been taken. A direction that wrongs all their souls. She cannot summon the spark of thought to do what she planned. She cannot be the thing she wanted to be to offer herself to spare the others. Now there is only waiting. The door is blocked and over a dozen men are watching. More are holding Charlie down.

'You,' Jonesy says, pointing at Marcy. 'Will do what I say or she,' he swings his arm to point at Charlie. 'Will get hurt...give her a smack, lads...'

'No!' Marcy cries out as fists lay into Charlie. 'Okay okay...whatever you want...please...'

The men stop hitting Charlie. The air thick and charged as they watch Jonesy smile cocky, broad and full of satisfaction. He winks at some of the lads then looks to Marcy. 'You're gonna kiss me, love...a nice big wet sloppy kiss with tongues...and you're gonna make it good...we got an understanding here? We reaching a deal? Yeah?'

'Whatever you want,' Marcy says.

'Good girl, now come here...oh yes...you gotta walk to me...come on...kiss for Sergeant Jonesy eh...good girl, now stop snivelling...I don't want snot in my gob. I might have a little squeeze on your norks while we snog.'

'That's fine...whatever you want.'

'It is fine,' Jonesy says, gripping her chin in one hand. 'Whatever I say is fine...you hear that?'

She nods. Her jaw clamped too hard to speak. He dominates her vision. His broad face edging closer as he savours the power of the moment. His hand relaxes. She locks her eyes on his, seeing the flecks of brown and gold in his irises, seeing the streaks of red and the grime filled creases in his skin. He licks his lips and cocks his head over slightly as he closes in. His rancid tongue pushes into her mouth. She wants to gag and pull away. She wants to lash out but her hands are bound. He pushes harder into her, his hands squeezing painfully. She wants to scream and bite his tongue off then suddenly she is kissing him back. He feels it too. He feels the passion she puts into it and her tongue in his mouth and it sends a jolt through his core. A rush of lust. He pulls back, his eyes stunned. She opens her eyes slowly, her lids seemingly heavy with lust. A look on her face.

'Everyone out,' he croaks.

'Eh?' one of the soldiers says.

'OUT,' Jonesy roars. He wants her alone. He wants her properly without everyone staring.

'What about her?' one asks as they start rushing to do what he says.

'What?' Jonesy snaps, turning reluctantly to see Charlie looking stunned and bruised. 'Leave her there...'

'Yeah but...'

'GET THE FUCK OUT...I SWEAR TO GOD I'LL SHOOT THE LAST CUNT GOING OUT THAT DOOR.'

P aula sits on the edge of the campbed. Her hands still bound but she is quiet and passive because she will wait for the chance to bite his fucking face off. She'll tear his jugular open and drink his blood and die knowing she killed him.

'Would you like me to stay, Sir?' Lieutenant Galloway-Gibbs asks hopefully as the soldiers file out. Forever the subservient aide willing to serve his master.

'Oh I don't think so,' Major Donaldson says, giving him a wink. 'I think I can manage one little lady...but do stay close...just in case she decides to play about.'

'Of course, Sir. I shall be right through here and the men are just outside.'

'Very good, lieutenant. I say, we shall have to re-think your rank. Captain is next eh?'

'Very kind of you, Sir.'

'I look after my men, Lieutenant. Loyalty counts with me. Now my fine filly. How about it? Going to be nice for the Major? Eh? Might promote myself you know. Lieutenant Colonel Donaldson. Yes. I think that is very apt considering my service and sacrifice. Now listen, my lads are right out there and will happily kick your teeth down your throat if you so much as grunt the wrong way...or perhaps they can go and visit your friends downstairs. Would you like that? Maybe one of them is your beau eh? Your lover. How about my men break his fingers and toes and set fire to his legs? Hmmm? Won't be me you hurt you see. It will only be yourself and your friends...'

A ll things end. All things must come to a close and Dave waits in the chair but without Jonesy and the Major the men are unsure. Trepidation shows in the looks they give to each other, all of them holding back to see if someone else will take the lead. Jonesy said to interrogate but they haven't actually asked any of them any real questions, just tortured them. That's what they have to do now. They have to torture him except no one wants to go first.

One goes forward knowing there will be hell to pay if they are caught delaying or holding back. He puffs his chest up and sets his jaw.

'Go on, Tommo...' one of the other men urges him on with relief that someone is taking the lead.

'Yeah go on, Tommo,' another says as more join in, urging the soldier on.

Tommo goes closer to Dave. A tall lad. Broad and muscular. He was hoping to be made Corporal when Jonesy got bumped up to Sergeant. Two of his mates are dead. He cannot process what just happened but the momentum sweeps them all along and there is no stopping now.

He reaches out to grab Dave's face, forcing the man to look at him. What he sees staring back are the coldest pair of eyes he has ever glimpsed. Spine chillingly cold. There is no life, no fear, no emotion. Nothing. He pulls away quickly, his heart beating like the clappers.

'Get the bucket...where's the cloth? We'll drown the cunt...'

J onesy unbuckles his trousers as Charlie lies on the table staring at the expression on Marcy's face.

M ajor Donaldson eases down to sit next to Paula. Her head bowed. His hand gently brushes her leg then moves across to grip her thigh.

D ave stares ahead. Tommo picks the cloth up. Another gets the bucket of water.

The lights go out.
'Fucking generator,' Tommo snaps.

'GET THAT GENNY GOING,' Jonesy roars, 'Either of you bitches moves I'll break your legs.'

'Damned good timing, wouldn't you say?' Major Donaldson whispers. 'We still have the moon after all my darling...'

'Chair in the centre. Hands behind back. Ankles nineteen inches apart. Three mil cable ties. Thirteen from fifty.'
'What the fuck did he just say?' Tommo asks.

'Fuck it,' Jonesy says. Realising he has enough moonlight streaming through the windows to see. He drops his trousers, his hands fumbling to free his penis from his boxer shorts. Charlie stares at Marcy. At the look on her face. The same look Howie has. That darkness. The intensity of it. The same thing Charlie felt in the café at the garden centre this morning. A power unleashing. She sees Marcy's mouth open and hears the words that come so full of resonance it sends chills down her spine. Three words spoken. Three words that make Jonesy sneer in confusion.
'How's your stomach?'

'Seriously,' Tommo asks to a few giggles sounding in the room upstairs. 'Who's he fucking talking to?'

'Paula, diagonal. Hallway. Two doors up. Forty feet.'

'What the fuck!' Tommo laughs. 'Special Forces my arse...special needs more like...he's lost the plot.'

The lights come on. Flickering weakly as the generator gets back up to speed.

'Ah now,' Major Donaldson whispers, his voice quavering with anticipation. 'We have light after all...' he rises to grasp the buckle of his trousers, his eyes fixed on Paula.

Jonesy looks up as the lights come flickering on. His hand rubbing away. A nasty smile on his face.

'Said how's your stomach?'

'Shut the fuck up,' he snaps. 'On your knees.'

'Two minutes.'

'What? What is? I'll fucking break your face...' his head twitches to the side. A fleeting grimace flits across his face. 'On your knees,' he hisses, shuffling with his trousers round his ankles to grab Marcy by the throat. 'Down...'

'No,' she whispers, her eyes blazing, her chin lifting.

He grimaces again. A twitch of his lips. 'Don't get brave now bitch...'

'Be what you were,' she whispers.

'What?'

'That's what he said. My little Reggie. Be what you were...'

'Dumb fucking...get down on your knees now or I'll shoot scarface.' His mouth sneers. His expression hardens. Muscles twitch.

'Guess what?' she whispers, leaning forward to hold her mouth but an inch from his. 'I'm infected...'

He staggers back. The pain searing so hard he drops to curl into a ball. Grunts and hisses sound out. He rolls into the chairs against the wall. Bucking and writhing. His legs spasm while he clutches as his guts. The soldiers in the corridor hear the grunts and bangs, nodding at each other with sick grins at hearing Jonesy going for it inside the room.

———

Tommo bursts out laughing again at the sight of Dave in the chair. The lights glowing again but dimmer now and flickering to dance shadows across the walls. 'You alright mate? Yeah? Had a nice chat with yourself?'

Dave remains as Dave is. Unflinching. Emotionless. His legs against the chair legs. His hands behind his back. Anger does not aid until anger is needed and can be used. His face changes. His eyes grow hard. Dave never shows expression. To show expression means you have to feel something to create that expression and Dave rarely feels anything. Until now. Now he feels Blinky's death. Now he feels the reaction to Mr Howie being hurt. To the lads being hurt. To all of it. Now he feels and his lip curls up as he brings his arms forward to show the knives held in his hands.

'I....AM...DAVE...'

———

Private Clarke saw the car coming into view and moved out still grumbling at the unfairness of everything. The car slowed and aimed into the small junction to the base access road. He heard the electric whine of the driver's window going down and clocked the beautiful lady inside. With his chest puffed out he strolled round with a what he hoped was a dashing expression.

'Hey sweetie,' the woman said with a big smile. 'Are you a soldier? I have been driving for hours trying to find somewhere safe and...'

'Yeah, British Soldier,' Private Clarke said, feeling a bit nervous at actually talking to an actual woman who appeared to be smiling at him.

'I see,' she said. 'I er...I like soldiers and...their big....guns?'

Private Clarke floundered for a second, trapped in her startlingly blue eyes and soft lilting voice. 'So you, what? Swedish?'

'I'm bloody Danish, mate. Why the hell does everyone in this country think I am Swedish?'

'What?'

Anja winced, her head pulling back in distaste as Private Clarke was taken off his feet with an explosion of force that took him down hard with a bone jarring crunch. 'Now that really was cuntish.'

'Double gate entry system with a vehicle trap. A long road to the glasshouse at the end. Fifty trained soldiers. All armed. The walls are too high and smooth to climb. Razor wire is everywhere. Patrols at the top, in the middle, at the bottom,' That's what Private Clarke said between pleading for his life. 'You won't get more than two steps without being shot.' He had a knife held against his throat as he spoke and a pistol aimed at his groin.

A suicide mission. Going into the base was to walk into death. Doing such a thing was a folly of an idea. Soldiers don't bite. They are trained to shoot back.

Mo and Maddox were also trained. Long years on a hard estate. Long years of burglaries and learning to scale, climb, move undetected and gain entry to places they should not be gaining entry to. Maddox tried talking Mo out of it. Mo said he was going. End of.

They used the Volvo to drive the long way round to the far side They used a tow rope to drag a section of the razor wire away then got the car against the side of the wall to stand on the roof. Mo went over first. Meredith didn't like the pup being out of sight so she ran at the car and used the roof as a springboard to leap to the top with Maddox surging up to push her over. Maddox went too because he heard Mo crying on the other side from the severing of the connection to Blinky.

They aimed for the generator. The huge noisy chugging thing at the back of the glasshouse. Maddox stopped with Meredith. Mo went on to climb and scale and do what he was trained to do. He found the skylight on the roof and worked fast to silently prise it open. The thing was old and damaged. It was easy. People worry about doors and windows. They never look up and think someone can come in from the roof. He counted while he worked and with the skylight open he waited.

Maddox also counted. He also killed the soldier that walked round to take a piss. A knife in his back while Maddox clamped a hand over his mouth and lowered him down. Brutal but necessary.

When the count was reached. Maddox killed the generator. Mo dropped in. Dave heard it. Mo followed Dave's voice. Ankles nineteen inches apart. Hands behind back. Thirteen in the room. Fifty enemy in total. He cut the cable ties and pressed the handles in Dave's hands and was already leaping back up to grasp the lip on the open skylight when Dave told him where Paula was.

Maddox reached the next count and turned the generator back on. He checked his rifle and the spare magazines were accessible, remembering the lessons Blowers had given him. A folly of an idea. A stupid idea. Taking on fifty is madness.

'Fuck it,' he whispers to Meredith. 'You ready?'

Diagonal. Hallway. Two doors up. Forty feet. Mo spots the skylight and runs fast to grasp the edge and start work. The lights come on below. The generator throaty and deep as it starts back up.

Lieutenant Galloway-Gibbs masturbates in the ante-room. He wants to hear the Major having sex. The thought of the voyeurism excites him. The whole end of the world thing is truly terrifying but at least here he has authority and role suited to his class and pedigree. Not that he ever strays more than a short distance from the Major or Jonesy. He is also slightly disgusted at having sex with a woman straight after someone else, but then everyone must make sacrifices in time of war.

Such is his state of arousal he doesn't hear the gentle thud behind him and only becomes aware of anything when his dick comes away in his hand from the blade slicing through it. He lifts his hand, staring at his penis. His penis that is no longer attached to his body.

'Is Mo Mo innit,' Mo whispers, clamping a hand over the lieutenant's mouth. 'You's gonna die now...' the blade, already bloodied from severing the officers' genitalia whispers across his throat. Blood sprays out. Hot blood released from the pressurised system within his body. 'You's feel that?' Mo whispers. 'That's you dyin' bro...that's for Blinky...'

'I...AM....DAVE...'

'Now's you's all fucked,' Mo whispers.

Thirteen against one. They don't stand a chance. Dave told Blinky to focus that rage and use it. He told Mo to hold his down and be cold. Now Dave does both. The clinical methodology of his work blends with the fury and thirst for revenge. Tommo is first. His nose broken as Dave runs into the middle of them. Two more fall away with hands to jugulars that spray blood in high arcs. Dave whips left and right, slicing and cutting. Bodies drop. Men scream out. Veins opened. Eyes stabbed and ears removed before the fatal wounds given. Some try and aim with rifles but they might as well be trying to throw stones.

'What on earth was that?' Major Donaldson asks on hearing Dave's thunderous voice. Paula's head snaps up. Her eyes blazing. Her heart hammering. Her muscles surging with energy. She looks up at the Major with a grim smile spreading across her face.

'He was going to rape me,' she growls glaring at the Major who screws his face up in confusion then hears the low sound of someone sucking teeth behind him. He falls from his Achilles tendons being cut. He lifts his hands in defence at Mo bearing down on him and watches in horror as his fingers fall away with stumps spurting blood and never before has he seen someone so very, very angry.

'Nobody touches my Paula.'

'My hands...' Paula whispers. Mo slices the cable tie through. 'Give me a pistol and a knife...'

'You's okay?' Mo asks, handing them over with his foot pressed on the Major's mouth, preventing him calling out.

'Dave's down the...'

'I done Dave.'

She grabs him to hug, holding him tight with pain and emotion surging through both of them. 'Blinky's dead,' she whispers.

'I know,' his voice quavers. Tears spill from their eyes. 'I's never let no one hurt you, Paula...'

'I know my sweetie, you've done so good...I'm so proud of you...' She pulls back to kiss his forehead. 'What happened?' she asks in concern at the welt across his head.

'S'nuffin,' Mo says quickly.

'Marcy and Charlie are somewhere...everyone is hurt downstairs in the cells. Hurt bad...'

'Okay,' he says, nodding rapidly, her eyes locked in his. The mother he never had. Someone who looks after him, who kisses his forehead and checks behind his ears for dirt. The woman who quietly puts clean underwear and his favourite snacks in his bag so the others don't see. She kisses his head again. Her hands so sore and painful but holding his wet cheeks so gently.

'Five outside the door...'

'Okay.'

'Want me to come with you?'

'Nah I got this.'

'You sure sweetie?'

'I got this, Paula...want me to kill this one?'

'No,' she says softly, 'this one is all mine.'

'I found Mads, he's got Meredith outside...'

'Bloody hell, Christ, Mo. How did you...never mind, I love you, I am so proud of you.'

'Love you too, Paula,' he whispers.

She wipes the tears from his cheeks, 'go to work now, Mo. You go to work. You kill all of them and get to Dave.'

J onesy writhes from the pain that's so bad he can't even breathe. It gets worse too. Every inch of him feels like it's on fire. The infection surges through his body. Invading. Replicating. Bringing him into the true state of being and Marcy watches. She watches him suffer and she hears the low cheer from the corridor outside when the lights come back on. The infection takes him and the newly promoted Sergeant Jones dies with his trousers round his ankles on the floor of a grotty back room in a decommissioned admin block once used as a military prison.

A pause. A silence. Charlie on her stomach on the table frozen in place at what she is seeing and Marcy waits. She waits for the feeling. For what she once had. *Be what you were.* Reggie is a clever bastard. Even after being beaten nearly to death he still outthinks everyone. Then it comes. Oh it comes. The feeling. There it is. She closes her eyes at the rush of it, at what she had before surging back. So organic and natural. Connections forming. Oliver Jones. Once a corporal in the British Army. His mind in hers. Not what he was. She never had that ability and she doesn't have it now. What she has is him. She can feel him. She opens her eyes as he sits up to stare out through red bloodshot eyes and Charlie draws a sharp breath.

'Get up,'

The infected rises. His eyes fixed on Marcy. His supplication hers and hers alone. A total and complete ownership of all that he is.

'Take your knife...hold it in your hand...'

Charlie watches, thinking Marcy will make it stab itself. She doesn't. She makes it cut her cable ties instead and after pulling Jonesy's trousers up walks over to cut those binding Charlie. She helps the younger woman from the table over to the far wall and lowers Charlie down. 'We're going to wait here, Charlie. Okay?'

Charlie nods. She can't speak. She cannot form words.

Go,' Marcy commands. *Marcy* commands. The Marcy from before. The Marcy that was. The Marcy that came to Howie. That Marcy. Full of power. Full of an energy that holds Charlie still.

The infected that was once Corporal Jones changes. His hunger given to him. His need to rake and bite. The desire inside only to pass it. A seething once human form of something that does not feel pain. A snarl, a growl, his mouth fills with saliva. His hand claw to talons and he surges for the door, bursting out into a corridor packed full of terrified, horny angry young soldiers who only see Jonesy acting like a twat.

Marcy reaches out to hold Charlie as the screams sound out from Jonesy biting into flesh. He moves fast. He is fit and strong. Blood is drawn as the soldiers try and run in the confusion, still too terrified to even think of grabbing or stopping what they think is Jonesy.

***

Mo opens the door and steps out with pistol in one hand and knife in the other. Five soldiers who heard Dave's voice then heard the screams from the room and figured the torture had started. Five soldiers who hear the commotion downstairs and figure it to be Jonesy and his team getting to have their fun first.

Five soldiers who blink in surprise at the sight of the young lad of Arabic appearance with wet cheeks and eyes so cold it freezes them to spot.

As Mo goes to work Paula lowers to a crouch beside Major Donaldson. A knife in one hand. A pistol in the other. He gibbers in terror. His fingers gone. Blood pouring out the stumps. He cannot feel his feet. His lips bleeding from Mo standing on his face.

'You missed one,' she says quietly as the thuds come from outside the door. 'His name is Mo. He's sixteen years old.'

Major Donaldson coughs from the blood going down his throat. His head shaking side to side. His whole body shaking in fear.

'Why?' Paula asks. 'Tell me what we did to you.'

The Major doesn't reply. Such is the terror gripping him.

'Done those five,' Mo says, leaning in through the door, 'going down to help Dave.'

'Okay sweetie,' she calls out over her shoulder then looks back down at the Major. 'See? Now, I am going to let you live...or rather...I am not going to kill you right now. You might bleed out of course but that's down to you. I'm going to check on my friends and then I'll come back and see you...I might break your toes and set fire to your legs...I might kick your teeth down your throat...you see, it's not me you are hurting, it's only yourself.'

She rises and steps away, stops, turns back and aims the pistol. 'On second thoughts...' she fires once into his pelvis then another into his guts. Two sharp bangs of the pistol lost in the chaos of the building. He still lives and Major Donaldson would scream from the pain if not for the blood pouring down his throat slowly choking him. She walks across the room and out into a corridor dripping with blood from the five young men who should have known better.

M addox drags Reginald down the corridor. Three bodies already here. One of them Blinky. He checked her as soon as he got inside but her death was obvious. Meredith licked her face with a soft whine but stayed there for only seconds. Death is death. Meredith feels the pain of the loss but the pack is formed from all and cannot be lost by the death of one. She found Reginald first and waited while Maddox found a weak slow pulse. Down the corridor to the last cell and the others all unconscious and hurt. Maddox moved swiftly, checking each in turn. Pulses and signs of life but the injuries severe.

Now, with one hand holding Reginald's wrist and his other holding the rifle aimed at the end of the corridor he drags the small man down and into the end cell. His eyes hurt from the tear gas. He coughs and feels the burn in his throat then goes back to the door, takes a knee, places his spare magazines on the floor and holds position while Meredith moves from body to body, licking and whining. The hive mind pushing images and feelings into the darkness within their minds. *Pack rise. Pack fight. The pup fights. Pack rise.*

M o walks into the room ready to fight. His knife and pistol gripped. His fighting stance ready to be adopted. What he sees is a blood-bath. A total annihilation. The floor thick with bodies and body parts. Blood so thick it forms pools. Blood dripping down walls. Blood dripping from the ceiling. The soaking wet body of Tommo in the chair. A cloth over his face. An empty bucket on the floor. Dave was angry and it shows.

'Fuck,' Mo says.

'Report,' Dave says, wiping the one drop of blood from his arm but otherwise looking as neat and tidy as ever.

'Paula's free...Mads is here, he's looking for the boss and the others...'

'Good. Pistol.'

'I's only got one, Dave. Paula's got my other one.'

'Have it,' Paula says, walking into the room without so much as a blink at the carnage.

'Give Paula your rifle,' Dave says, taking the pistol from Paula.

'Blinky's dead, Dave,' Mo blurts.

'Swallow your emotion, Mohammed. We have work to do.'

'Yes, Dave,' Mo says, stiffening from the gentle rebuke.

'Plan, Miss Paula?' Dave asks.

'Find Charlie and Marcy,' Paula says, finally looking round at Dave's work. 'Get to Howie and the others. We'll cover them. You two kill everyone.'

C harlie and Marcy stay by the wall in the filthy room listening to the screams of pain on the other side of the door as Jonesy's speed and ferocity becomes too much for the soldiers to handle. The corridor is narrow, dark and covered in debris that trips the soldiers as they try and flee. They scrabble over each other, impeding their escape. One makes it to the door and runs out screaming.

Maddox hears the scream and sees the camouflage figure come into view at the end. He fires a burst, sending the body spinning away into the base of the blood-stained stairs. Another runs away from the corridor to be shot down. A third the same. Jonesy bites and rakes. Jonesy snarls and does what his urges tell him while Marcy wills him on. Those that get over their fallen mates and through the doors get shot down by Maddox.

The screams. The gunshots. The noise of it sends the base into panic. The patrols run to each other. Men not on duty scramble to get weapons. Those on the gates and on watch leave their posts. Sergeant Hobbs guides his wife and child into a back room as his three good men come running into his house with their families.

The first one bitten by Jonesy sits up to open red bloodshot eyes. The next one mere seconds behind him and the ripple effect glides down the corridor. More and more die to come back.

Charlie feels the soft hands lifting her head and looks up into the eyes of a woman she barely recognises. Marcy's beauty is suddenly harsh, her aesthetic perfection suddenly a vicious joke used to hide something terrible. Charlie thought Howie was intense, Marcy's intensity is different, Charlie doesn't feel it, she can only see it. 'I will never hurt any of you...know that,' Marcy says. 'I'm in it to the end... stay here.'

With that she is gone. Striding for the door and out into a corridor of men dying who come back in the true state of being that sends connections to the woman staring round at them. Blue eyes close as they die, brown eyes, hazels and greys but all show red when they open. All show the mark of what they now are as Marcy feels the connections forming. 'Get ready,' she walks through them as they rise swiftly with instant rage flooding their systems. Chemical dumps within bodies that ramp aggression and make hands claw and muscles quiver with adrenalin. It takes just seconds for them to switch from benign creatures staring in adoration at Marcy to the wild beasts now so familiar and it takes just seconds for Marcy to reach the door and hold it open.

'Go.'

The surge is immense. The instant burst as they pour out from the corridor and through the hallway at the base of the stairs. The air fills with howls and snarls. With Meredith barking in warning and Maddox readying to fire before realising they aren't coming for him but going past and out through the doors. A solid press, fast and fluid, pumped and frenzied. Wild with hunger.

Meredith smells them. She gives voice to protect her pack. She teeth bared. Her hackles up. They smell different, not the same. The things but pack too. She tells them to stay away as Dave, Mo and Paula come to a sudden stop at the top of the stairs.

They hold position for a second. Dave as inexpressive as ever while Paula reels from seeing infected and a situation suddenly so much worse. Then the infected are gone. Surging past the stairs through the door and out into the base. A quietness settles. A strange few seconds of Charlie edging towards the door in her room, Maddox aiming down the corridor, Meredith growling and Paula, Mo and Dave waiting at the top of the stairs.

'Mads?' Mo calls out.

'MO...YOU LITTLE SHIT...YOU NEVER SAID WE'D HAVE INFECTED...'

'I didn't know, Mads,' Mo calls down.

'MO?' Charlie calls out, hearing his voice. She runs into the corridor and down to the door.

'CHARLIE?' Paula shouts, running down the stairs as Charlie comes into view. 'Charlie...my god...are you okay?' she clasps the girl, pulling her in tight. 'Are you hurt? Did they...'

'No,' Charlie gasps. 'We...I...did they hurt you?'

'No,' Paula says firmly. 'Mo got here...where's Marcy?'

'She...she...' Charlie sucks air to drag composure into her panicked mind. 'She turned them...'

'What?' Paula snaps as Mo looks over sharply.

'She turned them…one kissed her…she…she told him she was infected and he dropped…just dropped…'

'Fuck,' Mo whispers.

'She made him attack the others…' Charlie says.

'Was that them?' Paula asks, 'they ran through…was that them?'

'Yes…I…she told me to stay…she said she'd never hurt us… Maddox?' she balks at the sight of Maddox edging out of the corridor with an assault rifle held ready. 'What…how…'

'Mo found me,' Maddox says. 'They're in a bad way down there…'

'Shit,' Paula says, pulling away from Charlie to run down the corridor. She flinches in horror at the sight of Blinky, crying out at the awful injuries from which there will never be any coming back. She drops at Blinky's side, tears streaming down her cheeks. Pressure grows. Pressure builds. Pressure unrelenting. She lurches on, staggering on legs that feel drunk as Charlie gets to Blinky with hard sobs racking her body. Paula goes into the cell so full of tear gas that make her cough and gag. Her eyes mist but she goes low to find the bodies of the others. Clarence and Roy. Reginald and the lads. Howie. All of them so beaten. All of them with swollen faces giving disfigurement. All of them covered in blood. She goes from one to the next, desperately trying to stay calm while inside there is only panic. She finds pulses, some stronger than others. Reginald's so weak and slow. She hears breathing coming laboured and shallow. Chests rising but none of them waking up. All unconscious. All unable to defend themselves. All close to death.

Mo comes in. Instantly coughing at the chemicals in the air. The coldness he was trying to hold slips as he sees first Blinky dead then the state of everyone else. The same internal voice telling him this isn't right. This is not what they were meant to do. A wrong turn taken.

Charlie's heart breaks again at the sight of Cookey. The death of Blinky so raw but the sight of Cookey and the others takes the strength from her legs.

'We have to get out,' Paula says, her voice cracking from emotion and pain. 'We have to get out…' she looks round, her mind frantic. She is the leader now. She has to make decisions despite the jarring trauma. Blinky is dead. Reginald is close to it. Everyone else hurt so bad they can't wake up.

'We need to get out of here,' Maddox calls out from the door.

Paula pushes up to her feet. She has to think and lead. She has to get them out. 'Maddox...are you with us?'

'Seriously?' Maddox snaps. 'I'm here aren't I?' A sigh, a shake of his head and all without looking round. 'What do you need?'

'Will the Saxon pull this wall out?'

'How the hell...' he bites the retort off before running over from the door to look closer at the wall. 'Yeah, it's old as shit...hook the chains on the bars. Where is it?'

'Far end by the gate,' Paula replies. 'Can you get it up here?'

A pause. 'And how the fuck do I get down there? Can you hear the thing I'm hearing? That's gunfire and people dying...'

'Please,' she asks.

'I'll get it,' Mo says.

'Fucking kidding me,' Maddox mutters, looking round while shaking his head. 'Getting dragged into your lives...' he spots Blowers lying in the shadows, seeing his swollen eyes and broken nose, the blood covering his skin and the shallow rise of his chest coming from the laboured breathing.

'I'll go,' Mo says. 'Stay here yeah...'

'We clear after this, Paula?' Maddox asks, looking over at Paula.

'We're clear,' she says as firmly as she can.

'Do for me,' Maddox says tightly, swapping the magazine in his rifle for a fresh one.

'I'll come,' Mo says.

'No,' Maddox stays. 'Stay here.'

'They got Dave. I's coming.'

'You's ain't little bro. You's stayin'.'

'Don't tell me what to do, Mads.'

'You's fucking listen little Mo Mo,' Maddox seethes, striding across the room. 'You's good, you's good at fighting and killing and you don't give in but fuck me you are young, Mo Mo. You's don't know everything. You listen when people speak, listen and take it in. They need you. Howie is fucked up, Clarence and Blowers are fucked up. You get me? You stay here with your crew. Protect your crew. I'll bring the Saxon and if you suck your teeth at me I'll fucking whup you... Charlie, you said Marcy turned the soldiers...did they have weapons? CHARLIE...where are the weapons...'

'Corridor...in the...'

'I'll go for the Saxon...Mo, get some weapons down here...fuck me, you's gonna see a black man running through an army base...'

S he walks down the middle of the road. Screams everywhere. Soldiers in camouflage with blooded mouths and wild red eyes chasing men and women, taking them down in frenzied attacks. The whole street seething with motion.

Be as you were. Reginald told her what to be. Reginald said it. He knew what she was. He was there. He not only saw it but he felt the power of Marcy, of what she was and what she can do. Her role was never to work with Blowers. It was for this. She was held in reserve for when *this* was needed. Reginald knew. He knew she would offer herself. He knew she would take that pain inside from the bad things she did and offer herself in sacrifice and he knew she would pass what she had to them. A terrible thing to say. An awful thing to do. To tell her to go back to what she was but despite all the piss-taking, despite all the jibes, squabbles, arguments and digs they make at each other, Marcy trusts him implicitly and without exception. Reginald did not tell her to infect them. He didn't say to pass the virus. He said *be as you were.* Be that. Be the Marcy that was and bring destruction down upon this place to save the man they all follow. That's what Reginald meant. She is the atom bomb. She is the nuclear deterrent only to be used when there is no other option and by god and the grace of the angels that deserted them in their direst hour of need so she will detonate and bring death on a scale these people could never imagine.

A cold smile forms beneath hard eyes blazing with darkness. She wills them on. She pushes them harder, ramping senses and aggression. She feels the connections and strives to push and force the rage to unleash. There is no care for what suffering these people had before. There is only Howie and her friends who took her in after all she had done. She tried to kill them in the church on the Isle of Wight. She would have laughed while they died but they accepted her, they forgave her and gave not hatred in return but love. A twisted juxtaposition forms. She gives pain and suffering now to pay back for the love and forgiveness she was shown. She inflicts harm now in retribution for the lack of care her kind were given and she makes this place run with blood because they dared touch her Howie.

In that maelstrom of chaos, she spots four valiant men outside one of the little terraced houses. Sergeant Hobbs and his three soldiers desperately trying to protect their families inside the house. Assault rifles braced and firing. Frantic expressions etched on faces as they finally fight for that which they hold dear and the only thing necessary for the triumph of evil is that good men do nothing, and Sergeant Hobbs did nothing.

'Fuck you,' Marcy whispers. Blinky is dead. Howie is hurt. Her kind have suffered because he did nothing. They would have been raped and hung. These people are only alive now because Howie drew the other player to him and gave everyone else in this area a chance at living.

A flick of her head. A will sent. A command pressed and rammed into minds that make every single infected immediately stop what they are doing to look over at the four soldiers outside the house.

'Now,' she says clearly, her voice carrying despite the cacophony of noise surrounding them. The infected charge. All of them. Every single last one that she holds in her mind charges for those four. The soldiers open fire but they don't stand a chance. The rush is too fast and from all sides. Sergeant Hobbs screams out as he fights back into the house and he screams out when they take him down and sink teeth into his body. His men are taken. Their families are taken and with a single thought willed so the horde bursts away to continue their rampage. They surge into houses, into tents, they run everywhere the living are because these people did nothing while her kind suffered.

Her eyes blaze deeper. Her lip curls and the infected roar with greater fury. Fires break out from lamps overturned. She wills it more and they go faster and harder while she strides down the middle through it all.

More come to her mind. More connections join those already there. The essence of each is felt. The collective grows. The power magnifies and she wills them on to join her.

M addox runs from the building to the far side in the lee of the high wall where the shadows are deepest. The noises coming from the base are immense. Flames licking the sky cast dancing orange light on the walls. The base isn't that wide. Just a few metres from the wall to the edge of the buildings. He moves swiftly, berating himself for being here, berating them for dragging him back into their mess, berating everyone and everything while seeing what must be done.

A figure runs out. He fires a burst, sending the body spinning away. It's too dark to see if it was a person or an infected. A flatbed truck. Long and wide parked side on to a wide-open area. A crane on the back holding a dead soldier hung from the neck. He hunkers down for a second, gathering his wits and position in time and space before running on.

He reaches the end of what look like shipping containers and the shapes of mobile offices all giving rat runs and gaps through which people run screaming in terror. There is no way out. The walls are high. The gates are locked. A small helicopter fitted with a gun, the blades long and thin that appear as though drooping down. A mass of figures writhing on one side as they bite into the men and women trapped. Blood-curdling screams. Wails of terror and pain.

A large canvas tent on fire. The flames crackling with pleasure at the life they have. Smoke billows up. Gunfire sounds. A woman runs past him, heedless to his presence and concerned only with the infected soldier behind her. She turns to look round as she runs and slams into the wall, bouncing off and away as the infected soldier dives into her.

Maddox veers to go round them, running fast to reach the end of the base and the vehicles seen glimpsed through gaps in the structures. A hard impact from the side. A woman slamming him into the wall. The rifle drops from his hands as he tries to pivot but she clings on with nails raking down his bare arms. He goes down hard with the woman's open mouth sinking towards his neck. He punches out, snapping her head over but she comes back just as fast. He can't get his knife or pistol without releasing her weight and letting her drop on him. Movement in his peripheral vision. Another two running towards them. One a soldier, big and broad. The other a child. Both as frenzied and wild as the woman bearing down on him.

He twists hard, ramming the woman into the wall then back the other way, gaining just enough momentum to roll over her and surge up to jump back as the other two dive in. The child is fastest to recover and run at him. No time to think. No time for thoughts or to give voice to the scream inside that this is just a child. Pistol out. Shots fired. The child spins away. He aims into the other two and empties the magazines. The first few shots hit bodies and go virtually unnoticed save for the power of the round shunting their bodies. He adjusts to aim for heads, blowing skulls out. A second to gather wits and grab his rifle then on he goes. Firing only when he needs to at anything coming his way. Vaulting obstacles, hunkering down for seconds to let infected run past. He spots the curvature of the wall that loops round towards the gate and glimpses of vehicles seen through gaps.

As the building line ends he knows he has no choice but to run for it. He sprints out into the wide end of the road and sees Marcy striding towards him. Her head high. Her whole manner so different. Her golden skin reflecting the light of the fires. Her beauty in that second takes the breath from his throat. Not for any sense of lust or desire but the aesthetic quality of the visceral image searing into his mind. The flames, the smoke, the light cast, the way she strides and the flow of her hair. Powerfully strong but the look on her face is merciless and utterly cold.

A soldier runs from the side towards her. Blood glistening on his chin. His eyes wild. He sprints hard with an action that makes Maddox lift the rifle to aim then at the last second the soldier turns to position himself several steps ahead of Marcy. Another runs from the other side taking position in front. More come. More that fall in to perfect placement to form an arrow head of infected that only adds to the image of it, the sight of it and what it means. To have that power is a terrible thing. Maddox sees what she once was.

Jonesy runs in. His chin dripping blood. His eyes fixed with adoration on Marcy. When she stops walking they all stop walking. When she looks at Jonesy all the infected look at Jonesy.

'Not you...' she says in a voice now strong and defiant. 'This is too good for you...tear him apart.'

She walks on as they rush at Jonesy. He doesn't flinch but stays passive and if she could pull the infection back right now to make him feel his limbs being torn from their sockets and his flesh stripped from his body she would. It takes only seconds for the former soldier to be reduced to flayed lumps of unrecognisable meat with patches of camouflage material. Once done, the horde run to catch her up. Entirely compliant. Entirely subjugated.

'Maddox,' she says, coming to a stop without a flicker of surprise showing.

'Mo found me,' he says quickly, his intelligent mind processing everything he just saw. 'You okay then?' he asks, giving her a studied look.

'Paula?' she asks, holding his gaze.

'Mo got to her. Dave too...they er...they need a vehicle,' he says, nodding at the Saxon.

She smiles at the sight of the Saxon so familiar. Like coming home but a fleeting look of confusion shows. A yearning. A desire. A worry that reflects the depths of her soul. She thinks of Blinky. She thinks of the others and Howie and the power she has and the words Reggie said to her.

'But,' he adds, turning to look at the Challenger. 'They have a tank.'

'No, no take the Saxon,' she says, blinking to focus on the now.

'Other tank,' Maddox says, pointing at the Warrior APC.

'No,' she says. 'Saxon.'

'It's a tank, Marcy,' he says, buying time to assess, buying time to look and understand and see more infected rushing to gather behind her.

'They need the Saxon...it's like home to them.'

'It's a tank with a big tank gun,' Maddox says, noting she said *them* and not *us*.

'No.'

'Damn shame,' he mutters. 'You know that's not a proper Saxon don't you.'

'What?'

'It's a training vehicle.'

'How do you know that?'

He shrugs as nonchalant and casual as ever in an army base imploding and still full of the screams of the panicked and dying while all around him the infected ring Marcy. 'I know lots of things and proper Saxon's don't look like that.'

'You are not taking the tank, Maddox.'

'Just saying.'

'Take the Saxon.'

'Whatever,' he sets off towards it, his pace slow and easy. 'What you doing, Marcy?' he asks without turning, finally giving voice to the situation.

'I'll open the gates. Get them loaded.'

'You's think I'm stupid yeah?' he slips easily into the slang as he turns to look at her.

'I don't think you are stupid, Maddox.'

'Good, because I am not. Don't do it. Howie needs you,' he says bluntly.

'And you care all of a sudden?'

'Enough to have come back and helped. Enough to have got Mo into a fucking army base and enough to run down here...'

'Point taken.'

'Howie needs you. They all do. Don't do this.'

'We all have our path in life, Maddox.'

Maddox nods slowly before inclining his head an inch. 'I'm not one of you so I get to look in from the outside...and this is not the way, Marcy.'

'Take the Saxon, Maddox.'

'Howie loves you,' he says earnestly.

The words sting. The words hurt. A flash of rage shows, making the infected tense and growl. 'AND I WILL KILL EVERYONE ALIVE FOR HIM...' she roars with the power of what she is. With the glory of what she feels to mask the pain inside.

Maddox smiles. His clean white teeth showing so clearly in his broad handsome face that has seen too much now, hurt too much, lost too much. 'Nah,' he says easily. 'That ain't love, Marcy. Sometimes love is *not* doing a thing...anybody can become angry, that is easy, but to be angry with the right person and to the right degree and at the right time and for the right purpose, and in the right way- that is not within everybody's power and is *not* easy...'

'Nice quote,' she states icily, glaring at him.

'Aristotle,' he replies with a shrug. 'Seems to fit though. Be angry, anger is good, fuck...I know that more than anyone but not like this.'

'Take the Saxon, Maddox.'

'I'm on it.' He turns away with that disdainful casual air that infuriated everyone so much yesterday. 'You thought this through?' he asks, turning again as he walks.

'Take the fucking Saxon, Maddox.'

He sees the aggression rippling in the infected surrounding her, something close to Paco. Arms tensed. Heads fixed. Unrelenting monsters that will not stop, that do not hurt and will give everything for the will of one. The base behind them. Flames and smoke. Devastation wrought. A few screams sound out as the living still cling to life in the hope they can outrun the hundreds now turned who seek them out.

'Maddox...take the fucking Saxon,' she snaps, her voice hard, her expression furious and flushed with a sight Maddox has seen many times. The flush of power when it is denied. The flush of authority confronted with someone not doing as told.

'I am,' he says with a big sudden grin. 'But you know right? You know if you walk away now you stay away cos if I see ever see you near Mo Mo I'll put a bullet through you,' the smile fades, the man stares at her without a flicker of fear. 'You be infected you stay infected, Marcy because there is no way of knowing what side you're on...'

'I will never hurt them...'

'You already are you selfish fucking bitch. THIS. THIS WILL TEAR THEM APART...Blinky is fucking dead. Reggie is almost dead. Your people need you. Your crew needs you...these fucking things are not your people. You go this way then stay the fuck away from them because I *will* kill you and I will tell Dave and Mo to shoot on sight...'

'Reggie said to be what I was...'

'TO GET THEM OUT...TO HELP NOW...NOT TO STAY LIKE IT. The man had the shit kicked out of him. He's dying. He's fucking dying, Marcy...Ah you know what...' he turns away disdainfully, flapping a hand in her direction as he opens the door to the Saxon.

'You tell them, Maddox.'

'Fuck yourself.'

'You tell them I said I'm in it to the end.'

'Go play God, Marcy.'

'Tell Howie I love him.'

'I meant what I said. I see you again I'll kill you.'

CHAPTER FORTY-TWO

Pressure builds. Pressure grows. Pressure unrelenting. Paula stares into the darkness with the belief that Maddox is not coming back. Time stretches. Every second feels like a minute. Every minute feels like a lifetime. The air in the cell is thick with gas. None of them can breathe properly and some are so badly hurt that breathing this air will only make them worse. Charlie stays close to Cookey and Blowers as though even unconscious they can somehow give her strength. Maybe they are. Maybe just being close to them and knowing they are alive is the only thing keeping the girl from screaming in pain at the loss of her best friend.

Mo stays at the door. Dave, as ever, stays with Howie. Maddox isn't coming back. He'll revert to type and escape. Marcy? Paula has no idea where Marcy is. Charlie said Marcy turned them. Is that good? Is it dangerous? Will Marcy go back to what she was and send an army against them? Paula bows her head, her mind clogged from the loss, from the grief, from the worry and the injuries and the whole of it. All of it. Why? Why do this to us? What did we do? She looks up as though searching for a God that will answer the questions. She coughs from the gas. Her eyes hurt. Everything hurts.

A clunk. Metal on metal. Close too. She snaps her head towards the sound that came from outside. A voice shouting. Male. Deep. Her eyes narrow. Fresh fear coming back. She grips the assault rifle as Mo looks round and Charlie lifts hers. They'll fight to the last and she'll put bullets through the others before she lets the infected rip them apart.

A solid bang, a twang of metal pinging and a chunk of wall simply falls away with bricks raining down. The ceiling crumbles in the corner, chunks of masonry fall with a cloud of dust pushing into the room adding to the choking gas and fumes already inside. She coughs hard, unable to see properly.

'MADS?' Mo shouts, his voice breaking off in a coughing fit.

Paula feels the trigger under her finger, readying for whatever comes through.

'I'LL BACK UP...STAY THERE...'

'Thank fuck,' Paula releases the breath held at the sound of Maddox's voice. She hears the Saxon's engine roaring as it backs over the fallen bricks and chunks of wall. A sound that finally gives a glimmer of hope. The back of the vehicle pushes into the room through the hole, battering more bricks away. It pulls out, angles and comes back with a burst of speed to get deeper. The clouds of dust get worse. Thick and harsh. The noises of bricks falling on the Saxon. She stands slowly with her hand covering her mouth. She wants to rub her eyes but knows it makes them sting and stream with tears. She threads a careful route to the corner, trying to see the solid end of the Saxon through the murky air. She tries calling out but drawing enough air to speak makes her drop to her knees from coughing. She starts retching, gasping for air while her stomach heaves to expunge the contents except she has nothing to puke. Her stomach is empty. Bile comes up. Acidic and burning. She starts to panic, unable to see, unable to breathe. Dying in a room where no one can see or hear her. The back doors of the Saxon open but she doesn't notice. Hands lift her head. Water pours over her face. Gloriously clear cool water that cascades down, ridding the sting from her eyes. She tries to retch again but the hands hold her still.

'Easy...easy...breathe...'

She grabs at the hands for the contact of another person. For the feel of someone else. More water pours over her. A hand rubs down over her forehead and cheeks, clearing her eyes and nose so she can breathe. Soft words spoken.

'Maddox,' she gasps, clinging to the hands. 'I...I...you came back...'

'He did,' Marcy says, 'We're right here...breathe Paula...just breathe...'

'Marcy?' Paula grabs the woman, pulling her down, wrapping her arms round to hold tight.

'I'm right here,' Marcy says, 'right here...'

'Oh god...I thought...'

'Marcy?' Charlie calls out, coughing hard as she crawls over to find them.

'Here,' Marcy says, reaching out to pull her in.

'I thought you were gone,' Charlie whispers through the sobs, her face buried in the clasp of Marcy and Paula. All of them weeping at being together.

'Never,' Marcy whispers. 'We're going to be okay...I promise...'

'Marce?'

'Mo? I'm right here...' she calls back.

'Marce?' he gets to them, his face contorted with emotion and pain, his eyes red and streaming. 'I...' he tries to speak but chokes the words and drops into them. Arms hold him. Arms round each other. Heads bowed as the tears fall.

'Shush,' Marcy says, kissing the top of his head. She leans over to kiss Charlie then Paula. 'We're going to be okay. We're going to be okay.'

'Blinky's dead,' Mo breaks. The sheer agony coming out. His body heaving with sobs.

'I know,' Marcy whispers. Pulling them closer.

'She's dead...she...' Mo tries to speak, to say words to voice the pain. Dave said they have to be cold, to be different, to see different and he did. He did it. He did what Dave said and got inside to help them but it hurts so much.

'I'm so sorry,' Marcy says.

'I didn't think you'd come back,' Paula says.

'I'll never leave you...'

'Mads?' Mo calls out suddenly, lifting his head to look round.

'Right here,' Maddox says from a few feet away. His voice deep but showing the emotion while the filth in the air hides them from seeing the tears on his face.

'You's came back,' Mo says.

'Yeah...yeah we did.'

'You hurt?' Mo asks and Maddox, with his gift at seeing into the souls of men and the wishes they crave, that gift that pushes him away from everyone, that foresight of intelligence knows what Mo is really asking.

'Nah,' Maddox says softly, looming through the dust to lower at Mo's side.

'It fucking hurts, Mads...'

'I know,' Maddox says, taking him into his arms. Little Mo Mo who stopped at nothing to get inside. Little Mo Mo who killed thirty infected on his way to help his crew. Little Mo who broke into an army base now sobs in his arms. A sixteen year old boy so strong and capable, so young and vulnerable. 'You's did well little Mo.'

'Hurts,' Mo gasps. 'She's dead...'

Over their heads, Maddox and Marcy lock eyes. Both crying silently. Both knowing what almost happened and both knowing Maddox meant it when he said he'd kill her.

'We have to go,' Maddox says, 'there's a fire...it'll draw the infected and this place is full of munitions. We'll take Blinky with us. Bury her properly. She deserves that but we got to move now. Howie's hurt. They all are. We'll find somewhere...yeah? Paula? Your crew needs you. Need to switch on now. You said that yesterday. Told me to switch on. Gotta do it now. We need to move.'

They hold each other for the comfort it brings and the pain of losing Blinky while all around them the others lie with swollen faces, broken noses, disfigured and hurt and one small man stays impassive with his hand on Howie's chest.

CHAPTER FORTY-THREE

'It's a saline solution with Penicillin. No idea if it helped. I thought some of you might be allergic then I thought fuck it and did it anyway.'

Howie blinks slow and heavy, looking down at his hand as Maddox slides the cannula out. The long thin needle slipping from the flesh with barely a bubble of blood showing. Maddox presses down with a piece of sterile gauze, holding it in place as he looks up.

'Look like you done that before,' Howie whispers, his voice rasping and low.

'Bossman used to get smashed out of his face. He hydrated on a drip...and I did first aid in prison.'

Howie stares at the wounds on Maddox's arms. Long scratches caused by fingernails. The flesh opened but already scabbing.

'This where you say all skills are good skills?' Maddox asks.

Howie doesn't reply but snorts a blast of air from his nose that feels swollen and wrong.

'Blinky's dead,' Maddox says simply. 'I'm sorry.'

Howie nods once, closing his eyes. He felt it but hearing the words makes it real. 'How?'

'Shot in the head from behind...she tried busting out. Killed two though,' Maddox says while lifting the gauze from Howie's hand. 'She went out fighting...if that makes it any better.'

It doesn't make it better. Nothing will make it better. A great and terrible sadness inside his heart. An awful feeling of emptiness. Like he could shout in his soul and hear the echo. When he opens his eyes, Howie looks round at the sunlight streaming through windows. Golden and pure. The air is clear and the bedsheet over his body looks so white and clean. Dave stands close, watching Maddox like a hawk with one hand resting on the butt of a pistol.

The swim back to consciousness was not pleasant. Not pleasant at all. Dreams and images flashed through Howie's mind. Sounds of screams and gunshots and people dying. The emotional reaction to Blinky's death so strong. Then he was awake and opening his eyes to the sight of Maddox Doku tending his injuries with Dave, unmarked and as stoic and impassive as ever.

'Where are we?'

'House in the countryside,' Maddox says. 'It's safe.'

'Anyone else?' Howie asks.

'Reggie's in a bad way. The others...' he shrugs and stands back from the bed. 'Same as you, beaten to death but not dead.'

Questions form. Too many at once for Howie's mind still trying to catch up to being awake.

'Mo found me,' Maddox says, seeing the expressions cross Howie's face. Howie looks at him sharply. Maddox shrugs again. 'No idea how. He ran after you lot got taken away. Maybe the dog caught my trail. I don't know...'

'You helped?'

'Nah I hindered.'

'Just woke up, Maddox.'

'Yeah I helped. Do I get a medal?'

'Marcy? Paula? Did they...I...are they...'

'They're fine and no, they weren't. Mo got to them before it happened. You awake yeah?'

'I'm awake.'

'Sure? You taking this in?'

'Watch your tone, Mr Doku.'

Maddox smarts at the rebuke from Dave. A glimpse of annoyance that he swallows before nodding respectfully. 'It's just my way of speaking, Dave. No harm meant.'

'Mr Howie, you should rest,' Dave says.

'I'm fine, what were you saying?' Howie asks, looking at Maddox.

'Marcy is infected.'

'I know.'

'Nah, I mean contagious infected. She turned one of the soldiers in that base...'

Howie blinks, sitting up straighter as Dave rushes to his side to help him up. 'I'm fine,' Howie says, expecting the pain to be awful but finding it's barely there. Just a sense of fatigue and dull aches. 'Go on,' he tells Maddox.

'Fucker was going to rape her,' Maddox says. 'Made her kiss him... she didn't have much choice. Reggie told her to be what she was...she turned the soldier and sent him out.'

'Jesus, she okay?' Howie asks. 'Where is she?'

'With the others, Blowers came round first. Cookey and Nick a few minutes ago. Charlie and Paula are with them.'

'Fuck,' Howie whispers. His mind reels, his brain struggles to absorb the information.

'You needed to know,' Maddox says quietly.

Howie looks at him again, at the hesitation that signals Maddox is holding back. 'Spit it out.'

'Spit what out?' Marcy asks, walking into the room. 'Hey, you're awake. How you feeling?'

Howie spots the bruises instantly. Handprints on her face. Grip marks on her neck and arms. The anger rises instantly. A seething rage surging through that batters the pain and fatigue aside as his body readies to fight.

'No no no,' she says quickly, lowering down on the bed as he sits up. 'Take it easy, I'm fine. Just bruises...it's just bruises...'

'I'll fucking kill every last...'

'Already done,' she says.

'Understatement of the year.'

'Thank you, Maddox,' she says bluntly. 'Leave us please. Dave, you too. Howie needs to rest...'

'Not yet,' Maddox says.

'You can talk later,' Marcy says, turning to glare at him.

'Now.'

'Mr Doku,' Dave says, his warning clear despite his flat voice.

'Hang on,' Howie says, easing back from Marcy. 'What?'

'I want your assurance,' Maddox says.

'What? What for?' Howie asks.

'Not now, Maddox,' Marcy says.

'I don't want a bullet through my head from Dave or a knife slitting my throat...'

'I said not now. Paula told you Dave won't hurt you.'

'Yeah but Howie says jump and Dave kills everyone.'

'Dave?'

'Yes, Mr Howie?'

'Did Maddox help?'

'Yes, Mr Howie.'

'Don't kill him.'

'Yes, Mr Howie.'

'All I wanted,' Maddox says, easing away with his hands up. 'Tell him, Marcy.'

'Fuck off, Maddox,' she snaps.

'Tell me what?'

'Nothing, it's fine. Wake up a bit and we'll chat.'

'Fucking chat,' Maddox mutters as he walks out. 'Nice genocide chat.'

'What?' Howie asks, blinking rapidly. 'What's he on about?'

'Dave, you can go,' Marcy says.

'He isn't a fucking servant, Marcy. Tell me what? What happened?'

'Marcy killed everyone,' Dave says.

Silence. Stunned silence. Marcy winces, closing her eyes as Howie just stares at Dave who looks as impassive as ever.

'Do what?'

'Marcy, Mr Howie. She killed everyone.'

'Everyone?'

'Yes, Mr Howie. Everyone.'

'What does everyone mean?'

'All the people, Mr Howie.'

'What people?'

'In the base, Mr Howie. Marcy killed them.'

'Dave, let me explain it,' Marcy says quietly.

Howie exhales slowly, widening his eyes. 'How many?'

'Dave, please…'

'Over three hundred and fifty, Mr Howie.'

'I…Howie, listen…'

'I'm listening,' he says.

'Drop that fucking tone,' she snaps.

'Just woke up from being beaten the shit…having the shit…fuck it, whatever…I'm listening. Actually, I need coffee. Do we have coffee?'

'We've got coffee,' she says, pushing him down as he starts to rise. 'Wait.'

'How long I been out for?'

'Since yesterday.'

'A day? A whole day?'

'Nearly, it's early evening. Just rest…drink some water.'

'I don't want water. I want coffee…'

'Howie, please…we need to talk.'

'Were they attacking us?'

'Who?' Marcy asks.

'The people…were they attacking us?'

'It's not that simple.'

'Nothing ever is,' Howie mumbles. 'What happened? Maddox said you turned a soldier.'

'I'm contagious. Reginald told me…'

'Reggie? Where is he? Maddox said he's in a bad way.'

'Okay slow down, Howie. You're going too fast. Everyone is okay.

Reggie is hurt and still out of it but he's alive. Everyone else is waking up. We lost Blinky but…'

'Fuck,' Howie snaps, 'fuck…what the…I mean…' he flounders for words, aggression and grief rising and falling inside him. Anger one second. Loss and pain the next.

'Ssshhh,' Marcy takes his hands in hers, unfolding his clenched fists. The swelling round his eyes streaked with faint purples and blues from the bruises on his flesh. His nose now bent slightly. A big welt on one cheek. More on his neck, arms and hands and every single mark on him and the others shows what they went through. He breathes fast. His heart hammering. 'Dave, can you give us a minute please,' she says softly.

'Mr Howie?'

'Grab a brew,' Howie whispers, barely holding it in until Dave walks from the room but the second the man steps out so he lets go and sobs from the pain of losing Blinky. He weeps hard. Bereft and devastated. Marcy cries again. She's hardly stopped crying. None of them have, especially Charlie. They cling to each other, holding tight. Her arms wrapped round his neck and head.

A country house. Large, detached, isolated and surrounded by forests of pine. Miles from anywhere. Beds made up in every room. Drips hanging from metal stands feeding pipes attached to cannulas in backs of hands hydrating hurt bodies with Penicillin given for whatever help it may give.

In the next room along, Charlie holds Cookey as he weeps. Both of them crying hard from the news she just told him. Blowers in the same room staring at nothing through his one good eye.

Across the corridor, Paula draws the cannula from Nick's hand the way Maddox showed her. She holds pressure down for a second and stares up at Nick. 'I'm so sorry,' she whispers, the tears falling down her cheeks.

'Fuck,' Nick squeezes his eyes closed. Like the others, he felt it but it was all so surreal, so twisted in nightmares and images with emotional reactions. Here is the cold light of day and the confirmation given softly. The finality of it. He reaches out for her, consumed with pain. Paula holds him tight, kissing his head and feeling the pain of it as raw as ever.

Maddox is there when Clarence comes round. He draws the cannula out and waits for the spark of understanding to show in the big man's eyes. Roy stirs, murmuring as he wakes. Maddox turns to look, gaining an understanding of the thing inside of them. The thing that works on the same level to heal and fix to hold them under until it is ready to let them wake again. A thing that moves at the same pace through all. An infection that numbs the pain and makes wounds heal. He crosses the room to Roy, making sure the man can see him as he gains consciousness. A fleeting look of confusion. Maddox glances back to Clarence to see the same expression.

'Mo found me,' he says quietly. He waits another few seconds to make sure they are alert then breaks the news. Blinky is dead.

Howie slowly pulls away from Marcy. His face etched with grief. His head bowed.

'Clothes?' he asks quietly.

'Rest,' she says. 'Go back to sleep.'

She knows he won't go back to sleep. Not until he's seen everyone else. Marcy also knows Howie won't put jogging bottoms on or a gown and shuffle round in slippers. That's not their way. She rises from the bed to bring the washed and dried black combat clothes over. Fresh underwear. Big boots. Pistol on the belt. Knife too. His axe resting against the wall.

She watches him dress. Seeing the marks on his body that only add to the jigsaw pattern of bruises already on his skin. Lacerations. Bite marks. Fingernail cuts. Hardly a bare inch looks unhurt.

'Is there a toilet?'

'Through that door. Toothbrush in there for you.'

He flinches at the sight of himself in the mirror. He looks disfigured. His nose at a slight angle. His brows swollen. His face a riot of colours. The furthest yet from recognising himself. It's a different man. Not him. Not anything like him.

'You're still beautiful,' she says, leaning against the door frame.

'I look like roadkill.

'Handsome roadkill.'

Soft jokes said weakly but it helps. He empties his bladder, noticing with a grimace that even his penis is bruised. How did that happen? 'My willy is bruised.'

'I know. I saw it when I washed you.'

'Doesn't hurt that much. My testicles are a bit sore. I must have been kicked in the bollocks...who washed the others?'

'We all did.'

'They okay?'

'Same as you.'

'What? Bruised willies?'

'Bruised everything.'

He brushes his teeth and washes his face. She stands by the door, watching him closely.

'Your hair is almost long enough to tie back,' she says to break the awful weighted silence. 'Needs cutting.'

He nods as he dries his face on a fluffy white towel. His mouth feels cleaner. His mind coming awake more. Blinky is dead. He blinks and walks out to grab his pistol belt that he tightens round his waist. 'Rifle?'

'Other room,' she says quietly. 'Your axe is there.'

'Thanks. Did you sleep yet?'

She nods, 'in here with you.'

'You hurt?'

'Bit, not much...Howie, listen...'

'It'll be okay,' he cuts in. 'We'll talk later.'

'Sure...'

He follows her to the door. She stops to look at him, trepidation and worry in her eyes. 'I'm afraid.'

'Of what?' he asks.

'Of what you'll think of me...what I did to get you out.'

He stares back. Too numb to think properly. Too lost in his own mind to find words. She sees his hesitation and inability to speak so offers a sad smile and turns for the door. His hand reaches out. Turning her back. He doesn't say anything but just holds her hand, squeezing gently and sometimes an action is more than words. A passing of intent from one to the other.

A wide corridor lined with doors. White plaster walls. Varnished wooden floors and door frames. So neat and clean. So gloriously fresh and so stark against the weight and pain inside. As Howie steps out so does Blowers. Dressed and ready. Pistol belt on. Axe in hand. Black patch over his ruined eye. Bruises everywhere. Cuts and marks but still standing, still dressed and ready.

Nick comes out from his room. Hurt, bruised and marked but his head high.

Blowers moves aside to let Cookey and Charlie come out. Nick swallows. Cookey clears his throat.

A creak of floorboards, a creak of hinges and a creak of a door handle gripped by a huge hand. Clarence dressed and ready. His face a mess. His arms lacerated and nearly every inch is deep purple in hue. Roy behind him. The same as everyone else. The same pain in his face. The same state of readiness despite the utter desolation they all feel.

A moment in time. An air of expectancy of words that should be said. Words of comfort that could ease the pain. Howie can't think of a single thing. Only the raw void from where Blinky used to be. Her essence gone.

'Reggie?' Clarence asks, the word rough and low. He clears his throat, wincing at the pain from swallowing.

'In there,' Marcy says, nodding at a closed door.

Howie goes first, resting his axe against the wall outside before entering the bright room. Big windows showing gorgeous gardens full of rabbits eating content and growing fat. Birds singing. Squirrels on a bird table. A sight of utter tranquillity save for the broken form of Reginald lying inert in the single bed. A crisp white sheet pulled over his chest and legs. His face swollen and bruised. Howie moves in. The others behind him. The pain magnifies. Something went wrong. Reginald isn't a combatant. A staggering overwhelming sense of unfairness hits. Blinky is dead but she went out fighting. She killed two and showed them what she is.

'Who are you?' Howie asks bluntly.

'Anja,' Anja says, standing next to Reginald's bed. A cup in her hand with a straw poking out the top and the wet wipes on the side table show the care being given. The lads, Clarence and Roy take her in. Tall with long blond hair held back in braids and startling blue eyes that show a hint of fear at the sight of them all, and in that second she gains an understands how Mo did what he did. The black clothes, the weapons, the aura pouring off them. The sheer aggression that ripples out and to the last they have the eyes of killers and the injuries they carry only make the visual spectacle worse.

'She helped Mo and Maddox,' Marcy says, squeezing past Clarence to Reginald's bed. 'Don't be scared,' she says quietly to Anja.

'I'm not,' Anja says. 'Fucking terrified maybe but...'

A joke made with a smile offered and one given with warmth and the countenance of an honest person.

'Thank you,' Howie says to her.

'Thank you, Ma'am,' Blowers says.

'Thank you, Ma'am,' Cookey murmurs. They all say it. Nick, Clarence and Roy. Charlie smiles sadly at her, giving re-assurance.

'Roy?' Howie says.

'Here,' Roy whispers, his voice as bad as everyone else's. He lifts Reginald wrist, finding the pulse.

'I'm afraid there is no great change,' Anja says, watching Roy. 'His pulse is stronger perhaps. A little maybe. I am not sure. Maybe some more colour in his cheeks.'

Roy lowers the wrist then bends to rest his ear on Reginald's chest, listening for the rasp of fluid on his lungs. 'Sounds clear,' Roy says. He checks his eyes, seeing the pupils shrink from the light. 'REGGIE? REGGIE? CAN YOU HEAR ME?' With no response, Roy grabs Reginald's earlobe and tweaks once softly while watching closely for reaction. Nothing. He pinches hard, squeezing the fleshy chunk. 'There we go,' Roy says quietly, seeing the muscle twitch in Reginald's face and hearing the murmur in response. He pushes his hand into Reginald's and leans closer again. 'Reggie...squeeze my hand...squeeze my hand...REGGIE...SQUEEZE MY HAND...' a weak sensation comes back, Reginald's hand twitches, clasping weakly. 'GO ON, STOP PISSING ABOUT...' Reginald grasps, squeezing tight for a second. 'He's fine,' Roy says, patting Reginald on the shoulder. 'REST...YOU'LL BE FINE.'

'He okay?' Howie asks.

'How do I know? I'm not a doctor,' Roy says. 'He's responding to pain, no fluid on his lungs...he can hear me so just let the infec...' he trails off with a look to Anja.

'She knows,' Marcy says. 'I told her not to touch any blood or fluids.'

'Gloves,' Anja says, holding her hands up to show the surgical gloves.

'Let the infection work then,' Roy says. 'But like I said...I'm not a...'

'I think you know more than anyone else right now,' Marcy says, cutting in.

Howie goes closer, leaning over Reginald with a hand resting on his shoulder, 'rest mate. We'll wait for you.'

Clarence moves in as Howie steps away and places a huge hand on Reginald's shoulder, 'GET UP YOU LAZY SOD...'

Reginald flinches from the booming voice, a low murmur sounding clear. Howie snorts a dry laugh. Cookey's lips twitch but even he can't make a joke right now.

They file out and down to an open double doorway leading into a long open plan living area. Leather sofas round a solid wood coffee table positioned in front of a stone built fireplace. Enormous picture windows run the width of the room at the far end. An architectural delight. Howie glances round, seeing the subtle splendour like something from one of those posh house-building programmes for people with more money than sense. The air is clean yet subtly scented with vanilla and something floral. Candles flicker throughout the room. Small tea lights with tiny flames on saucers, in cups and on the stone fireplace. Fresh flowers in vases bursting with colour.

'Hey,' Paula says, standing in the wide entrance of the adjoining kitchen. She crosses to Howie, holding him for a second. 'Glad you're up.'

'You okay?' he asks.

She doesn't reply but moves on to Clarence and Roy, and any sense of awkwardness from yesterday is now gone. Too much has happened. Perspective has been gained.

An open door leading to a decked veranda. The sound of claws scrabbling and Meredith swooshes in, taking the turn through the door so fast she almost slips and loses traction. She aims for Howie, her tail wagging fast, her ears down then up then down again. Her huge tongue licking as she whines and pushes into legs. Hands find her head and back. Soft voices and smiles given. She can feel the energy inside them. One is gone. The pack is smaller now but the pack is still here. That's what pack is. It's the integrity of the whole that matters. *We mourn, we grieve but we keep going.*

Mo walks in through the open door. Two pistols worn. Knives in his belt. A very capable, very tough man but a sixteen year old boy who smiles sheepishly and even blushes slightly when everyone looks at him.

'Water's boiling,' Paula says, heading back to the kitchen. Anja follows her as Mo is engulfed by the others. Emotions high, the atmosphere charged. Tears in eyes. Handshakes, hugs, pats on backs. Low words spoken but not to any depth of detail, not yet, later maybe.

'Heard you were back,' Blowers says bluntly as Maddox walks into the room. He was outside with Mo and Meredith when they heard them all come in and held back, feigning a loose boot lace but giving time for Mo to see them before the shit starts. Now he holds his head high and feels the instant defensive sneer come onto his face. Pride and defiance at being faced with uniformed people who hold authority.

'Heard you lost an eye,' he fires back with that disdainful manner to deflect any power they think they hold.

Blowers takes the bait, bridling instantly at the tone. 'Bit scary in the real world was it?'

'Blowers, stop,' Charlie says.

'Yeah Blowers...stop,' Maddox says. 'You'll hurt my feelings.'

'Mads, leave it,' Mo says, stepping in front of Maddox as Charlie reaches out to pull Blowers back.

'Fuck this,' Maddox snaps, 'fucking mistake...'

'Fuck off then,' Blowers shouts.

'You can stop that right now,' Paula snaps. 'Maddox helped.'

'It's fine, Paula,' Maddox says. 'I'll get my kit and leave.'

'No, you won't,' Paula says.

'Mads helped,' Mo says earnestly.

'I did. I really did...' Maddox says with mock sincerity. 'I was a good boy, Corporal Blowers...'

'You fucking prick,' Blowers snaps, taking a step forward.

'Jesus,' Howie groans, pushing Blowers back. Clarence grabs his arm. Cookey and Nick move in but it only creates a divide with Maddox on his own and everyone else crowding round Blowers.

'Round two yeah? Go fuck yourself,' Maddox retorts.

'ENOUGH,' Paula shouts. 'Blinky just died for god's sake. Have some bloody respect.'

A harsh rebuke and the words sting. 'Sorry, Paula,' Blowers mumbles, lowering his head to drop the glare at Maddox.

'Sorry, Paula' Maddox says, earning a look from Howie. 'I'll get my shit and go.'

'No,' Paula says quickly, rushing to stop him walking out.

'Look, it's cool,' Maddox says gently, 'they're up now...'

'You are staying.'

'I don't want to stay. They're up. It's all good.'

'Let him go if he wants,' Blowers says, 'he's good at that...'

'Just hang on,' Paula says, shooting a glare at Blowers while trying to gently pull Maddox back. 'Maddox, please...'

'It's good, Paula. All good yeah. You take care now...'

'Or just fucking run away again...' Blowers says.

'MADDOX CARRIED YOU,' Paula shouts, spinning round to point at Blowers. 'He put you over his shoulder and carried you then went back for Cookey and Nick...he carried all of you...'

'Nah leave it,' Maddox says quickly. 'It's all good. I'll go...'

'You will not,' she clamps her hand on his and turns to look at the others, seething with anger. 'Mo knocked himself out for god's sake. Maddox found him...helped him and then went into an army base with over fifty soldiers to make sure Mo didn't do it alone. He killed a soldier to turn the generator off so Mo could get to Dave...'

'Please, just leave it, Paula,' Maddox says, shifting uncomfortably.

'Maddox then stayed with all of you until we got to him. Know what else he did? He went through that army base at the worst point to bring Marcy and the Saxon back and do you think any of us could have carried Clarence into the Saxon? We were on our knees. Broken and messed up. We couldn't function or even breathe properly... Maddox carried you, Blowers, he put you over his shoulder then went back for everyone else. *He* got us out. He found this place. He helped wash you and cleaned your injuries then went to a bloody hospital on his own to find drips and medicines and came back with Jess. He found the place they ambushed us and *looked* for her. Do you know what else he did? He went back to that army base on his own to bring Blinky's body here then spent the fucking afternoon digging her grave so we can bury her properly. He even made a...he made a...' her voice breaks with emotion, her chest heaving as she speaks. 'He made a cross for her...he's carved her name on it for god's sake...he carved Patricia on it and Blinky...he did that...' she chokes off with tears falling down her cheeks. 'He did that...he got guns from the base and brought them here...ammunition...he made a cross...he...he found white wood and...' the anger fades, her voice softens to a pained whisper. 'He held Mo when he broke down...he held me and Charlie when we had nothing left to give and he sat with Reggie and went from room to room checking on all of you so we could sleep...so please...please have some respect...and Maddox, you said you'd try. Please...'

Another silence. Another pained and heavy air void of words with raw emotions ramping that spin minds to flush anger one second then guilt the next.

'Sure,' Maddox whispers, his head turned away to hide the sting in his eyes. 'Sure thing.'

'You,' Howie starts to speak but the words come out thick and lost. 'You did that?'

'He did that,' Paula says, looking down at the floor. Her hand still holding Maddox's.

'Jess okay?' Nick asks quietly after a length, needing to break the silence.

'She's fine,' Charlie replies just as quietly.

A long exhalation from Blowers. A release of air as his head lifts. He walks over to Maddox and offers his hand. 'I'm sorry, mate,' he says simply, honestly.

'S'fine,' Maddox says, still turned away.

'Jesus, Maddox. Take the bloody handshake,' Paula says tightly.

A tut, a suck of air, Maddox turns to look at Blowers and takes the handshake. 'I'm sorry too...for the eye and...'

'It's fine,' Blowers says.

'And thanks. For getting me out with the kid.'

'Where is it?'

'It's a he. He's outside sleeping.'

'He okay?'

'Think so. Eats, sleeps, shits and cries a lot. Anja's taken over. I didn't have a clue.'

'Mate,' Cookey says, offering his hand.

'I ain't shaking hands with all of you,' Maddox mutters.

'Yes you are,' Paula says.

'Apparently I am,' Maddox says, shaking Cookey's hand.

'Thank you,' Cookey says.

'Maddox,' Clarence offers his hand and rests his other on Maddox's shoulder with a gesture too fatherly and close for Maddox who feels an instinct to pull back. He doesn't but only for Paula. He takes the shake and murmurs in reply as Nick and Roy take their turns. Awkward, weird and strained.

Howie stops in front of Maddox. Studying him closely. Maddox tries staring back but loses the battle quickly, Howie's intensity is too much, even for him, especially right now in this atmosphere. 'Thanks,' Howie says simply, offering his hand.

'Anytime,' Maddox says, taking the contact.

'You staying with us?' Howie asks.

'Ah you see, why you gotta ask that? Why? I'm here aren't I? It weirds me out when you ask shit like that.'

'I don't give a fuck what weirds you out, Maddox. I just wanted to know. Listen, thank you for...'

'Fuck off,' Maddox mutters, recoiling with another tut and shake of his head. 'Clichéd shit.'

'Know what?'

'What?'

'I still don't give a fuck. You with us?'

'Fuck's sake...Yes. Yes I am. For now...but I can go when I want.'

'Any one of us can go when they want.'

'For now then. Till you're all fit again...for Mo. I'll stay and keep an eye on Mo.'

'Fair one.'

'Fair one,' Maddox says back. 'Mr Howie,' he adds. 'That wasn't sarcastic. It sounded sarcastic but it wasn't...'

'It's fine,' Howie says. 'You brought Blinky here?'

Maddox nods slowly, 'she's outside. I wrapped her in a clean sheet.'

'Okay,' Howie says. 'We'll wait for Reginald to wake up.'

'I er...I wouldn't wait too long,' Maddox says carefully. 'It's hot.'

'Give it a few hours. She in the shade?'

'She is but it's still hot.'

'Okay, thanks, Maddox. What was the base like?'

'Fucked. Munitions went up. I tried bringing that tank back but couldn't get it working. We got more rifles though. Loads of ammunition. Pistols. Grenades, flashbangs and tear gas...grabbed a couple more GPMG's...and er...I got some fuel into the Saxon too...and brought Jess's horsebox back. I was going to get a new van for Roy but you all woke up. They got a chopper there if any of you can fly a helicopter...'

Everyone looks at Dave. Dave stares back. 'No.'

'Worth mentioning,' Maddox says.

'I'll give it a go,' Nick says.

'It's a helicopter,' Cookey says.

'Yeah. Can't be that hard...or the tank. Bet me and Roy can figure it out.'

'Maddox found that officer there when he went back,' Paula says, prompting Maddox to continue. Everyone looks at him with faces growing hard at the mention.

'How was he still alive?' Howie asks.

Paula clears her throat, 'Mo cut his Achilles tendons and chopped his fingers off then I shot him in his dick and stomach...'

'You shot his dick off?' Howie asks.

'He was almost dead,' Maddox says. 'Found him at the top of the stairs. I asked him why...'

'And?' Howie asks.

'Nothing...no reason...'

'Is he dead now?' Howie asks.

'He is.'

'How?'

'I hung him.'

'Okay.'

'Then I shot him.'

'Right.'

'And cut his head off.'

'Fuck mate.'

'So yeah. He's definitely dead. Especially when I ran over him in the Saxon...' he shrugs at the stares. 'Mo said he tried to rape Paula...I like Paula...she's been nice to me.'

Silence. Stunned and long. Howie looks at Paula, his eyebrows lifting. 'Remind me never to piss you off...you got Mo and Mads behind you.'

'I'm proud of them,' she says bluntly. 'Both of them...' she looks at Maddox for several long uncomfortable seconds. 'He's a good man.'

'Ah don't say shit like that,' Maddox groans.

'But yes,' she says, looking back at Howie. 'Don't piss me off.'

'I er, I am sorry to...to...' Anja says from the kitchen with a look of intense frustration as she stops to think of the right word. 'What is it? When you…oh cunting cunt…fucking…intrude! Got it. Yes, intrude…'

'She swears when she's perplexed,' Maddox says.

'Perplexed?' Howie asks.

'Confused,' Maddox says.

'I know what perplexed means, it was the way you said it.'

'Yes but the water is boiling now,' Anja says. 'Do you want coffee or shall I turn it down?'

'No, no coffee is good,' Howie says, smiling gently at her. 'Your accent? Swedish?'

'Are you taking the piss, mate?'

CHAPTER FORTY-FOUR

O n a golden evening in a sun dappled glade surrounded by mighty oak trees, on the twenty second day since the world changed forever, they bury Blinky.

A grave dug by hand. Six feet long. Several feet deep. The brown earth in a mound next to the hole. A starkness against the lush green meadow of long grass dotted with wild flowers. A beautiful spot on a hill with views of miles of unbroken countryside. A place to rest forever. A place to sleep eternally. A place for the body to be given back to the earth.

Reginald woke not long after Clarence bellowed at him. Who wouldn't be brought from unconsciousness after being shouted at by Clarence?

He was groggy, confused and scared for all of five seconds before his mind kicked in to run as it did before with assumptions made and calculated. He took the news as everyone did, with great pain and sorrow. A thing felt. A dream had. A knowledge deep inside that wasn't real until someone else spoke it. He rose from his bed to wash and dress despite the broken fingers on his left hand, the fractured ribs, the lacerations and the deep muscle bruising. A broken nose. Swelling to his face, joints and limbs but all with a distinct lack of pain. Some pain yes, but not the agony that should be there and the same as everyone else, he felt the conflicting reaction of having a thing inside so tainted with filth yet that same thing kept them all alive when by rights they should all be dead. A step closer to Paco.

Once up he listened to the accounts of the others told briefly. How Mo ran. How Maddox found him. The lack of questioning from the soldiers that reduced the experience to one simple staggering act of utter barbarity. Senseless and needless. A thing done seemingly for the sake of it and a reminder, a truly awful reminder of the savagery of the world now and that even they, with their might and experience in battle can succumb easily if they do not remain forever alert. The most jarring thing was that Reginald had no foresight of it. He did not ever think it could happen. None of them did. It was not factored or even considered.

He listened when Marcy said she infected the soldier. She asked him what he meant when he said be what you were. He declined to answer at that point, politely of course. He declined to answer because everyone else was listening and he did not know the woman with the blond hair in braids. Lessons learnt to keep his cards closer to his chest. Anja seemed fine, perfectly fine. A beautiful, warm and friendly person but still.

Clarence carried Blinky's body. Scooping her shrouded form in his arms to lead the procession across the grass and up the hill to the spot chosen among the majestic oaks. Fourteen people. Clarence flanked by Howie and Paula. The others behind with Jess and Meredith. Axes held, rifles slung. The sun beating down. Birds singing. Rabbits fleeing from the intrusion.

Clarence stopped at the end of the grave. His face a mask that showed his reluctance to let her go. That to do this would bring the finality of it. That it gives in somehow. He wanted to roar at the sky and challenge the gods for what they had done. He wanted to fight everyone and everything to bring her back. He wanted to beg for them to take his soul in exchange for hers. To hear her swear and belch, to hear the jokes and see that grin of utter fearlessness. He couldn't do that. He couldn't do anything and the single tear tracked down his cheek as he stared at the grave so deep and empty. He denied it. He refused it but all things have an end. All things must come to a close and so Howie came to his side and took hold of the sheet. Paula too. Blowers, Cookey, Marcy, Nick, Reginald, Roy, Charlie and Mo took hold of the sheet and together they moved as one to do a thing that must be done while Dave stood back to watch and scan, now more than ever he will be forever alert with his hands crossed over his body resting on the butts of his pistols.

Together they lowered her body into the earth. Together they sunk to knees to stretch down so she was laid gently, so gently. Together they wept and their tears dotted white blooms on the sheet that none of them could let go. None wished to break the connection. Meredith lay quietly. Her ears pricked. Her eyes sharp. Jess grazed and the birds sung in a world already moving on.

It was Blowers that let go first. His hand simply opening to release his grip. He moved to Charlie, enveloping her hand in his, soft and gentle. 'Let go.'

'I can't...'

'It's okay...let go...'

She released the grip, pulling back quickly to sink into him, weeping so hard her legs gave way. He held her tight. Paula moved to her. Cookey and Marcy. Minutes taken to compose to stand and draw back with every step a deliverance.

It was Blowers that gripped the shovel too and bent to scoop the earth back into the ground. No words spoken. Charlie crying hard. Everyone broken and lost and hearing the scrape of the shovel and the pattering of the soil falling on top of the white sheet. Maddox moved from Anja. The only other shovel in his hands. Blowers paused for a second, their eyes locking as Maddox stopped next to him. Both hard faced. Both wise beyond their years. A nod. Singular and shallow and they worked side by side. Bending to scoop the earth that rained down on Blinky lying within the grave.

Nick couldn't stand it. To watch idly. To suffer the pain without action to occupy his grief. Only two shovels. He used his hands. Joining the other two to feel the soil between his fingers. Mo followed him. Clarence and Roy a second after. Howie and Marcy. Even Reginald lowered wincing to his knees to use his right hand to throw the soil in. Paula held Charlie. The young woman unable to see her friend being covered so slowly.

Now it is done. Now the raw earth bulges from the land. Grotesque and swollen. A filthy nasty horrid sight but one filled with a raw poignancy. Now they stand with dirty hands and sweat soaked faces. Now they look down and accept what is, that they will never hear her voice again, never hear that laugh, never see her grin again. All of that is gone. The force of Blinky. The sheer unadulterated aggression that found a place in a world off the pitch.

The white cross is heart-breaking in simplicity. Two pieces of wood. One upright. One horizontal. Made by Maddox and now held by him and Blowers as they push the end into the earth and drive it down. Words carved by the point of a knife. Crudely done but breath-takingly beautiful for it.

Patricia
"Blinky"
To the end

N ow they stand with dirty hands and sweat soaked faces and look upon a grave marked with a name.

Marcy takes Howie's hand in hers. Her eyes streaming tears. She blinks and looks up at the sky, her lip trembling. Mo stares down with his eyes closed trying desperately to be like Dave and bring the coldness to take this pain away. Clarence stands with his feet planted and his arms hanging at his sides. He swallows and lowers his great head, closing his eyes to remove the sight of it.

Words are needed. Something needs to be said to mark the ritual but none can find anything to say. Charlie feels only the loss. An overwhelming feeling of pain at feeling the death of her best friend. Paula searches her mind for something to say. They all do. Reginald thinks maybe the place is his to speak out but right now even his incredible mind runs blank.

Anja moves past Howie and Marcy to lay wild flowers held together by green vines at the base of the cross. She kneels for a second to whisper words in her own language then draws back and notices that Blowers is the only one of them not crying. The only one that doesn't appear consumed with grief.

Still the silence extends. The things they do expose them to horrors beyond anything they could ever imagine. The hardship, the heat, the draining fatigue of fighting day after day against an enemy that has limitless resources who doesn't feel pain and one that will only get stronger and smarter. They did it willingly and have lost before, they've all lost before and suffered the grief of each but this is different. They felt this one when it happened. The severing of the connection.

'I read a poem in prison.'

They look over to Maddox who stares at the cross he made on the grave he dug filled with the body he went back for. He isn't one of them but he's paid his dues today and earned this right to speak. He lifted Blinky from the corridor in the admin block and carried her outside to the Saxon. He washed her face and hands then wrapped her body in the clean sheet.

'I er...I don't normally like clichéd stuff but...' he pauses, blinking a few times then clears his throat and when he speaks he does so clearly with a voice deep beyond his years that carries clear and strong. *'Do not stand at my grave and weep. I am not there. I do not sleep. I am a thousand winds that blow. I am the diamond glints on snow. I am the sunlight on ripened grain. I am the gentle autumn rain. When you awaken in the morning's hush, I am the swift uplifting rush...of quiet birds in circled flight. I am the soft stars that shine at night. Do not stand at my grave and cry; I am not there. I did not die...'*

Tears flows. Lips tremble but heads lift and backs straighten with a change in perception of a life lost but one given in service for the thing they do.

'Every action has a reaction,' Howie says clearly. 'Everything we do creates a ripple effect that influences everything around us...Blinky fought back when the rest of us were down. She took the fight to them, killed two and hurt more...and she bought time for Mo to get to Dave and Paula. She bought time for Marcy to think and react. If not for Blinky then Dave would be dead...she did that. Blinky did that. The hardest, most foul mouthed angriest woman I ever knew but fuck me, our lives is better for knowing her...'

Sad smiles show on faces. Blasts of air from soft laughs.

'She saved Clarence after he jumped from a moving vehicle...running through them to get Paco...'

'She did,' Clarence chuckles at the memory, rubbing the back of his neck while smiling and crying at the same time.

'Did you see her hip firing the GPMG?' Howie asks. 'Nuts...she was having the time of her life. Bloody hell, she volunteered for Dave training. Who does that? I've known Dave longer than all of you and I haven't done it... Blinky did.'

'She was good,' Dave whispers. Rare praise and the perfect timing is more by accident than design.

'She took a horde on single handed so Cookey could get to Blowers when he went down. She farted, puked, called Paula sir told us all when she needed a shit and gave Cookey dead arms and legs... she said fist me more times than anyone I have ever heard and she swore more than Nick and made it clear she wanted Dave's babies... but she also ran faster than all of us to get there first...Charlie, I don't know Blinky like you but I think if she could see us now, and know we got out she'd nod, fart, swear, make eyes at Dave and say job done...'

'She would,' Charlie whispers. 'She'd say fist me pencil dicks...get the fuck on with it and stop going blah blah...she was the toughest person I ever knew. We had a match once...about a year ago...the other team targeted me. Kept tripping me up, hitting my legs with the sticks...ramming, pushing...blocking...Blinky went to the pub they were in after the match and beat the shit out of them...' she stops to wipe the tears falling while smiling at the memory. 'The bouncers couldn't stop her...they called the police who had to tazer her to make her stop...'

'No way?' Cookey asks, his eyes as misted as hers.

'She did. Almost lost her place on the team but the other players were too embarrassed to press charges. She was my best friend. Coarse, rude, violent but the most loyal person I have ever met. The most honourable too. She never lied. Never backed down...she adored you, Mr Howie. You too, Blowers...all of you. She told me this was the happiest time of her life. I think she had crushes on all of you...and Mo? Blinky loved you like a brother. This hurts. It hurts so much...but...but she wouldn't change it. Not one minute of it. So,' she looks up and round, smiling through the sadness. 'Man up pencil dicks...'

'Man up,' Howie laughs, wiping his cheeks. 'Been an honour, Blinky. One of us.'

Blowers smiles as the murmur goes round the group. *One of us.* He adds his voice but still doesn't cry. The others don't notice so much. There's tough then there's Simon Blowers. It's not that reason that stops him crying. It's something else. He thought they might notice but then it was only for a minute or so and it was right at the point Blinky died so he figures it was lost in that maelstrom of angst.

Should he say something? Would it help? Maybe in a minute when they go back for a brew. He'll tell them then.

He'll tell them about last night when his heart stopped again.

CHAPTER FORTY-FIVE

Blowers dies...again

He surges up to his feet then staggers back. Confused and raging. His chest heaving. His hands balled to fists. He spins round, his hard face filled with the lust of battle but it fades away. All trace of the emotions he had ebb away and his breathing slows.

It's light now but grimy and grey. He's in a street so ruined and destroyed it looks like something from the Second World War. An old park lies in a square behind rusted railings. The slide has fallen down into a pile of rubble, rusted swing chains nestle amongst the yellowing grass. The sky is streaked blood red and the clouds look heavy and threatening. The place is unfamiliar. He looks round for the others but they aren't here. He's alone. A feeling of a presence. Something malevolent and evil that is coming closer. He can't see it but he can feel it.

'Fuck yes!' Blowers says, grinning widely as he turns. 'YES!' he bursts out laughing and starts walking with a feeling of being watched and hunted. An urge to run. He starts jogging then running then sprinting as fast as he can.

He looks behind to see dark shadows flitting between the ruined walls. Dark shapes of things that are evil with intent. A laugh echoes round, rolling to bounce off walls and buildings. The laugh becomes a dry hacking cough. Twisted and not right. Like a taunt. The fear grows inside him. They are coming for him. A certainty. A fact.

He stops running to stand proud. His hand comes up. His middle finger extends. 'DO ONE...' he shouts turning in a slow circle. Fuck them. He's been here before and he's not afraid this time. Not of them anyway. 'I'm right here bellends,' he calls out. 'No? Fuck off then...'

Movement on his right side. He spins to see a flash of black fur and a long tail running behind the broken wall of a house down the street.

'Bear?' he calls out, his voice hollow and strangely flat in this awful place.

A bark. It's her. He knows that bark anywhere. She comes running towards him. A furry black Exocet missile that streaks down the ruined road as he lowers to his knees readying for the impact. She comes in hard but pulling back at the very last second. Licking his face and spinning round as he laughs and rubs her sides and back. 'Good girl...you're a good girl...come on...'

He runs on through the whispers and inhuman sounds. Running over rubble and heaps of slag on the road. Veering round old cars rusted and left for years.

He takes the corner and slows to a jog to a walk while grinning at the unamused expression of Big Chris leaning against the doorway to the church while shaking his head.

'Making a habit of this, Corporal.'

'Sorry, Sergeant.'

'You're not bloody sorry,' Big Chris laughs. 'Cheeky sod.'

'How are you?' Blowers asks, offering his hand.

'Same as yesterday as it happens,' Big Chris says, engulfing Blowers' hand in his own with a firm grip. 'Come on in.'

'Marine Marine in a boat...being a twat that gets killed every bloody day,' Malcolm says, striding towards him. 'Para's don't get killed this many times you know...'

'That right is it?' Blowers asks.

'Has Clarence been here?'

'No but you are...' Blowers laughs.

'Cheeky fucker,' Malcolm says, taking a swipe that Blowers parries easily. 'In the shit again then?'

'Could say that,' Blowers says, the smile easing.

'Leave my corporal alone pencil dick...'

'Oh no...no no...' Blowers closes his eye at the voice. 'Please no...'

'Take it easy,' Big Chris says softly.

'Blinky,' Blowers says, turning round.

'Fist me...your bird is fit as fuck,' she says with an emphatic nod while walking towards him. Her hair in bunches, her clothing the same army fatigues as Chris and Malcolm. 'You never said you been here. Why didn't you say? So cool. Love it...'

'Mate, I'm so sorry,' Blowers says.

'Why? It's fucking awesome.'

'Is it...er...' Blowers hesitates, looking to Chris.

'Just Blinky,' he says quietly.

Blinky shrugs, 'But you're going back...whereas I get to stay and stare at your fit bird all the time...and all the other fit birds...loads,' she mouths, 'some gay ones too...I can tell...cos I'm gay. Some fucker shot me in the back of my head. Total cock...fuck him...Marcy tears him apart so bollocks.'

'Simon?'

'Haha...she calls you Simon,' Blinky snorts as Blowers steps out to see Meredith walking towards him down the centre aisle of the church. His heart whumps, turns upside down, flips over, sinks down, misfires and comes back to normal as he grins stupidly. 'Jesus...' Blinky says. 'You alright?'

'How are you?' he asks, enraptured, captivated, mesmerised. She smiles wryly with a comical tut.

'Back again?'

'I er...I think I died again.'

'I think perhaps you did,' she says, stopping in front of him.

'Am I staying?' he asks.

'I just said you're not,' Blinky says, earning a middle finger flicked up while Blowers faces away.

Meredith laughs with a sound of delight filling the huge room. A rush of warmth spreads through him. A feeling of absolute love. 'No, no you can't stay,' she says. 'But I love that girl...' she adds with another laugh.

'How long have I got?'

'Fuck me, how many times you been here?' Blinky asks.

'Just once,' Big Chris says. 'And it was only meant to be once...'

'Sorry, Sergeant.'

'Twat,' Chris laughs, walking past. 'Five minutes then you're back out.'

'Roger that.'

'I thought Marines said aye aye captain and tied knots round their white hats?' Malcolm asks, following Chris.

'I missed you,' Meredith says, moving in to touch his face. Her eyes studying him, pain and hurt showing but a deep profound still-ness that calms his soul. She stretches up to kiss him. Her lips so gentle against his. Her hands entwining in his. Everything she was before she is again. Pure warmth and light. Purity of grace and love. 'They hurt you,' she whispers sadly. 'Don't be angry at them, not all of them...they're just boys lost and scared...we'll take some here...'

'They hurt Mr Howie,' Blowers says.

'He'll live,' Meredith says. 'Keep going. You must keep going. Don't stop now, Simon. You can't. Now more than ever...'

'We were heading north...I told Reggie what you said.'

'You must keep going.'

'I will...we will.'

She smiles sadly, 'I wish you could stay.'

'I do too.'

'But,' she says with a sudden smile. 'I have Blinky to keep me company.'

'Who is about to puke from you two snogging,' Blinky says.

'They're going to be devastated,' Blowers says, looking at Blinky.

'Tell 'em to man up.'

'Charlie will be cut to bits,' Blowers says. 'Can I say I was here?' he asks Meredith. 'I won't if you say I can't...'

'I know...tell Mo I said he was a sneaky blind ninja fuckstick who can't see shit...I mean...how the fuck did he not see it?' Blinky says.

'See what?'

'Not telling,' she says instantly. 'And give Cookey this,' she pushes a hand into a pocket then pulls it out holding the middle finger up with an action that sets Meredith off laughing again. 'And tell Charles she kissed a girl called Natalie in a club after we won the league...she did it for a bet but she was drunk on tequila and so embarrassed after... be funny as fuck to tell her that...tell Dave I love him and even though there are fit gay birds here I'll wait for his babies...and tell Miss Paula Sir that I used Clarence's socks but I only realised after and I forgot to tell her. I didn't lie. I honestly forgot to say...tell Marcy she's fit as anything and I so would but she's alright too, like she worked hard today and got the job done. Good skills. She's not just pretty...tell Clarence thank you for helping me. Tell Roy he's really cool...tell Nick I said he was a cock but if I wasn't gay I would so fancy him. Tell Reggie to let Charlie do more cos she's getting frustrated. She's clever as anything, Blowers. She hates not knowing things...er...tell Cookey I will literally kill him to death if he ever hurts Charles, he won't though. I like Cookey. He makes me laugh...Maddox is alright, he'll take my place. Don't get wound up by his gob...um...and er...tell Mr Howie I said he was the greatest man I ever met. Tell him I said I wouldn't change it. Not one bit. I'm sorry I only got two and let the team down but...I'd follow him anywhere, and er...I ain't being soft but tell them I love them. I do...and er...like...cheers, Blowers. Never met anyone like you either. You're like the boss...I'd follow you anywhere. We all would. It's been an honour, Corporal...'

CHAPTER FORTY-SIX

Day Eleven

'And the big dog ran and ran. He ran very fast. He ran all the way home and wagged his tail lots and lots and that night he had an extra special dinner and a big bone...'

'Casseee.'

'Yes?'

'I hate that doggy.'

'Pardon?' Cassie asks, noticing the baleful glare coming from the boy staring at the black German Shepherd eating from the bowl in the big picture book.

'Bad doggy,' the boy says, screwing his face up.

'Why is it a bad doggy?'

'It bit Jennifer.'

'Jennifer?' she asks, leafing back through the pages. 'There isn't a Jennifer...do you mean Sally? The woman is called Sally...she wasn't bitten. She lost her doggy in the park.'

'Did the doggy bite her neck away?'

'What? No! She was crying because she lost him.'

'Sally should get a gun.'

'What for?'

'Make it go bang and shoot the doggy.'

'Okay...I don't think Sally wants to shoot her doggy.'

'It bit Daniel.'

'You said it bit Jennifer.'

'And Mohammed and Kate and Rachel and Oliver and...'

'I have no idea what you're on about,' she says, leafing back to the page she was on. 'Shall I finish?'

'Does the doggy die?'

'No.'

'Does Sally shoot the doggy?'

'No.'

'Is there another book?'

'There is,' she folds it closed and reaches for the next one.

'Does Sally shoot the doggy in this book, Casseee?'

'I doubt it very much. Why don't you like dogs?'

'It bit James and Karen and Jason and...'

'Okay,' she says pointedly, drawing the word out. 'Maybe time for sleep.'

'Fucking dog.'

'Hey, don't say that word,' she says sharply. 'That's a bad word.'

'Sorry, Casseee.'

'It's a rude word. Don't let Gregori hear it.'

'Okay, Casseee.'

She heaves up from the side of the single bed and bends over to tuck the sheet over his body then smooths his face while smiling at him. He smiles back then glances down from her face with a frown.

'Casseee?'

'Yes?'

'Why do your boobies hang?'

'What?' she says, pushing the material in on her low-cut top. 'They're not...'

'Will I have boobies?'

'What? No...no...women have boobies,' she drops to a squat

instead of bending over while thinking she should have put this top on *after* he was asleep.

'Why do women have boobies?'

'They just do...boobies make milk for babies.'

'Do your boobies make milk?'

'No. I don't have a baby.'

'If you had a baby would...'

'Yes, probably. Time for sleep.'

'Lizzie had a baby in her tummy.'

'Right. Who is Lizzie?'

'The doggy bit her.'

'Of course it did. Night night, sleep tight.'

'If the doggy comes will Gregori shoot it and make the brains come out?'

'Go to sleep.'

'And then you can have a baby and your boobies will make milk.'

'Go to sleep.'

'Night night, Casseee.'

'Night.'

'Love you, Casseee.'

'Love you too.'

She closes the door and shakes her head at the increasingly abstract conversations she is having with the boy. A sprawling one level cottage in the middle of nowhere. Forests and woods all over the place. Lakes in the distance. Beautiful but boring as shit. Gregori seems happy though. She adjusts her top, plucking it down to show the top of her cleavage and thinking she will bend over lots and lots of times to show Gregori her boobies. She stifles the giggle and plucks the top down a bit more, then a bit more, then she stretches the hem at the top to make it hang down then worries she's gone too far. Too far? Fuck that. Actually, screw it. She darts into her room, pulls the top off, unclasps her bra, throws it on the bed then pulls the top back on. Yeah, perfect. He'll have a choice of looking down it or seeing her nipples through it.

Yep. Tonight is the night. She will definitely, absolutely, totally and completely fuck Gregori. It has to happen. She'll explode if he doesn't. She might even point a gun at him and make him do it. That could work. He might even get angry and, you know, be rough. The plan is formed. Her list of things to do is ready.

1, Fuck Gregori.

2, Get the hell out of this dump and find somewhere else.

3, Make sure the boy has everything he could ever possibly need and want.

She pauses, thinking.

4...Fuck Gregori again.

Yep, perfect.

A bad new world.

A dangerous new world.

A wonderfully, deliciously violent blood-soaked new world.

'Hey,' she says as she walks into the kitchen. 'Hungry?'

'Yes.'

'Great...you'll need your strength for later.'

'Later? What later?'

'Yoga...'

ALSO BY RR HAYWOOD

EXTRACTED SERIES

EXTRACTED

EXECUTED

EXTINCT

Block-buster Time-Travel

#1 Amazon US

#1 Amazon UK

#1 Audible US & UK

Top 3 Amazon Australia

Washington Post Best-seller

In 2061, a young scientist invents a time machine to fix a tragedy in his past. But his good intentions turn catastrophic when an early test reveals something unexpected: the end of the world.

A desperate plan is formed. Recruit three heroes, ordinary humans capable of extraordinary things, and change the future.

Safa Patel is an elite police officer, on duty when Downing Street comes under terrorist attack. As armed men storm through the breach, she dispatches them all.

'Mad' Harry Madden is a legend of the Second World War. Not only did he complete an impossible mission—to plant charges on a heavily defended submarine base—but he also escaped with his life.

Ben Ryder is just an insurance investigator. But as a young

man he witnessed a gang assaulting a woman and her child. He went to their rescue, and killed all five.

Can these three heroes, extracted from their timelines at the point of death, save the world?

THE WORLDSHIP HUMILITY

#1 Audible bestselling smash hit narrated by Colin Morgan

#1 Amazon bestselling space opera

Sam, an airlock operative, is bored. Living in space should be full of adventure, except it isn't, and he fills his time hacking 3-D movie posters.

Petty thief Yasmine Dufont grew up in the lawless lower levels of the ship, surrounded by violence and squalor, and now she wants out. She wants to escape to the luxury of the Ab-Spa, where they eat real food instead of rats and synth cubes.

Meanwhile, the sleek-hulled, unmanned Gagarin has come back from the ever-continuing search for a new home. Nearly all hope is lost that a new planet will ever be found, until the Gagarin returns with a code of information that suggests a habitable planet has been found. This news should be shared with the whole fleet, but a few rogue captains want to colonise it for themselves.

When Yasmine inadvertently steals the code, she and Sam become caught up in a dangerous game of murder, corruption, political wrangling and...porridge, with sex-addicted Detective Zhang Woo hot on their heels, his own life at risk if he fails to get the code back.

THE UNDEAD SERIES

THE UK's #1 Horror Series

"The Best Series Ever..."

rrhaywood.com

Printed in Great Britain
by Amazon

73304158R00284